WICKED PROPOSAL

LOZHKIN BRATVA
BOOK 1

NICOLE FOX

WICKED PROPOSAL

Would you sleep with a villain to give your son a good life?

I'm a single mama.

And since the day my son was born, I've made one promise:

Never, ever miss a bedtime.

Then the devil offered me a million dollars to change my mind.

I said no.

Actually, I said hell no.

But then I started thinking about the holes in my son's shoes... the growl in his empty belly on the nights I couldn't even afford ramen...

... and I started to wonder what would happen if I took the deal.

One night.

One night on the arm of Yulian Lozhkin, the most arrogant, beautiful, condescending, filthy rich S.O.B. that the city of New York has ever spat out.

In return, all my troubles would go away.

Or so he said.

But one night with Yulian wasn't the end of my troubles—it was just the beginning of them.

WICKED PROPOSAL is Book 1 of the Lozhkin Bratva duet. Yulian and Mia's story continues in Book 2, WICKED REFUSAL.

1

MIA

Brooklyn in July is a war crime on my nostrils.

Hot asphalt, rotting garbage, and the tang of days-old sweat radiating all the way from the dude currently eye-fucking me from across the street.

I keep my gaze locked straight ahead, fingers tightening around the strap of my duffel bag.

My scrubs stick to my back like a second skin. They're damp from twelve hours of running codes, stitching gashes, and swallowing every catcall of *"Hey, sweet thing"* that various drunk assholes keep hurling my way as I try to hurry home for Eli's bedtime.

Sweet thing. The words slither down my spine, oily and familiar.

Brad used to call me that.

Brad, with his whiskey breath and knuckles like sandpaper.

Brad, who'd whisper, *"C'mere, sweet thing"* right before—

Nope. Not today, Satan.

I blink hard, shove that unwanted memory back into its coffin, and pick up my pace.

My sneakers slap against cracked concrete, dodging potholes and piles of dog shit. The dollar store on the corner blares reggaeton. Overhead, a dying neon sign whines like a wasp.

A group of teens loitering outside the bodega whistle as I pass. One of them yells, "Damn, ma, you workin' out or you *workin'*?"

I do manage to keep my middle finger holstered, but it's a very close call.

One of these days, I really might let it fly. Tonight, though, I don't have time to pick fights with teenagers juiced up on vape pens and testosterone.

I'm almost there.

Almost *home*.

It's four blocks to my apartment, which means four blocks to Eli. Four blocks to the brief seconds of peace I'll get burying my face in his sweet, perfect curls.

Then I have to change out of these stained scrubs, bolt back out, and hustle my way to my second job at a bougie med spa in Tribeca, where rich ladies pay eight hundred bucks a pop to get their labia steamed.

No judgment from me, though. I'm glad for the rich ladies.

Mama's got bills to pay.

I round the corner onto my street—and grit my teeth.

Because there's a car parked behind mine, blocking me in.

Not just any car. A black Maybach, polished to a liquid shine, prowling in front of my building like a panther in a junkyard. My beat-to-shit sedan—Rhonda the Honda—sits trapped behind it.

"You've gotta be kidding me," I mutter.

I scan the block in search of suspects. At first, I come up empty.

But then—*there*. Across the street.

A man in a gleaming black suit that looks utterly out of place in this decrepit armpit of the city is pacing the sidewalk, phone pressed to his ear. His shoes gleam like obsidian under the streetlight.

The rest of him is just as easy on the eyes. Stormy gray gaze. GQ stubble. Abs that look like you could grate a whole Parmesan cheese wheel on 'em.

I'm lactose intolerant, but I'd still take a bite out of him.

Or at least, I would—if I had time for that kind of thing.

Which I don't. My son needs his bedtime story, dammit.

I march over, duffel bag bouncing against my hip. "Hey! You the genius who parked in my spot?"

The man doesn't look up. Just holds up a finger.

Wait, it says. *I'm doing important things.*

That's strike one.

"Excuse me? Sir?" I step into his path.

He side-steps me, still talking. "—said to fucking *find her.* What part of that was unclear?"

There's strike two.

I plant myself in front of him, arms crossed. "Listen, Prince Charming. You're blocking my car, and I've got twenty minutes to kiss my kid goodnight before I'm late for work. Move. Your. *Shit.*"

For the first time, he actually deigns to glance at me. Those light eyes rake over my scrubs, my frizz-popping ponytail, the sweat stain blooming on my collar.

His mouth twitches.

Not a smile—a *dismissal.*

He turns away.

Oh, *hell* no.

Strike three.

"Cool. Cool, cool, cool." I yank my phone out, dial the number on the tow yard sticker plastered to the nearest hydrant, and unleash my sweetest customer service voice. "Hi! There's a massive, illegally parked car blocking my driveway on Sutter and Rockaway. A Maybach. Uh-huh. You can't miss it. You'll be here in five minutes? Perfect. You just made my day."

I hang up and stride into my building. I don't bother looking back.

~

Eli's laughter hits me the second I open the door—high, bright, the sound of ice cream trucks and sidewalk chalk.

He launches off the couch in a blur of Spider-Man pajamas and hugs me around the middle. "Mommy!"

Just like that, my day gets better.

"Whoa, bud!" I catch him mid-leap, staggering back. "Since when do you weigh a thousand pounds?"

"I do not!"

"Could've fooled me." I nuzzle his neck, breathing in baby shampoo and Cheez-It dust. No perfume has ever smelled so good. "You're turning into a dinosaur. A *Tyrannosaurus flex*."

"*Rex*," Eli corrects, pulling back to frown at me. "And I'm not a dinosaur—I'm a boy."

"Could've fooled *me*," my best friend Kallie chimes in from the kitchenette, where she's microwaving popcorn. "I found scales in your bed this morning."

"They were Goldfish!" Eli yelps in horror. But he still starts checking his forearms for signs of scaliness.

I set him down. But as I do, something snags my attention: dirty scuff marks on his shoes. And, now that I'm looking, there's a rip on the side that wasn't there this morning.

My smile curdles. These were new Jordans—well, relatively new. Thrifted last month in something close to mint-ish condition.

Now, though, the left toe is split open, foam peeking through like guts. I see his socked pinky toe wiggling in the gap.

"Eli, honey…" I kneel, thumbing the tear. "What happened?"

He shrinks down and mumbles, "Nothing."

I drop to my knees and clutch him close. "You know you can tell me anything, right?"

He keeps squirming, refusing to look at me. That lower lip starts to pout out and tremble, and my heart picks up some trembling of its own. "Some kids at recess… They said I run like a robot."

"And?"

"And they thought it'd be funny to tie my laces together." His chin quivers, but he drags his eyes up to mine. "I didn't cry, though! Not even when Mrs. Alvarez had to cut them apart."

My chest tightens. I feel all the single mom feelings, same as I always do in situations like this.

Rage at the unfairness of it all.

Fury toward the world that lets such cruelty go unchecked.

Sadness and crippling guilt because I can't be there to keep my baby safe every minute of the day.

But when I see him watching me, waiting to see how I respond, I do the same as I always do in situations like this: force myself to grin, so he knows that he's loved.

The rage, fury, sadness, and guilt are for me.

My son gets only my love.

I wink at him. "Guess we'll have to get you rocket boots next time then. Blast those haters to the moon."

Eli's eyes light up. "With lasers?!"

"Obviously! Now, go help Auntie Kallie with the popcorn before she burns it again."

As he scrambles off, tears forgotten, Kallie sidles over and hip-checks me with a sympathetic smile. "Long day?"

"Aren't they all?" I dig the heels of my hands into my eyes and sigh. "Shoes will be the death of me, I swear."

"Don't stress it, Mama," she reassures me. "I'll hit up the Buy Nothing group tomorrow. Someone's gotta have a size eleven."

"He's a twelve now."

"Shit. Boy is growin' up fast."

"Language, Kal." I point my chin at Eli, who is now enthusiastically shaking the microwave bag.

"Right. Uh, shizz." Kallie lowers her voice. "You okay, though, for real?"

"Peachy. Just need to pick up three extra shifts, sell a kidney, maybe start an OnlyFans—"

"Ooh, that's a good idea. Men love a girl in scrubs."

I snort as I look down at the murky stain on my thigh. "They sure do. My last patient tonight loved 'em so much he peed on me."

"Hm. On second thought, how much do kidneys fetch?"

"Mommy!" Eli shrieks with laughter as he holds up the bag, kernels exploding like gunfire. "It's *alive*!"

~

Half an episode of *Bluey* later, I'm perched on Eli's bed, tracing constellations on his palm. His eyelids keep drooping and struggling open as he fights sleep for as long as his stubborn little heart will let him.

"Promise you'll kiss me goodnight again later?" he mumbles. "When you get home?"

"Promise." I press my lips to his forehead. "Even if you're snoring like a walrus."

"Walruses don't snore. They... *blub*." He mimics a flipper.

"Then I'll blub you back. Now, sleep, E. Dream about happy things, okay? Rocket boots. Unicorns. Oceans filled with popcorn."

He smiles. "Okay. I love you, Mommy."

"I love you, too, superstar."

When he's asleep, I tiptoe out, grab my keys, say bye to Kallie, and steel myself for the night.

Outside, I'm relieved to see that the Maybach is gone. *Thank Christ.* I'm halfway to Rhonda the Honda when—

"You."

2

MIA

Suit Guy looms under the streetlight, all sharp angles and simmering rage. His tie is undone, jacket discarded somewhere, sleeves rolled up to reveal tattoos snaking down his forearms.

Up close, he's younger than I thought—late twenties? early thirties at most—with the kind of face that belongs on either a billboard or a wanted poster.

And right now, he looks like he wants to put *my* face on a *Missing* poster.

"Did you get my fucking car towed?" he snarls at me in a rasping, feral baritone.

I tilt my head. "I did try to tell you."

"You had no right." His jaw tics.

"Actually, if you had bothered to listen to me for even one second, I could've told you that was *my* driveway, and I actually have every right." I unlock my door. "Now, if you'll excuse me, I've got vaginas to steam."

He blocks my path. "Do you think this is a joke?"

"I think you're in my way."

"You made this much harder than it had to be."

I laugh right in his face. Buddy here doesn't know the first thing about how hard things can get.

"Life has a funny way of doing that, doesn't it?" I remark.

I try to sidestep him again, but he grabs my wrist.

Big mistake.

My body moves before my brain catches up. A twist, a shift, *pressure*—and suddenly, he's against the hood, my elbow jammed under his throat.

"Do *not* touch me," I snarl right back in the same growl he used on me.

He goes still.

Not scared, though.

Intrigued.

His gaze flicks to my fresh set of scrubs, my shaking hands, the faded scar on my throat that Brad left there.

"You're full of surprises, aren't you?" he murmurs.

The streetlight catches his eyes. Gray, with flecks of gold.

Dangerous.

I release him and step back. "And you're full of shit. Now, for the love of all that is holy, can you please move so I can get on with my life?"

He doesn't do anything of the kind. Just watches me, lips curving in a crooked half-smirk. "What's your name?"

"To you, it's Tow Truck Tina. For God's sake—"

"Tough act." He straightens his cuffs. "But that grip? You've had training. Nursing school doesn't teach you that. That's *more.*"

I freeze. *How the hell did he know—?*

He smirks and rakes his eyes up and down my body. "Scrub pants, sneakers, adrenaline shakes. You know how to handle yourself. But you learned it the hard way, didn't you?"

"Wow. You're a detective *and* a dickhead. Multitalented."

I reach for my car door, but his hand shoots out, pinning it shut.

"Wait." His voice drops, barely audible above the street noise. "I have a proposition for you."

I bark out a laugh, right in his smug face. "I'm not interested in any proposition from a guy who can't read a 'No Parking' sign."

"What about one that could solve your financial problems?" His eyes flick to my worn-thin scrubs, to the fraying strap of my bag, then back to my face, which is worn-thin and fraying in its own kind of way. "*All* of them."

Something in his tone makes me pause. The streetlight casts shadows across his face, but his eyes are clear. Calculating.

He means it.

"Three minutes," he presses. "That's all I'm asking. I'll tell you what I need and why you're perfect for it, and when you tell me yes—"

"—*if* I tell you yes—"

"—*when* you tell me yes," he overrides, "then I'm going to put a large amount of cash in your hand, and you're going to thank me for the easiest money you've ever made in your life."

I should tell him to fuck off, then knee him in the groin and run. As a matter of fact, I'm about to do exactly that—

But then I think of Eli's shoes.

Of the pile of bills on my counter.

Of the three jobs that still aren't enough, have never been enough, have only ever felt like hole-riddled pails I desperately use to bail out a sinking ship that keeps taking on more water, and more water, and more, more, more, dragging me and Eli alike down to the bottom of a black ocean that never gave a damn whether we lived or died.

"Two minutes," I hear myself say. "Not a second more."

The man's smile stretches wider.

3

YULIAN

THIRTY MINUTES EARLIER

"Blyat'!"

I barely restrain myself from hurling my phone across the street.

Maksim's update has been nothing but shitty news: Nikita still hasn't been found. Not at her apartment, not at her usual haunts, not even at HQ.

Maks is my best friend and second-in-command, but he's still getting my full wrath right now. Mostly because I have nowhere else to vent.

"Boss—"

"Did I fucking stutter?" I interrupt. *"Find her."*

"I've got all our men on it," Maksim sighs. "Did you find out why her GPS signal died in Brownsville?"

"Hey!" someone pipes up down the sidewalk.

I ignore that voice behind me.

"No," I mutter to Maksim. The truth is, I don't have a goddamn clue why Nikita's GPS would lead here at all.

She lives in Manhattan, for fuck's sake. There's nothing in this armpit of New York that could have lured her here—

Unless…

Unless she found a lead.

"Excuse me? Sir?" The voice behind me is closer now. More insistent. "Your car is—"

"Shh." I hold up a finger to silence the nagging woman. Whatever she wants with my car, she can wait until I'm done. "Maks, you got anything else?"

"Not really," he answers. "I just— Wait, hold up. I just got word that the man we captured is awake."

My hackles rise. "Put him on the line."

"You're already running late to the gala, Yul. Let me handle this. I can—"

"*Now,* Maks."

My second gives a frustrated sigh. "Alright, fine. But I'm not driving your ungrateful ass halfway across the city during rush hour."

"You will if I need it."

He bites out a curse in Russian. He knows I'm right. He knows he'll never say no to me, even if I'm the one making myself late for tonight's event.

Maksim is a lot of things, but disloyal isn't one of them.

Not when it comes to me.

Which is why I don't doubt for a second that he'll do as I say.

There's a little scuffling at the other end of the line. I walk into an alley and lean against the graffitied wall. It isn't exactly a private setting to carry out an interrogation by phone, but it's as private as it'll get right now.

"No!" a new voice cries out. "I don't know anything! I don't—"

"According to his ID, his name is Boyan," Maksim informs me. "Just so you two can be on a nice, friendly, first-name basis."

"Hello, Boyan." My tone goes as cold as the fucking grave. "I'm going to ask you a few questions now. If you answer them, I'll ensure that you don't suffer. If you don't... Well. There's only so much I can do."

"I don't know anything!" Boyan repeats, panicked. "I never met her! I just—"

"Maksim," I cut in, "break one of his fingers."

He doesn't hesitate. A second later, a sickening *crunch* echoes across the line, followed by a scream.

"Let's try this again," I growl. "I will ask. You will answer. Say you understand."

Boyan's wails turn to silent sobs. "Y-yes. I understand."

"Good. Then tell me how you knew Nikita."

"I d-didn't," the man sniffles. "I swear, I—"

"Maksim. Break another."

A second *crunch.*

A second scream.

"T-that wasn't the deal!" Boyan cries. "I answered your question!"

"And I didn't fucking like it," I snarl. "So do better."

"I was hired! I-I swear, I—"

Bingo.

"Tell me what they hired you to do," I demand. "You have five seconds."

To Boyan's credit, it only takes him two to answer this time.

"T-to clean up!" he blurts. "I was s-supposed to clean her place. Like, wipe down the surfaces, get rid of traces."

"Doesn't sound like a normal cleaning gig to me."

"I needed the money," he sobs. "I c-couldn't be picky. Please, sir, let me go, I promise I won't tell—"

"Name your client. Then I'll consider it."

Boyan's breath stutters. "N-name?"

"Yes," I grit. "I want a name."

"I c-can't—"

"*Maksim.*"

"Please, no!"

I hear scuffling, then another familiar sound—the sweet snapping of bone.

"*Arghh!* I don't know! T-they never say who they are! They hire through notes and pay cash! I swear, I have no idea who it is!"

They never say who they are.

Boyan's words burrow deep into me.

My blood turns to ice water, carrying a numbing cold through me—the cold of suspicion.

Of memories.

Blood on the floor. Blood everywhere. The smell of gunpowder in the air, the echoes of screams.

White tablecloths stained red, red, red—

"Maksim," I bark, "kill him."

"No! Please, have mercy! I swear I don't know anything! I—"

BANG.

Boyan's body thumps to the ground.

Thank God. Motherfucker was starting to give me a headache.

Moments later, I hear Maksim's voice again. "So? We believe him?"

"I don't know. He pissed me off."

My second barks a laugh. "God, I fucking love working for you. Never a dull moment."

"Good to know employee satisfaction is high."

"I mean, the dental benefits suck, but I digress. Anyway—what about tonight?" Maksim asks, a swift change of subject. "You still going to the event?"

"StarTech's future depends on this deal," I say. "And I don't need to remind you what else is on the line."

"I'll take that as a yes."

I grit my teeth. Maksim's cheer clashes with my mood on the best of days, and today's not a good day to begin with.

Not by a long shot.

"Without Nikita, I'm fucked. Find me a replacement date."

"That's gonna be hard on short notice."

"I don't give a shit." My phone cover cracks in my hand as I clench it tight. "And keep looking for Nikita. I want her found."

Before Maks can answer, I hang up.

Fucking hell.

This had to happen *tonight,* of all nights?

Plus-ones are a status symbol, as much as a good suit and an expensive watch. And the man I'm meeting tonight, Baldwin, is exactly the kind of shallow bastard to care mostly about the arm candy I bring for him to gawk at.

If I show up alone, this deal's as good as dead.

Meet me there with my date, I type quickly to Maksim.

But as I walk to my car, I realize the problem with that plan.

My car isn't there anymore.

"What the—" My eyes fix on the bright orange sticker on the ground. A towing company's details. "*Blyat'.*"

Furious, I type in the towing company's number and call.

"You have my car," I spit the second someone picks up.

An automated voice answers me. "You've reached Brownsville Towing Trucks. If you want to report a car, press—"

"I want to talk to a fucking human, goddammit."

The robotic voice keeps blathering on. " … To get your car back, please show up with your documentation between 9:00 A.M. and 6:00 P.M."

I glance at my watch: *8:34 P.M.*

"Fuck."

"To go back to the menu, press—"

"FUCK!"

I toss my phone across the street. It lands with a loud *crack* on the concrete, shards flying every which way.

I don't need this shit. Not today of all days. Not when the thing I've been chasing after for so long is finally within my reach.

A way to find my family's killers—to get my revenge.

But it can't happen without Baldwin's alliance.

I pull out a spare phone. I'm about to type another text to Maksim…

… when I see *her.*

Messy purple scrubs. Ash brown hair, pulled up in a haphazard bun. Tired blue eyes, without a smudge of makeup. A beauty mark just under her chin that draws my eyes like a target…

… and a shit-eating grin like the cat who ate the canary.

All at once, I know what happened.

I stalk towards the woman. As I get closer, I realize how tiny she is—barely reaching my shoulder.

But if she thinks she's getting my merciful side, she'd better think again.

That shit does not exist.

"You." I stop in front of her. "Did you get my fucking car towed?"

She freezes. Then she turns with steel in her spine, her shoulders held up, chin raised in defiance.

For a tiny thing, she's a spitfire.

"I did try to tell you."

"You had no right."

I can tell my closeness rattles her, but she hides it better than most. It's a refreshing novelty. The way she holds my gaze. The way she doesn't back down, not even for a second.

It's been years since anyone's spoken to me like this—like I don't fucking scare them.

That can only mean one thing.

She doesn't know who the fuck I am.

Just like that, I get an idea.

Whether it's a good idea or a bad idea remains to be seen.

4

YULIAN

My offer has her head spinning.

I'll tell you what I need and why you're perfect for it, and when you tell me yes, I'm going to put a large amount of cash in your hand, and you're going to thank me for the easiest money you've ever made in your life.

Her face goes through all the colors of the rainbow. I can practically see the gears in her brain working overtime. Cataloging bills to be paid. Clothes to be bought. Dreaming of a vacation, maybe, for once in her overworked life.

It's like everything she is has been splayed out before me. I can taste her despairing midnight tears, the ones she doesn't dare show anyone. I can feel the heartbroken clench of her fists as the world frustrates her again and again.

She's been beaten down by it.

This is a leg up she taught herself long ago never to expect.

"I need a plus-one," I tell her succinctly. "My date is... indisposed, on short notice. You'll take her place."

"I'm not a *whore*," she hisses, cheeks bright red.

"And I don't pay for sex." I send my location pin to Maksim so he comes to collect me and my new date here. "Ten thousand. That's my final offer."

Her blue eyes go wide. "T-ten...?!"

"Ten thousand dollars. For one night of your time. You'd be stupid not to accept."

I can see more emotions clashing in her eyes. Pride versus practicality.

It's easy to see which will win.

"I have conditions," she says carefully.

"Name them."

"Nothing illegal," she blurts. "Nothing sexual. And no names."

Her boundaries amuse me. As if she has any idea what real danger looks like.

By stepping into my world for even one night, she's already in deeper than she realizes.

But it costs me nothing to humor her. To pretend her little boundaries mean anything at all.

"Sure thing, Nurse Winters."

Her gaze darts to her nametag. I find myself enjoying the blush creeping higher and higher along her cheeks. Can't help but wonder if the skin beneath her collarbone has the same delicious scarlet hue.

"Look—"

"I don't give a shit," I interrupt. "You have fifteen minutes to make yourself presentable. Go, or the deal's off."

I can tell she wants to mouth off some more, but she must realize how badly she's rushing against the clock.

With a final glare at me, she rushes back upstairs.

The second she does, I pick my phone back up.

"Maks. It's me. Run a full background check on a 'Nurse Winters' living in Brownsville, right near the pin I just sent you."

I adjust my cufflinks and feel a smile slowly widening on my face. Muscles I rarely use, now warming up again.

That nurse's attitude, her utter refusal to bend the knee…

It makes me want to see how far I can push her before she breaks.

5

MIA

My heel taps nervously against the sidewalk.

I'm still processing the craziness of the past half-hour. I couldn't even explain myself properly to Kallie and Eli. I just took the fastest shower in history and ran back down in my third-hand Cavallini heels.

Cue the most awkward seven minutes and a half of my fucking life.

Mr. Cheese Grater Abs is impatient.

Very impatient.

He keeps checking his phone, snarling at passing cars, going through the five stages of pissed off and then starting over again at the beginning.

Whoever's keeping him waiting, I wouldn't want to be them.

But do you want to be his date?

In short: fuck no.

He's right about one thing, though: I do need the money.

Upstairs, my kid has a pair of basketball shoes filled with holes that I can replace if I do this. My bills, my loans—I could pay it all off for a month or two.

I could *breathe.*

I just need to get through tonight.

The purr of an engine snaps me out of my thoughts. A sleek black limo rolls up, stopping right in front of us.

"Yo, Yulian!" A big guy with facial tattoos and a wicked grin waves from the driver's seat. "How's it hanging, new girl? I'm Maksim."

"Mia," I blurt before remembering we weren't supposed to be doing names. *Fuck.* "I mean—"

"Get in." The man—*Yulian,* apparently—throws the car door open. "Now."

It's the least gentlemanly way anyone's ever held a door open for me, to say the least. Someone ought to teach him what "please" means or what a "smile" is.

But a payday's a payday, so I grit my teeth and slide into the limo.

Yulian doesn't sit in the front. Instead, to my mounting horror, he sits right next to me.

"Drive," he barks to Maksim.

The car merges back into traffic. I stare wistfully at my beaten-up Honda as she disappears into the distance, wondering if it's too late to change my mind.

"Put this on."

I startle at the item in Yulian's hands. "What's this?"

"Your dress." His gray eyes rake over my midnight blue A-line. "One that doesn't come from a thrift store."

"Hey! It's pre-loved."

"It's a disaster. Change."

I gawk in confusion at the opaque garment bag he thrusts in my hands.

Conflict twists my chest. I may need this money, but no one ever said anything about having to strip naked in a car with a stranger to get it.

In fact, I was pretty clear on this *not* happening.

But Yulian is still staring at me, gray eyes cold as stone, fingers drumming impatiently on his thigh. "Put it on, Ms. Winters. Unless you'd like to back out of our deal."

With a swallow, I unzip the bag. "Fine. But you're turning around. And—*oh.*"

The words die in my throat.

Cool, pale blue silk shimmers in my hands, spilling through my fingers like water. I've never seen anything this beautiful, let alone touched it.

The fabric, the handiwork—it's exquisite. A far cry from any "pre-loved" dress I've ever owned.

This piece has never been loved before.

I'm its first.

"And?"

I startle back to the present. "What?"

"You said 'and.'" A faint smirk paints Yulian's lips. He's having the time of his life watching me squirm. "I'm turning around, *and...?*"

Pettiness flares inside me. "And I'm keeping the dress," I snap. "Now, do your part, Bright Eyes. Sit and spin."

With that smug smirk still firmly in place, Yulian obliges.

Yulian.

I roll his name on my tongue as I strip.

It sounds way sweeter than the man it belongs to.

My hands fumble every step of the way. The limo may be big, but it isn't *that* big. No car is big enough for someone to get naked next to someone else without accidental contact. Every near-brush with him makes my heart leap up into my throat.

I swallow my nerves and do the only thing I can think of to make this bearable: conversation.

"So, uhh... you do this often?"

It's a lame joke at best, but Yulian doesn't even pretend to play along. "You'll have to be more specific than that."

"Bribe women into being your date," I bite back acidly. "Is that a typical Friday night for you, or do you sometimes score *without* the help of your thick, fat wallet?"

I could swear I detect the faintest hint of a laugh dancing on the edge of his voice. "Nothing about this is typical. Well, that's not quite true. You're far from the first woman to strip naked in my car. But you are the first one who's in it because you got my car towed."

My face heats up. I said nothing sexual, but we're thirty minutes into this absurd scenario and I'm naked, he's talking about all the women he sleeps with, and we're both probably picturing things we definitely shouldn't be.

"To be fair," I mumble, "you deserved it."

"I thought nurses weren't supposed to cause harm?"

"I'm sure your car is perfectly fine. And no one at NYU told me that cars fell under the Hippocratic Oath."

"So that's where you got your degree," he muses. "NYU."

Goddammit. I told myself I wouldn't let this man know anything about me. Now, he knows my name, where I live, what car I drive, and where I went to school.

Nice going, Mia. Why don't you give him your Social Security number, too?

Think he knows that your blood type is O-neg?

What about the freckle on the inside of your thigh? Why not just give him a peek of that for good measure?

"Maybe," I say, trying to sound casual and mysterious and sounding more like I'm unsure about my own alma mater instead. "Maybe not."

It's a pathetic attempt. I know it, Yulian knows it—hell, even Maksim probably knows it.

Five minutes I've been in this car, and I've already made myself ridiculous in the eyes of all its occupants.

"Alright, I'm decent. You can look—"

Now, I wanted to say, but my breath catches halfway.

Because there are hands on the zipper at my back.

And they're not mine.

"Keep still," a hot, gravelly voice whispers behind me. I can feel his breath on my neck, the warm pressure of strong hands. "We wouldn't want to rip your new dress, would we, Ms. Winters?"

I hate the way he says my name.

My *not*-name, the one I resurrected from my great-grandmother's diary when my real one became unusable.

But at the same time, I'm glad it's not my *actual* name he's saying.

Mia Winters—she's tough. She can take it.

Euphemia Collins—the name I was born with—absolutely could not.

But then again, Euphemia Collins couldn't take a lot of things. That's why she's dead and buried. That's why I'm Mia now.

"I told you not to look," I hiss, hating the way my voice trembles.

"I wasn't. I turned around, like you asked." He sounds way too pleased with himself. "Towards the window."

Which is a reflective surface. Of fucking course. Talk about malicious compliance.

"You're awful."

"I've been called worse things." Again, that hot breath on my neck, closer than sin. "You should know—you said several of them."

Yulian's fingers deftly work the zipper up, one hand still buried in my hair to keep it from getting caught. I feel myself go slack under his touch, pliant, malleable. Play-Doh in his hands.

All things I haven't let myself be in a long time.

Desperate for a distraction, I turn my attention to the window. The limo is gliding smoothly over the Brooklyn Bridge now, city lights blurring as we zoom past.

But no matter how hard I try to pretend otherwise, I can still feel Yulian's gaze on me.

"So, uhh… What's this event we're going to?"

"You'll see."

Great. Thanks. Really helpful.

"You're not a big conversationalist, are you?"

"I'm a man of action, Ms. Winters," he whispers into my ear. "Not words."

My mind runs off with it—the image of Yulian in action. The question of just how much this dark stranger is capable of.

It paints a vivid picture, starting with the tattoos I can see crawling up his hands and wrists.

I catch myself wondering how far they go. How they might flex and curl around his muscles in motion, if by some wave of my fairy godmother's wand, his suit was to suddenly disappear…

"If I had a nickel for every time some fuckboy said that to me, I wouldn't have had to take you up on your stupid offer," I retort.

It's a little feisty—I'm definitely biting the hand that's literally feeding me—but something tells me that Yulian here will appreciate a spark of defiance.

Sure enough, he's not bothered in the least. In fact, he makes a humming sound deep in his throat, like a purring jaguar. It vibrates through every inch of my skin.

"What would it take?" he murmurs, tracing the line of my shoulder strap. Goosebumps bloom where he touches me, a thousand tiny alarms. "For you to believe me?"

I want to tell him.

I want to tell him *exactly* how he could convince me—with his tongue, hands, lips—of anything he wanted me to believe.

God, I want it so bad.

"I..."

And then, suddenly, Yulian's phone rings.

He growls in his throat as he pulls away. "One moment."

He glances at the screen. His eyebrows furrow, and all the heat that had been simmering in the air disappears beneath the smog of his irritation.

"Tell me you're not seriously calling me from the driver's seat, *mudak*."

As if by magic, the partition slowly sinks, revealing Maksim's face. "What? You might've been busy."

"I was." My cheeks flush at the thought of just what he'd been busy with—*me*. "Start talking before I chuck this at your head."

Undeterred by Yulian's threats, Maksim grins. "Just got a quick question for ya. The men are taking care of the, ah, *Boylan problem.* Only, the usual dumping ground is a no-go. Apparently, there's a construction site right over it."

"Then melt him and turn him into fucking soap," Yulian snarls. "I don't care how you do it. Just make sure there's nothing left to find."

Welp, that's a mood killer.

Literally.

The illusion shatters. My thoughts sharpen again, fog clearing all at once.

Suddenly, I remember.

I remember way, way too much.

There's a man in New York. A hotshot CEO, constantly at the top of Forbes *40 Over 40* and *Most Eligible Bachelor* lists.

A man who's rumored to be involved with the Russian criminal underworld. Nothing anyone can prove, but enough that the whispers are barely even whispers anymore.

And his name is Yulian Lozhkin.

Yulian.

Fuck. I can't believe it. Of all the people in this city—all the rich assholes with money to throw at their problems…

… Did I seriously just land in a car with the most dangerous one of them all?

6

MIA

Shut up, Mia.

Just shut up. Pretend you know nothing.

Otherwise, you'll be the one in the acid bath, right next to poor Boyan.

But I'm freaking out as the car stops.

As Maksim announces, "We're here."

As Yulian steps around to open my door, takes my hand, unfolds me from the backseat.

His eyes stay riveted on me. Grayer than gray, stormy, intent. Like he's testing me.

Is she dumb enough to run? To flag down cops?

But I know better than that.

I worked so hard to run away from men like him. To leave it all in the rearview mirror for good. I'm not going to get sucked in again—not for all the money in the world.

But as I think about sprinting for the closest exit while screaming like a chicken with my head cut off, I remember Eli's shoes.

If I do this, I can take him to the store first thing tomorrow.

I can watch his little face light up again, bright like Christmas lights.

All I have to do is get through tonight.

And for him, for my boy, my little angel, I'll do anything.

Even make a deal with the devil himself.

So I take a deep breath, look at Yulian, flash a smile, and step through the white-lilied arch of the wedding venue.

The cameras keep flashing. Yulian's hand stays planted firmly on my lower back, steering me up the marble steps.

I don't like it there, in large part because it makes me feel giddy and sweaty and all too aware of how huge he is next to me, how good he smells, how intimidating he looks.

But I can't exactly swat it away in front of the whole paparazzi army, so I just deal with it.

I plaster on the fakest smile I can muster, wave like the freaking Queen of England, and wait for the venue to swallow us up.

"Can you take your hand off my ass now?" I hiss through my teeth.

Without a word, Yulian obliges.

Just like that, a chill snakes down my spine. I'm cold again as soon as he's not touching me. Lost. Unmoored.

As much as I hated his hand being there, I hate it being gone even more. It's so unbelievably dumb that my body reacts like this. My own biology despises me.

But then again, I guess it always had a thing for bad boys, huh?

Whether I liked it or not.

"Better?" Yulian asks, his own smile perfectly in place.

"Much."

As a scantily dressed hostess takes our coats, I let my eyes roam over the venue. Someone clearly spared no expense. It's just marble pillars and gold chandeliers as far as the eye can see.

Apparently, rich people like to recreate Greek temples in their spare time.

I can't deny that it's beautiful, though.

Yulian's voice breaks the spell. "Like what you see?"

"This stuff?" I quickly shape my face into a scowl, as if I'm not impressed. "No."

"So that's a hate-stare, then."

I roll my eyes. "It's beautiful, don't get me wrong. But…"

"But?"

"It's like whoever's getting married tonight thinks they're hosting the Met Gala. Like they're convinced they're just that important."

"Maybe they are."

"Please. The press? The Playboy Bunny waitress? The freaking gold leaf in the drinks?" I scoff. "Either Kim Kardashian's moving onto her next victim, or the happy couple has delusions of grandeur."

Yulian snorts. "Fairly accurate."

I do a double-take at the noise coming out of him. The Ice King can *laugh?* Who knew?

I let Yulian lead me around the ballroom. This place really does look like a fairy tale come to life. Except for a few classless choices, like the waitresses' ass-length skirts, it's clear whoever did this handed a blank check over to an army of interior decorators.

I wonder whose name was on the check. My eyes dart around the little groups mingling together. Even the guests look like they came straight out of a fashion magazine: cool, attractive, rich. Effortlessly at ease in such opulence.

Very unlike me.

It makes me feel like an imposter. Like a poor, stupid wannabe. Like—

You're a nobody, sweet thing.

Who'd believe you over me?

"Relax," Yulian whispers in my ear. "You're drawing attention."

"I highly doubt that," I mumble.

"Yes, you are. These people pick up on nerves. And if they think you're nervous?" He leans closer. "They'll know you don't belong here."

"Well, I don't," I snap. "You know that. You literally picked me up off the street."

"You belong wherever you decide you belong, *kotyonok.*" His voice is practically scraping the floor, so low and rough I can *feel* it. Like he's touching me in all the right places, all without lifting a single finger. "Most importantly, where *I* decide. And tonight, you belong on my arm."

Yulian's words leave me flushed and breathless. I have no idea what I loathe more: the fact that he's right—that people really *are* looking?

Or that he thinks he owns me?

But he does, a tiny voice in my head reminds me. *Tonight, he does own you.*

Whatever comfort I could have found in his words is eclipsed by that fact. A simple, cruel fact of life.

He's rich. I'm poor.

He's powerful. I'm not.

He's someone, and I'm nobody.

The rest of the night makes it even more apparent. As Yulian drags me from group to group, greeting people of importance without so much as introducing me, I realize that's exactly the role I was meant to play: arm-candy.

Nothing but a well-dressed prop for him to show off.

See? I own her. Like I own this watch, this suit, this world.

After the fifth conversation like that, I say, "You could at least introduce me."

Yulian flicks me a flat look. "I believe it was you who insisted on 'no names.'"

"Right. But since you do, in fact, know my name—"

"It sounds to me, *Ms. Winters,* like you're already regretting your own rules." He says it with the barest hint of a smirk, just enough to let me know how self-satisfied he's feeling about this.

Asshole.

If I had a drink in my hand, it'd already be on his face. His smug, flawless, unfairly attractive face.

"I need some air," I say. "I'm going to the bar."

He doesn't so much as blink. "I'll expect you back here in five. See that you're on time."

I swallow the childish urge to mock his own words back at him and stomp out.

The outdoors bar is nestled into a pretty, curated garden, lit up by an odd combination of mason jars, naked bulbs, and fairy lights. Like three separate wedding planners had a fight over it and some disinterested groom just told them to do whatever.

But hey, if the bride's happy…

"What's the strongest drink a girl can get around here?"

The bartender laughs. He's a tall, dreadlocked guy with an easy smile, the kind Kallie would fall head over heels for. "Depends on how bad a night you're having. How would you rate your pain on a scale from one to ten?"

"Eleven."

He winces. "That bad, huh?"

"Yup." I pop the *P* all the way and slump gracelessly on the counter.

"Friend of the bride?" he asks as he mixes. "Or the groom?"

"Neither. You're looking at someone's Rolex."

"Then I guess I finally see the appeal of those."

The casual flirtiness in his tone makes me smile. Innocent bartender ways, no doubt, but at least it's not flat mockery like Mr. Cheese Grater Abs.

He slides my drink towards me. I take a sip and—*whoa,* okay, definitely on the strong side. "Would you believe that's the nicest thing anyone's said to me all night?"

"Then you need to find yourself a better date."

"And I suppose that would be you?"

He grins like he's been waiting for me to ask that exact question—which, obviously, he has. The bartender opens his mouth to deliver his knockout line.

But before he can, someone steps between us.

A very large, wealthy, pissed-off somebody.

"Not if I have anything to say about it," he growls.

My drink disappears from my hand.

"Hey!"

I try to get it back, but I'm too slow. All I can do is watch with mounting horror as Yulian tips the glass back, drains the whole thing, then thumps it down in front of the bartender.

"Thanks for the drink," he drawls with simmering venom. "If I find out you've served my date another one, though, I'll shatter it and shove the broken glass down your throat."

The bartender is stunned into silence. I'm not totally sure what you'd say to that kind of thing, anyway.

Because Yulian looks like he fucking *means* it.

When the silence stretches to a satisfying length, Yulian nods once. Then he turns to me. "Let's go."

Just like that, he grabs my arm and drags me back to the hall.

As soon as we're there, I yank my arm out of his grip. "What's your problem?!" I ask furiously. "I was just—"

"Flirting. You were *flirting.*" His voice is scalding now, fire smoldering just beneath the ashes of his gray eyes. "I get that you don't do this for a living, Ms. Winters, but let me give you a tip: If you're looking to get paid for your services, running off with the help is not the way to do that."

"Running—? Oh my *God.*" My cheeks burn with shame. "I was literally getting one drink. *One. Drink.*"

"Seems to me you were out to get more than that."

"Not even a little bit! He's not my type whatsoever. He was just—"

"I don't care who wanted what or why," he snarls. Suddenly, his Ice King aura is nowhere to be found. I can see rage burning in the depths of his irises, hot and blazing. "Until the sun rises, you are *mine*. So do not wander off again. Have I made myself clear?"

Tears prickle at the corners of my eyes. I force myself to

swallow the lump in my throat, the bitter disappointment that this is what it's come to: me, being treated like property.

Again.

You belong to me, sweet thing. Now and always. Brad's voice just will not leave me alone tonight.

"Crystal," I bite out.

Yulian considers me for a moment longer. The smoldering ashes of his eyes revert back to the cold, smooth surface of a frozen lake.

"Good," he says. "Now, keep up. And give me your phone."

I blink. "My—?"

"I don't like to repeat myself, Ms. Winters." His face clouds over again. "You're here to perform a job. I won't have you be distracted again."

Right. Tonight, I'm not my own person.

I'm not my own anything.

"Fine," I snap, handing him my phone with all the lack of grace I can muster. "But I need to be reachable for emergencies."

He doesn't even bother answering me. Just pockets my phone like that's his property, too, and beckons me to his side.

For the rest of the night, I keep my feelings close to my chest. I don't let him see how hurt I feel, or how badly he's disappointed me.

I steel myself. I smile at all the right times, nod in all the right places, laugh politely at every joke. Once or twice, Yulian even remembers to introduce me.

Then the announcement rings out.

"Esteemed guests, please make your way to the chapel."

Fucking finally. The sooner we get this ceremony over with, the better.

We step into a side room fitted with everything a chapel would have: cascades of flowers, lacquered wooden benches, more of that odd mix of fairy lights and naked bulbs from the garden.

We take our places on the groom's side. For the first time, I realize I have no idea who's even getting married here.

How does Yulian know them? Is this business, or does he, too, have friends?

But one glance at his emotionless face tells me all I need to know. Whoever's tying the knot here tonight, he couldn't care less.

Then I see him.

Tall. Blond. Decked in white from head to toe, waiting for his bride at the altar, his curls slicked down with gel and a lily in his breast pocket, and...

... the face of my worst nightmares.

No. It can't be.

My palms go clammy. My heart starts hammering, wild, the heartbeat of prey caught out in the open, defenseless, hopeless.

I try to make myself small in my chair, frantically looking around for an exit route, but the other guests are blocking me in.

At that moment, the march starts playing.

If I stand now, he'll see me, I realize, panic rising through my throat. *If I stand—*

But he sees me anyway.

I feel it in my gut—the second our eyes make contact.

The moment I know, irrevocably, how fucked I am.

Because my abusive ex just recognized me.

Brad.

The man I ran away from.

The man I changed my name for.

The father of the child he thinks I lost.

7

MIA

It happens like in the movies.

The nuptial march starts playing. Heads turn at the sound of clacking heels. The room *oohs* and *ahhs* at the sight of the bride, walking up to the altar in a cascade of white lilies.

But the guests in the front row, decked out in all the hues of Gaudy Gold and Pretentious Pink money can buy, aren't looking at the bride.

They're following the groom's gaze.

And at the end of it is *me*.

Me, who wasn't supposed to be here to begin with.

Me, who had no idea it was *my ex* getting married here tonight.

Me, who needs to get the hell out.

"Are you alright?"

A voice next to me snaps me out of my trance. A deep, rough voice, like hot sand and gravel. Mere moments ago, that voice was getting on my last nerve.

Now…

"Mia?"

Now, I cling to it with all I've got.

I take in the man at my side. Gray eyes, designer stubble—everything a woman could possibly want in a date.

Too bad it's all fake.

"Mia," Yulian demands, with all the authority he's capable of. The authority that, according to the rumors, keeps the Lozhkin Bratva in line. "Answer me."

"Let me leave," I whimper, not caring how pathetic I sound. "Please, let me leave."

But I know, even as I'm asking, that it's already too late.

He saw me.

He fucking saw *me.*

And the groom's wicked smirk seems to agree.

The music stops. The priest starts talking. The groom's eyes don't leave mine for a second.

Fuck.

If this were a different kind of movie, the song would shift into something hopeful. Soft notes, slowly rising in a crescendo, right before the groom's grand gesture of romance.

If this were a different kind of movie, the priest might be asking the love of my life, who'd look suspiciously like Hugh Grant, "Do you love someone else?"

But this isn't that kind of movie.

There is no Hugh Grant here.

And that groom—tall, square-jawed, imposing—is *not* the love of my life.

This is my worst nightmare come to life.

"Mr. Bradley James Baldwin," the priest says uneasily. "Do you take Miss Constance Julia Lovegood to be your lawfully wedded wife?"

Pause.

Pause.

Waytoofuckinglongofapause.

Then, my nightmare decides to one-up itself.

"No."

Brad's grin grows bigger as he shrugs off the priest's question and steps away from his bride like she's nothing.

"I want *her* instead."

Then he points.

At.

Me.

Chaos erupts. Several guests gasp deep enough to suck the air out of the chapel.

Me? I'm not getting any air at all. If not for the rabbit-quick heartbeat in my chest, I'd think I stopped breathing the second Brad laid his claim on me.

This can't be real, I tell myself, despite every evidence to the contrary. *This can't be happening.*

Not to me.

Not—

"Not again," I find myself pleading, voice small and brittle. So brittle, in fact, that only the person next to me seems to hear it.

Too bad he'll *never* help me.

I'm paralyzed. I can't move. All I can do is watch Brad walk towards me in long, confident strides.

He'll get you back.

He'll get everything back.

And then, he'll get Eli back, too.

That's what snaps me out of it.

Terrified, I leap up and sprint down the aisle. My legs feel like jelly, stumbling with every step. The crowd is acting like molasses, trapping me, keeping me from fleeing the chapel like I so badly want to, when—

"You can't have her."

Hands grip me around the shoulders. Strong hands, but not cruel.

Nothing like Brad's.

Just a few paces away, Brad sneers. "What the hell did you just say to me?"

My eyes dart to Yulian's. His expression is unreadable, a mask of cool, smooth ice. To anyone else, he would look perfectly calm.

Except that I'm close enough to see what his eyes really look like.

And it's a fucking storm up there.

With a swift motion, Yulian grabs my hand and tugs me behind his back. I'm left speechless, my mind struggling to catch up to everything the rest of me is witnessing.

Yulian, getting in the way.

Yulian, stepping between me and Brad.

Yulian, *protecting me.*

No one's ever done that before.

"I said you can't have her," Yulian growls. "She's *mine.*"

Wait, what?

My heart jumps in my throat.

Mine, he said. *She's mine.*

Warmth explodes at the center of my chest. I have no idea why, or what it's about. I just know it's the second time tonight that Yulian Lozhkin has done something for me no one else ever dared. The second time he *saved* me.

What I don't know is *why*.

My gaze flies between Yulian and Brad. Brad's face is twisting with fury—a very predictable reaction.

But Yulian?

He doesn't let go of me.

He doesn't budge.

He *stays.*

God only knows what that means.

8

YULIAN

"You can't have her. She's *mine.*"

After I speak those words, I realize three things at once.

One: the room has gone silent. *Dead* silent. All whispers have ceased, every scandalized gasp fizzling out like an old soda can. Even the bride has stopped hyperventilating.

Two: Mia's fallen silent, too.

It's concerning. This filterless woman, who hasn't stopped sassing me all night long—*now,* she decides to be quiet? It makes me wonder just who the hell this guy is to her.

And why she looks so damn terrified of him.

Three: my business deal just went out the fucking window.

Brad Baldwin. Around five years ago, the smarmy piece of shit inherited Baldwin Construction, his father's multinational conglomerate. Ever since, he's been swimming in money, luxury, and lucrative requalification deals. Deals I'd wanted to get into badly enough that I chose to willingly suffer through a whole night of socializing at his wedding.

A wedding that is clearly no longer happening.

Brad smirks, stepping towards Mia again. As if he already owns her. As if I'm just some poor schmuck who hasn't gotten the memo yet.

"Yours?" He sneers. "I'm afraid that's not possible. You see, she belongs to me."

"No," Mia tries to protest, but it comes out broken, brittle. "I'm not yours."

"But you are." His lips curl, revealing a row of white, perfect teeth. His left canine is slightly crooked, like a fang grown too sharp. "I've been searching everywhere for you. To think this is where I'd finally find you. Couldn't stay away, could you, sweet thing?"

Behind me, Mia's body starts shaking. I can feel her hand crushing mine, holding on for dear life. As if begging me not to let her go.

It makes dark fury bubble up inside me.

"That's okay," Brad croons. "I knew you'd come home eventually. Shoulda known you'd wait until the last second to make an entrance. You always did love your drama."

I expect Mia to lash out. To tell him to go fuck himself, threaten to shove a syringe up his ass and fill him up like a balloon.

The woman I met in Brownsville, the one who got my car towed and didn't show an ounce of remorse afterwards—she would have done that and more.

But this one isn't doing anything.

I turn, incredulous, and see her staring at the floor. She's biting her lip hard enough to draw blood, and still, she isn't saying a damn thing.

React, I want to roar. *For fuck's sake, just say something.*

Just then, Brad lifts a hand. A single hand, headed straight for Mia's cheek.

And Mia doesn't move.

Like she can't get her body to do it. Like she's too scared to.

So I do it for her.

I snatch Brad's hand out of the air. My fingers clench around his wrist, *hard.* Any harder, and they'd be crushing his bones like a little bird's.

To his credit, Brad doesn't cry out. Just emits a quiet grunt and grimaces. "Get off me."

"No. I don't think I will."

"This doesn't concern you," Brad spits. "She's mine. She always has been."

The whole room is watching us with bated breath. As if they're wondering who'll throw the first punch. Whose blood will spill first, hm?

Their curious eyes drift to Mia, puzzled, almost asking, *Why her? What's so good about her?*

I don't give a shit. Let them look. No one's taking her away.

She belongs to *me.*

The flash of possessiveness takes me by surprise, but I don't dwell on it. My whole focus is on Brad—on keeping his filthy hand away from her.

Tonight, I paid Mia to be my date. I put her in that dress, brought her here on my arm, and taught the guy flirting with her at the bar a lesson in manners.

I taught everyone what happens when you touch what's mine.

And Mia Winters is mine. Until the sun rises, she is *mine.*

Certainly not Brad fucking Baldwin's.

Brad's expression turns vicious, cruel. It falters between a grin and a snarl, like a feral dog with a bone. "I'll say it one more time: that girl isn't yours. So get the fuck off me."

His voice is dripping with entitlement. I catch Mia flinching at his words, her body shaking harder against mine.

Don't let go, her blue eyes beg me. *Please, whatever you do, just don't let him touch me.*

I decide then and there that I won't.

Not ever.

"You're mistaken, Mr. Baldwin." My grip tightens, just enough to draw another wince out of Brad. I'm not looking to break bones yet, but that can change. "Mia Winters is with me now."

"Mia Winters?" Brad barks out a laugh. "So that's what you went with? Your great-grandmother's maiden fucking name? I should have known you'd do something like that. You've always been sentimental."

Mia's face has gone pale now. She looks like she could faint at any time. Like she's staying upright by sheer force of will.

I let Brad's wrist go and shove him off. If Mia's going to faint, I need to be able to catch her.

Brad massages his wrist. "You have no idea who she is, do you?" he laughs, mocking and bitter. "Do you even know her real name? What she's done?"

"I don't need to," I say. "I know enough."

"No, you don't. Otherwise, you'd know that she belongs to me." His leery eyes fix on Mia. "And I don't share."

"What a coincidence," I growl. "Neither do I."

The tension could be cut with a butcher knife. A new murmur rises through the crowd. Now that the spell's broken, the guests seem to have a lot to say about the recent developments.

They thought they were getting a wedding, after all. The side of the bride is furious, every single one of them.

But they're also afraid. Afraid to displease their illustrious host, to fall out of his good graces.

So most of them are directing their angry glares at Mia instead.

The powerless one, the inoffensive one. The one who's to blame for nothing, but cannot hurt them. The *easy fucking target.*

These people make me sick.

I tuck her closer to me, shielding her from the crowd's rage.

Then, finally, the bride snaps out of it.

"*Her?*" She picks up her skirts and stalks this way, her face a mask of fury. "Are you fucking serious, Bradley?"

"Shut up, Connie. I don't want to play with you anymore."

He tosses his arm back casually, making the girl stumble. It's such a cruel, dismissive gesture, I can feel Mia flinching hard behind me. Her hand shoots forward out of reflex, trying to catch the bride's elbow even though she's too far away.

A bridesmaid darts forward, saving Connie from a horrible fall. Brad doesn't even notice. He's too focused on Mia.

It makes me disgusted to see it. How can anyone treat their woman like this? Their bride, the person they supposedly *love?*

And even if there's no love there—even if this is just a merging of fortunes—how the hell can you look yourself in the mirror after acting like this?

Behind me, Mia doesn't seem surprised. I find myself wondering even more about their history, about whatever ties her to Brad.

Was she his bride, too, once?

Was she wearing white and stepping up an altar to marry him?

Was she, too, discarded like she was nothing?

I don't get to demand those answers. I don't get to do anything at all.

Because one second later, bullets start flying.

9

YULIAN

I don't think.

I don't wait.

I don't waste one goddamn second.

I grab Mia and throw her to the floor under me.

She lets out a scream. I can feel the shock in her body, her wide eyes staring up at me without understanding. "Yul—?"

"Stay down!" I bark. "Keep your head low."

For once, she doesn't argue.

Around us, the other guests are screaming, running every which way. In their panic, they end up straight in the line of fire.

I watch their bodies drop like flies, one after the other, blood spraying mercilessly on the toppled flower arrangements.

The lilies, once white, turn red within seconds.

When I realize Mia is staring at the scene, too, I pull her head in the crook of my arm. "Close your eyes," I growl. "Don't look."

She gives a quick nod. I can feel her bury her face against me, like I'm the only safe place she's ever known.

My protective instincts surge, stronger than before. Stronger than ever.

I tuck her close and wait for the rain to pass.

Memories are crowding my mind, pushing against the walls of my skull, but I won't let them. No matter how insistently they demand my attention, I'm not going to give it.

Right now, I need to stay lucid. Need to keep my focus no matter what.

The past has already happened.

Bullets, flying in through the windows. A shower of broken glass and gunmetal. The smell of gunpowder, so strong I can't breathe.

Blood. Blood. So much blood.

I can hear them scream—my parents, my sister, my family. The only family I've ever known.

And Kira, too, dropping like a stone at my side.

I plant my nails into my arm, force myself to snap out of the unwanted memory. The pain grounds me, turns my focus razor-sharp again.

Then the bullets stop.

It's my chance. The only chance I might get.

"Let's go."

Mia stumbles after me. Pulling her upright takes longer than I'd like, but after that, it's only a matter of keeping her steady and running. Her body weighs nothing compared to mine.

We rush past the corpse of a bridesmaid and head for the garden.

As we make our way through the grass, Mia doesn't say anything. Her feet are uncertain but quick, tripping along like a newborn fawn. My arm is around her waist, and her face—tear-stained, makeup-streaked, the spaces between her freckles spattered red with blood—is still tucked into my side.

I hear her exhale, soft and shaky. As if she thinks we've made it past the worst.

She has no idea that *this*—getting away, getting out alive—is the most dangerous part.

Whoever opened fire on us won't want us to live to tell the tale.

"Wait."

I pull Mia to me and flatten myself against the wall, one hand pressed to her mouth. She looks up at me then, her blue eyes lost and confused, but I don't have the luxury to explain.

Instead, I press my free finger to my lips.

She nods once, trusting me.

A few people rush out of the church, running ahead. They don't see us—they can't. They're too agitated, too blind with fear to pay attention to the darkness.

Then they start dropping.

The shots are quiet. Silenced. They whistle through the air and that's it: one dead, two, three women fall like marionettes in the grass.

Mia chokes a scream into my hand, eyes gone wide and terrified.

"Don't look," I whisper again.

Her eyes flutter shut. I can feel something wet on my hand, dropping down my fingers like pattering rain.

Tears, I realize. *She's crying. For strangers.*

"Maks," I mutter into my phone. "Bring the car. Now."

Moments later, Maksim's limo skids to a stop next to us. He must've already been on his way. "Get in!"

I don't need him to tell me twice.

I throw Mia into the backseat head-first, then I follow. Before I've even shut the door, the engine is already roaring again, Maksim's foot slamming on the gas pedal.

Then we're off into the night.

I wait until the shots fade, then turn to Mia. "Are you—"

Hurt, I want to ask, but the word dies in my throat.

She isn't wounded, not physically. But her eyes are still huge, unblinking, her mouth forming words that won't come. Her hands, rigid like blocks of ice, still haven't let go of my arm.

I don't make her.

"Mia." My voice drops low, as soft as I can ever make it. "It's over now. You're safe."

She's shaking like a leaf. I can hear her teeth rattling, can feel her sharp intakes of breath like she's forgotten how inhaling and exhaling works.

The protective thing inside me roars, fierce. It roars for her—for Mia Winters, or whatever her real name is.

I have no idea why. She's nothing to me.

Then why are you still holding her?

I chalk it up to the memories. Once, a long time ago, I lost people just like this. People who actually meant something to me—people who meant everything. I tell myself that's all this is: me, projecting. Feeling what I felt then, like an echo of a long-forgotten song.

And yet, it's hard to make myself believe it.

Not when every inch of my body wants to wrap around hers and never let go.

I swallow down the urge and stay where I am. This is why I don't date for real: it's too fucking inconvenient. Being with someone means getting attached. It means giving a shit about them, tying yourself to them.

It means that, when a bullet goes through their chest, you *feel* it.

Like it was your own damn heart.

That's a weakness I can't afford.

"Mia," I whisper, "talk to me. Tell me you're alright."

I tell myself it's just insurance. I don't want to waste my time driving her to the hospital, or filling out police reports, or paying for her therapy. After all, she signed up for this, didn't she?

Except she didn't. She had no idea who you were.

But now, she does.

Next to me, Mia finally moves. It's so imperceptible I almost don't catch it: a slow, shaky nod.

"Yeah," she croaks. "Yeah, I—I'm good."

Strong. It shouldn't be the first word to come to mind, but it is. This woman, whoever she is—she's way stronger than she seems.

Way fucking stronger than Brad Baldwin seemed to be giving her credit for.

But she isn't strong enough to go home right now.

It's a split-second decision, but like all the other choices I make, I don't second-guess it.

"Do you trust me, Mia?"

Trust. It's a word I'm not used to anymore. It's been ages since I spoke it. Since I meant it.

There's no reason she should say yes, but she does. "Yeah. I do."

"Maks," I bark, "turn left. We're taking a detour."

10

MIA

We pull up under a lone neon sign in the middle of nowhere.

I have no idea how long we've been driving. How long it's taken me to come back to myself.

Even now, I'm not sure I'm fully *here.*

Not when part of me is still *there,* crushed to the chapel's floor, Yulian's cologne in my nostrils and the roar of gunfire in my ears.

Yulian. He's opening the door now, climbing out and reaching in with his hand. This time, there's no trace of forced gallantry.

"Come. We're here."

His hand is warm, strong. *Real.* I accept it, let it anchor me to the here and now.

When I'm outside, I take a deep breath of cool night air. That, too, helps ground me. We're far from the city, somewhere green still exists outside of concrete squares, somewhere without lights.

If you squint, you can even see a handful of stars.

But it still doesn't tell me where "here" is.

"Here meaning…?"

"A twenty-four-hour diner," he explains. "They won't ask questions. You can clean up in the bathroom, get changed."

"Why would I need to…?" Finally, I glance down at my dress. My beautiful pale blue dress, now spattered with red. "Oh."

I feel dizzy. Right on cue, Yulian's hand finds my shoulder. I find myself leaning into the touch before I realize it's supposed to steady me. Like, in case I'm about to faint.

"Does the sight of blood bother you?"

Suddenly, I feel the hysterical urge to laugh. "No, no. I'm a nurse. I—I'm used to it. It's just…" My eyes travel down the stained silk. Just like that, the urge to laugh morphs into an urge to cry hysterically instead. "I ruined your dress."

"Technically, it's *your* dress." Yulian's lips quirk slightly. "You get to keep it, remember?"

That almost-smile—it makes me feel warm inside. Way warmer than I have any right to feel after a night like this.

"Right."

"Though I'd advise getting it dry-cleaned."

That manages to drag a small smile out of me, too. "That's probably a good idea."

With that, Yulian shepherds me into the diner. I'm surprised by how gentle his demeanor has turned. When he puts his hand on the small of my back now, I don't even think of batting it away.

In the course of a few horrifying hours, he's gone from pain in my ass, to downright rude, to emotionless, to savior I didn't know I needed—and now, to comfort I didn't know I was going to need to depend on.

It's been a roller coaster, to say the least.

The diner is, as promised, empty. "Get changed," Yulian says. "I'll get us something."

The authority in his tone propels me into motion. My feet, frozen until moments ago, start moving again on their own. Like they were waiting for him to tell me what to do.

I duck into the bathroom and disappear behind the sliding door.

I go through the motions without looking in the mirror. I don't think I could take it—seeing the full extent of the damage.

Not because of the dress, but because of what it means.

All the people I didn't get to save.

Some nurse I am.

I hold no delusions, though. Those gunshots were professional work. Straight to the head. I couldn't have saved anyone, not even if I'd sprung right into action.

And yet, the images of those bodies dropping in the night... that will haunt me as long as I live.

But I've seen my fair share of horrors, too. I've seen people die. It comes with the territory of being an E.R. nurse—not knowing when death will strike.

Maybe that's why I'm back to myself so soon: death is no stranger to me.

And neither is Brad.

Brad. When we rushed out of the chapel, I saw him crouched under the pulpit, taking cover in the safest spot of all.

For one second, our eyes met.

I knew, then, that he'd survive.

There's no doubt in my mind even now. Brad is alive. Untouched, unscathed—and coming for me.

He knows my name now. He knows I'm in New York. How long will it take him to find out the rest?

Where I work? Where I live?

How long will it take him to find out about Eli?

My son. *Our* son. The son I spent the last four and a half years hiding from him.

A familiar sensation grips me: the urge to bolt. To hurl us into my beaten-up Honda and drive across state lines. Just me, Eli, and the open road.

But bolting isn't an option. Not this time. When I left home over five years ago, I had a clean slate. I didn't have loans, or debts, or problems with the law.

That's all changed now.

I lean over the sink and force myself to breathe. In, out, repeat—like I teach my patients. Finally, my eyes meet their reflection in the mirror.

I look like a mess. My makeup's all ruined, blotting around

my eyes in dark, looming circles. I can see red smears on my skin that have nothing to do with lipstick.

I scrub until it goes raw.

Calm down, Mia. Breathe. I try to fish out my therapist's mantra, but somehow, it's not her words that come to mind.

It's Yulian's.

It's over now. You're safe.

I don't know why, but I believe him.

Slowly, the tremors ease. My heart stops racing. When I glance at myself in the mirror again, I almost look like I did when I left home.

All thanks to him.

He saved me. The realization hits like ice water: Yulian Lozhkin, the ruthless CEO-slash-criminal mastermind, *saved me.*

He shielded me with his body, protected me with his life, and made sure I'd be safe.

And he protected me from Brad, too, before all that.

But he's a killer, that nagging inner voice reminds me. *You heard him in the car. He was having a freaking corpse melted.*

Yeah. He was. But somehow, right now, I can't find it in me to care.

No one ever helped me when I needed it. Not the cops, not the neighbors, not anyone.

The system that was supposed to keep me safe? It failed me, over and over again.

So, if the devil gives a shit? That's who I'm sticking with.

My mind made up, I finally emerge from the bathroom.

I find Yulian at a corner booth. "Sorry. I made you wait."

"Not at all." He slides a cup my way. "Coffee's still warm."

Gratitude wells inside me. *He ordered me coffee. He didn't have to, but he did.*

"Thank you," I whisper.

I take a long sip. The coffee burns on the way down, grounding me. Warmth starts spreading through my body again, slowly bringing me back to life.

I end up downing the whole thing in one go.

Yulian's eyebrows rise. "Rough night?"

Somehow, I find myself laughing. "Not the roughest I've had," I offer. "You should try manning the E.R. triage desk on the Fourth of July. If that doesn't take away your faith in humanity…"

Yulian's lips twist. He has a dimple, I realize—just a slight one under his right cheek. It makes this rare smile of his feel even more precious. "I'm afraid that dried up a long time ago."

"Smart man." I refill my mug from the pot at the center of the table. "Though I'll say you haven't lived until you've had to look someone in the eye and ask them how exactly they *'accidentally sat'* on their empty beer bottle."

The dimple deepens. I find myself hypnotized by it—the only true physical indicator I have of how amused the Ice King really is.

"Sounds like tonight wasn't even that eventful by your standards."

I wish.

"Look, I… I'm sorry," I whisper. "About how things went down."

Yulian stares at me. "You're… apologizing?"

"Well, yeah."

"Why?"

"I—" my voice catches. "What do you mean, why? I ruined your night. I made Brad make a scene. I…"

"Mia." Yulian leans across the table. His piercing gray eyes hook me into place. "You didn't do anything. You were just sitting there. So explain to me, kindly, why I should accept your apology."

I bite my lip. I'm not used to this—being excused. "I guess I just… feel responsible."

"But you're not."

"I'm not sure Brad would agree."

He makes a show of looking around the vacant diner, then back at me. "Brad isn't here."

"Right." I give a wry laugh. "Sorry. Old habits."

Yulian watches me carefully. As if he's caught between wanting to ask and wondering why he should.

I don't blame him. He has no reason to care about me. To him, I'm a stranger. A girl he hired for a job.

He saved my life tonight. That's already enough.

"Brad…" He trails off. "He knew you."

"It was a long time ago," I murmur. "A lifetime, really. Guess I just… wasn't expecting to run into him again in this one."

"Mia—"

"It's just like him, though. To get us shot at." I force a laugh out of me. "Seriously, typical Brad. Always screwing with the wrong people."

Yulian goes still. Suddenly, I wonder if I've said the wrong thing. After all, Yulian did take me to Brad's wedding. Maybe they really are friends?

But no, that can't be. The way Yulian snatched Brad's wrist out of the air, keeping him from touching me…

That wasn't a friendly gesture.

"The wrong people, huh?" Yulian echoes eventually. "Sounds like he keeps bad company."

"The worst," I assure him. "He always had a knack for hanging out with dangerous crowds. Guess he thought it'd make him dangerous by association."

"Dangerous crowds," Yulian muses. "More dangerous than me?"

I consider him. His commanding manner, his tattoos. His hot-and-cold flashes, never letting you understand if he cares or if he doesn't. His expensive suit and cologne, the kind no clean money can buy.

His stormy eyes, filled with a thousand dark promises.

"I wouldn't know," I decide. "I haven't seen how dangerous you are yet."

Something passes through his eyes. Something close to amusement. "That's for the best."

It's an odd close to the conversation. I feel like I've missed something—some crucial piece of it.

But then Yulian's rising, leaving a few bills on the table for us, and I know the moment is over.

So I follow him out and back to the car.

"Mia." A warm hand shakes me awake. "We're here."

I startle back to life. "What…?"

"We're at your place."

I plaster myself to the window. The sky's much lighter now—too light. Over the horizon, dawn has already broken.

"Shit." I fumble with my bag. At some point, Yulian must've slipped my phone back inside, because I can see a thousand missed calls on it. "I have to go. I'm sorry, I—"

"It's alright," Yulian says. "I said you'd be mine until the sun came up. It's not your fault that it did."

Despite my panic, that drags a laugh out of me. Before I know what I'm doing, I find myself blurting out, "Look, I know this is really weird, but would you maybe want to—I don't know, get coffee or—"

Then I turn and I see it.

A big, fat wad of cash.

"For your troubles," Yulian says coldly. "And for your service."

Service. Right. Of course.

What was I thinking? This was work. A job—nothing more. One that I didn't even perform that well.

What exactly was I expecting? That he'd rescue me from my shitty life? That he'd come over to my shit-stained side of the world, when his side is made of luxury cars and fashion-magazine people?

I guess I was at least expecting that he wouldn't look at me like I meant absolutely nothing to him.

Yulian sees me hesitate. "It's all there," he says, as if he thinks that's the problem.

That, right there, is my answer.

I *do* mean absolutely nothing to him. I never will. I'm a tool he used for a job, and now that the job is over, I am irrelevant.

I take the cash from his hands. The motion must be too abrupt, because Yulian's eyes squint just a fraction. "Mia—"

"Thanks," I mumble. "Guess I won't be seeing you around, then."

Something settles in his expression. Somehow, it feels like a door closing.

"Guess not."

I get out of the car, slam the door, and slump back to my side of the world.

Shit stains and all.

11

MIA

I count the money anyway.

It's a petty gesture, I know. After all, like Yulian said, *it's all there.* But it gives me a dark rush of satisfaction—to focus all my attention on it. The one thing that matters.

Because *I* sure as fuck don't, do I?

Calm down, Mia. It's that voice inside my head again, the reasonable part of me. *You got what you came for. Isn't that enough?*

More than enough, in fact. As the numbers add up, I finally realize just how much this money is going to change my life. Ten whole grand—for one night's work.

It's a drop in the ocean, but it's more than I've ever held in my hands at once.

With this, I can replace Eli's shoes. I can pay my bills, keep the bank quiet for one more month, fill up my tank. Next time I come back from work, I won't have to deal with Drunk Tom staring at my ass. Won't that be a dream?

Then why am I still so fucking sad?

Because it wasn't his money you wanted, that nasty voice in my mind answers.

I shake my head. That coffee in the empty—that's what I choose to blame my unease on. How shaken I was, how badly I needed comfort. Yulian gave me that. He sat across from me, filled my cup, and made me laugh.

Then he shoved cash in my hands and sent me coldly away.

I have no idea what changed between that moment at the diner and our arrival here. If he finally realized what a poor substitute for his usual dates I was. Not rich enough, not beautiful enough, not easy enough.

God, I'm so pathetic. What the hell is wrong with me? A guy shows me basic human decency, and suddenly, I'm DTF?

"Forget him," I snap under my breath as I climb. With the elevator perpetually out of service, I have no choice but to carry my heels. It looks every bit like the walk of shame it is. "Forget Yulian Lozhkin. You never had a chance. You've got bigger things to worry about. Like..."

Brad.

As I search for my keys, I realize just how thoroughly fucked I am. Brad was never supposed to know where I was. But tonight, he found me.

And if he found *me...*

No. Absolutely not. Brad has no reason to suspect Eli exists. No reason to look.

And if he does—

Well, then I'll do whatever it takes to protect my kid.

"Kallie? Eli?"

"Aunt Kallie's gone."

I follow that tiny voice to the living room. Relief washes through me as I see him: my son, watching cartoons with a bowl of cereal in hand.

"She tried calling you," he scolds. "But you weren't picking up. She had to go to work."

Right. Of course. Kallie had a morning shift—how could I forget? She asked me specifically to come back early. And there I went, off gallivanting with a stranger at the shittiest wedding of the year.

I want to say I'd take it all back if I could, but the weight of Yulian's money in my jacket pocket would make me a liar in a second.

"I'm so sorry, baby." I kneel by Eli and stroke his curls. "So much happened tonight, and I… I didn't realize how late it was."

"It's okay." Eli shrugs, his attention still fixed on his cartoons. "I don't mind. Aunt Kallie looked upset, though."

"I'll make it up to her," I tell him. "I promise."

"I didn't touch the stove."

"I know you didn't. You were very good."

"She left you a note in the kitchen."

"Okay." I press a kiss to his forehead. "I'll go see. You want anything?"

"Can I have juice?"

"Of course you can. What do we say?"

"Pretty please?"

"Good boy. I'll be right back."

Kallie's note is way less angry than I deserve. She had every right to scream at me. Instead, her handwriting just reads, ***Had to run to work, tried calling. Told Eli not to touch the stove. TEXT ME!!!***

Texting her is the first thing I do. ***Sorry—crazy night, couldn't get to my phone. Back home now. I promise I'll explain everything.*** Then, with a fresh pang of guilt, ***Thank you for staying as long as you could. I love you, I do not deserve your kindness, and at your earliest convenience, I will spend two straight hours massaging your feet and groveling for forgiveness. Pinky swear.***

I grab the juice and cuddle up to Eli on the couch. "Did you have fun with Aunt Kallie last night?"

"We watched Carmen Sandiego." He slurps loudly through the straw. "Why did you come back yesterday? You got all pretty."

"Why, thank you."

"Mom."

I ruffle his hair. "It's a long story. But I've got good news—"

Before I can say another word, the doorbell rings.

"We're not expecting mail, are we?" I frown, realizing as I say it that it's way too early. I check the time—7:35 A.M.

I open the door—

"Good morning, Ms. Winters."

—and it's *them.*

12

MIA

The social workers blink at me placidly from the hallway.

"Mr. Lee." I force myself to smile. "Mrs. Deloera. What brings you here so early? I thought we didn't have another visit scheduled until next month?"

"We don't," Howard Lee says, his nose already up in the air like a sniffer dog. "May we come in?"

Can I say no? I want to snark, but swallow back the impulse. Knowing Mr. Lee, he might actually write that down in his godforsaken little notepad.

"Please." I smile through my teeth. "Make yourselves at home."

"Thank you, dear," Itzel Deloera says. Her eyes crinkle behind her half-moon glasses. "We'll only be a minute."

Her colleague, on the other hand, just plows right in. "Where's the child?"

"Eli?" Itzel calls, soft and grandmotherly, her head peeking into the living room.

"Aunt Itzel!" Eli jumps down from the couch, forgetting the cereal in his hands entirely.

The bowl rolls, then spills all over the floor.

"Oh…" Eli goes, panic flitting over his little face. "Oh, no, no—"

"Don't worry, baby." I stroke his head, calming him down before he can have an episode. "I'll clean this up. Why don't you go color a little with Mrs. Deloera?"

"But I made all this mess, Mommy…" he sniffles. "The cereal…"

"Cereal's very cheap," I reassure him. "We can buy a fresh box whenever we want. And luckily, hardwood floors are easy to clean. See?" I wipe at some of the mess with a paper tissue nearby. "Good as new, yeah?"

Slowly, his lower lip stops trembling. "Okay," he mumbles.

"Now, why don't you show Mrs. Deloera your new markers?"

Eli trudges towards Itzel. She smiles kindly down on him. "There's my favorite young artist! Come on, let's find your sketchbook…"

She takes Eli's hand and they disappear into his room. I've gone through this song and dance countless times, and yet, I still can't get used to it—seeing my kid being led away by a stranger. Fortunately, Mrs. Deloera's as inoffensive as they come.

If only that could be said for her colleague.

"Can I offer you anything, Mr. Lee?" I force out. "Coffee? Water?"

A laxative? Help removing the stick that's surgically inserted up your ass?

Lee scowls at my living room. He doesn't seem to be appreciating the mess of plushies and toy cars strewn all over the floor. "No, thank you."

Then, as if drawn by a sudden realization, his eyes zero in on me. Like, *really* zero in.

"When did you come back last night?"

"What?" I blink. "Why is it any of your—"

"Kindly answer the question, Ms. Winters. Where were you last night?"

His icy voice sends a shiver down my spine. I take one look at myself and realize what he must have seen: a woman in a night dress, barefoot, hair all mussed up and makeup haphazardly washed off—and two deep, black bags under her eyes.

Like someone who's been out all night partying.

Shit.

Panic swirls in my stomach, but so does fury. "When my shift was over," I grit. It's the truth—technically. "What exactly are you implying, Mr. Lee?"

"Do I need to spell it out?" he asks. "I believe the conditions for custody were very clear, Ms. Winters: You were to keep your job, foster a safe home environment—"

"—which I *have*—"

"—and never leave your child home alone again." His eyes narrow. "We don't want history to repeat itself, do we?"

Cold sweat breaks down my back. Guilt swims up my throat. I force myself to swallow, to hide from Mr. Lee how badly he's rattled me.

We don't want history to repeat itself.

"I'll ask you once more, Ms. Winters: *where were you last night?*"

"With me."

We both turn to the tiny voice in the hallway.

"Mommy was here," Eli insists. "She tucked me into bed and kissed me goodnight."

Mr. Lee stares at Eli. I feel like I must be doing the same, too shocked to speak.

"Eli," Lee says, his tone marginally gentler, "you know it's not good to lie, right?"

"I'm not lying!" Eli cries out, suddenly ferocious. He isn't very intimidating, but I can tell he's trying to be. His fists are balled up at his sides, his tiny brow furrowed as far as it can be. It makes that horrible guilt stab me even deeper.

He's doing it for me.

He's trying to protect me.

God, I don't deserve him.

"Okay," Lee concedes reluctantly. "But she mentioned a shift. Who was with you then?"

"Aunt Kallie."

"And when did Aunt Kallie leave?"

"Just now." He points at the toppled bowl of cereal. "She made me breakfast. I didn't touch the stove."

Mr. Lee doesn't look convinced. "Eli…"

"It's getting late, isn't it?" Itzel's gentle voice breaks through. "We'd best be on our way, Howie."

Lee—no, *Howie*—stiffens, visibly irritated. "Mrs. Deloera," he says with the barest minimum of patience, "we aren't finished here."

"I think we are." Her grandmotherly smile spreads softly on her wrinkled face. "Everything seems to be in order. We found Eli in the care of his mommy, didn't we?"

The vein on Mr. Lee's forehead starts bulging dangerously. "But—"

"Didn't we, Howie?"

Finally, his stubbornness gives. "I suppose we did," he mumbles, like he's being forced to swallow a particularly sour lemon.

"Good. Then off we go." Itzel waves. "Goodbye, Eli. Goodbye, Mia, dear. Be good for me, won't you?"

"Yes, Mrs. Deloera," Eli says politely.

"We'll be good," I promise.

Mr. Lee glares at me. "See you next time, Ms. Winters. Eli."

Then they're out.

I slump against the door, face in my hands. My body slides to the floor. If I'd been five minutes later…

If, for some reason, I hadn't made it back in time…

They would have taken him. My son.

I feel a tug on my sleeve. When I peek through my fingers, a worried little face blinks back at me. "Are you okay, Mommy?"

"Of course," I lie. "Why wouldn't I be?"

Eli curls up next to me. "I'm sorry," he whispers. "It's my fault they keep coming."

"Oh, baby." I pull him into a hug. "No, no, no. You didn't do anything wrong. In fact, I'm the one who should be apologizing. You lied to cover for me just now, didn't you?"

His lips press into a thin, guilty line. "Am I in trouble?"

"Of course not." I hold him closer. "Thank you. I'm sorry you had to do that."

He shakes his head. "I want to protect you, Mommy. Like you protect me."

My eyes grow wet. I force myself to blink back the tears. "Hey," I whisper. "Wanna know the good news I had for you?"

Eli peers up at me. "What news?"

"I have the day off." I grin. "Wanna go shoe shopping?"

Eli's face brightens instantly. "Can we?!"

"Only if you get dressed real fast."

I watch him hurtle towards his bedroom like a tiny tornado.

Happy—like kids are supposed to be.

For the first time in hours, I feel like I've done something right.

13

YULIAN

I'm staring out the windowed wall in my Manhattan office when Maksim bursts in with a folder.

"You were right," he announces. "It's them."

That's all he has to say. We don't say the name anymore, because every time I do, it's ash on my tongue and fire in my veins and it takes many, many sessions of spilled enemy blood before I can calm myself enough to think clearly again.

So it's just them.

Them.

Prizrak—that's what they're called. It means "specter." A syndicate of men who do not exist in any government database.

They are ghosts. Spooks. Bloodstained phantoms in the dark.

Originally from Bulgaria, they hire themselves out as contract killers to anyone with the cash to pay and the balls to dare. Allegedly, they've been behind every major unsolved assassination since the Fifties.

And twenty years ago, someone hired them to destroy my bloodline.

It took me twenty-four hours to find out who did the paying. To learn who had the cash and the fucking balls.

A friend—or so I thought. I tied cement blocks to his ankles and fed him to the Hudson. Ever since, I've refused to speak his name, even in my mind.

But it's taken me twenty years longer to get even a whiff of the bastards who actually pulled the trigger.

I've sworn to kill them all. I won't stop until it's done.

Only then can my family rest in peace.

Only then can I move on with my life.

Because, as it turns out, they're still carrying out their task: "Destroying the Lozhkin bloodline."

They've taken a creative approach this time, I'll give 'em that. Instead of shooting at me, they're shooting at every woman I'm seen with more than once.

It's why I've been bringing a different woman to every event, showing up with a different date on my arm every night. It's why Nikita was the perfect choice for last night.

Because she's a woman I have no feelings for, who can handle herself as well as any of my men. A true Bratva lieutenant.

But somehow, they got to her, too.

Funny enough, it's not Nikita that my thoughts go to. It's not that I don't want to find her—she's given me her loyalty for years, and I'll spend my last breath hunting for her if that's what it takes.

But I know that, wherever she is, she's giving her captors hell.

So it's another woman who draws my attention.

Mia.

Mia, who came there with me.

Mia, who was so shaken she almost forgot how to speak.

Mia, who didn't doubt for a second the attackers had been after Brad.

I didn't correct her. Didn't bother. Didn't tell her the truth about last night, not even when she gave me the perfect chance to explain things at the diner.

Those attackers—they were never after Brad.

They were after *me.*

Whoever shot up Brad's wedding venue… They were the same people who shot up my estate. The same people who killed my family. Who killed Kira.

Prizrak.

Them.

"Why now?" My fists ball up at my sides, knuckles going white. "Why there?"

"Haven't the faintest." Maksim shrugs. "You?"

You know why. My skin has been crawling all night with suspicion.

Mia.

You can't have her. She's mine.

I replay those words in my head. I was pissed off, angry that some entitled daddy's boy thought he could just take the woman on my arm.

As if I'd ever let that happen.

But *Prizrak* must have thought differently. They must have thought Mia meant something to me.

That I intend to marry her.

The same thing they thought I intended for Kira.

"*Blyat'!*" I slam my fist on my desk, the sharp crack of wood bouncing off the glass walls. "These fucking *mudaki.*"

"We'll get them," Maksim vows. "They've shown their cards now."

I shake my head, because if I keep dwelling on the rage, it'll consume me. I need to do what I've always done: focus. Plan. Prepare.

"Update me on Nikita," I order.

"No news, I'm afraid," Maks sighs. "But we found her getaway bag. Which means she didn't take it."

"Which means she didn't run."

"Exactly."

Of course she fucking didn't, my instincts snap. *Nikita wouldn't run. Not when she's got as much skin in the game as I do.*

"Find her," I growl. "I want men looking for her 'round the clock. No one sleeps until she's back."

Maksim inclines his head. "Yes, boss."

I make a mental tally of the past twenty-four hours.

Nikita, gone.

Mia, shot at.

Fuck knows how many wedding guests, dead or traumatized.

All because of their tenuous connection to me.

All these years, I've been asking myself one question. It's a piece of shrapnel lodged in my skull, a splinter I haven't been able to pull out no matter what: why go after my women? Why not just kill *me*?

Why, when their task has always been to obliterate the Lozhkin family?

There's only one answer I've been able to come up with. Only one that makes sense.

Torture.

This isn't just about destroying me. This is about revenge. They don't simply want me dead—they want me to suffer.

To always be looking over my shoulder, waiting for the moment everything I care about will be taken from me again.

They want me to be alone, die alone, leave my empire up for grabs. It's a long, cruel game, one where I'm king and pawn at the same time.

But joke's on them: solitude suits me.

I cast a telepathic thought out toward those ghouls, wherever they are hiding. *Stop aiming at innocents and come for ME, motherfuckers. I fucking dare you.*

"Oh, that reminds me." Maksim snaps his fingers in the air. "I've got that thing you asked for. The background check on that nurse."

Immediately, my thoughts take a hard swerve. "Go."

He plops down across from me. "Bullet points: her financial situation's not good. Actually, it's kind of a mess. Debts, loans, overdue bills—you name it, she has it."

I flip through the file he hands me. Mia's driver license picture is right at the top. She's younger in it—nineteen, tops. Her face is rounder, her blue eyes brighter. Her hair, pulled back in a braid over her shoulder, is dyed a rich, dark brown.

I glance up at Maks. "How much debt?"

"Quarter mil, give or take."

I frown. "That's a lot of money for a nurse to owe."

"My thoughts exactly."

"There's student loans in there, I gather?"

"Around fifty grand of it." Maks turns the page and points. "The rest is from… this."

My eyes narrow as I see what he's pointed out. "A settlement?"

"Yup. Last year. Record's been sealed, but people talk. There was a fire at her old place. Rumor has it, her kid set it."

"Her kid?"

"Oh, yeah. She's got a rug rat. Little boy of four, going on five."

I do the math in my head quickly. "She must have had him young."

"Wasn't even twenty-one." Maksim flips through a few more pages. "Here's his birth certificate."

I scan the document quickly. *Eli Winters, male.*

"There's no father listed here," I note.

"No father anywhere I could find," Maksim confirms. "He's either a ghost, or very much not in the picture."

Suspicion spreads through me, but I push it aside. It's not like it matters who the father of Mia's kid is.

But it does matter to you, doesn't it?

I shut that voice up and turn to Maks again. "You mentioned a fire."

He pages back to the incident report. "Apparently, she left her kid home alone over a night shift. Probably thought she'd be back before he woke up."

"But she wasn't."

"No, she wasn't," he sighs. "Kid woke up, started playing around with the stove. Luckily, he managed to run off to a neighbor before the fire spread."

"He was unharmed, then?"

"Why?" Maksim ogles me with a cheesy smirk. "Looking to adopt an heir?"

His smug face irks me. "Keep reading," I snarl. "And keep your idiocy to yourself."

"Oof. Yessir."

The truth is, I've got no idea why I asked. Why is the thought of Mia and her kid's well-being on my radar at all? Mia's business is her own—it doesn't concern me.

"Anyway," Maksim yawns, "that's pretty much it. Landlord sued for damages; she settled. Most likely wanted to avoid a full-blown court case."

"Or a jury," I muse. "Might not have looked kindly on a mother leaving her kid alone overnight."

"That's what I thought, too." He shrugs. "Unfortunately for her, child protective services got involved anyway. To paraphrase their report, she's on thin fucking ice."

"Is that all, then?"

"Almost." Maksim's face splits into a grin like he's been waiting for this exact question. "Wanna know the kicker? Until five years ago, Mia Winters didn't even exist. At all."

That finally catches my attention.

"And you waited until *now* to mention it?"

"You know me, boss. Got a flair for the dramatic."

I ignore my idiotic best friend and focus on what he just told me.

Five years ago.

Didn't exist.

I knew Brad a lifetime ago, she told me.

"A lifetime ago," I mutter aloud.

"What's that?"

"Nothing." I shut the file. "Any luck tracking down her real identity?"

"Not so far, but I haven't looked hard. Want me to keep digging?"

"Yes." I hand the file back to him. "Look for a connection to Bradley Baldwin, too. Those two have history. I want to know what it's about."

"Sure," Maks says. "I'll do that. But honestly, Yul? This right here is just about enough to wrap anyone around their finger. That's what you were looking for, isn't it? Leverage?"

Is that what I've been looking for? I'm not certain.

Last night, I just wanted to get under the skin of the nurse who got my car towed. Now…

Now, a plan is forming in my head.

A wild, reckless plan.

My enemies think Mia matters to me. They think I care—enough to make it worth trying to kill her. Once I drop out of her life, I doubt they'll try again.

But what if I didn't?

What if I stayed in her life?

Most importantly—what if I kept her in mine?

"You're thinking it, too, boss, aren't you?" Maksim murmurs, sober and serious for once. "That this is our chance?"

Mia's presence already drew out my enemies once. Which means she can do it again. And again, and again, however many times it takes me to catch them.

She'll be the bait.

They'll bite. Oh, they'll fucking *bite.*

And then I'll have my revenge.

"Draw up the paperwork," I order. "Make sure it's ironclad."

Custody troubles. Crippling debt. A fake identity and a secret past.

It's perfect.

She's perfect.

It'll be the easiest "yes" in history.

"Sure thing," Maksim says. "Should we warn her of the danger?"

"No. The less she knows, the better."

I rise. Manhattan spreads out under me, pieces of an empire. *My* empire.

Now, Mia Winters can help me secure it for good.

14

MIA

The rest of the weekend goes on in a peaceful haze.

Eli is over the moon about his new shoes. He wears them around the house all Saturday, then falls asleep in them. On Sunday, I have to bribe them off his feet with Fruit Loops.

It's the best weekend I've had all year.

When I have to go into work for my night shift, I tuck in Eli and kiss him goodnight. "Be good with Uncle Reese. I'll pick you up in time for school, okay?"

"Promise?" Eli pleads. His tiny hand clings on to my sleeve, as if afraid I won't show up. That I'll leave him on his own again.

It makes guilt pierce me even harder.

"I promise," I whisper.

I mean it.

Never again.

Things are gonna be different from now on.

At work, Kallie is surprisingly understanding when I give her the whole insane rundown. "Oh, you poor thing," she says when I finished my story. "I can't believe I was mad at you!"

"To be fair, you had every reason."

"No, I didn't! You got caught in a *shooting,* Mimi. That's a get-out-of-jail-free card if I ever saw any." She hugs me tightly, almost squeezing me to death. "Are you sure you're okay?"

"Positive," I croak. "Can I please have my lungs again?"

"Nope. All mine now."

Afterwards, Kallie tries to grill me about the mysterious billionaire-slash-bad boy who hired me to be arm candy for ten thousand smackaroos.

But I'm not ready to get into all that yet—especially not the Brad part—and so she reluctantly lets me off with another bone-crushing hug and a rain check for tea and yap.

The shift is, of course, grueling.

By the time I've dropped Eli at preschool on Monday morning, I'm beat. All I want is to curl up into bed and shut off my brain for a couple of hours. Forget about my wild Friday night and sleep like the dead.

Unfortunately, it seems the universe has other plans.

"Ms. Winters. We need to talk."

When I see him on my doorstep, all dark suit and husky voice, my first thought is: *Oh, no. He's back.*

And then: *Oh, no. He's hot.*

I slap myself mentally. The fact that he's here cannot be good news—at *all.*

I don't care how good he looks in those tailored slacks and that barely-buttoned shirt: Yulian Lozhkin is trouble.

With a capital fucking T.

"Mr. Lozhkin." I steel myself. "What a surprise."

The corner of his mouth curls. "Not that much of a surprise, it seems. You've done your research."

"And you've done yours," I bite back. "Otherwise, you wouldn't know at which door to loom."

"Is that what I'm doing? 'Looming'?"

Focus, Mia.

Don't get distracted by his abs, Mia.

You've got no cheese left to grate, Mia.

"You tell me," I say with a nervous swallow. "You're the one blocking me out of my apartment."

He looks at me with a hungry glint in his eye. An intense, predatory look, the kind that makes you suddenly realize how interesting the floor between your toes is.

Slowly, he takes a step towards me. "First, I was blocking you in," he drawls. "Now, I'm blocking you out."

I force myself to hold his gaze. "Points for consistency, I guess."

We stay like that for a while, in silence, just staring at each other. Waiting to see who will blink first.

Get comfortable, Mr. Lozhkin, I seethe at the back of my mind. *'Cause it sure as hell ain't gonna be me.*

Eventually, he takes a step back and concedes. Not like someone who's lost, though—like someone who's got much bigger games to play.

Somehow, it gets even more on my nerves.

"Aren't you going to invite me in?" he asks.

"No." I cross my arms and plant myself in front of my door. "Whatever you have to say to me, you can say it right here."

"It's cute that you think a locked door could stop me."

"It's cute that you think I'll let you in where my kid sleeps."

His lips twitch again with that quicksilver smile. I hate that he's getting a laugh out of it. Out of *me.* It makes me want to fist that perfect shirt and scratch those perfect abs and—

Nope. Wrong train of thought.

Still, the sentiment stands.

Eventually, Yulian plucks a manila envelope from under his arm. I was so preoccupied with him, I hadn't even noticed it.

"Read," he says, with the calm confidence of a man who expects to be obeyed.

Warily, I take the file.

My eyes narrow as I scan it, but every word I read pries them wider. At one point, I'm convinced it must be a prank. Yulian doesn't seem the type to clown around, but who knows? Maybe he's secretly a big joker.

Or maybe I'm the clown.

"This is a contract," I blink.

"An astute observation."

"To be your *fake fiancée.*"

"Again, glad to see your reading skills are up to the task."

I grind my teeth into dust. God, what I wouldn't give to just grab his face and—and—*urgh!*

"Yulian, what the hell is this?"

His pupils widen—just a fraction. Belatedly, I realize this must be the first time I've called him by his first name.

He recovers quickly, though. "As you so cleverly noticed, it's a contract of employment."

"To be your girlfriend."

"*Fake* girlfriend."

"For the next six months."

"If you're fishing for compliments, I'm afraid I've already said everything I'm going to about your comprehension abilities."

"How about *your* comprehension abilities?" I cry out. "You realize I'd have to be crazy to say yes, right?" I thrust the papers back to him. "I mean, last night—"

"Turn to article five."

"Excuse me?"

His tone grows darker. "I'm not in the habit of repeating myself, *Mia.*"

The sound of my name in his mouth sends a shiver down my spine. Suddenly, my legs feel like jelly.

I don't know why I obey, but I do.

"Article five," I read flatly. "'Compensation.'"

"Go on."

I'll tell you where you can go. "For six months of service," I grit, "the Employee will be paid…"

Then I stop.

I blink.

I reread the number.

Then I count the zeroes again, and again, and again, because it can't possibly be—

One million dollars.

But it is.

I turn my gaze back to Yulian. "You're—you're serious?"

"Like I said," he rumbles, "I'm always serious."

One million. One *freaking* million. My eyes are crossing, reading the number over and over, like it might change at any second.

I have to fight the urge to pinch myself, if only because I know Yulian would be insufferable about it.

Of course, he decides to be insufferable anyway.

"Not bad for six months' work," he points out. "It's certainly more than you make right now."

"How do you know what I—?"

"I have my sources," he says vaguely. "Besides, you're a nurse."

The dismissive way he says it makes my blood boil. Like nurses are just a disposable category—people you don't really *need*. People who, when it comes down to it, can be replaced in a heartbeat.

It's the way every hospital administrator in history has felt about us. The way every hotshot doctor treats us.

I want to tell him to shove his contract up his ass, but I can't.

Because the truth is, it's a lot of fucking money.

More than I make in six months, he says? Fuck that—it's more than I'd make in *ten years.*

I bite my tongue, but I doubt there's a point in secrecy. It's not like my ratty scrubs and the bags under the eyes aren't giving Mr. Bad Boy Billionaire the full picture anyway.

"You'll be my plus one at events." He fixes his cufflinks, not even looking at me as he speaks. "You'll accompany me wherever I choose, whenever I choose. You'll wear what I say, do as I say, and behave like a true Lozhkin fiancée would."

It irritates me to no end—the way he says it.

Like I've already accepted.

Like it's unthinkable I wouldn't.

Like he can just waltz into my home and *buy me.*

"In exchange for that," he goes on, oblivious to the dark glare on my face, "I'll take care of all your debts. I'll take care of your needs. I'll make sure you never have to set foot in a shithole like this again."

He knows about my debts. It's like a bucket of ice water straight to the face.

Until now, I'd been downplaying how dangerous Yulian Lozhkin is, how resourceful. How capable of getting whatever it is he wants.

But now, I can't ignore it anymore.

Yulian's gaze flicks back to me. Calm, unbothered—like he's already won.

In a way, he has.

There's no world where I say no, is there? No universe. No version of reality. This is one million dollars we're talking about. It's life-changing money. It's—

"I'll even throw in an investment fund for little Eli."

At that, I see red.

"Keep my son's name out of your fucking mouth," I snarl.

Then I slam the contract into his chest.

Yulian's eyes widen. Just a little, but enough to betray his surprise. If I didn't know better, I'd even call it shock. "You're refusing."

"No shit, Sherlock." I plant my fists on my hips. "What? You thought you'd just show up here and—and *buy* me?"

"You need the money," he says again, like it explains everything. "Clearly, you do."

"And clearly, you're not the great negotiator you thought you were." Forgoing all thoughts of self-preservation, I get all up in his space again. I may be half his size, but I'm fairly certain I'm carrying twice the rage he's capable of right now. "You come here, you insult my profession, you insult my home—"

"I did not—"

"Yes, you did!" I snap. "This 'shithole' that you despise so much? It's *home* to me, Yulian. To me and my son. And you do not get to come here and play sugar daddy with us."

Yulian's face is a mask of barely-concealed fury. I watch his throat work, his jaw set tight.

"If I have offended you," he growls, "then you have my apologies."

It feels like it costs him to say it—like he just had to swallow a lemon whole. I get the impression that the word "apology" is not usually a part of Yulian Lozhkin's vocabulary.

"That said," he adds, cold as ice, "I fail to see how what you're doing here is smart."

"What you fail to see," I retort acidly, "is that I've had enough of rich men thinking they can own me."

"You're saying you won't even consider it."

"I'm saying—"

Suddenly, my pocket starts vibrating. I pull out my phone, and—

—and the preschool's number blinks back at me from it.

"Shit," I curse. "I have to go."

"We're not finished here."

"Yes, we are."

"Mia—"

I drop the papers at my feet and rush off.

Yulian's stare burns holes in my back the whole way.

15

MIA

When I get to the principal's office, my heart sinks. "Oh my God. What happened?!"

Eli trudges towards me, sporting a fresh black eye. He doesn't answer—just drops the bag of frozen peas and tucks himself tightly against me.

"Baby?" I get down on his level, stroking his hair and trying to coax words out of him. "Does it hurt?"

He shakes his head, but flinches when I touch the bruise.

My heart breaks in a thousand different places. Here is my son, my world, and I couldn't protect him.

Again.

Before I can ask anything else, the secretary's head pops out. "Ms. Winters? Principal Johnson is ready for you."

"I'll be right back, okay?"

I squeeze his arms, press a kiss to his head, and duck into the office.

The principal is waiting by the window. "Mia," she greets without a smile. "Take a seat, please."

I swallow. Somehow, the Happy Hares Preschool principal always makes me feel like a little kid all over again—one who's just gotten into huge trouble.

Which makes no sense. It's *my* kid out there with a black eye, isn't it? This is probably just an incident report.

Diane sits across from me, massaging her temples with a sigh. She's a stout woman in her fifties with a gray-streaked afro and a no-nonsense attitude. Despite how uneasy I feel in her presence, I've always liked her as a principal. She's the kind of woman who does no harm but takes no shit.

Unfortunately, her "take no shit" glare is now currently fixed on *me.*

"There's no easy way to say this, Mia…"

"I know," I cut in quickly. "I saw Eli outside. His eye—"

"—was almost entirely his own doing, I'm afraid."

Wait, what?

Fury mounts inside me. My mama bear claws are pushing to come out, but I restrain myself. "That can't be true."

"He assaulted his classmate Bobby."

"Bobby *Perkins?*" I explode. "Mrs. Johnson, you don't understand. That kid—he's a bully! The other day, Eli came home with his new shoes filled with holes. I had to buy him a replacement, one I almost couldn't afford. He's—he's the worst!"

Diane lifts a plucked eyebrow. "A four-year-old child is 'the worst'?"

"Yes! No—I mean—"

"Look." She steeples her fingers and leans on the desk. "Bobby has behavioral issues. Now, while I wasn't aware of this particular incident, I'm aware of the bigger picture."

"Great!" I blurt. "So why is *my* kid in trouble?"

"Because it wasn't Bobby who escalated things this time."

I blink. Diane's words feel like water, going right through me. "What are you saying?"

"I'm saying that Eli threw the first punch."

"Wha—" My mouth hangs open like a goldfish's. "No, that can't be true. Eli—he's not a violent kid!"

"Maybe not," Diane concedes. "But he's hotheaded, impulsive, and won't listen to anyone once something sets him off. You're aware of his episodes, I presume?"

"That's just anxiety," I protest. "Ever since the fire, he's been feeling out of control. His therapist said it's normal."

"The court-appointed therapist he only saw three times?"

Something in Diane's tone makes me feel defensive. "Yes," I grit out. "Is there a problem with that?"

For a long moment, Diane just stares at me. Then she takes off her glasses and sighs. "Mia, can I be frank with you?"

Maybe it's the exhaustion in her voice that makes me put down my arms. The dark bags under her eyes, so much like mine.

"Of course."

"We both know Bobby's a little shit. Ms. Keane agrees that he was, indeed, trying to ruin Eli's shoes."

"See?!" I throw my arms up. "Then—"

"That doesn't change Eli's reaction was completely disproportionate," Diane interrupts. "He pounced on that kid, Mia. You think Eli looks bad? It was a miracle Bobby didn't need stitches."

My heart drops. "Stitches?"

"Eli took his scissors from him. He was hacking at his shirt when Ms. Keane managed to drag him off."

I blink. My mind feels blank, frozen. I keep trying to picture Eli acting so violent and just—can't.

My kid wouldn't do that, would he?

Would he?

"What are you saying?" I murmur. "That Eli's—what? Aggressive?"

Diane's expression softens. "Eli's a wonderful kid," she says. "But he isn't getting the support he needs. Not here, and definitely not with those three isolated therapy sessions."

It stings to hear her say that. Like I've somehow failed him. "You think he needs more therapy? About the fire?"

"I don't think this is about the fire at all."

Then Diane pulls out a questionnaire.

"Every year, we test the students we feel meet the criteria." She slides the paper my way. "These are Eli's results."

"Test?" My hackles rise. "Test for what? Why wasn't I informed?"

"Because it's a harmless questionnaire," Diane shrugs. "And because you would have said no."

"All the more reason—"

"Mia, don't get me wrong. Almost no parent wants their kids tested for this." She levels me with her gaze. "And almost every child suffers for it."

That gives me pause. The thought of Eli suffering—it's the one thing I can't bear.

"What am I looking at?" I sigh.

"A preliminary test for neurodivergent traits," Diane says. "Eli's score suggests he'd benefit from an ASD assessment, as well as an ADHD evaluation."

It takes a moment for all those letters to sink in. "You're saying Eli's… autistic?"

"I think there's enough evidence to warrant digging deeper."

My mind reels. "But… he's verbal. He's social, he interacts, he—"

"—can still be on the spectrum," Diane interjects. "Even with all of that."

"So, his episodes…" I swallow hard. "You think they're meltdowns, then?"

"I do." Diane taps on a chart at the bottom of the page. "I also think he's been regularly behind his developmental milestones, if only by a little."

"B-but…" I shake my head. "Eli's smart. Like, *really* smart. And—and kind, empathetic, curious. He loves spy movies, you know? He's always tinkering with his building blocks to make gadgets. If he had ADHD, or if he was autistic, or both—wouldn't I have noticed?"

Wouldn't I have known my son needed more from me?

Shouldn't I have seen?

Is all of this my fault?

Diane squeezes my hand. "I think you and Eli have been through a lot already. It's not easy to pick up on these signals when you're a working single mom. And I think—though it's only my opinion—that Eli saw how thin you were spread. Like you said, he's a smart kid."

There are tears in my eyes now. Not because Eli might be autistic—I've always hated parents who turn their kids' diagnoses into personal tragedies—but because, if what Diane's saying is true, *I've* been failing him.

"So he was masking?"

"It's pretty early to call it that, but yes. In a way, he was. And when he wasn't, it was easy to mistake the signs for long-term effects of his trauma."

My voice is a broken, hopeless thing when it wobbles out of my throat. "So what do I do?"

"Honestly?" She fishes around her desk drawer. "If it were my kid, I'd do this."

Then she hands me a pamphlet.

Rainbow Infinity Private School.

"This is…?"

"The support he needs," Diane fills in. "Don't get me wrong. You won't find anyone who believes in public school more than me. But the truth is, here?" She gestures around at the crumbling plaster and ancient, scratched furniture. "We're barely keeping our heads above water. There's no way we can splurge on a specialized teacher. And Ms. Keane? God, I love her, but she's thick as a brick." She taps on the pamphlet with her fingernail. "If you want to do right by your son, this is your best bet."

My eyes scan the pages. Smiling children beam up at me, happy and diverse, with a rainbow shining behind them in an infinity shape.

It's... nice.

Way too nice.

"How much is it?"

"Fifty thousand a year."

The cogs in my brain screech to a halt. "That's more than I make before taxes, Diane."

"I realize that. Normally, I wouldn't even be bringing this possibility to your attention."

"So why are you telling me?"

"Because Eli's special." Her shoulders slump. "He's bright, and he's driven, and he hates injustices with all his heart. He's also way too trusting and with his head in the clouds far too often. You think Bobby Perkins is bad? Wait to see what happens when he starts *actual* school."

"You think he'll get bullied?" My hands start trembling. "Like —seriously bullied?"

"I've seen it happen way too often to discount it. And not just with other kids."

Diane's words stab straight to my chest. "You're saying teachers might...?"

"I know they will. Some of them, at least."

"But..." I blurt. "But you must be able to do something. Fire them, or—"

"And hire who?" Diane gives a bitter laugh. "Our district's been defunded to hell and back. We're losing our best teachers every year. Even the ones who want to stay... they just can't afford it. I'm already scared enough for the rest of our kids as it is, but a special needs boy? He won't survive here. Even if I do my damnedest to protect him—which I will —it won't be enough. Sooner or later, he'll be scarred. And I think he's already got enough scars for one lifetime." Her eyes meet mine. "Don't you?"

I think back to the fire.

To every night I gave up my meal for his because we couldn't both afford to eat.

To the ratty shared apartment my son was born in.

To the father he doesn't have.

"I do," I whisper. "But fifty thousand a year..."

It's impossible. It's unreachable. Add up the rest of his schooling years, and that's more than half a million. More than I could possibly make in a lifetime.

Unless...

Unless nothing. There was only one chance to pay for this, and I already turned it down.

I'm not so sure I regret it, either. Yulian's proposal felt like a double-edged sword. It felt like the kind of deal you make with the devil.

And I'm not ready to sell my soul quite yet.

But what if it was the only thing that could save my son?

"Thank you," I rasp. "I'm sorry for the trouble Eli has caused. Please, extend my sincerest apologies to Bobby's family."

Diane gives me a warm, two-handed handshake. "Don't you worry about that. I'll handle the Perkinses. You just sleep on this, okay?"

"Okay. Thank you, Mrs. Johnson."

When I exit the office, Eli takes one look at me and hangs his head. "Did I make more trouble for you, Mommy?"

"Of course not." I pull him close. "How about we go get ice cream?"

"Really?!"

"Really." I press a kiss on the top of his head. "Then, once we're home, we'll talk a little more. Okay?"

"Okay, Mommy."

As we walk back to the car, my heart fills with all sorts of feelings. Guilt is the worst of them.

My kid needed me. He needed me, and I wasn't there.

~

By the time we make it home, Eli's bouncing around with grocery bags filled with tubs of all sorts of flavors. I know I'm going to need to give him a stern talking-to about his attack on Bobby, but for now, I want to put him at ease. I want to see him smile again.

Then I see the crumpled envelope lying on the welcome mat.

"Mommy?" Eli peers down at it. "What's this?"

"Nothing," I say quickly, squirreling it under my arm. "Just mail."

But I can't ignore the anxious thumping of recognition in my chest, nor the Post-It stuck on top of the contract.

You have three weeks to decide.

Three weeks. That's all I've got.

Three weeks to figure out my kid's future.

Three weeks to decide whether to sell my soul or keep it.

Three weeks to shake hands with the devil.

16

YULIAN

"*Blyat*," Maksim curses as he nearly trips. "Pothole. There's nothing but potholes here!"

I tune him out and focus on my breathing. Jogging always clears my head. There's nothing like a good workout to get the blood pumping, but today, the gym didn't feel like enough.

Today, I wanted to keep my body in motion.

Today, I wanted to be *here.*

Which is an odd thing to feel about Brownsville.

Maksim's phone pings. "Nikita?" I ask as he checks it.

He sighs. "Another dead end. Fucking hate dead ends."

"Not as much as I do."

He must feel the growl of warning in my tone, because he leaves a wide berth between us as we jog down Brooklyn's asphalt asshole. "It's like we said, man. Whoever did this is a ghost. Which fits a little too well with everything else that's happened."

He means the shooting at the wedding.

"Any news on Brad?"

"Alive and kicking, unfortunately," Maks replies. "And kicking up a storm with the NYPD. He's demanding the perps be found."

Good luck with that. I've been on their tail for two decades and turned up jack shit. If Brad actually manages to get anything done, I'll send him a fucking fruit basket in gratitude.

But he won't. I know it in my gut: No one else will bring down my enemies.

That duty belongs to *me*.

Gunfire. Spilled wine on the floor. Blood, mixing with it. At some point, I stop being able to tell them apart.

There's a girl next to me under the table. A girl I've known all my life. A girl it never crossed my mind to marry—we were friends. Too good friends to ruin it.

But my enemies don't know that.

"Stay down," I growl. "Keep close to me, Kira. Don't let them—"

Then her body slumps forward.

"Kira?!" My hand shakes her shoulder. "KIRA!"

But it's too late.

I shake my head and pick up the pace. Those images never do me any good. I don't need my wrath to be fueled—I need it to be sated. I need vengeance.

And fucking hell, I need to find Nikita.

Last time, it was too late to save my family. Too late to save Kira.

I won't let it be too late again.

"We're stopping?" Maks asks hopefully, more than a little out of breath.

"No." I take a swig of my water. "Why? Tired already?"

"Just eager to preserve my neck from all these damned potholes."

"Or maybe you've been behind a steering wheel too long." I chug down the rest of the bottle, then crumple it in my hand. "Can't remember how to work those legs."

"Very funny," Maks deadpans. "I'll remember that next time I kick your ass on the ring."

"Sure. In your dreams."

"Speaking of dreams," he pants, "why are we in this nightmare of a neighborhood anyway?"

As if on cue, I hear it.

Her voice.

I look up. From across the road, I can see her through the open kitchen window: in her pajamas, flipping pancakes, a big grin on her face.

I thought she looked gorgeous in the dress I gave her. Then I thought she looked gorgeous in her ratty scrubs. Now, I'm not surprised to realize she just might look gorgeous wearing anything.

Or nothing at all.

My cock twitches in my shorts. They're wide enough to hide it, but not if it gets any more interested. And I know better than to get interested in an asset.

Because that's what Mia is: an asset. A pawn. A means to an end, no matter the cost.

That cost, I realize, could very well be her life.

Those same old memories flash before my eyes again: the blood, the bullets, the bodies. I was nineteen then. I'm not nineteen now.

But the thought of someone dying for me still doesn't sit well in my chest.

My men are trained for this life and the death it might bring. They know what they're getting into. From the moment they're sworn in to the instant a bullet takes their lives, they breathe for *me*. And they get their fair dues in return.

What I offered Mia was more than fair, but she still turned me down.

It was a surprise. More than that—it was new. No one has ever turned me down before. Not as CEO, not as *pakhan,* and certainly not as a man.

But Mia Winters refused all three.

Why?

Why would she turn down a million dollars? Why, when it could change her whole life? It can't be just because she thought I was rude. That would be absurd.

And yet, I can't find any other reason.

She has no idea I was the target at Brad's wedding. Or rather, that *she* was. I doubt she could have figured it out on her own, given her limited resources.

My past is a secret I've guarded carefully. The only explanation left is that, somehow, she caught wind of how dangerous I am. That she's scared of me.

Call me crazy, but she sure as fuck didn't look scared.

Suddenly, another head pops into view. Smaller, shorter—a little boy. *Her son,* I realize. The curtain is waving in the wind, hiding him from view from one moment to the next, so I don't get a clear look. I'm not so sure I want to.

Because, if Mia ends up saying yes, I'll be looking at the boy I might turn into an orphan.

An orphan like me.

I shake that thought right off. I can't let it sink its claws into me. Whatever Mia's life looks like is none of my concern. Whoever gets hurt isn't, either.

My revenge takes precedence above all.

Besides, I'm not the kid I used to be. I'm strong now—strong enough to protect what's mine.

"That's her, isn't it?" Maksim is grinning next to me. "Should we wave?"

"Do it and I'll cut your fucking hand off."

He backs away, eyes wide. "Fine, fine. Geez, you're touchy. No wonder she dumped you."

"She didn't *dump* me. We're not a goddamn couple."

"Not with that attitude."

"You—"

A flash goes off behind me.

I turn, already pissed to hell and back, but don't see anyone to vent my anger on. "Who the fuck's taking pictures at this time of day?"

"Construction crew?" Maks shrugs. "They work with blowtorches. Sometimes, those look like camera flashes."

"Shitty fucking neighborhood." The longer I'm here, the more I'm convinced my description was accurate: This *is* a shithole. Mia can get mad all she wants—she's just mad I'm right.

She could leave, though. If she'd only take my money, she could buy a place in the heart of Manhattan. Live at the top of the world.

So why won't she?

"You know, you could hire someone else," Maksim floats out there. "For this scheme of yours."

"No," I spit too quickly. "It has to be her."

"Why?" he presses. "Because your enemies think it's her already? We both know you could orchestrate a pretense twice as good as that. With a professional, that is."

"I don't want a professional," I snarl. "I want—"

I swallow it before I can say it. It feels far too real. Maksim wouldn't understand. He's a fucking romantic.

Me? I'm a beast. A starving, savage beast.

It's not my fault Mia's scent feels like the only thing that could sate me right now.

"I want it to look real," I tell Maksim. "Mia does that. A professional won't."

"If you say so."

"I do. So stop fucking questioning me."

My gaze flicks back to the window. Mia is moving away from it now, the smell of half-burnt pancakes wafting down for a couple of seconds longer. She heaps the carnage into a plate, ruffles her kid's hair, and disappears.

I jog back to the car, Maksim close at my heels. "Put more men on Nikita's search," I tell him without looking back. "Turn the heat all the way up. We can't afford to lose her."

"Understood," Maks wheezes as he climbs into the driver's seat. "Should I turn the heat up on Mia, too? Talk her landlord into an eviction, make her reconsider?"

I look back towards her apartment building. "No," I say. "Let her come to me."

"And if she doesn't?"

"She will."

And once she does, she'll be mine.

17

MIA

"Wait." Kallie's eyes go wide as saucers. "He offered you how much?!"

"Shh!" I glance nervously around the E.R. "Lower your voice! What if Gwen hears?"

"Oh, she'll know either way," Reese chimes in from Bay Three over the sound of his patient throwing up. "Last week, she knew what I had for lunch. On my day off. In my own apartment."

In Bay Five, Kallie shivers. "That's so creepy."

"C'mon, guys." I fasten the tourniquet around my patient's arm. "Gwen's a little strict, but she's not, like, a Bond villain. She rides us hard because she *cares*."

"Or because she gets a kick out of it," Reese mutters, pulling his patient's hair back as she hacks up every piece of bad sushi she ever ate. "It's called sadism. Look it up."

I ignore him and turn to my patient. "Alright," I say with a bright smile. "Where does it hurt today, Mr. Konrad?"

"Everywhere," Mr. Konrad complains.

"Business as usual, then?"

"It's different this time." He gestures across his body with his free hand as I prepare the blood draw kit. "This pain starts here—" He points at his right shoulder. "—then jumps and picks back up over *here*."

"Your abdomen?"

"Belly button," he specifies. "Then it zigzags all the way down, right here, under my—"

"Okay!" I push him gently back down on the cot. "Make a fist with your right hand for me, yeah? Real tight, like we always do."

"Should I turn away?" he asks with an edge of panic. "M-my brother always faints when he's doing this. I heard it can be hereditary. I read an article saying—"

"All done," I interrupt before he works himself into a hypochondriac frenzy. I pat Mr. Konrad on the back. "I'll send these to the lab while we wait for your consults."

"Already?" He glances in disbelief to the gauze on his arm. "Wow. I didn't feel a thing! You've really got the touch of an angel, Nurse Winters."

I can't help but preen a little. Gratification in this job doesn't come cheap—I'll take what I can get. Even if it's from Hypochondriac Kevin.

"Why, thank you."

"Also, I think you should take the sugar baby job."

"Me, too," Kallie joins in. "Then I can become *your* sugar baby."

"Haha. Very funny."

"Hey! He's hot, rich, and willing. I say go for it. What do you have to lose?"

Hot is an understatement.

Rich, even more so.

But…

"I don't know." I wince. My heart flutters with a thousand conflicting feelings. "He didn't strike me as the most reliable person on the planet. Or the most considerate."

Flashes from that diner keep overlapping with his coldness on my doorstep. The way he ordered me coffee, made me smile, brought me back to myself. The way he *took care* of me. Those are all good things.

Then there's the way he dismissed me like a cheap hooker.

It's been three weeks since he left that ultimatum on my doorstep. Three weeks of his contract burning a hole in my kitchen drawer, right next to the knives and just as sharp.

Today, at midnight, the offer will expire.

"I'm with Mia on this," Reese offers. "Sorry, but it sounds like a serial killer podcast waiting to happen. No one pays that much money for a girl, let alone a fake girl. No offense."

I sigh deeply and sit at the foot of Mr. Konrad's cot. "You're right. It's madness."

But without Yulian, how am I going to afford Eli's school?

I keep swinging back and forth on that. One second, I'm crying myself to sleep, thinking of all the ways I've failed him since he was born.

The next, I look at my son's smiling face and feel like we're gonna be okay, fancy school or not.

And then there's the whole Yulian situation. His smirk, so rare and sharp I could cut myself on it. His million-dollar clothes, million-dollar cologne.

Million-dollar abs, my horny mind supplies.

No. Nuh-uh. I'm not gonna fall for it. I'm not gonna let myself get tangled up into some entitled billionaire's power schemes, whatever they may be.

I've already seen the damage it can do.

"Break time, is it?" a sneering voice interrupts.

We all spring to attention. "Gwen! We were just, uhh—"

"Comparing treatments," Reese cuts in helpfully. "For emesis."

"I think I'm gonna throw up, too," Mr. Konrad mumbles.

Gwen—our head nurse—surveys the scene. Her expression is, as always, unreadable. I've never seen a sixty-odd woman who's shorter, grayer, and more severe-looking than her. She's like one of those Roman statues whose age and mood are shrouded in mystery.

"I see. How's *your* patient doing, Kallie?"

Kallie goes green as she glances at the empty bed that her discharged patient vacated half an hour ago. For a second, I'm worried she might throw up, too. "I-I'll go do another round of the bays."

"Good idea," Gwen agrees snidely. "'Right now' would be perfect."

Kallie scurries away. I cringe inwardly for her. Getting scolded by Gwen Zimmermann is never great. Sometimes, it feels like she can stare into your skull and read your mind. Like she knows every corner you've ever cut and she feels nothing but scorn for your weakness.

As if on cue, her narrowed eyes zero in on me.

"You don't look well," she notes.

"Haven't had a chance to hit the salon lately." I laugh awkwardly, but it goes over like a fart joke.

Gwen isn't swayed. "It's not that. You look… tired." Her eyes, if possible, narrow even further. "Make sure to take care of yourself. Otherwise, you won't be able to care for your patients."

Then, sermon delivered, she marches off to the next victim.

Reese and I share a look. "Unbelievable," he breathes. "She's worried about you. I didn't know she could do that."

"Do what?"

He gestures wildly. "Care!"

I roll my eyes. "She's not that bad, you know. She taught us everything, remember?"

"How could I ever forget the Gwen Glare?" He shivers. "I see it in my nightmares all the time."

I shake my head. Reese loves being dramatic. He's got one thing right, though: I cannot accept Yulian's offer. Not now, not ever.

I glance at my phone. My shift is almost over. The calendar blinks back at me with a date circled in blue.

August 2nd. The day of Eli's first basketball game—and my deadline.

But that's okay. I've already decided. Turns out, I decided this one a long time ago.

Never again.

By the time I get to the school, I'm so excited I could burst. It's Eli's first game, and I can't wait to see it.

He looked so happy practicing at home with his plastic hoop. Seeing him like that, I forgot why I ever considered calling his therapist back in the first place.

The more the days go by, the more I convince myself Principal Johnson got it wrong after all.

How can such a happy kid be struggling with anything?

All the families will be here, too, which is more good news. Maybe I can take the chance to extend an olive branch to the Perkinses. If he's going to be moving next door for grade school with everyone else in a couple of years, I want him to be on the best of terms with everyone. It'll make things easier down the road.

Or so I think.

Then I arrive, and I realize how misguided all that hope really was.

When I enter the gym, Ms. Keane's face is white as a sheet. "Oh, Mia! It's terrible." She runs up to me, her thick glasses bouncing on her nose. "We can't find Eli anywhere."

I freeze. "What do you mean, you can't find him?"

"We've looked everywhere." She looks close to tears. Behind her, children in tiny jerseys are already warming up on the court. "I was about to call you. I—"

"It's okay," I lie, because yelling at Ms. Keane won't make me feel any better. Because my son's missing, and right now, that's all that matters. "I'll find him."

I rush out of the gym and start searching.

I look in the classrooms, the bathrooms, the cafeteria. The school isn't big, not by a long shot, but there's no sign of him anywhere.

Soon, I move into the courtyard.

My heart is racing. My worst fears are crowding my head.

What if Brad found out? What if he came here for him? What if—

What if this morning was the last time I ever got to see him?

But then I hear it: soft, choked sobs, just off into the shrubbery.

I push the branches out of the way—

"Eli?"

—and there he is.

Thank God. I let out a breath I fully knew I was holding. *He's safe. He's okay.*

But when I look closer, I realize he's not okay at all.

He's got something in his hands: a pair of shoes.

Destroyed shoes.

They're ruined, full of holes. On the ground, I can see three separate rolls of duct tape and a pair of round-edged scissors.

He's crying. He's crying so damn hard.

"Mommy," he sobs, "I'm sorry. I couldn't stop Bobby. I—I tried fixing them, but it won't stick! Why won't it stick, Mommy?"

"Oh, baby." I scoop him into my arms. "It's okay. Don't worry about it."

"It's not!" He starts hyperventilating, a telltale sign he's in the middle of an episode. His cheeks are all red, his little nose runny and sniffling. He throws his supplies away, then clings to me and wails. "I hate it here. Everyone's mean. They say I'm a weirdo and a freak, but they're the freaks! They break everything and they're *evil!*"

My own eyes are wet now. I try to tell Eli I'm sorry, that it's all going to be okay, but nothing comes out.

All I've ever wanted is to give my kid a good life, but what kind of life is this? No money for shoes, no time together, no way to protect him?

"I don't want to come back here, Mommy," he sniffles into my chest. "Please, don't make me come back."

I think back to Principal Johnson's words. To her warnings I ignored. To the contract, burning a hole in my drawer.

"Okay," I rasp. "Okay, baby. We don't have to come back." I pick him up and press a kiss to his teary cheek. "I'll fix this, okay?"

"Okay," he sniffles. "I'm sorry, Mommy."

No, I am.

All this time, I've been so selfish. I've been in denial, afraid to face the reality of my son's needs. I've been acting like I've got options when I don't. When it's obvious there was only ever one choice to make.

Luckily, I'm still in time to make it.

So we go home. I tuck Eli into bed and hold him until he falls asleep.

Then, two minutes before midnight, I make the call.

"It's me. I'll do it."

18

MIA

The day after I sell my soul to the devil, I call Eli's therapist back.

He gives me a referral for a colleague who specializes in early development and ASD. It's three hundred bucks a pop, but I still make the appointment.

I take Eli twice over the weekend, paying extra for the speedy sessions. Then I splurge on a fancy daycare for the rest of the month, because even though he won't be going to preschool anymore, I've still got double shifts every other day.

It burns through every cent of Yulian's money. But Eli takes to his new therapist—a Dr. Summers, which makes him giggle every time—like a fish to water. And, by the end of his first appointment cycle, he has a preliminary diagnosis.

ASD with a side of ADHD-c.

"Mommy?" Eli asks from his booster seat on the way back from therapy, slurping his new organic, sugar-free juice. Because, apparently, regular junk food is extra bad for neurospicy kiddos with dopamine troubles. "Why do I have to go to Dr. Summers?"

"Why? You don't like her?"

"I do! She lets me play with her building blocks."

"That's nice of her." I grin at him from the rearview mirror. "Maybe next time you can bring Mr. Bunny to meet her?"

"Yay!"

Inside, I try to steel myself for the conversation to come. Dr. Summers said there's no perfect time to talk to a child about their diagnosis, and that Eli's too young to understand anyway.

But she also said honesty is important, and that his questions should be answered with as much truth as he can handle.

I happen to agree with her. When I had Eli, I swore I'd only tell him one lie. One big lie to keep him safe, then no more.

That his father died before he was born.

Of course, there were little lies over the years. White lies, like Santa Claus and the Tooth Fairy and *"Bambi's mommy is absolutely fine, just napping."*

But on big things? Serious, trust-building things?

Never.

"You see..." I bite my lip. "Principal Johnson, from your old preschool, said you were having a little trouble."

"Because I hit Bobby?"

"That's a good example."

"I said I was sorry," he mumbles with a pouty lower lip.

"I know, baby. And hey, Bobby was really mean to you, so it wasn't all your fault. But you know how you sometimes space out? And get really upset and don't remember what happened after?"

"Yes…"

"Well, Principal Johnson thinks Dr. Summers can help with that. Even if you're not going to her school anymore, she wants to make sure you're taken care of."

Eli is quiet for a while. Then he murmurs, so low I almost don't hear him, "Am I sick, Mommy?"

"What?" I crane my head and meet his eyes. "Of course not, baby. Why do you ask?"

"Because Dr. Summers is a doctor."

I laugh. "There's all sorts of doctors out there, honey."

"So I'm not sick?"

"You're not," I promise. "You're just… just… a little fish."

He gives a big, theatrical blink. "I'm a *fish?*"

"Yup. A cute, adorable fish. But sometimes, little fish get put in the classroom with little squirrels. And while the squirrels are really good at climbing trees, fish are good at other things."

"Like swimming?"

"Exactly!" I snap my fingers. "Dr. Summers… She's there to help you find what you're good at. As a little fish."

He pauses for a long, thoughtful moment. Maybe I underestimated my boy. Maybe he does get it, does understand, is old enough to grasp the things at play here. He opens his mouth and...

"Does that mean we can get a pool?"

I can't help but laugh. "Maybe, baby."

I don't tell him that, with Yulian's money, we could get a whole damn mansion and burrow there for the rest of our days, far away from the Bobby Perkinses of the world.

It'd be way too tempting for both of us.

"First, you gotta learn to swim, though," I add. "And do math. And take long, big breaths when you're mad."

"I can't read yet," Eli points out. "I don't think I can do math, either, Mommy."

"Well, I can't do math, either, so that makes three of us."

He giggles at the joke. "Can I still play basketball?"

"Of course! I happen to know little fish can be *very* good at basketball. Or at least, this little fish right here."

With an ear-to-ear grin, Eli starts bouncing on the car seat, excited to be playing again at some point in the future.

Me? I'm not thinking about the future at all. Instead, I think back to the day he was born: pale, wrinkly, small as a puppy.

I remember holding him close to my chest and promising him: *You're safe with me. I'll always protect you.*

"Hey, munchkin?"

"Yeah?"

"I love you to the moon and back."

Eli's face spreads into his biggest, dimpliest, most gap-toothed grin yet. *Love you to the moon and back*—that's our phrase. My bit, at least.

"I love you to the stars, Mommy!"

"Whaaat? All of them?"

"All of all of all of them!"

I see myself smile in the rearview mirror. *That's my kid.* My beautiful, neurospicy kid with a heart bigger than the whole universe.

And we can handle whatever the world throws at us.

Even Yulian Lozhkin.

19

MIA

On Monday, the world starts pitching curveballs.

It's now been two days since I sold my soul to the devil. Two days since the devil has been ghosting me, making me lie awake at night, wondering if it was all a dream: the diner, the wedding, everything.

On those nights, I pad to the kitchen and pull out the contract to read.

It's real, I tell myself as my fingers brush over the printed words. *He'll call. He will. He's probably just busy.*

When I go take out the trash on Monday morning, however, I realize exactly what Yulian Lozhkin has been busy with.

"Ma'am." The gorillas at my door salute in unison. "Good morning."

The garbage bag dangles from my fingers. *The hell... ?*

"Let us get that for you."

One gorilla plucks my trash from my hand. The other plants himself in front of the door, as if daring anyone to try and come in. Which is a bit inconvenient, because I was kind of hoping to get back in there.

"Okay, what is this?" I demand. "Who are you? Why are you guarding my door?"

"Boss's orders," one grunts.

The vein at my temple starts pulsing. "I never gave permission for this."

"You didn't need to, ma'am."

"You're welcome, ma'am."

Say "ma'am" one more time. I'll shove it up your ass faster than a suppository. "I want to speak to Yulian. Now."

"That's not possible, ma'am."

"He doesn't want to be disturbed, ma'am."

"Well, tough." I fish my phone out of my pocket. "He's about to be."

Then I storm back into my apartment and slam the door.

I type the text with shaking hands. Not out of fear, but rage. ***Why the hell are there mobsters at my door?***

Yulian's reply comes way too quickly for a busy man. ***Insurance,*** he types back.

My vein pulses harder. *I fucking knew it.* Give a billionaire an inch, and he'll take the whole damn neighborhood and bulldoze it to pave the way for luxury condos.

Too bad I'm not going to let him have his way. I've had enough of this attitude—I know where it leads.

This time, I'm nipping that shit in the fucking bud.

My place, 3 P.M., I type. ***Ghost me and the deal's off.***

Then I put my phone on silent.

"Mommy?" Eli whispers as we head out. "Are those spies?"

"Not at all." I force a smile. "Just… new friends."

I calm myself on the drive to the Upper East Side. Rhonda the Honda splutters and splatters, echoing my state of mind.

Yulian—how dare he? How dare he put my building, my *family,* under surveillance?

I may have promised him my soul, but my freedom stays mine.

When we get out of the car, Eli's eyes go wide. "*This* is my new school?"

"Could be." I take him by the hand and lead him through the gates of Rainbow Infinity. "If we like it."

With every step we take, his eyes grow wider. I can't blame him—this place looks nothing like Happy Hares. That school looked like it was held together with spit and plaster.

But this?

White walls. Green gardens. Clean corridors. The outside looks like a miniature college campus—and the inside? It's like those blonde-wood-and-lush-green-plants millennial offices using bouncy balls as desk chairs.

"Ms. Winters!" A smiling, middle-aged man comes to greet me. "I'm Principal Garcia. So glad you could make it." His eyes crinkle as he crouches down. "And this young knight must be Eli."

Eli nods, not quite meeting Mr. Garcia's gaze, but Mr. Garcia doesn't look put off in the slightest. He doesn't try to touch him or invade his personal space in any way. Just gets back up with the same benevolent smile and says, "You're right on time for our mid-morning snack."

We're shown into a big, bright room. I leave Eli to the care of a Ms. Lawrence and the attention of eleven curious pairs of eyes.

"I'll be right back, okay?" I tell him.

"Okay, Mommy."

Then I follow Mr. Garcia into his office. Again, I'm amazed at how well the walls are holding up.

"Coffee?" he offers. "Water?"

"Water would be great, thanks."

He gives me a glass with cucumber in it. I almost want to cry —everything here is so damn *nice.* Is this what it's like to be rich?

Mr. Garcia gives me the gist of the school: stimulating activities, Montessori method, the whole shebang. When I ask about their handling of AuADHD kids, he seems perfectly at ease. He assures me every teacher has specialized training in neurodiversity, as well as diversity training in general.

"We want this school to be a safe space," he explains. "Here, you're met with acceptance and support, no matter your needs. We also have zero tolerance for bullying."

Tears prickle at my eyes. Mr. Garcia discreetly slides a box of tissues over to me. "Diane is a dear friend of mine. She mentioned you've both been through a lot."

"Yeah," I rasp. "It's, uhh—it's been a bit of a ride."

"You're safe here," he assures me. "Both of you."

Safe.

What a concept.

"It's wonderful," I laugh, my voice wobbling a bit too hard. "This place. It's—it's a dream."

"But an expensive one," he says, as if reading my thoughts.

"Yeah."

"I understand. Believe me, I do."

"I—I might be coming into some money soon," I blurt. "I'm not certain it'll pan out, but if it does…"

"We've got a spot open right now," Mr. Garcia says. "Usually, you'd have to be put on our waitlist, but like I said, Diane's a friend. I can hold your spot until the end of the month."

"You'd do that?"

"Of course. It's the least I can do."

It's the first lucky break I've had in ages. I hadn't even realized how badly I needed it.

"Thank you," I croak. "Really. I just… Just, thank you."

By the time I've dried my eyes and made my way back to the classroom, Eli bounds up to me, his shyness completely gone.

"Mommy!" he squeals. "I made friends!"

"That's wonderful, baby!"

"Can he stay?" a little girl with cornrows pleads. "Please?"

"Please, Mommy?" Eli joins in.

I want to say *yes* so bad. "Not today, munchkin. We need to get our ducks in a row first. Lots of paperwork to do."

"Then can I stay after the paperwork?"

"If everything goes smoothly." It's the most I can promise without lying. "Now, say goodbye to your new friends. We'll be late for lunch with Aunt Kallie."

I watch Eli part with a whole gaggle of kids. It makes my heart crack in my chest—that I don't know if I can give him this.

We drive back to the apartment. Kallie's supposed to meet us at the bagel place two blocks over in half an hour. I unbuckle Eli, pick him up—

—and see a black Maybach parked right across the street.

20

YULIAN

No one has ever made me wait.

As CEO, I command respect. As *pakhan,* I inspire fear.

No one dares to cross me unless they're very stupid or have a death wish. Meetings happen when I say so; executions take place when I arrive. No earlier, no later.

But Mia Winters has kept me for half an hour under her window.

And she isn't answering her goddamn phone.

Considering the people we're dealing with, it wouldn't be strange if they already got to her. If the reason she went radio silent on me was because she was feeding the fish in the Hudson.

And yet, my instincts tell me that's not the case.

Mia is alive and well.

She's just ignoring me on purpose.

"*Blyat*." That woman. She pushes me like no one else. Worse, I doubt she even knows she's doing it. She just loathes my ways so much, she's willing to cross lines no man in their right mind would ever cross.

It makes me want to do unspeakable things to her. Remind her who's *really* in charge between us.

Her ash brown hair in my fist. Her back, arched as I fuck her senseless. Her moans bouncing off the walls, her full breasts spilling from my fingers. Her tight, wet—

An angry knock on my window snaps me out of those thoughts. Relentless, impatient, rude.

I don't even need to look to know it's her.

"What the hell, Yulian?" she yells at me as soon as I roll the window down. "You're *three hours* early."

"I had time now." My voice goes cold. I have no idea who this woman thinks she is to take up that tone with me, but she's gonna have to rethink her priorities. "You should be grateful I made time at all. I'm a busy man."

"Oh, I'm plenty grateful," she snarks. "I'm *so* thrilled my son almost saw you."

I glance around the empty street. "I don't see him."

"Because my friend dropped everything to come get him early!" she hisses. "You realize other people have lives, right? Real, actual lives."

"And you're free to get back to yours," I answer. "I can go right now, if that's what you wish. But I'll take my million with me."

She holds my gaze. I can see her weighing her options in her head, like she thinks she has any. Like she still hasn't gotten the memo.

It's a simple lesson.

When I want something, I *get* it.

Finally, she breaks. "Then at least come inside. I'm not doing this like it's a drug deal."

Come inside. I can almost picture those words in a whole different tone, her voice twisting around them in a sultry whisper. A plea. Like she'll combust if I don't do what we're both dreaming of doing.

I chase those thoughts off and climb out of the car.

Mia walks briskly up the stairs. She's wearing a pair of low rise jeans that look older than she is. Every step makes her ass bounce.

If I'm not careful, I'll be collecting her contract rock-hard.

When we get to her door, she glares at the bodyguards I put there. "Here we are," she mutters. "Home sweet compound. Make yourself comfortable."

One glance around the place tells me it's easier said than done.

The apartment isn't dirty, per se, but it's… colorful. Toys and puzzle pieces are strewn every which way, with no rhyme or reason. When I step inside, I almost put my foot right into the back of a toy truck.

"Careful with that," she warns. "Social worker almost took a dive down the stairs, skating on it. Was real fun to watch, though."

She doesn't apologize for the mess. She doesn't invite me to sit. She doesn't offer me coffee, or water, or anything a good host might.

Instead, she clears the kitchen island from a pile of haphazard plushies with one arm and unlocks her knife drawer.

I raise an eyebrow. "If you're going to make an attempt on my life, I'd recommend something that keeps you out of arms' reach."

"I'm not." She pulls out the contract from the back of the drawer. "But don't tempt me."

More threats. It's kind of adorable, really. She couldn't harm a hair on my head and still, she pretends that it's an option. That she has control.

"I take it you've signed it?"

"Not yet." She hands me the contract. "I've taken the liberty of making a few suggestions."

I take in the mess of red pen on it. Another act of insolence that would have left anyone else short of the hand that did it.

"Have you, now?"

She puts a hand on her hip and holds my gaze again. "Yes."

It's a cute bluff. We both know that she needs this deal. That she's fucked ten ways from Sunday if it falls through.

But it doesn't keep her from putting on a brave front.

That, at least, I can respect.

"Very well." I take a seat across from her. "Let's hear it."

She taps on the first page. "First, no invasions to my home life. Those gorillas out there? I want them gone faster than you can say—"

"No."

Mia blinks. "What do you mean, 'no'?"

"I don't believe I stuttered." I lean over and hook that delicious, flustered blue gaze of hers. "I'm the boss. I decide what gets done, when, and how. And your bodyguards aren't going anywhere."

She grits her teeth. "This isn't how negotiating works."

"I never said I'd be negotiating with you. That was your assumption."

Her face twists with displeasure, but I can tell she's not done fighting. "Why would I even need bodyguards?" She throws up her arms. "I'm not becoming the fake girlfriend of Prince Henry. Unless your king-of-the-world complex really is that big."

"My men stay." I stare her down. "That's final."

She stares me down right back. "One," she growls. "One man, downstairs. Or on thc roof, or in the plumbing—I don't care where he stays, so long as it isn't in front of my apartment. My kid's already going through a lot—he doesn't need to worry about Bond villains at his door, too."

My kid's going through a lot. I file that tidbit of information away, remind myself to set Maksim on its trail.

Whatever's going on in Mia's life, I want to know it. A pawn as crucial as her is not allowed the luxury of privacy.

"That's quite the characterization," I remark.

"My kid's quite the Bond fan."

She doesn't drop my gaze. I can see her swallowing with nerves, the subtle tremor of her fingers giving her away. But despite all that, she's still pushing back.

I can't say I dislike it. Infuriating or not, she's got guts. And if this plan is going to work, I'm gonna need that attitude.

"Fine," I say. "One guard, in his car. But I want a camera on the door. Live feed, 24/7."

"Can you make it small?"

"I'm the CEO of StarTech. I can make anything."

"Then that's fine with me."

She doesn't look impressed with my declaration. Instead, she flips right to the next order of business. "Condition two—reasonable notice."

"Sure," I deadpan. "I'll check with your assistant. Maybe you can send me your Calendly. Oh, and have we connected on LinkedIn yet?"

She makes a frustrated noise. "I have a *job,* Yulian. I'm a single mom. And on top of all that, sometimes, I actually have a life, too!"

"Congratulations. Where should I stick your gold star?"

"Stick it up your ass," she retorts. "I want a week's notice for every assignment. That's non-negotiable."

"I don't think you understand—"

"No, *you* don't understand," she interrupts. "I have a kid. I won't risk leaving him unattended. Not—" She sucks in a breath, like she's swallowing back a word she hadn't meant to speak. "Not ever."

"Wouldn't be the first time, from what I hear."

She reels back as if slapped. I feel a slight, unfamiliar prick of guilt at her reaction.

"If you know that," she says slowly, collecting herself just enough to speak rather than yell, "then you know why I need notice."

Our staring contest resumes.

Goddamn stubborn woman. I haven't got all day here—not by a long fucking shot.

"Fine," I say. "Twenty-four hours."

"That's not—do you have any idea how hard it is to get a sitter on such short notice?!"

"Do you have any idea," I murmur slowly, "how dangerous it is to keep pushing me?"

She blanches and falls silent. But not for long.

"Forty-eight hours," she tries. "And you'll send a sitter if I can't find one."

My instincts tell me not to give in. To get up and have Mia chase me down the stairs—to make her *beg*.

But a part of me doesn't want that. Somehow, this little game is proving more interesting than I'd anticipated. And besides, like I said—I don't have all day.

"Fine," I concede.

"Good. Okay." She lets out a relieved breath. "Thank you."

"If that's all—" I rise from the table, but she grabs my sleeve.

"Wait!"

I look down. Her fingers are shaking where they're holding on to me, her blue eyes suddenly terrified.

"I..." She swallows thickly. "I want an advance. On the payment."

It's a bold request. Even I'm surprised by it.

"That's not how this works," I tell her.

"I know, but—"

"But what?"

"I need to know you're serious about this." Her gaze isn't leaving mine for a second. It looks panicked, urgent. "About us."

Us. I savor the way she says it. Like we're not just playing pretend. It makes me wonder what it would be like—not to be playing.

"Name your price, then."

She hesitates. "F-fifty thousand."

I almost want to laugh. *Just that?* After having the guts to demand this of me, she doesn't even want half the total sum? Fifty measly thousand?

She needs it for something. Suspicion oozes at the back of my mind, dark and cloying. *Something that wasn't in the file.*

"It's quite the request."

"I told you," she mumbles, "I need to know you're serious. I—"

"Done."

"—what?"

I enjoy watching her flounder. She wasn't expecting to win this—that much is clear. And whatever that sum is about, I'll find out. Maksim will make sure of it.

"I said I'll give you your advance." I glance downward. "Provided I can get my sleeve back."

She blushes furiously. "O-of course! I—sorry, I just—"

I fix my cuff. "My turn now."

"I—sorry, what?"

"You've got your rules. I've got mine." I turn fully towards her, towering over her as I speak. "A daily selfie with geolocation, to prove you're still here."

Mia blinks. It takes a moment for my odd request to sink in.

Then, once it does, she bristles. "And where else would I be?"

"You could run off with the money."

Her face colors even harder, but not from shame. "You—!"

"Second," I interrupt, "no skipping assignments. Ever. I'll be demanding that advance back if you do, every cent of it."

"Yulian, I have a kid! I work in the E.R., I—"

"Every. Fucking. Cent."

Her brow creases, her cheeks puffing up like a hamster's. It'd be cute if she wasn't absolutely fucking furious, but that's none of my business.

This is life or death.

Whether she realizes that or not.

"Third," I drawl, tilting her chin up with my fingers, "no getting *ideas*."

I can feel the heat of her skin where our bodies touch. It's such a small connection, but I'm already burning from it. I've never toyed with an employee like this. Never thought I'd be doing it with her of all people.

But now, I find myself getting high on the thrill of the chase.

Even though it won't lead anywhere.

Even though I *can't* let it.

"You're not allowed to fall for me," I whisper, inches away from Mia's full, plush lips. "In lust, or in love, or in anything between."

She glares at me, like a caged beast ready to maim as soon as I set her loose.

And yet, I can see the truth in her eyes. Her pupils, pinpricks until moments ago, have eaten away at her irises almost completely. A black hole, swallowing the sea.

"I wasn't planning on it," she snaps.

"Doesn't matter. We'll be playing a very dangerous game together. Anything could happen."

My mouth travels close to her ear. As I speak, I can feel the shell of it against my lips. It drives me fucking crazy—how little it would take to bite it. To nibble until she mewls and writhes against me.

"But you can't be the future Mrs. Lozhkin," I add. "No one can."

She struggles free from my grasp and fixes me with a glare that could melt glaciers. "Don't worry, *Mr. Lozhkin.* I'm not interested in ever seeing you again after this is over with."

Liar.

"Then we have a deal."

I offer her my hand.

She stares at it like it could bite her. But eventually, she gives a firm shake.

"Deal," she says, like she was ever an equal partner in this. Like she ever had any power in our little "negotiation."

I turn to leave. "Oh," I remember at the door. "Get ready for tomorrow night. I have a business meeting. You'll be needed."

Mia's mouth gapes. "That's too soon. I—I can't. I have a shift, I don't have a sitter, I—we just agreed on forty-eight hours!"

"Yes," I agree. "And going forward, you'll be given your precious notice. But tomorrow, you will be where I need you to be."

Without another glance back, I climb down the stairs.

"Hey!" Mia's voice follows me, then her footsteps. "I'm not done talking to you!"

My patience is hanging on by a thread. If I stay any longer, I won't be able to control my actions. I'm unpredictable on my best days, but around Mia Winters?

I have no idea what I'll be capable of if she keeps pushing me.

She chases me out the front door. Her breaths are heavy by the time she's caught up with me, hands-on-knees kind of heavy. "You can't—you can't just walk away!"

I glance back at her figure. Bent, sweaty—exactly the way my worst instincts would want her. "I just did."

"You…!" she heaves. "You arrogant, cocky, entitled son of a bitch! I am *not* going to dance to your fucking tune just because you want me to, you got that?!"

Finally—*finally*—the thread snaps.

It happens faster than I can process it. One second, I'm standing in front of my car, and the next—

"Hey! What the hell?!"

—I'm dragging Mia into an alley.

I bracket her against the wall with my right arm, slamming my palm hard into the concrete. Plaster crackles and falls at the impact. Mia's gaze snaps to the spot I crushed, takes in the consequences. Immediately, a shiver goes through her.

Good, the dark side of me preens. *Fear me. Hate me.*

And show me some fucking respect while you're at it.

I lower my gaze, meeting hers. She looks terrified, and yet, at the same time, ready to pounce. I've never seen such a mix on a person's face before.

"You seem to be under the mistaken impression you can call the shots here, Ms. Winters," I growl, low and dangerous. "Let me assure you, you cannot."

"I—"

"Quiet." My hand flies to her throat and clamps down. Not enough to hurt, but enough to keep Mia from moving a muscle, her quick tongue included. "I'm talking now."

I draw my face closer to my doe in the headlights. Like this, I could do anything to her.

I just might.

"I will decide when we meet, where, and how. I will decide how you dress, how you act, what you say, when you say it. If I'm displeased with any of it, I won't hesitate to tear that pretty contract of yours to shreds."

We're close. Way too close. Enough to kiss or kill each other.

Right now, I can't decide which one I want more.

"Tell me you understand."

Mia's eyes fill with fire again. The kind of fire that makes me want to draw closer to the flame, see how bad it can burn.

All this time, I've been the one burning down empires left and right.

Never have I let another's flame touch me.

But Mia's heat almost matches the intensity of mine.

"I'm not your property," she says. "I'm not—"

"Yes, you are. You are *mine.* Until the sun comes up six months from now, you belong to me and only me. And I won't have you questioning me."

"Or what?" She trembles. "You'll hurt me?"

"No, Mia. I'll never hurt you. I'll never need to." My lips graze her cheek, just shy of her quivering, open lips. "There are much easier ways to teach someone a lesson."

She shrinks into the wall, but I don't let her go. The fear in her eyes has a delicious undertone to it.

Mia Winters is a liar. I've known that from the day Maksim handed me that file on her.

No—from the day I fucking met her.

She has secrets up to her beautiful blue eyes, thick enough to drown her. She has a fake name, a fake life, and a fake notion of who she is.

Right now, she thinks she fears me.

But I know the truth.

The body doesn't lie.

Mia's pupils aren't shrinking. They're blown, black and full, wider than ever before. Her breath hitches, coming out in short little gasps that make me want to do the unspeakable to her.

I'm hard as a fucking rock, but like hell am I gonna let her notice.

Rule number one of power plays: Never let your opponent know how much they have over you.

And Mia, as loathe as I am to admit it, has done quite a number on certain parts of me.

When I speak next, I mask my desire. Instead, I fill my voice with implied violence. "Tell me you understand, *kotyonok.*"

She's panting now, her breasts brushing against my chest with her every breath. I know she feels it, too—the heat pooling between us, the circle of gasoline around our bodies.

One spark, and it'll catch.

"I understand," she whispers.

Only then do I let her go.

"Tomorrow," I say once more. "Don't be late."

With that, I leave her.

I leave her in that alley. I leave her gasping, shaking, with tears in her eyes and tremors in her thighs.

I leave her and curse myself, over and over, in the car.

Blyat'. I let myself get carried away. I let her lead the game. Even if she doesn't realize that's what happened, I know it did.

I lost it. I lost my cool, lost my head.

And I'm still hard as a fucking rock.

21

MIA

I can still feel his lips against my cheek.

I should be repulsed. I should be terrified. I should have taken one look at Yulian's true face, the way he cornered me in that alley, and ran for dear fucking life.

Instead, here I am one measly day later, waiting for him on the sidewalk in front of my apartment, all dolled up for him.

I can practically feel the feminism leaving my body, along with my hard-won self-respect. *Goodbye, my friend! It's been good knowing ya.*

And all the while, I can still feel his lips against my cheek.

Mere steps from me, that alley he cornered me in gapes wide open, like a dark, hungry maw ready to swallow me whole.

But this isn't about self-respect. That's for people whose lives aren't this royally fucked-up, who don't attract trouble like flies to honey. For those who have *choices.*

Me? I've run fresh out.

Because the truth is, it doesn't matter how much of an asshole Yulian is. It doesn't matter how badly his closeness rattles me, with fear and something else.

I don't even dare unpack that—I'm terrified it would land me exactly where I was five years ago, at the beck and call of Local Rich Dick who thought he could treat me however he wanted because he bought me nice gifts. When I thought I was in love.

Wow. The Venn diagram of my life really is a circle, isn't it?

Except that, this time, it's not about love.

I'm not that delulu little girl anymore, the one who thought slaps were caresses and punches were kisses. The one who believed having her phone checked five times a day was a sign of care. Who hoped that, one day, he'd realize she wasn't going anywhere and stop trying so hard to keep her. That her body's bruises would fade, her soul's scars would heal, and she'd land into the fluffy clouds of "happily ever after."

No—this is business. Cold, hard business.

Nothing less, nothing more.

I've seen enough of Yulian Lozhkin to stay away for the rest of my life.

Six months. It's such a small price for freedom, but when I count the days in my head, it feels like forever. Three times I've met him, and three times I've come away burned.

How long before his flames consume me?

How long before I don't have a life to return to?

But you have Eli. You have your son.

It's that voice in my head that keeps me going, keeps me steady enough to endure Mr. Choke-Me-Daddy's knockoff Christian Grey attitude. If swallowing my pride is all I have to do to secure one million dollars—my son's future—then I'll open wide and say, "Pretty please."

After all, I've already done it once for free.

One million. Suddenly, all the things I could do with that money crowd my head. I could pay off my debts; I could buy us a house. I could keep Eli's tuition paid and his therapist covered, could take him for pizza and ice cream every weekend. I could buy him all the sports gear he wants, fill his room with new toys instead of hand-me-downs. I could spend more time with him. I could…

Make him happy.

And I could *keep* him.

I'm not stupid. I know CPS is going to pounce at the first infraction. The second that my bank account goes under, that I miss a payment on my loans, that I so much as misspell a word on a check, they'll swoop in like vultures.

They'll take Eli, dump him into foster care, and…

No. I slap my cheeks and force myself to stop thinking. I'm about to be a freaking millionaire—CPS won't be a problem anymore.

With Yulian's money, I can hire a whole team of custody lawyers. I can make the case go away. I can disappear, far away from here, where Mr. Lee won't find us.

Where *Brad* won't find us.

And then, maybe, if I pick my studies back up… if I can finish what I started…

If I can get the degree I *really* wanted...

Then we won't have to worry about money ever again.

Just as I'm nursing that thought, Yulian's Maybach pulls up. The window rolls down.

"Get in."

And fuck you, too, I want to say.

But I slide into the backseat instead.

Yulian is there, all broody darkness and devil-actually-doesn't-give-a-shit scowl. He doesn't greet me, so I don't greet him.

If silence is how he wants to play this, that's fine by me.

"Hiya there, Nurse Wonder!" Maksim grins from the driver's seat. His tattooed face peeks into the back. "So glad you decided to join the team."

Did I have any other choice?

"Hi, Maksim." I smile back. "Thanks for driving us."

Out of the two Russian mobsters I've now tied my fate to, he's by far the better hang. Polite, too, not that Yulian would know what that means.

"Hear that?" He wiggles his burned-off brow in Yulian's direction. "She has *manners*. Refreshing, isn't it?"

Yulian grunts something unintelligible. Then, "Drive."

Maksim doesn't need to be told twice.

We zoom off into the night. For a while, no one says anything. The tension in this car could be cut with a machete

—and I don't doubt Yulian's got one stashed away in the mini-bar.

"I see you've managed to make our appointment," Yulian notes eventually. "Despite the lack of… ah, *notice.*"

His tone makes me want to break every oath I've ever sworn. Repeatedly.

"My best friend is a saint," I say instead. "It's not the first time she bails me out of an emergency. Though I'm not sure this qualifies."

"No?"

"You know what they say." I smile tightly. "'Lack of planning on your end does not constitute an emergency on mine,' and so on, and so forth."

His eyes glint with amusement. "But she came through."

"She always does."

"Seems like you had nothing to worry about, then."

God, please give me patience, because if you give me strength, I'll end up on the news.

"Good friends are hard to find. Thankfully, I found her. Which is extra nice, because I can't imagine having to hire someone every time I needed help. I'd be broke *and* sad." My smile widens. "Good thing I'm just broke, huh?"

Yulian's amusement flickers. Something else mixes with it—not quite anger, but close. A simmering annoyance, perhaps. The kind of dry kindling you don't want close to a spark.

Then, seemingly out of nowhere, he says, "Nice dress."

I look down. The black lace ruffles around my middle and snakes up my arms in floral patterns. The butterfly sleeves give me something to torment with my fingers, though I won't give Yulian the satisfaction of seeing it.

He can't know how nervous I am. Last time we sparred, I blinked first.

Now, it's his turn.

"Thanks." I smooth down my skirt. "I got it off a clearance rack."

His lips quirk. "A better rack than last time, I'm sure."

He isn't wrong—I *did* splurge a little. As in, way more than I ever thought I could spend on a single item of clothing. That receipt will be giving me nightmares until I die.

"Figured I'd need a work closet," I say with a shrug.

Yulian hums appreciatively. "You could have done worse."

I get the feeling it's the most praise he's ever given anyone. "I'll try harder next time. To do worse, I mean."

"No need." He fixes his cuffs—a habit of his, I've noticed, even when there's nothing wrong with them—and turns to me. "I'll be handling your 'work closet' from now on."

It should be a relief, but I don't like the way he says it. Like I'm his thing to dress up. A doll he bought, and now gets to play with however he sees fit.

But I let it slide. It costs me, but I do.

It's just work, after all, isn't it? My body, my person—for the next six months, they're his. He made it abundantly clear yesterday, in that alley.

I can still remember how it felt. His hands on me, his cologne around me. His husky voice, scraping my self-respect straight out of my brain.

It's the only reason I didn't freeze up completely: The man who was cornering me, who was grabbing me and threatening to do whatever he wanted with me—he was clearly *someone else.*

He was clearly not Brad.

But that doesn't mean he can't be worse.

I'll have to tread carefully. Yulian Lozhkin is no fairytale prince, that much is for certain. He won't open the door to the carriage for me, won't gift me priceless dresses because he wants me to be happy wearing them, won't shower me in luxury for my sake.

Everything, from the first silk thread to the last diamond drop, will be for *him*. To any other woman, he'd be the villain of the story.

Luckily for him, I've already filled that role.

Suddenly, I find papers being thrust in front of me.

"What's this?" I ask.

"Your contract." Yulian's voice is cold, businesslike. "Amended, like you wanted."

You mean like you *wanted, too.* It's uncanny how quickly he's managed to forget half of these changes came from him.

I take the contract. It's weightless, which is appropriate. It's like Yulian said: One wrong move, and he'll tear it up.

Only one of us is truly protected by it.

"Here." Yulian passes me a pen. "In case you actually don't own one."

You swore an oath, Mia. Hippocrates would be really upset with you, Mia. You can't punch the cocky Russian asshole who pays for your son's schooling, Mia.

Swallowing back my anger, I take the pen. I also don't stab him with it, which I count as my good deed of the day.

My teeth have been gritting nonstop since I've met Yulian Lozhkin—it'll be a miracle if I'll be able to eat anything other than soup by the time these six months are up.

But fine. With his million, I can pay for a damn dentist, too.

I scrawl a signature on the papers and hand them back to him. "Here," I say. "All done."

I try not to flinch when his hand grazes mine. Try not to shiver, either.

His closeness drives me crazier than his attitude. If I'm going to survive this, I'll need to learn how to deal with it.

But that's not going to happen tonight.

Because, the second the car stops, Yulian offers me his arm. "Shall we?"

Deep breaths, Mia. You can do this. You can survive one night with the devil.

And then another, and another, and another.

"Yeah," I say. "Let's go."

I take his arm. I let him lead me through two heavy, gilded doors, the word ***GOLDENROD*** gleaming on top in a golden arch.

I let him shepherd me through a luxurious lounge, all marble floors and chandeliers and glassware that's worth more than all my organs.

I let him pretend I belong here, but I don't.

"Relax," he whispers. "You're with me, remember?"

You belong wherever you decide you belong, kotyonok. Yulian's words on that first, fateful night linger in my mind, warm and soothing. *Most importantly, where* I *decide.*

So I take a deep breath and try to act like it. Like I was born for this. Like this is all I've known all my life.

Like I'm the future Mrs. Lozhkin.

And then, out of the blue, a hand slaps my ass.

22

YULIAN

I feel Mia freeze.

Then I see why.

A hand.

On her ass.

It slaps her once, then it's gone.

And everything I see gets tinted blood-red.

"Yuli!" an older male voice booms cheerfully. "*Blyat*," look at you! You've grown so big!"

I turn to look at the man who spoke. My hands are flexing and unflexing, knuckles popping, as the surge of blood into my muscles wakes up every last nerve ending.

I'm going to hurt this man. I'm going to do it slowly and painfully and publicly.

But not yet.

"Ieronim," I greet coldly. "You seem to have misplaced your hand there. Did you want to lose it permanently?"

Ieronim Salnikov—one of my parents' closest friends.

Once, he was a legend in the Bratva world. Then he started clinging a little too close to his liquor, and the legend faded into myth. Now, the Salnikov Bratva is a footnote in New York's history.

I'm about to wipe it the fuck out of existence for good.

I pull Mia closer to me. The room falls silent around us, every other businessperson gathered here suddenly too busy staring at their drinks to come greet us. Waiting for the storm to pass, too scared of getting caught in it.

Clinking ice cubes in glass tumblers go still.

Murmurs cease.

The red tide in my vision darkens.

Finally, Ieronim seems to realize just how badly he fucked up.

"Now, now," he says in an attempt to pacify me. "You know I can't resist a good piece of ass when I see it. Besides, I hear you're not the type to get attached. What's the harm in sharing, right?"

I can smell the alcohol on his breath as he speaks. A haze of bourbon and unbrushed teeth.

Fucking vile.

"Why are you talking to me, *friend?*" I say.

He blinks. "Pardon?"

"Don't talk to me." I jut my chin toward my date. "Talk to her. Apologize."

Ieronim blinks again. Drunk, confused, or stupid, I'm not sure which and I don't fucking care. All I know is that his abject, groveling, and heartfelt apology is the only thing that will stop me from ripping his head clean off his spine right here and right fucking now.

"For…?"

"For daring to lay a single one of your greasy fucking fingers on a woman of her stature."

His jaw drops.

From my side, Mia blinks at me, eyes wide. Like she can't believe what she's hearing. Like the thought of me defending her clashes with some deep-set conviction that this is not what's supposed to happen when some gropey, idiotic stranger takes liberties with her body. "T-that's really not nec—"

"I insist." My voice goes cold as ice. "Ieronim. Now."

He doesn't catch the threat in my tone. Instead, he gives another booming laugh. "So sorry about that, Miss! Like I said, you're quite pleasing to the eye. Can't blame me for being tempted, yes?"

Nor can you blame me for filleting you like a fucking fish.

I'm opening my mouth to say exactly that when Mia cuts in with a laugh, too shrilly to be natural. "Not a problem! I, um —I'll go see what the bar has to offer. Yulian, do you want—"

Ieronim pipes right up. "A scotch would be nice, dear."

She gives a tight nod and heads straight for the bar. Unease swirls in my gut—I don't like leaving her out of my sight. She has no idea where she is tonight, what kind of club I brought her to.

Yeah, 'cause you sure as fuck didn't tell her.

I silence that nasty voice in my head before it gets wildly out of hand.

I've got two choices in front of me. One is to shred Ieronim limb from limb. The other is to go after Mia, because this room is full of vultures who will make Ieronim look like a harmless little guppy. If I leave her alone, a hand on the ass will be the nicest thing that happens to her all night.

You brought her here. You put her in danger again. It's your *fucking fault if something happens to her.*

So, with a discontented growl in Ieronim's direction that suffices as a goodbye, I turn and go after her. If only so I can protect the only thing in this whole cursed fucking room that's actually innocent enough to deserve protection.

I see her. Beautiful, curvy, a vision in black lace. Fuck, she looks incredible as hair tumbles down the curve of her throat.

It strikes me, not for the first time, how lucky I am that she stumbled across my path. Or rather, that I parked along hers.

For her to be not just tough, not just desperate, not just feisty, but also gorgeous enough to make me pause in my tracks in a room full of dangerous men? To stop and stare while my enemies lurk in the shadows?

To drool?

To lust?

To *need?*

What the fuck did I do to deserve that?

I snap myself out of my reverie. I don't know how I got so lucky, but I do know that I have uses for Mia Winters tonight, and abandoning her to the jackals will only waste her potential.

I take one step in her direction, desperate to put my hand where Ieronim's was, but—

"Good evening, Mr. Lozhkin."

Suddenly, it's like flies flocking to shit. The greetings multiply, my name crooned over and over again.

I'm swarmed by business associates I cannot easily brush off, department heads of manufacturing companies and CFOs of office buildings sporting our cybersecurity technologies.

That's what nights like these are for—making more lucrative deals.

And greasing the palms of dangerous men.

I'm one such man. Ieronim is another. I can spot at least half a dozen more: the Neri patriarch, the Alexopoulos heir, Yamazaki's eldest daughter. Everyone here is rich, but not everyone got there through legitimate means.

It's why we gather at the Goldenrod, the most exclusive club in New York. Not just because membership is a hundred grand per month, but because, by night, the usual golf-doctors-and-lawyers clientele is gone.

Instead, access becomes restricted to only a certain kind of elite.

Men like me.

And I don't want Mia alone near men like me.

It takes a while before I manage to extricate myself from the conversation. When I do, I see everyone's dolled up plus-ones lounging by the couches, colorful drinks in hand and light laughter floating in the air.

Ideally, that's where I'd want Mia to be, too. If not by my side, then at least with her ilk. At least to be safe.

But when I finally lift my eyes back to the bar, I can't find her.

I promptly abandon every man demanding my attention.

"Tell me where she went," I snarl as I approach and slam my hands down on the counter, rattling bottles of champagne.

The bartender blinks back at me, confused. "Pardon me, sir?"

"The woman. Short, petite, black lacy dress."

He gives me another lost look. With a glance at the couches, I realize I'm describing almost every girl in here.

"Brown hair, light," I tell him, my patience slipping. "Blue eyes. She's got a beauty mark right here, under her lip."

Finally, the bartender's expression lights up. "Oh! Yes, of course. She went to the smoking terrace with a gentleman."

I fucking doubt it.

No one here's a gentleman, least of all one who'd take another man's woman to the "smoking terrace"—a well-known code for something else around here.

But it wouldn't be well-known to Mia, would it?

This is your world, not hers.

You *brought her here.*

You *did this. You did all of this.*

So what are you gonna do if something happens to her?

I head to the smoking lounge without a second's thought. The elevator pings next to me, but I don't pay it any mind. Instead, I take the stairs two by two, praying I'm not too late.

If something happened to her... My fists clench, fury exploding in my knuckles. *If* I *let something happen to her...*

That dark, amused voice in my head chuckles. *Then what?* It grates against the walls of my mind. *That's the whole point, remember? For something to happen to her. Get shot at, kidnapped, dismembered—you name it. Anything to get you closer to your goal.*

So what if it happened tonight?

"No," I spit under my breath. "No one touches her. Not until I say so."

I'm a fucking hypocrite. I know that. But now is not the time to deal with introspection.

I just need to find this fucking woman.

"Stop," I hear as soon as I step out into the terrace.

A woman's voice.

Mia's voice.

"Aren't you a coy little one?" Ieronim slurs. He's way too drunk to be standing. Definitely way too drunk to be shoving his hands up Mia's dress, squeezing her ass like it's the only thing keeping him upright. "So demure. Making me work for it, are ya?"

"N-no," Mia gasps. It's brittle, quivering, terrified. "I—I don't want—"

"C'mon, sweet thing." He takes a whiff of her neck and grinds her harder into the railing. "You know you want it."

Mia freezes. Like a deer in the headlights. A doll with her strings cut.

She just—stops. Stops doing anything.

Stop pushing him off, talking, resisting.

Like…

Like she doesn't think it'll make a difference.

The next time I blink, Ieronim is screaming.

I realize, dimly, his arm is in my grip. His wrist, to be exact.

And it's hanging at a very awkward angle.

Odd. I didn't even hear the bone crack.

"Arghhh!" he yells into the night. "God, Yulian, don't— Stop, please—!"

"'Please, don't stop'?" I echo. "If you say so."

I twist harder.

Against the railing, Mia is staring wide-eyed, horror on her face. But it's a dim, distant sort of horror. Like she isn't fully here yet. Like she's still wherever she went when Ieronim called her—

Sweet thing.

Suddenly, Brad's voice echoes in my ears. I remember him using the same exact words with her—the same lecherous tone.

Back then, Mia froze, too.

Blind with rage, I yank Ieronim hard. He goes careening into the floor, blood spurting from his nose and staining the beautiful Portuguese tiles.

"Are you out of your fucking mind?!" Ieronim coughs. "Jesus, Yulian, she's just your whore for the night! You think I don't read the articles? She—"

"She isn't yours to touch," I boom. "So do not fucking touch her."

"I—*ARGHHH!*"

I feel his fingers snap under my heel. This time, the *crack* echoes loud and clear. Impossible to miss.

"And do *not,*" I grow, lower and darker and angrier than I've been in a long fucking time, "call her a whore."

When I kick him in the head, he goes out like a light.

Then I turn back to Mia.

She's still staring at me, but something's different in her gaze. More present. More here.

"Let's go," I bark, grabbing her hand.

She blinks down at it. My fingers wrapped tight around hers. Like she can't quite make sense of it. "B-but your event—your meetings—"

"I don't give a shit," I snap. "We're going home."

Home. Like it's something we share. If I was in a better state of mind, it'd make me fucking laugh.

When's the last time I've shared a home with someone?

When's the last time I've shared anything?

One thing, though, is for certain.

I will *not* share Mia.

Not as long as she's mine.

23

YULIAN

When I step into the underground ring beneath the Goldenrod, the crowd roars.

It drowns out everything else. Drowns out my thoughts, too, which means it's working.

But soon, the images resurface.

Mia, with Ieronim's hands on her.

Mia, frozen in terror.

Mia, looking at me afterwards like I was a hero.

But I'm no fucking hero. Never have been, never will be.

And this—violence, blood, the cold snap of broken bone—is a reminder that I'm exactly where I'm supposed to be.

Certainly not home with her.

It's been a week since it happened. A week since I dragged her out of that meeting, lost out on potential billions, and shoved her into the backseat of my Maybach.

A week since she spoke those words to me.

The car ride is quiet. Too quiet. I've never struggled with silence, but as Mia fidgets with her sleeves at my side, I realize I'm not good with this one. A silence that could mean anything.

I want to know what Mia's thinking. If she's okay. If she's not. If she's about to cry. If she's only holding it in because she doesn't want to look bad in front of me.

She has no idea she could never.

That thought surprises me. Catches me off-guard like a sucker punch. As the engine purrs beneath us, I wonder when exactly I stopped thinking of Mia like a nuisance and started thinking of her as a person.

Maybe I didn't.

Maybe tonight's just getting to me.

"We're here," Maksim calls from the driver's seat. "Your stop, Miss."

She gives Maks a quick nod, but stays where she is. Slowly, her blue eyes find mine.

"Do you want to come upstairs?"

"Hellooo?" Maksim snaps his fingers in front of my face. "Earth to Yulian?"

I shake myself out of those thoughts. Turns out, a roaring crowd is not an effective remedy against Mia Winters. Whatever the cure for that disease is, it hasn't been found yet.

"Do that again and I'll bite them off," I warn him.

"Oh, good, he's back." Maksim winks. "Thought I'd lost you for a second there, buddy."

"Call me 'buddy' one more time and I'll—"

"Yeah, yeah, yeah." My second waves a hand to cut me off mid-threat, still grinning from ear to ear. "That's the Yulian we all know and fear."

He starts taping my hands. I don't let other people touch me unless it's absolutely necessary, but this is a little tradition of ours. When I was just starting out, a kid of nineteen with a lot of anger and nowhere to put it, Maksim was always there for me.

C'mon, boy. Can't punch your daddy's killers if you don't got hands no more, can ya?

We've come a long way since then. I've grown into my *pakhan* shoes, commanding respect from everyone under my authority. From the highest-ranked *vor* to the lowest recruit, no one dares treat me with anything less than absolute deference.

But Maksim's different. He's the exception. He's seen me at my worst and never deserted me, never once wavered in his loyalty.

And for that, he takes a whole lot more liberty than anyone else would dare.

"Looking a little spacey tonight," he notes as he finishes winding the wraps around my knuckles. "If I were you, I'd tap out early. Go find the girl who's making your head spin."

"I don't tap out." I flex my fingers, test the tape. "And there's no fucking girl."

Then I step into the ring.

My opponent looms, tall and large. His muscles are bulging in a way that screams steroids and shriveled dick, but hey, whatever makes him happy. It won't save him either way. Nothing will.

Then the bell rings.

I duck the first punch, then the next. Whoever this motherfucker is, he doesn't waste time circling. It speaks to poor strategy and a brain even more shriveled than his balls, but he makes up for it in viciousness. He's feral, lunging and swinging and snarling every time he gets close.

A slow grin spreads on my face. *Exactly what the doctor ordered.*

I lose myself in the thrill of the fight.

But as my opponent's moves start growing repetitive, my mind picks up the thread again. That worn, dangerous thread I swore to myself I'd never follow to the end.

"Do you want to come upstairs?"

There aren't many people in the world who can make me speechless, but somehow, at that moment, Mia does it.

"It's not—" She hesitates, embarrassment creeping up her cheeks in a delicious shade of red. "I just thought you might want coffee. Or water. Or—or something."

"Something," I echo.

"It was just an idea." There's a note of defensiveness in her tone. "My kid's sleeping over at Kallie's, and I feel bad for how... how the night went. I know I can't make up for it, but I wanted to try."

Make up for it.

Those words fill my head, crowd it with promises. I know, rationally, she isn't offering me sex, but the way she says it... it's tempting. More tempting than she realizes.

"It's just..." Her fingers are tormenting that lace into shreds, but I can't tear my eyes off of it. It's hypnotic. "It's my fault you had to leave. You hired me to make things easier for you, not cause trouble. I—"

"It wasn't."

She blinks. "What?"

"Your fault," I clarify. "You said it was your fault. It wasn't. Ieronim should have kept his hands to himself."

For a long moment, she's silent. Like she can't wrap her head around it—something not being her fault. At Brad's wedding, she had the same reaction.

I wonder if this is what she's used to: thinking every man's lack of decency is on her.

I wonder if she thought it of me, too, in that alley.

"So, then..." she clears her throat awkwardly. "Coffee?"

I'm tempted to say yes. So, so fucking tempted.

Because the truth is, Mia's vulnerable right now. She doesn't want to be alone. She wants someone to touch her in all the right ways, to chase Ieronim's grimy hands out of her memory. Replace the experience with something better.

I could give her that.

I could give her the best.

"No."

She looks stricken, but only for a second. "Right," she mumbles. "Next time, then."

I don't say anything to that. I don't make promises I can't keep.

And I know, if I climbed up those stairs, I'd end up breaking every promise I've ever made to myself.

"Sorry again," she breathes, all at once. "And... thank you. For saving me."

Before I can say anything to that, she bolts out of the car and into the night.

Pain explodes in my jaw, snapping me back to the present. A hook, right in the face.

"Damn," Maksim whistles as I hit the ropes. "You really are off tonight, brother."

"Shut up."

"That's what you get for letting a cute nurse mess with your head, you know. They don't always make boo-boos better."

"I said—" I spit a glob of blood on the ground. "*Shut. The. Fuck. Up.*"

Then I jump back in.

The pain is jarring, but welcome. Because Mia Winters has somehow managed what all those other women couldn't.

She got under my skin.

And I've got until our next night together to figure out why.

I decide to stop toying with my opponent. When he bull-rushes in yet again, roaring, sweating, heaving like a fucking wildebeest, I slip his wild uppercut, step to the side, and unload a crisp knockout blow right to the sweet spot on his jaw.

He goes down without so much as an *oof.*

"Nice save," Maks grins as I saunter back to my stool. "Almost thought you were gonna blow it."

I don't bother replying. I just step out of the ring and walk toward the locker room.

But when I get there, I don't stop. Hands still taped, knuckles still bloody, I keep striding right out into the night.

The cool night air hits my face. It should be soothing, but all I can think about are Maksim's warnings.

I hate that he dared say something like that to my face, but what I hate even more is that he might be right. Mia cost me billions in deals, first with Brad and now with Ieronim—and somehow, I still haven't had enough of her.

I must be on edge. That's gotta be why. My enemies are closing in, their scent alive and buzzing in the air, and that's making me restless. It's making me itch to act.

By the time they come knocking, I have to be ready. Ready to face them, to swing at them and *win.*

And ready to sacrifice Mia.

24

MIA

"Mommy! What color do I do the petals?"

I smile at my son, my arm held out like a coloring book. "How about blue?" I suggest.

Eli beams, picking up a cornflower shade eye pencil. "Look, Mommy, it's like your eyes."

"Then I'd say it's perfect."

Happy with his choice, Eli starts coloring in the petals on my tattoos. They're small, insignificant drawings, but for some reason, my kid loves them. Loves turning them into little works of art with my makeup bag.

"We watched Bluey today at daycare," he says. "It was that episode where..."

As he starts chattering off, I fix my gaze on my arm. There are tiny flowers on them, with leaves popping in between. A couple of stars, too, and suns and moons to match. The center of the suns and the flowers is blacked in, but the rest is just line art, which makes them the perfect canvas for a child with artistic pursuits.

Underneath the ink, the scars have almost faded.

When I went to the tattoo shop, I'd just stopped breastfeeding. I was barely making it through with what I had, but a friend of a friend got me a discount.

It was a patient's idea, actually. A young woman, no older than eighteen, who'd been admitted after a neighbor called the cops on her deadbeat live-in boyfriend. She kept insisting she was fine.

But I knew the signs.

So I opened up to her. With domestic violence victims, it helps to show them they're not alone, that it's okay to ask for help. I showed her my scars, told her their story, convinced her it didn't have to be hers. That she could be free of her abuser the way I was now free of mine.

I hate that he gave you these scars, she told me later, as I was drawing her blood in preparation for the kind of kit no one ever wants to give. *I hate that, one day, your kid's gonna ask how you got them.*

I'd already decided not to lie to my son then. He was only two years old, but soon, he'd grow.

Soon, he'd start asking questions.

So I went to this friend of a friend's tattoo shop. I explained what I needed, why I needed it. She suggested this design: flowers, stars, suns, moons.

Good, happy things to hide the ugliness beneath.

The first time Eli asked about my arm, it was to know if he could color in the lines. I knew then that I'd made the right choice.

"Are you listening?" Eli scolds me, bringing me back to the present.

"Sorry." I wince. "Might've gotten a bit distracted. Start again from the top, please?"

He gives me a full pout. "Maybe you should get tested for ADHD, too."

I gasp. "Eli Joshua Winters, did you just sass me?" I tickle him until he squeals.

"I'm sorry, Mommy! Please, no more!"

"Fine," I harrumph. "I'll grant you mercy. But only because you might be right. After all, they do say ADHD is hereditary."

"What does that mean?" he frowns. "Her—haradi—"

"Hereditary?" I laugh. "Just that it's a trait you get from your parents. Or grandparents."

He pauses, lost in thought. "Did Daddy have it, then?"

Bang. Shot to the solar plexus. My heart aches the same way it always does. At times like this, the one lie between us weighs on me like a thousand of them.

"I don't know, honey," I say, and it makes me feel horrible. Even if it's the truth. Even if it's the best I can do for him.

He accepts my answer. When it comes to his dad, he always does.

"I wish I could ask him."

"I wish you could, too."

He goes back to coloring. I take a long, deep breath to keep my arm from trembling.

"Green for the leaves?" he asks after a quiet minute. "Or orange?"

"I think green. It's still summer, isn't it?"

"Good point."

The grown-up way he says that makes me laugh. He gets it from the cartoons he watches—new phrases, new sayings, every day. I love that for him. I love seeing him grow, even in little ways like this one.

Soon, if Yulian's advance comes through, he'll be getting his new words from friends at school.

I watch him finish his masterpiece. He's added little clouds in white highlighter pencil, and used lipstick to paint butterflies. Once, these scars were a symbol of my pain. Now, they're my son's favorite pastime.

Kids are gifted like that, aren't they? Returning innocence where it was once lost, without even knowing it.

It's why I have to protect him at all costs.

I can't let Brad take away Eli's innocence, too.

Suddenly, there's a knock at the door. "Yeah?" I call from the kitchen.

"It's Boris," my last remaining bodyguard announces in a thick Russian accent. "I have a package from the boss."

The boss. I roll my eyes.

Right away, Eli's eyes go wide. "It's the Russian spy?"

"He's not a spy," I tell him. "He's just… new security for the building."

Not technically a lie, since he provides security for *us,* who live in the building.

"Why?" Eli asks.

"Because someone decided it."

"Why?"

"Because sometimes, adults make decisions without consulting anybody else."

"Why?"

Because they're rich, entitled, stuck-up assholes.

"Beats me, munchkin."

I open the door. Boris looms there, a huge box in his hands. I can feel Eli shrink behind me, his little voice whispering, "He's *totally* a spy."

"I'll take that." I swipe the package from his hands as fast as I can. "Thanks, bye, take care!"

Then I shut the door.

"Open it, open it!" Eli starts jumping up and down excitedly. "I wanna see!"

I put it on my bed—the only surface large enough—and pop the top open.

Oh. My. God.

I thought the blue silk dress was stunning. I thought it was the nicest thing I'd ever touch.

But this, right here?

It's fit for a fucking queen.

I lift it up, mouth agape. The sage chiffon flows smoothly down, cinched at the waist by a golden belt. It has a Greek neckline, with two rose gold circles tying the shoulder straps together.

It's a dream.

It's a fantasy.

It's also mine now.

"That's for *you?*" Eli balks in dismay.

"Unless you want it," I shrug. It won't do to let Eli see how shocked I am—he needs to think this is normal. No need to let my four-year-old son know about the big, bad wolf who pays the bills now.

Eli puts a hand to his chin and tilts his head to the side.

"I think it's too big for me," he decides solemnly. "Look, there's shoes!"

I follow his gaze and realize he's right. At the bottom of the box, there's a set of matching heels in rose gold, along with a smorgasbord of glistening jewelry.

Then, beneath it all, a note.

Saturday, 8 P.M. Don't be late.

I roll my eyes. I can practically hear his bossy voice as I read it.

Which reminds me: I still haven't sent proof of life today.

Ever since our contract began, I've been taking pictures at the end of every shift, adding in a copy of today's paper out of spite like I'm a hostage victim.

They weren't good selfies, not in the slightest. Eye bags, dirty scrubs, messy hair, the whole shebang. Was it on purpose?

Little bit, yeah.

But now, perhaps because of this gorgeous dress in my hands, I'm feeling generous. Call me a material girl, but I haven't held something this nice since that blue silk gown was thrust into my hands over a month ago.

So I hold up the dress, flash a grin, and take the snap.

Got your package.

Then I hit send.

I'm not expecting a reply—there's never been one—but this time, a tiny bubble pops up at the bottom of the screen. My breath stays caught in my chest until…

Good. I'll expect you to wear it.

Before I can think better of it, I fire back, ***Say please.***

It's a dangerous game, pushing Yulian's buttons. But I can't help myself. That cool, icy composure—I want to see what happens when it melts.

His reply comes even faster than before.

I don't beg.

But you'll thank me later.

"Right." I roll my eyes. "Yessir." How he manages to be this bossy even through text, I'll never know. Though I hate to admit, he's right—this dress is making me feel *very* grateful. Leave it to Yulian to have great taste in women's fashion.

I'm about to pocket my phone when, unexpectedly, another text comes.

P.S.—Check your bank account.

With my heart in my throat, I do.

I click on the app. I put in the password. I wait for the home page to load.

And then I see it.

One hundred. Thousand. Dollars.

Dizzy, I lean on my dresser for support. There's no way I'm reading it right—there must be a mistake. Either my eyes are starting to go, or my mind is.

But no matter how many times I refresh the page, those zeroes stay.

It's double what I asked. It's more than I've ever had all at once. It's…

Kind. I realize that suddenly. *This is Yulian's way of being kind.*

Warmth seeps into me. Slow, gradual, undeniable. A thrill fills my chest, the kind you get when luck finally turns your way. When you can let go of that pent-up breath you've been holding all your life.

Then I see the transfer note.

To prove how serious I am. —YL

They're my words. My own words, staring right back at me in Yulian's curt, bossy style.

"I want an advance," I'd told him, gathering up all the courage I never had. *"To show me how serious you are."*

And there, right there, is the answer.

He's serious. He's *so* fucking serious. He isn't conning me, isn't having a laugh at my expenses, isn't toying with the girl next door.

He's…

Committed.

To me.

I sit down on the bed and stare into space.

It's just business, I repeat in my head like a mantra. *This thing with Yulian is just business. See that ridiculous amount of money? That's proof.*

"Mommy?" Eli's tiny voice breaks me out of my reverie. "Are you okay?"

"Yeah," I rasp. "I'm fine. More than fine, actually."

Because, finally, I can take care of you.

Eli hauls himself onto my knees. He peers up, his curious gaze boring into mine. "Are you crying?"

"No," I sniffle, drying my eyes. A little white lie. "Mommy's just really happy right now."

"Because of the dress?"

"Yes," I laugh. "And because of you. You're the best kid in the world, you know that?" I ruffle his hair.

"Stop," Eli laughs, "it tickles!"

"Say, what if we went out to dinner?" I whisper conspiratorially. "Just the two of us."

His face lights up. "Are we getting pizza? Or ice cream?"

"How about we get both?"

While Eli runs excitedly around the house, chanting "Ice cream and pizza! Ice cream and pizza!", I text Yulian back.

Thank you, I type, even though it's not nearly enough. ***Seriously.***

Before going out, I snap another selfie.

Going for pizza AND ice cream!

I don't expect him to text back at all, but he does.

Careful,* kotyonok. *Gratitude looks good on you.

Those words make me dizzy all over. I remind myself of every reason this means nothing: the transactional nature of our relationship, Yulian's wild mood swings that make it impossible to tell what he's really thinking, the vow I swore to myself.

No more men.

No more mess.

No more scars.

And no more falling where no one will catch me.

25

MIA

On Saturday night, I meet Yulian again.

It's another business meeting at the Goldenrod. This time, the night passes without incident.

I cling to Yulian's arm like the good piece of candy I'm supposed to be, laugh politely at every bad joke, and show off Yulian's spectacular sage dress and jewelry.

Somehow, it's our coldest date yet.

It leaves me puzzled for the rest of the night. There was no shooting, no violence, no lecherous men pawing at his prize. I saw him shake hands, make deals, secure millions for his company.

By all standards, it was a success.

And yet, Yulian felt like a piece of ice all the way through.

We've gone out exactly twice more since then, all in the span of a single week. Every time, I've wanted to teach my soul to crawl out my body and astral project back home, with my sleeping kid and my deli lasagna and none of the thirty-plus forks that rich people dinners seem to have.

I guess I shouldn't be surprised. After the text exchange, I got my hopes up. It's not like I expected Yulian to suddenly turn decent and renounce his life of crime, but maybe we could be… friends? Companionable colleagues? Have a boss-employee relationship that doesn't revolve around threats or strangely hot acts of borderline violence in alleys?

"Unrealistic," Kallie decides once I'm done venting to her. "Repeat after me: men are pigs. Even smoking hot, GQ-stubbled men with abs of steel."

"That's not helping, K."

"What's not helping?" Eli mumbles, rubbing the sleep from his face as he walks into the bedroom. Then his eyes go wide. "*Another* dress?!"

"Whatcha think?" I grin, doing a little spin. This one is lilac satin with a high neck and a wide skirt. The box it came in also held a pearl-studded waist belt and a matching purse, as well as a stunning pair of Sophia Webster ivory heels. "Good enough for a Bond girl?"

"*Duh,*" Eli gapes. "You look like a mother-freaking-princess, Mommy!"

"Now, where'd you learn that word?"

"April Labeene. Ms. Spencer at daycare makes us dance to her songs."

"Yellow flag for the fancy daycare?" Kallie winces as soon as Eli's out of earshot.

"Kind of, yeah." I'm starting to think the "fancy daycare" I spent a fortune on is probably not as fancy as it made itself sound. Just ridiculously expensive. "But August's almost over. Might as well make it count."

"He's starting the new school, then?" Kallie brightens. "The one Mr. Definitely-Not-A-Sugar-Daddy is paying for?"

"Okay, first: he is *not* my sugar daddy." I hold up a finger, then two. "Second, *I'm* paying for it."

"With his money."

"That's called 'nitpicking.'"

"And that's called 'denial.'" She sits me back down on the bed and pulls up a chair across from me, rummaging through my makeup purse for anything resembling lilac. "Now, hold still while I beat your face."

"I'm pretty sure that qualifies as grievous bodily harm."

"Only if I make it look ugly." She topples the purse on the bed. "Christ, it's like an expired eyeshadow cemetery in here."

As Kallie—metaphorically—beats my face, I list in my head all the reasons she's wrong.

Yulian is my new side-boss. That's all this is. The rules are clear on that: nothing is going to happen. No hugs, no kisses, no dancing the horizontal tango in luxury hotels.

Just stunning dresses, daily selfies, personal security, expensive dates, a shit ton of cash, and—*oh.*

Oh, no.

"I'm not his sugar baby," I repeat, though this time it's more for my benefit. "He's paying me for a service."

"The service of being pretty in front of his peers?"

"Yes!" I blurt. "And I hate it!"

"You're right," she says flatly. "I see how wrong I was now. You're definitely not his sugar baby."

"Thank y—"

"If anything, you're his salt baby."

She fastens my new pearl necklace around my neck. I grimace at the cool weight of it against my skin. If I put together the price of everything he's sent me this past week, it'd probably add up to more than my advance.

God. What if Kallie's right? What if I *am* a sugar baby?

"He doesn't want anything from me," I sigh, frustrated with myself. Frustrated with my best friend for always seeing right through me. "Not—not like *that.*"

"You could sound less sad about it."

"I'm not—!"

"Also, dude, I'd totally tap that ass. If I could. Like, if I was into girls and you weren't my best friend and shit." She dabs a little blush on my cheeks. "You can't tell me Mr. Matching Lingerie hasn't thought about your *assets*. The stuff he sends you? Straight from the spank-bank."

I cringe. I'd been trying not to think about the matching lingerie part. "He's probably just obsessive," I blurt. "Doesn't want a random gust of wind to ruin the perfect picture he's painting."

"Oh, he wants to paint something, alright. With his thick, wooden brush."

"You are so—!"

"Done," she interrupts.

I stand up and walk to the mirror.

My jaw falls.

It's nothing like when I do it. The hues blend seamlessly together, complementing my skin without looking gaudy. Even though Kallie used bold colors to match Yulian's choice, including a purple lipstick I haven't worn since my goth phase, I look…

"Beautiful," she whispers. "You look beautiful, Mimi."

I turn to Kallie. My best friend, my ride-or-die, the one who's always there for me. Who's been there for me ever since we were ragtag roommates in a moldy shoebox apartment, one pregnant, the other orphaned.

We've been clinging to each other for so long, I can't even think about how painful it would be to let go. How cold it would feel.

"Thank you," I rasp. "It's incredible."

"*You're* incredible." She smiles sweetly. "And if he doesn't wanna bang you after this, I can introduce him to Reese."

"Kallie!"

Then the doorbell rings. It's Boris, warning me to come down if I don't want to be held in contempt for Criminal Lateness.

I hug Kallie goodbye. "Text me if anything comes up, okay? Anything at all."

"Don't worry," she says. "The most adventurous thing that can happen tonight is a *Skyfall* rewatch. With popcorn, if we're feeling daring."

"Popcorn?" Eli pokes his head in from where he was playing in the hallway. "Can we have it, Aunt Kallie? Please, pleeease?"

I kiss Eli goodnight, grab my new purse, and run like the wind.

26

MIA

When I get downstairs, Yulian is already there, leaning against his sleek Maybach. His eyes widen as he sees me, but he schools it quickly.

"You're late."

I glance at the Cartier watch he sent me. I haven't checked how much it's worth—I'd be too tempted to sell it. "By two minutes?"

"Time is money," he says flatly. "Especially my time."

I roll my eyes and head to the car. Yulian's gaze doesn't leave me for a second, a gray storm I can't decipher. Hot, cold, and everything in between.

Then, as I'm about to open the door, I hear it.

"Mommy!" Eli comes hurtling like a bullet into the empty street, waving his hand wildly. "You forgot your phone!"

From the staircase windows, I can see Kallie wheeze, struggling to keep up.

Shit.

Until now, I've done everything I could to keep my two lives separate. Everything to prevent the darkness of Yulian's world from tainting Eli's innocence.

Now, I can do nothing but watch them clash.

Yulian sees Eli. His gray eyes, stormy and intense until moments ago, go wide.

Just a fraction.

Just enough to tell me he's not pleased about this.

Oblivious, Eli jogs forward. "Hello," he says shyly.

"Hello," Yulian echoes in his deep rumble.

"Are you a spy?"

Please, Earth, swallow me whole.

"No," Yulian answers, a little taken aback. If this wasn't a PR nightmare for me, it'd almost be fun to watch. After all, how rare is it for the great Yulian Lozhkin to stumble? "I'm… not."

"Are you sure?" Eli crooks his head. "You kind of look like Boris. He delivers our mail now."

"Does he, now?"

"Mhmm. Mommy says he also keeps us safe."

"That's good," Yulian says. "You can never be too safe."

"I still think he's a spy, though. He's got the accent."

"Bond villain accent," I explain awkwardly. "He's—very into spy movies."

Yulian's gaze flicks to me. If I didn't know better, I'd say he looks almost amused. "I remember. You mentioned."

"Are you Mommy's boyfriend?"

Before I can be put through the emotional blender of answering that horrifying question, Maksim slips out of the car.

"Who's the little one?" he chimes in, sounding amused. "Ah, a friend of Mia, I presume?"

"Heh." I smile awkwardly, pulling him to me. "This is Eli. My—my son."

Eli's eyes fix on Maksim now. "Are *you* a spy?"

"Maybe," he says with a shrug and an air of mystery. "Wouldn't tell ya if I was, would I?"

Eli seems to consider it. "That's fair."

"Alright!" I pocket my phone and ruffle Eli's hair. "Now, Mommy *really* needs to go, so—"

"Sorry!" Kallie blurts, finally catching up to us. "I told him I could do it, but he said he was faster, and—well, he's right, haha."

Yulian doesn't spare her a glance.

Maksim, however, immediately steps between us. "Well, well," he drawls, "Mia never told us she had such a pretty friend. *Enchanté.* My name is Maksim Goncharov, but you can call me your most fervent admirer."

Then he takes Kallie's hand and brings it to his lips.

Oh. My. God.

I freeze. That's gonna be trouble. Kallie isn't one to tolerate unwelcome advances, not even for the sake of keeping up appearances. Last time a guy tried to dance her up at a bar, she threw her drink on his crotch and told him to sip his own straw.

Sorry, Maksim. Looks like you're in for a world of—

"Oh! U-um, likewise. I'm Kallie. Well, Kalinda, technically, but everyone calls me Kallie, so..."

—Wait, what?

"Kalinda," he croons, like he's savoring it. "I hope you won't mind if I call you that. Such a beautiful name is not made to be shortened, *mademoiselle*."

Next to me, Yulian's foot starts tapping. Never a good sign.

"Quit pretending you're French," he barks at Maksim. "No one's buying it."

"I lived in Marseilles for two years," he says proudly. "I'm French-adjacent."

He still hasn't let go of Kallie's hand. To make things worse, Kallie is blushing furiously, like she's suddenly turned back into a schoolgirl.

I've known her for five years, and I have *never* seen her like this.

"W-well, we really need to, uh... get going now. It was lovely to meet you, Maksim." She flicks her gaze to the side. "Yulian."

Yulian's eyes narrow. Shit—was I not supposed to tell Kallie his name? Was there an NDA somewhere in all those papers? Am I going to be sued for all I'll ever own?

But Yulian just says, "We're late."

"Right," I interrupt, finding my voice again. "Thanks for the phone, guys. Bye!"

"Bye, Mommy!" Eli waves. "Bye, Maksim! Bye, Yulian!"

Yulian blinks, caught off-guard. But soon enough, Eli disappears back into the building with Kallie, and it's just us again.

Cue the crickets.

"Look," I blurt, "I'm sorry about—"

"Let's go."

He doesn't sound particularly angry, but I also don't want to test it. There's still something off about him. Something that began the second he saw my son.

I tell myself to forget it and climb into the car.

27

YULIAN

"So, um... got any kids?"

Mia's question catches me off-guard.

"What?" I ask.

"Kids," she repeats, like she thinks I didn't hear her the first time. Her cheeks, even in the darkness of the car, are red like summer cherries. "I was asking if you've got them. You met mine, but I realized I never asked you if..." She trails off, face burning, eyes downcast.

Fucking hell. Of all the topics of conversation, this is the one Mia had to choose for tonight's awkward car ride. I'd much rather she be silent.

"No," I answer shortly. "I don't."

Mia nods. Her hands are twisting the fabric of her skirt, betraying how nervous she feels. "And do you... want them?" she ventures. "Kids, I mean?"

Kids? Don't make me fucking laugh. Children, family—the possibility of any of that has been taken from me the day the tablecloths in my mansion were soaked red.

I *had* a family.

It's gone now.

I won't seek out another.

Family, to me, is weakness—nothing more. It's the blind spot that kills you.

And I intend to survive.

"If you're looking for a pay raise," I growl, "I'm afraid you're going to have to look elsewhere. I'm not looking to fill that particular position."

"I wasn't suggesting—!"

"Weren't you, though?"

"I wasn't offering myself up, asshole," she hisses. "Believe me, one solo trip to the delivery room was enough. I'm not looking to be single-mothered twice."

"And you assume that's what I'd do?" I ask. "Enjoy the perks and leave you to fend for yourself afterwards?"

Her jaw hardens as she turner her face toward the window. "In my experience, that's exactly what men do."

"Then you haven't met a true man yet. A man never abandons his family. Not his blood, and certainly not his woman."

She averts her gaze, embarrassed. "Then she'll be a lucky girl," she mumbles. "Whoever you choose to make a family with."

I don't bother answering. This shit is not why I hired her, not why I've kept her, not why I'm bringing her with me again and again. It's irrelevant.

She has a job to do.

So do I.

That's the beginning and end of the matter.

Or at least, that's what I intended to be the end of it. But...

"I'm sorry."

Mia's voice catches me by surprise. Her hand on my arm, even more so. For a second, I can do nothing but stare, the warmth of her skin seeping into the ice of mine.

"I don't want your pity."

"It's not pity," she insists. She offers me a small smile. "I've... been separated from my family, too. It's hard enough not to see them, but I can't imagine what it would be like to know they're not waiting for me."

I keep staring into Mia's eyes, hoping to find something there. A flash of sharpness, of betrayal—anything.

Instead, there's just warmth.

It's ridiculous. *She's* ridiculous. I'm her enemy. I am the man who shoved her against a wall and threatened her. The one who holds all the power in our relationship.

Anybody else would be looking for a weapon. Something, anything they could use to even the scales.

But she's not doing that. She's just—listening. Even though I haven't said a word about what happened. Even though she has nothing to gain.

Which means *she* must have something to gain.

There's no other reason to be kind. If there's one thing I've learned, it's that.

And if it just plain old kindness—

Then she hasn't seen what this world is capable of.

I shake my head, yank my arm away. Mia's savior complex is none of my fucking business. Just like my past is none of hers.

Then, mercifully, the car rolls to a stop. "We're here," Maksim announces.

"Here?" Mia tilts her head, trying to make out the venue out the tinted window. "'Here' where?"

"The back entrance to the Goldenrod," I tell her.

"Why the back?" she frowns. "Why aren't we going in the usual way?"

"Because the usual way is for business," I explain. "This is for something else."

I step out of the car and offer her my arm. It's just for show, but the way she clings to me sends a stab of guilt through my chest. Like I'm plunging her into the deep end with no safeguards.

"Yulian… where are we going?" Mia whispers.

"You'll see soon enough."

~

We take our seats at the front of the table, Maksim to my right, Mia to my left.

Mia. She's been a decent actress so far, but tonight, she's borderline useless. She keeps fiddling with the silverware, trying to figure out which spoon to use first, even though the food hasn't been served yet.

If she keeps this up much longer, my *vory* are going to realize something's wrong. I can't have that.

For this ruse to work, everyone must be convinced. Otherwise, there's no way Prizrak will be.

I cover her hand with mine. She stops fiddling immediately, the tremors dying down. Centered, once again.

She takes a big breath, exhales. Finds her focus.

I take in the sight of my *vory,* sitting at their places in silence, eyes fixed on me and the woman at my side. It could almost pass for a company dinner. The thought strikes me as somewhat amusing.

Kazimir Smirnov—Department Head of Bribery, if we had any such thing as departments—is smiling politely at us. He's my youngest *vor,* barely even thirty, easy to underestimate. That's his strength.

Slavik Pushkin—Director of Money Laundering—is sipping his water, calm and calculating. His eyes miss nothing.

Anton Volkov and Zhenya Volkova—Twin Managers of Illicit Entertainment and Violent Debt Collection—are sitting next to each other. Anton is half-asleep, waiting for his sister to say or do anything he can agree with. He's an oily son of a bitch, but an effective party planner, provider of drugs and girls and whatever else our patrons may wish for. Then, when it's time to pay the pied piper, Zhenya comes into play. She's got none of her brother's reservations and an impressive collection of crowbars.

Finally, at the other end of the table, Rurik is glaring down at us. He's my oldest *vor*—been with the Bratva since my father's time—and he never misses a chance to throw his weight around. He handles the gambling dens, our primary source of cash flow.

There couldn't be five more different people at this table. And yet, right now, every one of those people is thinking the same thing:

Who the hell is that woman?

The waiters carry in heaped plates of Russian cuisine: *borscht, pirozhki, shashlik, blini, pelmeni.*

But before anyone can tuck in, Slavik clears his throat. "I understand this meeting was urgent."

"It was," I reply. "Haven't had a decent Russian meal in ages."

"Enough with the fuckery!" Rurik snarls, slamming his palms on the table. "What the hell are we doing here? Our time is—"

"Valuable," I cut in, rising from my chair. "As is mine. More, in fact, if we're comparing net worth."

Slavik clears his throat, but says nothing. Out of all my men, he's the most seasoned and the least prone to conflict.

Rurik, on the other hand, is as ornery and disagreeable as old mobsters can get. He used to be my late father's *brigadir*, and because of that, he isn't afraid to push me.

"You'd do well to remember you're not ruling alone, Yulian," he scoffs. "We all contributed to this empire, and I, for one, am sick of hearing you talk like you're—"

"The *pakhan,*" I cut him off. "That's what I am, Rurik. Something *you'd* do well to remember. Which brings me to the reason I've gathered you."

Then I pull Mia to her feet.

"*Vory,*" I announce, "meet your future *pakhansha.*"

The table falls silent.

Every whisper ceases.

Slavik's the first to recover. "That's... a surprise," he admits, but bows politely at the waist. "But a welcome one. Pleased to make your acquaintance, *moya pakhansha.*"

The other *vory* rise as well, one after the other. "*Pakhansha,*" Kazimir greets with a pleasant smile. He's the most easygoing of the bunch, but beneath that soft exterior and silver tongue, he's as venomous as everybody else. "It's an honor to finally meet you."

"Hmpf." I don't even need to turn to know who made that sound: Zhenya. "Could've been an email."

"She doesn't mean that," Anton, her twin brother, laughs as he digs an elbow into her side. "We are, of course, delighted."

Mia gives an awkward laugh. "It's, uh... it's very nice to meet you all. I'm Mia."

"At least it's easy to remember," Zhenya adds.

Everybody else introduces themselves then, with the exception of Rurik. He stands off to the side, his face a mask of displeasure.

It's enough to prickle my nerves. "Something wrong, brother?"

It's a warning. A chance. His relationship with my father is the only reason I haven't put him in the ground for his insolence yet. The only reason I'm giving him an out.

But Rurik doesn't take it. "Where to even start?" he laughs scathingly. "She's a nobody. She's got no connections, or else she would have said so. Instead, all she gave us is a first name. Like a goddamn stripper."

"Careful," I warn.

"Is that what *you're* being?" he challenges, stepping forward aggressively towards us. "'Careful'? Because from where I'm standing, it sure as fuck don't look it. Just looks like you decided to marry your latest whore." He spits on the ground. "If only your father could see you now."

My hand darts to my gun. *That's it.* No matter how much Otets valued him, I cannot keep around a man who'll show me such blatant disrespect.

But before I can whip out my weapon, a smooth voice intervenes.

"I understand your concern," Mia smiles, far too gently for someone with her temper, let alone one who's been called a stripper and a whore in the last minute. "It's reassuring, honestly. It means you really care about my Yulian."

My Yulian. The words stick in my brain in a way I cannot explain.

"But—" And here her voice takes a dangerous, icy plunge. "—I believe you know him well enough to realize what he will or won't tolerate. Don't you?"

Then she takes my hand, guiding it away from my gun.

That's when I realize she's shaking.

Of course. This whole thing is an act. A shockingly well-executed one, but an act nonetheless.

Mia wasn't bred for this. She has no idea what it takes to be a true *pakhansha.*

Could've fooled me, though.

Rurik grits his teeth. I can see the urge to fight back on his face, but then Kazimir steps in, smooth as silk. "Well said, *pakhansha,*" he praises. "Now, I think we've all gotten a bit carried away, yes? Maybe we can apologize to the lady for keeping her from the banquet in her honor?"

Rurik goes red. But I can tell something's changed. That, somehow, Mia changed it.

"Of course," he forces out. "My apologies."

Then everyone sits back down.

"You can let go," I mutter to Mia. "I'm not going to shoot him. Not tonight, at least."

"Is that supposed to reassure me?"

"Mostly."

With a shaky exhale, she lets go.

The rest of the dinner is much smoother sailing. Mia carries herself well, bantering with Kazimir and trading political opinions with Slavik. At one point, she even manages to drag a snort out of Zhenya.

I've never been more turned on in my life.

Once everyone leaves, Mia turns to me, her face suddenly

uncertain. "How did I do?" she breathes. "I didn't overstep, did I? I'm sorry, I just really didn't want you to k—"

I don't let her finish that sentence.

I push her against the table and kiss her senseless.

28

YULIAN

I can't take my fucking hands off her.

"Yulian—" She gasps into my mouth, driving me crazy with want. We're in the elevator, heading up towards the Goldenrod's luxury suites. *My* personal suite, where I've taken all my one-night stands.

Because, if I take her there, then that's all she is to me.

"Wait," she whispers, so close I can fucking feel it. "Maybe we should—"

"Quiet," I growl against her lips. "From now on, you only make noise when I tell you to."

Then I'm on her again.

She moans, soft and keening. Opens up to me like I'm all she's ever wanted. I can't believe I've waited this long to do this. Every sound out of her mouth goes straight to my dick, turning it harder than goddamn stone.

When the elevator doors finally open, I don't waste a single second.

I pick her up, swipe my card, and carry her into the suite.

It's not gallantry.

It's not seduction.

It's pure, raw animal instinct.

Drag her into your territory and make her yours.

She wraps her legs tight around my middle. Her dress rides up, exposing those creamy thighs. I sink all ten fingers into them, relishing the little moan she gives in response. Like I'm hurting her in all the right ways.

But it's not enough for me.

I want more.

When I toss her on the bed, her eyes go wide with surprise. Around her bent legs, her dress flares. It's an expensive piece —easily worth a small fortune.

I rip it up like it's nothing.

"Yulian!" she gasps. "That—that was your—!"

"Don't care," I growl. "*This* is mine, too."

My gaze travels over her body, ravenous. Every inch of her is like a banquet laid out just for me. I want to eat her whole.

It's never happened before. Not like this. Until now, I've never met a woman whose form I actually appreciated. They were all just warm bodies, distractions for a night.

With Mia, I never want to stop looking.

But the urge to touch is too strong.

She's wearing coordinated lingerie. Lilac lace and purple satin. The sight of it on her is enough to drive me insane, possessiveness rising through me like poison.

I yank her panties down and rip those up, too.

Mia's cheeks flush. Her hands move automatically, trying to cover up what I've already seen. "D-don't stare like that! It's—"

"Beautiful." It's not what she wanted to say, but it's the only word in my mind. *"Blyat', kotyonok.* Do you even realize what you do to me?"

Before she can answer, I sink between her thighs.

"Yul—!" she chokes, fisting the sheets. My tongue licks ravenously into her pussy, like it's the first meal I've eaten in ages. Like it's the only thing that can curb my hunger.

But the more I taste of her, the more I want.

I suck her clit, drinking in the sounds she makes. Hot, desperate, like she doesn't get a say in what happens to her body now. Doesn't get to decide how much pleasure she can take.

She's got that right.

Tonight, *I'll* decide how many times she's coming.

Her thighs wrap around my head, pushing me harder against her. I'm not certain she even knows she's doing it: every time I glance up, all I see is the quivering mountains of her breasts, still regrettably clothed in lace, and her head thrown back.

I reach out and grab her chin. "Look," I command. "Look at

what I'm doing to you. If you take your eyes off even for a second, I'll stop and walk out that door."

It's a bluff. I couldn't stop if I wanted to. Even taking my mouth off of her long enough to speak is sending me into withdrawal, but I can't have Mia thinking she's got the upper hand here.

She can't know how deeply she's crawled under my skin.

Slowly, her eyes meet mine. The black of her pupil has eaten away at the blue, leaving only thin rings of ocean around the abyss of her desire.

I dive back into her, fucking her with my tongue.

Her manicured fingers sink into my scalp. "Ahh, Yulian…!"

I palm my cock through my pants, seeking relief. It makes me crazy—how hard she's digging her nails into me. Like it's all she can do to hold on for dear life as I strip her self-control away.

And finally, I feel it: that telltale contraction, her hips bucking wildly into my mouth, seeking *more.*

She's so close already. I haven't even fingered her yet, haven't tortured her clit with my thumb as she begs for mercy, and yet—

"I'm coming," she gasps, all helpless need. "I—*ahh*—"

"Come," I growl into her pussy. "Show me all those pretty noises you make."

She moans, high and desperate. I lap into her harder, suck her clit and torture her entrance and yank her thighs flat against my shoulders. When she comes against my face, I want to *feel* it.

And I do.

It's wild. *She's* wild. This is who Mia Winters truly is, under that tough exterior and spitfire attitude: a warm, quivering mess of *need.*

She spends her life taking care of others—when's the last time someone's taken care of her?

When's the last time someone's made her come like this?

As she shakes apart, I lap up all her juices. I'm drunk on the taste, drunk on her voice, drunk on her body shuddering against mine. All I want is to push into the tight, wet heat—but what happens once I cross that line? Once I sink into Mia once and for all?

Get her out of your system. It's that cold, dark voice at the back of my mind, the *pakhan* in me. *Fuck her out of it. It's the only way.*

She's panting now, her chest rising and falling as her blue eyes slowly find their focus again. Her fingers have loosened, no longer digging in, but stroking. Caressing.

It makes me fucking furious. *She* makes me furious. How dare she do this to me? Make me lose sight of my priorities—make me lose control?

"Yulian?" she whispers. "Is everything—*ah!*"

"Quiet," I snarl, rising to my feet and pulling her flush against my crotch. "I'm not done with you yet."

Her eyes go dark again. She wants this, wants *me*—perhaps just as bad as I want her.

But if she thinks this is going anywhere, she's dead fucking wrong. This night will stay within these four walls. I'll make damn sure of it.

I can't afford a distraction like her.

I shrug off my shirt, then pin her down by the wrists. My cock is throbbing in my pants, begging for release. I haven't been this keyed up since I was a teenager—what the hell is this woman doing to me?

Fuck her. Get her out. Get it over with.

Fuck her, then forget her.

... if you can.

Mia's hands work my cock out of my pants. I hear a small gasp when she realizes what a struggle it is to wrap around it completely, but she quickly schools her surprise, picking her rhythm back up.

I suppress a shiver, the feeling of those delicate fingers playing with my shaft driving me fucking crazy.

I tear her bra off and take her breasts into my mouth, one after the other. They're so full, so sensitive, nipples hard as pebbles under my tongue.

Mia whimpers, rubbing my cock along her seam, as desperate and impatient as I am. "Get inside," she begs. "Fuck me, Yulian."

Blyat'.

I can't wait anymore. Can't hold off one more fucking second.

I grab Mia's thighs, spread them open, and *thrust.*

"Ahh—!" she moans as the head of my cock breaches her. Her walls stretch around it, too full, too much. She's so petite, I feel like a giant inside her.

But when I force myself to slow down, she urges me on, her hips bucking wildly against mine. "D-do it. I can take it," she stutters. "Fuck me, need you, need your cock—ahh!"

The last thread of my restraint snaps completely.

I pull her hips up and fuck into her, hard and fast and deep. It's a brutal, savage pace, but Mia's moans are anything but pained.

"Yes," she says, over and over. "Yes, like that, don't stop—"

"*Blyat*," I curse, pulling almost all the way out and then slamming back in. I can feel the whole length of my cock dragging against her walls, the obscene slaps of skin-against-skin echoing in the four walls of the suite.

It's borderline pornographic, but I can't fucking stop.

"You little minx. You've wanted this all along."

"N-no," Mia gasps, "I—"

"Don't fucking lie to me." I pick up my pace, voice twisting into a snarl. "I've seen the way you looked at me. You wanted my cock the second you towed my car."

"I-it wasn't—"

"Oh, yes, it was." I spread her legs wider, sink my cock in deeper. "Were you hoping I'd fuck you right there? That I'd drag you into an alley and make you regret it?"

I can see it in her eyes when the fantasy sets in. "Yes," she breathes, too far gone to deny it. "But you wanted me, too."

"Did I now?"

"Y-you bought me," she says. "You made me undress in your car. You wanted me to bend over and beg for it, didn't y—*ah!*"

There you are. I hold her hips a little higher and pound into that sweet spot all over again, making her scream. "Naughty little kitten," I snarl. "Always so disrespectful. But that's an act, too, isn't it?"

"Ahh—"

"You want everyone to think you're tough," I rasp, the pleasure making it hard to talk, to *think.* "You act like you want to be punished, but I know the truth."

"W-what's that…?"

"You want to be a good girl for me." I wrap one arm around her waist and rub her clit with the other. She moans so loud at that, I'm convinced the whole floor must be hearing her. It drives me crazy with possessiveness—the thought of anybody else witnessing this. Seeing how delicious she looks when she's so close to breaking. "You want to be good so bad, it's killing you."

She flushes crimson. It tells me all I need to know: that I'm right about what makes her tick, what makes her come.

"I… I—"

"But you know what, *kotyonok?*" I push her flat against the mattress, chest flush to hers. The next time I speak, my lips brush her ear. "Tonight, you've been a *very* good girl."

It's uncanny—how quickly it happens. How quickly her thread, too, snaps.

"I-I'm gonna—!"

"Come," I order.

Her head rolls back. Her body seizes. Her pussy tightens into a vise, trapping me so deep, I couldn't pull out if I wanted to.

But I don't want to. Tonight, I want to claim every inch of her.

Inside and out, she is *mine.*

She comes so hard, her nails break the skin on my back.

That's the last straw. I buck into her, sink deeper than ever before, and see white.

It's the hardest I've ever come in my life. Mia's body milks me for every drop, her legs locked at the small of my back, her walls fluttering wildly around my cock.

I don't even realize I've been kissing her until we break apart.

The second Mia's eyes meet mine, I know.

The second her arms wrap around me, warm and inviting, I know.

I've just made the biggest mistake of my life.

29

MIA

I wake up to fresh sheets, perfumed pillows, and a four-poster bed.

Shit.

I sit up like a cartoon spring, minus the sound effect. Memories of last night flood my mind, turning my cheeks redder by the second.

Yulian kissed me. After the meeting with his vores or whatever, he—he *kissed* me.

And I let him.

Then he did a whole lot more to me, and I let him do that, too.

Panicked, I check the other side of the bed.

Empty.

Which doesn't mean what happened last night was a fever dream, though. At least, a very specific part of me seems to remember every detail.

Oh. My. God. We fucked. Like, seriously fucked. I saw his cheese grater abs and every other kitchen implement he's been endowed with by nature, and holy shit, the tabloids did not lie for once.

I bury my face in my hands. This is the most mortifying day of my life. I didn't just fuck my boss—I begged my boss to fuck me. I was so far gone, the brain upstairs took its PTO while the brain downstairs overhauled every single rational decision I've ever made.

That's what you get for letting cobwebs grow down there. I can hear Kallie's voice like she's physically here, snickering at my expenses.

Then I remember.

Kallie.

Eli.

Shit!

I glance at the snazzy curtains again and realize it's light outside. Double-triple shit with a cherry on top.

I spring to my feet before realizing I'm still naked, then wrap the sheets around me. The effect isn't quite modest-but-sexy Hollywood starlet, but I couldn't care less. Yulian isn't even *here,* for fuck's sake.

I try not to linger on how empty that thought makes me feel. That, after last night, he couldn't even stick around.

Instead, I rush into the bathroom to grab the fastest shower of my life—

—and I collide with a brick wall.

No, not a brick wall. A *cheese grater* wall. The very same eight-pack I've been ogling since day one. What's that they always say in children's movies? *"Careful what you wish for"*?

"You're in a hurry." Yulian's husky voice snaps me out of my panic. It isn't a question—it never is.

"Sorry," I blurt, "it's just, it's super late and I was supposed to be back last night and I can't even remember if Kallie had a shift and—"

"Car's downstairs," he cuts me off. "Maks will take you."

It's only then that I finally meet his gaze.

Cold. It's the first thing I notice, a feeling more than a thought. A chilly, unwelcome sensation spreading down my naked body.

Last night, there was a storm in Yulian's gray eyes. It was a storm of desire, of *want,* so raw no one could possibly deny it existed.

Now, they're as cold as steel.

He sidesteps me, giving me space to enter the bathroom.

"Wait," I call after him. "That's it?"

Slowly, he turns. "You'll have to be more specific."

"We just had the craziest, most unhinged sexathon ever, and that's all you've got to say to me?"

His gaze turns sharp. I try to ignore how much it hurts—or how familiar it feels.

"It seems," Yulian starts, as glacial as I've ever heard him, "you're under the mistaken impression last night meant something."

Hurts, hurts, hurts.

Fucking hurts all the way to my heart.

"Didn't it?" I rasp, too raw to be anything less than vulnerable right now.

But Yulian doesn't grant me the courtesy of handling me with care. He's ice and steel, flat and unfeeling. Whatever was in his eyes last night isn't there now. Maybe I just dreamed it up.

"No," he says, cold and final. "It didn't. It never does."

It never does. Those words sink their claws into me, right into the scars I've done my damnedest to cover up. To heal ugly and fast, anything so they'd just stop bleeding.

I'm no stranger to being used. To being treated as a warm body, a servant, a thing.

But somehow, I thought Yulian...

Thought what? my rational mind mocks. *That he'd be better? That he wouldn't be just like any other bad boy billionaire who's ever made you suffer?*

That he'd be different?

"Right," I answer tightly, pushing past the lump in my throat. "How silly of me."

Then I slam the door and lock it.

I take the fastest shower of my life, blinking back the tears under the spray. But once I'm done, I hesitate to open it again. I don't want to see Yulian—not like this.

When I peek my head out, no one's there.

He left. I don't know why the realization leaves a bitter taste in my mouth. Isn't it better this way? That I don't have to face him again so soon?

You wanted him to stay.

"Shut up," I say out loud. "Just—shut up."

I find women's clothes in the dresser. With a flash of outrage, I realize where I've landed: Yulian's fuckpad. His man cave. His playroom, though with an astonishing lack of whips and leather handcuffs.

Right. He probably keeps the good stuff at home. Why waste his Bad Dragon haul on the help?

I pick out a dress and underwear—still with their price tag, thank God—and hurtle down at the speed of light. I don't head for the Maybach, though.

Instead, I flag down a good, old-fashioned cab and disappear into Manhattan traffic.

~

I pay the driver extra to ignore all traffic laws. Some physics laws, too, judging by the way we're zooming through the city.

I try to reach Kallie the whole drive over, but her phone's off.

Please, let him be okay. For the rest of the drive, I swing wildly between the five stages of grief.

It's not that late after all. Denial.

Why the hell didn't Yulian wake me up?! Anger.

Maybe Kallie's still there. Maybe she's called Reese to take over. Maybe she brought Eli with her to the hospital. Maybe she didn't have a shift at all and they're both still asleep. Maybe they're making pancakes. Bargaining.

I'm such a horrible mom. How could I fall asleep like that? How could I let last night happen at all? Depression.

And, finally—

No fucking way.

"Ms. Winters." Howard Lee greets me from my own door in his perfectly pressed suit. "We were starting to wonder if we shouldn't send out a search party."

"Mr. Lee, I—" I fade off, not knowing how to end my sentence. My heart is sinking with every thought.

CPS is here.

They beat me to it.

They're going to take Eli.

I'm never going to see my son again.

All for stupid Yulian Lozhkin.

At his side, Mrs. Deloera gives me a sad, pitying look. Somehow, I feel like I've disappointed my favorite teacher. Like she's telling me, *I really wanted to save your ass, but you just couldn't keep it in your pants.*

Worse—I've disappointed my son.

"Now," Mr. Lee urges, "are you going to let us in?"

My shoulders droop. Dejected, I put my key in the door.

I turn it.

I push.

And then I blink.

Because this can't be my apartment, can it?

Clean floors. Like, *super* clean floors. Tidy surfaces, every single one of them. Toys neatly tucked away in colorful boxes, organized by type.

And fresh, *unburnt* pancakes on the counter.

"Hello, Ms. Winters!" a jovial, unknown female voice greets me.

Mr. Lee's eyes are practically bulging out of their sockets. I can only imagine what mine must be doing.

"Hi," I breathe, not knowing what else to say.

"I took the liberty of tidying up a little." The unknown woman smiles. She looks about my age, only with a way better skincare routine.

"Hello," she says to the CPS caseworkers. "I'm Tamara, Eli's new babysitter. Nice to meet you. Mia here has said so many good things about you."

Mr. Lee's eyes immediately narrow with suspicion. "She did?"

I did?

"Of course." She welcomes them in, even going so far as to help Mrs. Deloera with her cane. "Eli's still asleep. I'm afraid I couldn't quite make him stick to his bedtime." She gives a little apologetic shrug that probably endeared every single red-blooded man in the span of ten miles, even though they didn't see her. "I made breakfast, though. You want some?"

"No, thank you," Mr. Lee bristles, as immune to feminine wiles as ever. "But I'd like to see the child."

"I'll take tea," Mrs. Deloera chirps cheerfully. "Two sugars."

Shaking his head in defeat, Mr. Lee heads for Eli's bedroom. I follow.

And there he is.

Sleeping. Tucked into bed. Hugging his favorite Bluey plushie.

Safe.

A weight lifts from my chest. I don't care what weirdness is going on right now—my kid is okay. He's safe.

That's all that matters. "Satisfied, I hope?" I ask Mr. Lee with a touch of acid.

Mr. Lee grunts his assent and heads back to the kitchen, presumably to swap out my sugar with rat poison.

By the time my two caseworkers leave—one looking very satisfied and the other looking murderous—I turn to Tamara. "Who are you?"

"I'm Tamara," she repeats, all smiles. "Mr. Lozhkin sent me last night. He said you'd be needing my services. I was to take over from the other girl and stay as long as you needed me to."

The other girl. That must mean Kallie. "And, um, how did you convince her to go?"

"She wasn't very keen," Tamara admits. "She made herself… ah, *comfortable* on the couch. Left just after dawn, and only once she'd spoken to Mr. Lozhkin."

So she slept over. Part of me feels guilty, but another part is relieved. Kallie wouldn't leave Eli with a complete stranger—not unless she knew he was safe. Apparently, she demanded that assurance from Yulian.

Yulian. So this is why he didn't wake me. Granted, the sitter thing was in our deal, but that was for work. And last night… that didn't count as work.

Unless it did for him.

"Will you be needing anything else today?"

Tamara's voice snaps me out of it. Even now, she's being annoyingly perfect.

For some reason, I can't stand it. Can't stand wondering if this is the kind of girl Yulian likes, all tall and flawless and Russian.

"No," I almost snap. "Thank you, Tamara. You can go."

With a nod of her perfect head, she leaves.

As soon as she's out the door, I let out a breath. Yulian kept his word. He saved my ass. He saved my kid from being flushed down the foster system by Mr. Lee.

So why can't I forgive him?

30

MIA

It's been a week since I've last heard from Yulian.

A week since the best sex of my life.

A week since he broke my heart.

I haven't been sending in my daily selfies. Call me petty, but I don't particularly feel like posing for the man who stomped all over my feelings.

Not that I even had *feelings,* but—okay, fine, it's complicated. Capital C and all.

Let's stick to the facts, shall we?

Fact: I don't *love* Yulian. How could I? He's selfish, rude, bossy, and always acts like he's owed the world. I couldn't stand being in a relationship with a guy like that. I've already done it once, and it ended with me faking a miscarriage, changing my name, and packing up my life.

Not exactly "happily ever after" material.

But after last night… I was vulnerable. I was raw. It's not like I expected breakfast in bed and cuddles, but the way he treated me? It made me feel cheap. Replaceable. Like everything we'd done was just another transaction between us, and I was the only one who hadn't gotten the memo.

It was humiliating.

"Hurry up, Mommy!" Eli bounces up and down at the door, backpack already strapped to his tiny shoulders. "We're gonna be late for my first day of school!"

I snap back to the present and grab my keys. "Coming!"

As we walk out the door, I glance at the hidden camera on the wall. It's too small to be seen, but I bribed Boris to show me the exact spot he planted it. After all, if *I'm* not the mark, why shouldn't I know where it is?

I blink at it once, twice. I considered learning how to spell "fuck you" in Morse code, but figured it was too much effort for the intended audience.

Here's your selfie, asshole.

Then I take my kid downstairs.

He spends the car ride in a state of bouncy excitement. His juice spills everywhere on the upholstery, but I can't quite find it in me to scold him. Seeing him so happy makes me happy, too.

Happier than I've been in a long time.

The second I drop him off, he hurtles towards the playground like a bullet, calling out the names of his new friends. "Ally! Marcus!"

"Eli!" The little girl with cornrows waves, flashing a gap-toothed grin. I remember her as the one who begged me to let Eli stay the day we came to visit. That must be Ally.

The kid next to her—Marcus, I suppose—doesn't lift his gaze from his video game, but once Eli's there, he shifts to make room, letting him watch.

His first friends.

That realization hits me all at once. I'm on the verge of the ugliest cry in Single Mom history. Eyes red, nose dripping, blubbery and ugly and just overwhelmed.

My son turns to wave goodbye, his smile brighter than I've seen it in ages, and I notice it's the first time he doesn't linger by me.

The first time he doesn't cling to my leg, or ask when I'll be back to get him.

He just grins.

Then he turns and goes to play.

"Emotional first day?" Principal Garcia appears at my side, eyes crinkling behind his thick glasses.

"Sort of." I quickly wipe the tears away with the back of my hand. "It's just... It's been a while since I've seen him like this."

"Kids here band together fast," he says. "They're drawn to each other. The quirks that push others away out there—they're the same thing that makes children click together in here."

"Same wavelength, huh?"

"In a way." He nods towards a couple of kids hanging out by themselves. "There are those who prefer solitude, and that's all perfectly fine, but there's peace in knowing you can have that here without being ostracized for it. And then, sometimes, those solitary kids learn to be solitary together."

He points at the sandbox, where a little girl is drawing shapes and another is counting ants just outside of it, in the grass. They aren't speaking or looking at each other, but their silence doesn't feel tense at all. "Parallel play. We encourage that a lot."

Suddenly, I'm reminded of Eli coloring by my side while I sort the bills. The lump in my throat grows tighter.

"I… I can see why."

After I've collected myself, Principal Garcia shows me the way to the accounting department.

I thank him and bid him goodbye, then step up to the front desk. "Mia Winters. I'm here to pay for my son's tuition."

"Little Eli, right?" The woman at the front desk grins. "We've got his registration papers right here. So thrilled to have you join our little family here."

I spend a couple of minutes filling in everything—birth date, allergies, family details. I write my contact information on the ***"Parent/Guardian #1"*** field.

The second one, I leave empty.

Instead, I add Kallie and Reese's contact info under "***Others***." I tick the box for pick-up so they'll be allowed to bring him home if I can't. After a moment's hesitation, I also add Tamara's name, just to be safe.

On the fourth empty row, my fingers start writing a "Y," but I quickly cross it out.

Let's not get carried away, right?

"Here you go," I tell the clerk.

"Perfect!" She gives a satisfied nod and tucks the papers away. "Will you require a payment plan for the tuition? We have a very good one that breaks it up in five installments over the year, no interest."

She says it without the slightest hint of judgment. Like this isn't just a rich kids' school, but one that tries to be fair.

Wouldn't have made a lick of difference without Yulian's money, though.

I banish all thoughts of Yulian from my mind and shake my head. "That won't be necessary. I'll pay in full."

I sign the check and hand it over. The number of zeroes still makes my head spin, but I feel light, too. Almost dizzy with excitement.

I just paid Eli's tuition in full. Pride swells in my heart.

Right on its heels is relief. *I could do this for him. For my kid.*

All thanks to...

As I walk out, taking a deep breath of fancy Upper West Side air, I think back to that night. How good it felt to be touched, to be wanted.

Then I think back to this morning. How happy Eli was to meet his friends again, how kind Principal Garcia was to me. I think back to all the ice creams and pizzas I could buy Eli last month, to his new and final pair of basketball shoes, to his shiny new toys.

To Tamara, saving my ass from CPS.

That was all Yulian's doing, too. Despite how cold he was to me, he also thought of me. Thought about my needs. If he hadn't sent Tamara, I wouldn't be taking my kid to school today. Wouldn't be taking him anywhere.

Slowly, all the anger I've been nursing starts to ebb away. Yulian Lozhkin… I don't understand him. Most likely, I never will.

But that doesn't mean I can't be grateful to him.

Before I can think better of it, I lift up my phone and snap a selfie.

First day of school. Couldn't have swung this without you, so… thank you. For everything.

It's not quite forgiveness, but it's as close as he'll get.

Our relationship is work. I need to remember that. What happened that night… It was just a one-time thing. Unpredictable, unstoppable, unforgettable—but also unrepeatable.

As long as I don't get too close again, I'll be fine.

Because, if I do, there's no way to tell what's going to happen. Whether I'll get frostbitten…

… or burned to ashes.

31

YULIAN

It's been a week since it happened.

A week since I had real sex with my fake fiancée.

A week since I stopped sleeping.

I'm used to nightmares. After my family was murdered, it was all I could do to pass out wasted for a couple of hours a night.

But no matter what I took, drank, smoked, or snorted, I still saw them.

These aren't nightmares, though. They're a whole other beast, one I've never had to fight before: obsession.

When I close my eyes now, it isn't the dead bodies of my family members that greet me on the other side of sleep. Instead, it's *her* body: naked, alive, warm and willing under my touch.

Our night together replays over and over in my mind, like a movie I can't stop.

It's driving me to madness.

I fucked her to be free. To stop thinking about her so goddamn much. I took her where I took everyone else, fucked her where I fucked everyone else, and left her the way I left everyone else.

And it hasn't.

Fucking.

Worked.

If anything, it's worse. Before, all I had to go by was stolen glimpses in the backseat of a car and my imagination to build Mia's body in my fantasies.

Now, I've seen it all: what she looks like taking her pleasure, what she sounds like when she comes, what she *tastes* like.

She's not out of my system. Not by a long shot. Instead, she's crawled in deeper, under my skin and into my bloodstream, like a goddamn infection. I cannot scratch her out.

I've tried. Over and over again, I've tried.

And then there's her eyes. The way she looked at me when I told her what we did had no meaning… I've broken hopes before—mainly the aspirations of supermodels who already saw themselves on a double spread in Forbes.

But Mia's face… it was like I'd broken her fucking heart.

So what? that cold voice inside me whispers. *It's not like you care about her. She's your bait, nothing more.*

Right?

Right. This is why I should have kept my distance. From the

start, I've let Mia get too close. She has everything to gain from seducing her billionaire boss.

But me? I've got everything to lose.

She's a distraction. I can't afford distractions. If I was just the CEO of StarTech, I could roll into bed with whoever and cash my checks from home.

But that's not all I do.

I'm Bratva. I'm the *pakhan.* If I so much as blink at the wrong moment, I'm dead. And with me dies every man under my command.

So why can't I stop thinking about her?

"*Blyat!*" I push all the papers off my desk and slam my fist on the lacquered mahogany. The noise bounces off the glass walls, startling the assistants sitting outside my door.

"Whoa," Maksim says as he sticks his head in. "Which one of those R&D reports pissed in your coffee this morning?"

I don't bother replying. "Fire the new assistant," I bark as I drain the dregs of said coffee.

"Why? Don't like his brew?"

"If he can't even work an espresso machine, he can't work here."

Maksim lets loose a long-suffering sigh. "That'd be the fourth one this week. I get that you're as all-powerful as it gets, but assistants don't grow on trees. Not even you can make that happen."

"Then get R&D to speed up their robotics research," I retort. "I'm sick of hiring people who can't tell their ass from their face."

He gives me a pointed look. "Wow. Someone really did piss in your coffee. That, or you're back to staring holes in your ceiling until the sun comes up. When's the last time you slept, man?"

Goddammit. Leave it to Maksim to hit the nail right on the head. "That's none of your concern," I snarl.

"Kind of is, when you're being a dick to everyone else. 'Cause then they come to *me*. You know, the Yulian Whisperer." He makes jazz hands as he says it. "If that's gonna be a permanent role, I want a pay raise."

I turn away from Maksim and his annoying chatter. I'm in no mood for it. "Give me a status update on Nikita," I demand, my glance sweeping over the city at our feet.

"Yessir." I hear him flip through pages. "So far, we've checked all the neighboring states—"

"The short version, Maks."

"Alright. Short version: no dice."

My knuckles pop. "There has to be something."

"There isn't," he sighs. "We've got to start considering that—"

"Don't fucking say it," I interrupt.

"Doesn't make it any less true if I don't say it." Then, because he's Maksim, he says it anyway. "She could be dead, Yul. All this expenditure of men and resources—it could all be for nothing."

"I don't care if it's for nothing!" I rise, slamming my palms on the desk. "Nikita is *our* soldier. She's—"

"Kira's sister," Maksim cuts in. "And that's been clouding your judgment since day one."

My gaze goes frosty as I turn it on him. "You seem to have a lot of opinions about my judgment lately."

"I'm just saying…" He shrugs. "You don't usually ditch me to spend the night in the Maybach unless there's an emergency. And as far as I remember, there wasn't one last weekend."

"Since, as you so keenly observed, I haven't been sleeping," I snap, "wake me up when you get to the fucking point."

"Oh, you slept, alright," he says with a saucy wink. "Just not alone."

I punch the desk. "It's none of your fucking—"

"Kalinda called me. She asked me where Mia was."

"Who the hell is Kalinda?"

"*Kallie.* Mia's gorgeous BFF? Moonlights as a babysitter? Smells like a tropical paradise?"

Finally, the pieces click.

"I wasn't aware she had your number." *Sure as fuck explains how she got mine, though.*

"Slipped her my business card when I kissed her hand." He makes finger-guns and winks. "See? This old man's got rizz."

"Mazel tov," I growl. "Now, explain why that's my goddamn problem."

"Because, if you've been getting it on with Mia, that means you're not objective anymore." He fixes his stare on me. For once, there isn't a trace of humor on his face. "You've got to fire her, Yulian. For everyone's sake."

Fire her.

My blood boils. The thought of someone else on my arm—of *Mia* on someone else's arm—is enough to make my temples throb.

"I will do no such thing."

"It'll put her in the clear," he says in a diplomatic, pacifying tone. "It'll keep the plan going and it'll keep her safe—"

"*I* will keep her safe!" I bellow in Maksim's face, all patience gone. "Mia signed a contract. She sold herself to *me.*"

"She didn't sell her soul," Maks shoots back. "She didn't sell her life. Something that, in light of recent developments, you should be keen to preserve."

"She means nothing to me." I spit those words out like venom. "And you're no one to tell me what to do. I'm *your* boss, not the other way around."

"And I'm your *friend,*" Maksim counters. "I don't want to see you getting hurt, man. Not again."

With that, the fury fades.

The haze clears.

Finally, I see Maksim's challenge for what it is: concern. Misplaced, but well-meaning. The concern of a true friend.

I sigh and slump back into my chair. "I won't."

"You will if you keep letting her in," he protests. "That's just what happens, Yulian. That's—"

At that moment, my phone vibrates. A text—from the only number I haven't put on silent except Maksim's.

MIA: ***First day of school. Couldn't have swung this without you, so... thank you. For everything.***

A thousand potential replies crowd my mind. Flirty, teasing replies that would bridge the past week's distance between us.

I don't type any.

Instead, I shut my phone and pocket it.

"Let's go."

"Where?"

"To look for my missing soldier."

32

MIA

Yulian doesn't reply to my text. Or the one after that. Or the one after the one after that.

He's never been particularly loquacious—except for that flirty reply that one time—but this much radio silence? After we slept together *and* I slammed a door in his face?

Suffice it to say, I spend the night staring at the ceiling, counting how many years it'd take me to pay his advance back. Because, at this point, it's clear I've blown it.

I shouldn't have stopped sending selfies, I scold myself over and over. *I shouldn't have reacted like that. I shouldn't have been so unprofessional.*

But then another, softer voice inside me says, *He shouldn't have broken your heart.*

I toss in bed and force myself to close my eyes. My heart was never on the table. I'm not in love with Yulian Lozhkin—I'm in *lust.* Dark, bottomless lust, but lust nonetheless.

Love has nothing to do with it.

Love is for schoolgirls without cigarette burns on their arms.

On the third day, I'm fresh out of hope. I take Eli to school, kiss him on the head, watch him trot to his new friends, and then break down crying in my car.

I fucked it up. The job, Yulian, everything. It was my son's only hope, and I fucked it up.

Why can't I stop ruining everything?

At home, I'm getting ready to call the bank and beg when Boris knocks on my door.

"A delivery," he announces in his deep, accented baritone. "From the boss."

I toss the box on the ground and throw my arms around his neck. "Thank you," I hiccup.

Boris freezes. He pats my head awkwardly, like he's not sure what he's supposed to do with an armful of tiny, crying woman. "You're… welcome, Miss."

Once I'm alone again, I rip open the package. Inside is another dress—and another note.

Saturday. 7 P.M. Don't be late.

I laugh through the tears. It's a little burst, hysterical and just a bit mad, but God, the relief is overwhelming.

I'm not fired.

I'm not done.

I can still care for my kid.

With that, all my qualms about Yulian melt like fresh snow.

He was a dick. So what? What if he used my body, stomped on my heart, and ghosted me back just to scare me? Just because he could?

It doesn't matter.

None of it matters.

Only Eli matters.

When he was born, I swore to myself I'd do anything for him. Anything to give him the life he deserved. So, if I have to put on a pretty dress and dance for the devil?

Cue the fucking music.

~

"Mia! We've got another code red coming through!"

I rush to the E.R. doors and flank the stretcher rushing in. "Male, thirty-two," the EMT rattles off. "Another victim of the pile-up on I-278. Fell off his motorcycle and flew into the bushes. Wasn't found until he woke up and started screaming."

"I WANT TO SEE MY WIFE!" the patient yells, thrashing on the stretcher.

"Sir, calm down," a fledgling nurse at my side urges. "We're going to take care—"

"TAKE ME TO MY WIFE!"

"Pushing 1 mcg lorazepam," I say as I hook him up to an IV.

The new nurse frowns. "You can't prescribe—"

"I'm a nurse practitioner," I answer without looking at her.

The words roll right off my tongue from how used I am to saying them. "And right now, I'm treating this patient."

"You should still wait for the doct—"

I ignore her and stick the syringe in.

The patient's eyes flag, then his body goes limp.

"There," I tell her. "Much better, yes?"

Dr. Kitagawa rushes over. "What's wrong with this one?"

"Pupils are clean," I inform her. "He doesn't have a concussion, but his leg's broken. He's also feverish and delirious. Had to sedate him."

"Good call," she approves, examining the leg. "Yep, not gonna go two-stepping anytime soon. No head injuries or internal bleeding, though. Lucky guy."

"Pays to wear a helmet." The EMT shrugs.

"Less work for all of us," she agrees. "Alright, take him to ortho and—"

"—put him on a cycle of antibiotics," I finish for her, smiling as I hold up a fresh syringe. "Got them right here."

Dr. Kitagawa's shoulders slump with relief. "Thanks, Mia. You're a lifesaver."

Then she zooms off to the next stretcher.

"Sorry," the new nurse mutters as we roll our patient into the elevator. "I didn't mean to question you, it's just—"

"Your first day?"

She sighs. "Yeah."

"Welcome to your fire baptism." I smile at her and pat her shoulder. "I promise it never gets better, but you do get used to it. Sort of."

The elevator dings. We head to ortho, where a dozen other stretchers are lying around, waiting to be sorted into rooms we do not have. By the looks of it, it's gonna be yet another slumber party in the hallway.

"How do you do it?" my new fan asks, starry-eyed. "It was like you knew exactly what to do."

"I've got my secrets." I wink. "Stick around long enough, and maybe you'll learn some."

It's a lie. Alright, maybe only half a lie. Truth is, when you quit medical school a year shy of graduation, the knowledge tends to stick anyway.

But medical school would have meant a residency. It would have meant years before I got a real salary. Years I did not have.

Not with a tiny life growing inside me.

Still, the E.R. nurse life isn't so bad. It's just way less money than I'd have made in the long run. Plus a constant battle to be taken seriously.

Oh, and overtime. Lots and lots of overtime. So much overtime, it barely registers anymore.

Which is why, when I check my watch, I almost have a heart attack.

7:45 P.M.

Shit.

I rush to find Gwen, who's barking orders left and right at the E.R. entrance. "I am so sorry, but I really have to—"

"Go." She waves me off briskly. "We're sorting the last ones. We'll manage."

I take in the sight of the EMTs rolling stretchers in. So many people wounded. So many patients in need.

"I'll help," I tell her.

"You don't have to—"

"We're short-staffed again tonight, aren't we?" One glance at Gwen's tight brow tells me I've hit the nail on the head. "C'mon. It'll be easier if there's two of us."

With a grim sigh, she nods.

We triage the last handful of patients from the pile-up with quick, silent efficiency. By the time I'm rushing out the doors, I have twelve missed calls from Yulian.

I immediately dial back. "I'm so sorry," I pant, "there was an emergency and I'm—"

"Still at work," his voice says, much closer than I'd expected it. "I can see that."

My stomach drops.

It's been two weeks since we saw each other. The last time we did, I was naked, wrapped in Yulian's sheets and Yulian's scent. I was wrung out, reeling from more orgasms than I'd ever had in my life, the sweet ache of him still pulsing inside me.

Now, as I collide with his firm cheese grater abs, his cologne hits me with full force, yanking me back into those memories. Back into the feeling of his body on mine, his arms around me, his—

"You're warm." Suddenly, his hand is on my cheek. "If you caught something there—"

"I'm fine!" I squeak, a little too shrill. "I, um—I'm okay. Shift just ran long is all."

"An hour and a half long," His gray eyes pierce me, cold, unreadable. "You're late."

Any other day, I'd be getting right back into his face, snapping about priorities. But if there's something the past two weeks taught me, it's how badly I need this job.

So I hang my head and say, "I'm sorry."

He seems surprised by that. "What, no backtalk? No excuses?"

"Would it make a difference?"

"No," he muses. "No, it wouldn't."

I look up into his eyes. My fingers are twisting his shirt, but I'm only distantly aware of it. Not nearly enough to stop.

"Please," I rasp, "don't fire me."

He falls silent. For the longest time, he doesn't say anything at all.

This is bad, I realize, my heart sinking into my stomach. *He's going to fire me, isn't he? I've fucked this up beyond repair, I—*

"You were saving lives." His deep, husky voice snaps me out of it, bringing me back to the present. Back to him, still pressed against me, as close as that night. "You don't have to apologize for that."

I'm stunned. I stare at Yulian's face and try to figure out if this is his idea of a joke, if his lips are going to quirk up at the edges, flashing that handsome dimple one last time before he kicks me to the curb.

But he doesn't do that.

Instead, he turns to his Maybach. "Maks," he calls. "Go to Mia's place and pick up her dress. You can take her car. Then meet back up with us at the venue."

"W-what?" I stammer.

"You don't trust Maksim with your precious Honda?"

"That's not the issue!" I look between the two men, utterly lost, but neither of them seems to be batting an eye at this. To make matters worse, Yulian is already heading for his Maybach again, expecting me to follow blindly. "I need to get ready, I—where am I even gonna shower?!"

Yulian throws me an amused look. The kind of look that melts ice and makes knees go weak. "My place."

Then he climbs into the car and shuts the door.

33

MIA

My jaw drops. "You *live* here?"

Yulian's gaze flicks disinterestedly to the humongous skyscraper towering over us. "Yes."

"This is your company," I point out. "It says so right there."

He follows my line of sight to the giant ***StarTech, Inc.*** neon sign. "Acute observation."

"How can you live in your own company building?" I gesture wildly to the suits walking in and out of the revolving security doors. Behind me, a camera flashes, probably to capture the magnetic silhouette of Mr. Most-Eligible-Bachelor. "You've got employees here! And paparazzi at the door!"

"It's more convenient this way. Also, paparazzi are for movie stars." His gaze flicks to the direction the flash came from. "That's probably just a photographer sent to cover the event."

Right. The event we're supposed to be at. Guilt pricks me, but not for long. I'm way too distracted for that.

"I mean, I get it, your work is your life, but this is too much," I say. "It's like if I hunkered down in the morgue. Gwen would chase me out of there with a broom."

"Then it's a good thing no one can chase me out of my own building." He pulls out a black key card, shiny and sleek, then leans in. "And we're definitely not going down."

The way he says it makes me weak in all the wrong ways.

Stop thinking about it, Mia! I scold myself all the way to the elevator. *It was one time. It's over. He's been abundantly clear on that. Where's your goddamn self-respect?!*

Probably somewhere under those sheets at the Goldenrod.

The doors close. Yulian presses a gold button at the very top, with the letter ***P*** on it. Private? Penthouse? Pad for fucking while clocked-in?

"Make yourself at home."

The second those doors slide open, my jaw falls.

Hot.

Fucking.

Damn.

It's like those interior decor catalogs you flip at the pricey dentist's office. The ones you cut out and make mood boards with as a teenager, way before the financial reality of the world has set in, thinking dreamily to yourself, *One day, I'll live here.*

Except that he *does* live here. Yulian's life *is* actually that catalog.

Pick up your jaw, Mia. No floor is that clean.

And yet, as I wander around the penthouse wide-eyed, like a kid's first trip to Coney Island, I realize I could probably eat off the furniture here.

It's like Yulian barely lives here at all. Like nothing's been touched since it was set into place.

And what a place it is.

Marble floors. Leather couches. Countertops so shiny I can see my reflection in them. A whole wall that's made up entirely of glass, the city of Manhattan spread out like an ever-changing postcard.

It's like Batman and Christian Grey somehow fell in love, got shotgun married in Vegas, and merged their assets to buy this.

Actually, scratch that: they couldn't afford this between them.

"It's that way."

"Huh?"

"The bathroom." Despite the absence of a smile, Yulian somehow manages to seem more and more amused by the second. "Unless you were planning to wash up in the kitchen sink…?"

It's almost as big as a bathtub, so why not?

"Right!" Somehow, the thought of showering at Yulian's place doesn't do much to banish the horny thoughts. "I'll, uh, I'll go do that. In the bathroom, I mean. Definitely not in the kitchen sink."

"I can give you a boost, if that's your thing."

"Ha-ha," I snark, trying to cover up how embarrassed I'm actually feeling. *Please, God, let him miss how red my face is.* "Very funny."

The bathroom is as luxurious as the rest of the place. The shower alone is bigger than my kid's bedroom. It pisses me off in an *eat-the-rich* way, but it also fills me with envy.

And thoughts. Lots and lots of thoughts.

Because this shower is definitely big enough for two.

I spray myself with cold water to banish the images. Then, because I can't resist the temptation, I test how hot it can get.

And oh. My. *God.*

It's the best shower of my fucking life.

There's a variety of soaps, all as expensive-looking as everything Yulian owns. I lather myself generously, figuring I might as well take advantage while I'm here.

When am I going to get another chance like this? In twenty-four hours, I'll be back to my spluttering spray and lukewarm heater and Trader Joe's two-for-one soaps.

I wonder if this is what Cinderella felt in her Fairy Godmother's dress, spinning at that ball with the prince everybody else wanted. Granted, it's just water pressure, but you get to appreciate these things as an adult.

Speaking of adult things...

My gaze falls to the mirror on the wall. It's misted up, but when I swipe at it with my palm, I can see my body clear as day.

On my hips, the bruises Yulian left have completely faded.

I touch the spot they used to be, searching for that soft, pleasant ache I felt in the days after our night together. Whenever I pressed on them, I'd remember how Yulian's fingers felt, dug so deep into my skin I knew they'd leave a mark.

In fact, they're the first mark I've ever gotten that wasn't unwanted. In all likelihood, Yulian didn't even mean to give them to me.

Unlike my scars.

I trace my fingers along the other marks he left: a faded hickey on my neck, the memory of a bite mark on my breast. The sore ache between my legs, now melting back into need.

Stop, drop, and roll, girl.

Don't do anything you'll regret.

I rinse myself, turn off the shower, and climb out.

I pick up the only bathrobe and fold it over myself. It dwarfs me, way too big for my body. As I bury my face into the fabric to dry up, I catch notes of an oddly familiar scent. Pinewood, maybe, or amber.

Or…

Yulian's cologne.

It's his bathrobe. I'm wearing *his* bathrobe.

Ohmygodjustkillmenow.

I look for anything else I can swap it out for, but there's nothing. I mean, yeah, there's towels, but they're way too high up. This place was clearly designed with Tall Russian Hunk as the target user, not Bite Sized Woman who still buys her sneakers in the kids' section.

I do a little jump, but the towel slips through my fingers. "Dammit."

I do another. And another. And another.

And then, when I've finally almost got it—

"You alright in there?"

—he walks in.

And the bathrobe *falls open.*

34

MIA

The staring contest goes a bit like this:

He stares.

I stare.

He stares.

I try to cover myself up with the bathrobe and accidentally drop it fully on the ground.

He. Stares. Harder.

This is it. He's gonna fire me. He's gonna sue me for sexual harassment, take me for everything I don't *own, and then he'll—*

Wait, why is he walking?

Why is he walking towards me?!

"*Blyat*." That foreign word spills like a curse from his lips. "You think you're clever, don't you?."

"Wait, it wasn't like that! I didn't—I—what?"

He's looming now, him fully clothed, me very much not. "Always teasing. Always just out of reach."

"Please don't—"

Whatever I was going to ask him not to do dies when he bends down to ravage my mouth.

He licks my tongue like he owns it. Like I'm his and always have been. It makes my head spin, sends me right back through the locked door of that night's memories.

"Yulian," I pant, "we can't—"

"No," he agrees, pulling away sharply. His voice is a husky rasp, scraping me raw. "We're late enough as it is."

"Right."

"So we'll just have to be quick about it."

Then he slips his fingers between my legs.

I toss my head back. "Yulian, wait—" I'm trapped against the sink with no way out. My hand curls against his eight-pack, tense and taut through the clothes. "This is a bad idea. We shouldn't—"

"Should've thought of that before you flashed me, *kotyonok.*"

"It was an accid—*ahh*—!"

He's so rough with it. So rough with *me.* I can feel every ridge of his calloused fingers on my clit, torturing it to madness, moving quick and sharp against it.

It shouldn't feel good, but fuck me if it isn't the hottest thing in the world.

Shit, do I have a caveman kink?

"So naughty," he growls into my ear. His free hand cups my breast, squeezing it hard. "You think you can just tug on the leash all you want, hm? That it won't fucking snap?"

"N-no," I gasp. There's something absurdly hot about this—me begging him to stop, even as my hips roll into his touch with every stroke. Because the truth is, I don't want him to stop. "Please, I—"

"Tell me to let you go," he snarls. "Tell me you don't want this."

I can't. He just started touching me, but I'm already so close, it's unreal.

"Yulian…"

"Say the word, *kotyonok,*" he demands. "Or else I'll keep going until you scream."

I open my mouth. Whether to moan or to stop him, I don't know. It doesn't matter how badly I want it: if I let it happen, it'll end in disaster.

Just like last time.

But then, just as I'm about to find my voice—

"Mr. Lozhkin?" a feminine voice calls, knocking a few times on the door. "I've got an urgent delivery for you from Mr. Goncharov."

Yulian's fingers slip from me. I mourn them immediately.

"Fuck," he curses, pulling away. "Time's up, kitten. Your dress is here."

Then he brings his fingers to his mouth and licks them clean.

My head spins.

He leaves me there, naked and panting against the sink. Like he didn't just throw my world into disarray again. Like he didn't just almost make me come.

I stay there, trembling, catching my breath, until I feel like I can walk again.

Then I pick up Yulian's bathrobe and head into the bedroom.

My dress is already laid on the bed. It's another stunning piece, just like the one he sent a couple of days ago to my place: a black, tight-fitting bodycon dress that leaves nothing to the imagination, just classy enough to whisper "business" instead of screaming "whore."

Only…

"There's no underwear," I note.

He just shrugs. Completely unrepentant. "Pity."

My face catches on fire. On one hand, I'm glad Maksim didn't have to go rummaging through my panty drawers, but on the other hand…

"So you just want me to—?"

"Yes." His voice drops an octave, dark with desire. Held back, but just barely. "Now."

Swallowing, I pull the dress on. With nothing else underneath, like Yulian demanded.

It's infuriating.

It's humiliating.

It's also the hottest thing in the world.

Yulian's bossy attitude… I used to think I hated it. But watching it play out here, within the four walls of his bedroom, commanding me to wear a dress with no panties underneath… It's nothing like being ordered around at a party. That drives me crazy in the brain, but this? It drives me crazy in a whole other place.

It makes me want to *obey.*

But it makes me want to push back, too.

Just a little.

He zips me up. I can feel his fingers on my exposed neck, lingering just a moment too long. He smooths down my dress, his rough palms sliding down my curves, feeling up every inch of my body.

He exhales through his nose, his grip tightening just a little. "We should go," he growls. "We need to be—"

"No."

Before I can think better of it, I grab his hand. I lead it where it was moments before, lifting up my dress just enough to make room.

"You started something," I rasp. "I want you to finish it."

Silence falls behind me. I realize that this must be a rare occurrence for Yulian—being told no.

But eventually, his hand starts moving again.

"Fuck, *kotyonok,*" he breathes, inhaling my scent deeply. "You'll be the death of me."

Then he sinks one finger into me.

I shiver, hard. He makes a noise of appreciation at that, then starts slowly pumping in and out of me.

"More," I moan.

"Greedy little kitten," he scolds me. "You don't get to make the rules here."

I fist his hair behind me. It's all I can do to hold on to him, lean into his body and let him support me as pleasure mounts inside me. My legs are already shaking—if I'm not careful, I'll fall to my knees right on his bedroom floor.

Would it be the worst thing in the world?

"Yulian..." I whimper as he adds a second finger. His thumb tortures my clit from above, while his middle and ring fingers reach deeper with each thrust.

"Fuck. Look how much you like it."

Boldness overcomes me. Or maybe it's need. I have no clue anymore.

"I like this more," I whisper, tilting the angle of his wrist just a little.

I feel his lips curve in the crook of my neck. "Yeah?"

"Yeah," I gasp. He's picking up the pace, and it's so much sweeter like this. With every thrust, he's fucking straight into that spot that brings me to tears. "Just like that, God, don't stop."

Yulian growls into my neck, sucking a bruise just past my hairline. It rips a moan from my throat, loud and obscene, and suddenly, I'm wondering where that line between "business" and "whore" was.

But if this is what it's like to be Yulian's whore, I'll sign on that dotted line again and again.

"You want me to fuck you again."

It's not a question, but I answer anyway. "Yes."

"How?" His finger-fucking grows wilder, rougher. There's the slightest edge of pain there, and it feels fucking amazing. "How do you want it?"

"I don't care."

"I don't believe you." He circles my clit once, twice, and the pressure is so strong, it's a miracle I haven't come yet. "You've thought about this. Touched yourself to it."

I don't deny it. I *can't*.

"Yes."

"In those dreams, did I fuck you on your hands and knees?" His voice drops even lower, a sandpaper whisper, and the picture it's painting drives me insane. "Did I fuck you from behind, just like this?"

"Yes."

"Did I make you come on my cock?"

"Yes!" I cry out. "Please, fuck me, make me come—"

Yulian groans, rocking his hips against me, his fingers crooking with every thrust.

I'm so wet I can't breathe. All I want is release, but Yulian won't give it.

Every time I'm about to tip over the edge, he angles his touches slightly away from where I need them. I try to guide his hand, but he doesn't let me.

Frustrated, I reach behind me to palm at his cock. He hisses in pleasure, but twists my hand back against my thigh moments later, forbidding me from touching him. From taking his cock out and plunging it inside me from behind, exactly the way he promised me.

But he didn't promise anything, did he? He built a fantasy—that doesn't mean he'll let me have it.

The thought hurts more than I thought possible.

"Please," I whimper. "I need it, need you to fuck me from behind, need you to treat me like your whore!"

"*Blyat!*" A thrill shoots down my spine as I feel Yulian's left hand release my wrist, getting to work on his belt. His cock springs free, the hot head brushing against my seam. I should be scared at how big he is, but all I want is to feel it inside me—all of it.

"You little… fucking…!"

He pushes me down by the neck, like a dog. Like he's about to fucking mount me.

Then he grabs his cock and guides it right up to my pussy.

I'm on my hands and knees, gaping open for him, so close to my orgasm I could cry. I feel him line up with me, feel his head start to push in—

BANG, BANG, BANG!

Knocks on the door. Loud, impatient knocks.

"Lovebirds!" Maksim's voice breaks in, teasing and amused. "You're both wanted at the party! Come on down before all the snacks are gone!"

I like Maksim. I really, really do. He's polite, funny, and my best friend's new crush.

But right now, I could kill him with my bare hands.

"Fuck." Yulian's cock, so close to breaching me seconds before, pulls back. "We have to go."

"No!" I protest, close to tears.

"Yes," he groans, no happier than I am. "He wouldn't be knocking unless someone was about to come up here themselves."

He traces the edges of my glistening pussy with his fingers, making me shiver. "Besides," he drawls, "if I start fucking you now, there's no way I'll stop before morning."

That promise keeps me sane. *If I start fucking you now.* It means he can fuck me later, once this party business has been wrapped up.

It means I can still have this.

Even if it's the worst idea in the world.

I struggle to my feet and smooth down my dress. Then I catch it again, from the corner of my eye: Yulian, licking my juices off his fingers.

He notices me staring. He smirks, wolfish and mischievous. "Something wrong, kitten?"

"No," I lie, my face ripe as a strawberry. "Not at all. Just—getting ready for the party."

"Good." He tilts my head up with that same hand. "Because it wouldn't be proper for you to get impatient. Like I said, you don't make the rules here. *I* do."

It sends a shiver down my spine. Like there's no question of him being in command, out there or in here.

We make ourselves decent. I'm throbbing between my legs, but I force myself to ignore it. The wetter it gets down there, the worse the "no panties" problem will become.

I can do this, though. I can hold off for a few hours. I can smile and wave and shake hands with people I don't give a shit about just so my boss-turned-lover will reward me all night long for it.

And I can definitely pretend it means nothing.

Right?

35

YULIAN

It happened again.

No—*I* let it happen again. I could have walked out of that bathroom any time, but I didn't.

Instead, one look at Mia's naked body was enough to break all the promises I'd made to myself: keep her far, keep myself cold, keep us on the right side of the line.

But what line is left now?

I can't help it. Apparently, neither can she. Whatever this chemistry between us is, it's clear we can't control it.

I've never had that problem before.

At my side, Mia stands perfectly composed, as if we hadn't been about to fuck like animals just fifteen minutes ago. There's a slight flush on her cheeks that could be makeup, but I know for a fact isn't.

It's a last, lingering trace of everything we did upstairs.

Everything we *almost* did.

Everything we'll do once I wrap this stupid party up.

I didn't even want to throw it. Parties, events, galas—I hate them with every fiber of my being. They're a well-dressed circus, a show we put on to pretend our money makes us better than everybody else.

But true success isn't about making money. Money is just what happens when you claw your way to the top. If you're strong enough to get there, the world is your oyster.

That's what tonight is all about for me: securing the world, one deal at a time.

And to make deals, you need to showcase what you're offering.

"So, this party…" Mia licks her lips, uncertain, her stare fixed on the closing elevator doors. "Is it, like, a company party, or…?"

"There are no company parties at StarTech."

She huffs a laugh, rolls her pretty blue eyes. "Of course not. That would imply fun."

"Are you complaining about lack of 'fun' in your position?"

"No." Her gaze flicks to me, a cheeky smile playing on her lips. "You're a lot of things, *Mr. Lozhkin,* but you're not boring."

The elevator doors slide open. Reluctantly, I pry my hand off Mia's ass and slip it into my pocket.

Showtime.

"Wow," Mia exhales. "This is..."

I follow her stunned stare to the display of opulence before us: waiters flitting around with trays of tarts and flutes, dripping crystal chandeliers on the ceiling, a champagne tower in the middle of the room.

"Adequate," I decide.

"That's it?" she scoffs, laughing in disbelief. "Just 'adequate'?"

"My staff did their job. Nothing more, nothing less."

"Gee. I'd hate to be getting performance reviews from you."

"You have nothing to worry about." My voice drops to a whisper. "So far, your 'performance' has been... more than adequate."

Her eyes go dark. "Maybe I'll up my game, then. Shoot for better scores."

Blyat'. If this goes on, we won't make it five minutes into this godforsaken party. I'll end up dragging her into a supply closet and fucking the life out of her before I've shaken a single hand.

"Mr. Lozhkin!" A familiar voice interrupts my train of thoughts. "There you are!"

Mia tilts her head curiously at the young man who's just bounded up to us like an excited puppy. It's not the way most people greet me.

But then again, Tikhon isn't most people.

"The prototype for the ingestible GPS is ready!" he chirps excitedly, his tunnel vision blocking Mia from sight entirely.

With anybody else, I would take offense, but I've known Tikhon long enough to understand his brain only has one concern: his dear prototypes.

"Our trials have improved significantly, and almost no one is getting diarrhea from it anymore—well, there's Bob, but you know Bob, always keeping his mayo out of the fridge—so I've been thinking we can hand it over to packaging in time for Christmas. Keep your pets safe, your kids safe, and find out if your husband's double-dipping. How's that for a slogan? Oh, oh! We should get billboards for this one! Like that one we did in Times Square? Or maybe—"

He doesn't take a breath the whole way through. That, too, is expected.

"Mia," I cut in, "this is Tikhon Baranov, lead engineer of StarTech. Tikhon, this is Mia Winters. My fiancée."

Tikhon's gaze finally zeroes in on Mia. "Hello!" He beams, lighting up. "So nice to meet you! You know, when I first heard the rumors our fearless leader had gotten hitched, I couldn't believe it, but now, I totally can!"

"Uhh… thanks?" Mia says, watching her hand being shaken up and down like a ragdoll. "That's, um, very kind of you."

"Have you seen the prototypes yet?" Tikhon continues, eyes shining behind his thick glasses. "Come! I'll take you for a tour of the hall."

Mia throws me a quick glance, seeking permission. I grant it with a nod.

Ordinarily, I wouldn't let anyone take her from my side, but there's far too much heat between us tonight.

Better let it cool down a bit.

"Separated from your princess?" Maksim smirks, appearing at my side with a glass of champagne.

"She wanted to see the prototypes."

"More like Tikhon wanted her to see his tech babies. If you're not careful, he'll steal her away for the rest of the night."

"I'm sure his husband will catch up at some point."

Maksim barks out a laugh. "Dammit. I was hoping you didn't know that."

"Why? Wanted to make me jealous?"

"A bit." He snatches a tart from a passing tray and shoves it in his mouth with zero grace. "Maybe then you'd have realized you care."

Care. That word stabs me right in the gut. "You're wasting your time."

"Nah, I don't think I am." He grabs a few more tarts and shoves them into his jacket pocket. "Kalinda is convinced you're either going to save her or break her heart. And I know for a fact you're not here to play white knight, so that only leaves one option."

"I didn't ask for your girlfriend's opinion."

"Hah!" he laughs again, but this time, it comes out bitter. Sad, almost. "If only I was twenty years younger. Hell, even ten."

It's enough to make me listen. Enough to put my anger on hold. I've known my second long enough to realize when he isn't joking around anymore, and right now, that sadness feels far too real for comfort.

"Kalinda didn't seem to mind the age gap," I remark, studying Maksim's reaction closely.

If he's distracted—if he can't be objective about our plans anymore—then I have to know now.

"Ah, she was just embarrassed." He waves my words off. "Even if she's got a thing for silver foxes, that's not the kind of thing that lasts. And I'm afraid I'm not like you, Mr. Playboy. One night isn't enough to scratch off my itches."

Me neither.

Not anymore.

"If I didn't know better, I'd say you're in a pining mood."

"What's the use in pining for men like us?" he sighs. "Besides, Kalinda isn't made for this life. Her soul is still pure. I'd hate to drag a good girl into a bad mess."

The guilt stabs even harder now that Maksim isn't trying to make me feel it. *Good girl, bad mess*—it's Mia and me in a nutshell.

And I'm the one who dragged her in. I'm the one who isn't going to let her out of it until I've reached my goals. The one who's putting her in danger.

The one who doesn't care if she gets hurt.

The wild, primal part of me howls at the thought. That part has long claimed her.

Mine, it snarls even now. *Mine to use, mine to own, mine to keep.*

Mine to protect.

I won't let anything happen to her. Not because I care, but because I'm damn good at what I do. Mia is bait—that doesn't mean she has to be there when my enemies bite. It doesn't mean she has to be swallowed whole.

What kind of *pakhan* would I be if I couldn't keep a single woman safe?

If I let my enemies take from me again?

When I snap out of my thoughts, Maksim is watching me. Closely, his eyes narrowed, like a hawk. "Whatever you're thinking," he says slowly, "remember the goal, Yulian. You can't afford to split your focus. Either you're willing to sacrifice everything, or you'll end up with nothing."

Maksim's warning hits the mark. I want to snarl at him, tell him to shut the fuck up and mind his own damn business.

But for once, the words don't come.

Because I know, deep inside, that he's right.

"Boss!" Tikhon swoops in again, out of breath. "You won't believe the idea Mia had!"

"It was just a thought!" Mia protests, hands up as if to fend off praise. "There's no need to bother—"

"Sure is!" Tikhon pulls out a tablet and shows me the specs of another prototype. "I was working on a fitness smartwatch, but there's already tons of those out there, so I ended up scrapping it. But Mia pointed out that, if we could make an ingestible chip that monitors vitals, that'd be super useful in hospitals."

"Hospice, most likely," she corrects. "Short-term patients are already monitored, but long-term ones—"

"They could stay home!" Tikhon pipes up. "Be with their families! And if anything's wrong, *PING*! Signal straight to the caregiver's phone. If we can make them accurate enough, they could even call 911 on their own."

It's... a surprisingly good pitch. One that could make us billions.

"Make it," I command.

"Hell, yeah!" Tikhon moves to high-five me, then thinks better of it. He offers his hand to Mia instead. "Great knowing you, Mia. Gotta dash. Be sure to drop by!"

Once we're alone again, Mia slumps into my shoulder. "He's... interesting."

"Hyperactive." Her warmth seeps into me. I clench my fists, force myself to ignore what her proximity does to me. Even like this, she's gasoline for my fire. "But that's why I hired him."

"He gets the zoomies more than Eli." Her lips twitch with amusement, but not mockery. "I could see him doing this, when he grows up. Tinkering in a lab, making the world a better place one gadget at a time."

"'Gadget'?"

She cringes. It's fucking adorable. "Blame it on the spy movies. My brain's fried."

"We should unfry it, then." I hand her a champagne flute from a passing tray. The second her lips touch the glass, I regret that action. I watch her throat bob with her first sip of bubbles and my cock hardens. "Let's go."

Mia follows without question. Puts her arm through mine without hesitation. Like a lamb that has no idea it's being led to slaughter.

But that's not where I'll lead her. I'm stronger than I was twenty years ago. Now, I can protect her.

"Well, well, well."

Or so I tell myself.

Mia freezes. Her arm goes limp in mine.

I turn.

And there, smirking like the cat that just caught the canary, is Bradley Baldwin.

36

MIA

It's him.

He's here.

Again.

For me.

"There you are. I've been looking for you all over."

His words sink like stones in my gut. I try to speak, but the lump in my throat won't budge, won't let me.

Instead, I break out in a cold sweat, palms clammy and slick even as I wipe them on my dress.

Yulian's hand grabs mine. His warmth lets me breathe again, but it also anchors me, and right now, I don't want that. I've fallen prey to an old terror, one I never fully learned to fight, only outrun.

But now I'm stuck in place, and all I can feel is Brad's dark eyes on me, glinting with cruel amusement.

Brad's presence, inching closer into my personal space.

Brad's mocking tone, slithering around me like a snake, dripping with venom and promise.

Brad's claim, all over again.

"Finally." Brad smirks, pure self-satisfaction and smug entitlement. His crisp white suit crinkles as he steps closer. It's his signature color, even off the altar. "I've got you now. Be a good girl and come with me, and no one's going to get hurt."

I'm thrust back into the body of the little girl I was five years ago. Too young to know what was good for her. Too lovestruck to recognize the monster who held her by the throat.

He's back. He came to get me. I'll never be free.

I'll never—

"Don't make promises you can't keep." It's Yulian's voice, snapping me out of it. Yulian's dark, deep rumble, cold as Siberia and dangerous as frostbite. "You're in my house, Baldwin. *I* decide who gets hurt."

Finally, Brad's eyes flick to Yulian. Bored, annoyed—like he's just another obstacle on the road to his undisputed victory. "Is that how you talk to all your guests, Lozhkin?"

"You're not a guest," he snarls. "You're a pest."

"Really?" Brad pulls a sleek, black letter from his breast pocket. "And here I thought your invitation was an olive branch."

The word "invitation" lands straight on Yulian's nerves. I can feel his grip twitching with barely-suppressed anger.

"A secretarial mistake," he growls. "Surely, you couldn't think I'd want you here."

"Maybe not," he concedes, tossing the invitation on the floor. His eyes veer to me. "But someone else does. Isn't that right, sweet thing?"

My hands start shaking. Or maybe they've been doing that all along, and I'm only now noticing. I have no idea. All I know is what I heard, and what it's doing to me.

Those two words—*sweet thing*—keep echoing in my panicked mind, sending it further into a tailspin. Reminding me of all the other times he's said them.

You know you want it, sweet thing.

C'mon, sweet thing. Don't make me hurt you.

You're mine, sweet thing. All mine, forever.

He reaches for me. Like that night in the church. Like countless nights before.

I squeeze my eyes shut, bracing myself for it—

But his touch never comes.

When I open my eyes again, Yulian's hand is wrapped firmly around Brad's wrist. I can see Brad's fingers turning pale, the blood flow cut off.

"This again?" asks Brad, masking his fear behind disgust.

"I'll give you a choice," Yulian says icily. "You can leave here on your own two legs, or you can leave in a body bag. Your call."

I can't tear my gaze away from the scene. From Brad's wrist caught in Yulian's vise, like a butterfly about to be crushed.

How often did I dream of this, back then? That someone—*anyone*—would swoop in and save me?

And why is guilt all I can feel now that it's happening?

Because you know how much it's costing him, the wicked voice at the back of my head whispers. *His business will suffer because of you. His company will suffer because of you. Even that young, peppy engineer that just talked your ear off for half an hour—they'll* all *suffer because of you.*

Everybody suffers because of you.

Even your own son.

After a long staring contest, Brad clicks his tongue in disdain. "Fine," he scoffs. "Don't get your panties in a twist, Yulian. There's nothing worth doing here anyway."

He sneers at me as he says it. One last, vulgar humiliation.

Yulian doesn't let go.

"Boss," Maksim's voice comes in a whisper. "Your investors are looking."

It's true. There's a small crowd around us. As the argument got more and more heated, the guests must have gotten curious.

Again, everyone is watching.

Again, it's all my fault.

Finally, Yulian throws Brad's arm back down. "Go," he spits. "And stay out of my sight."

Brad rubs his wrist, his lips curled into a grimace. He was always good at that—pretending nothing touched him. That pain wasn't pain unless he willed it to be.

"Gladly," he replies.

Then he turns to me.

His smirk falls back into place. Cruel, sharp—a weapon. "See you around, sweet thing."

It's a promise. Like all those horrible promises he made to me over that wretched summer.

You're mine. All mine.

You belong to me. No one else can touch you unless I say so.

I will never let you go.

The second he's gone, I bolt towards the door on the opposite end of the hall.

"Mia!" Yulian calls after me, but I barely hear it. My head is pounding, blood rushing in my ears, drowning out all sound.

I run to the end of the deserted hallway. My left heel twists and snaps off, throwing me off-balance, sending me careening into the pristine white tiles.

The pain barely registers.

You're mine.

Suddenly, I can't breathe.

All mine, sweet thing.

Suddenly, I can't see.

I will never, never, NEVER—

Hands press on my shoulders. I fend them off in a frenzy, like a cornered animal fighting for her life. "Stop!" I gasp, trying to yell and failing. "Don't touch me! Don't—"

"*Blyat'*, Mia, calm down!"

My eyes snap open.

Yulian.

I take him in piece by piece, through a wall of tears and fog.

Dark hair—check.

GQ stubble—check.

Gray eyes—check.

"Help me," I croak.

Yulian doesn't make me say it twice. "Follow my lead."

At times like this, I get why he's the *pakhan.* How he can command thousands with a single gesture.

He puts my left hand to his chest, then places my right one on mine. "Breathe," he instructs. "In, hold, out."

"I can't," I sob. "I can't, I—"

"Yes, you can," he cuts me off. "Now, do as I say. *Breathe,* Mia."

Mindlessly, I obey.

I have no idea how long it lasts. How long it takes before the world slowly comes back to me, in bits and pieces.

Smell returns first. Then touch. I feel Yulian's cologne surrounding me, his arms a wall of protection around me. Comforting, familiar. *Warm.*

My voice comes back last. "Sorry," I rasp. "I think I just had a panic attack."

"No shit, Nurse Winters."

For some reason, that makes me laugh. "You've got an awful bedside manner, you know that?"

"I've been told." His lips quirk, that precious dimple appearing just off to the side.

"Really?"

"No. Actually, you're the first."

The first. I don't know why, but those words manage to thaw the last piece of ice in my heart.

"Yeah?" I whisper.

"Yeah."

It doesn't happen like in the movies. There's no montage, no chorus, no soft notes rising through the air. My makeup is smeared, his suit is rumpled. My hair's a mess and his gun is peeking from under his jacket, ruining the illusion of Prince Charming kneeling at Cinderella's feet.

And yet, it's perfect.

This time, he kisses me slowly. Without hunger, without urgency. With all the caring he pretends he doesn't feel, his ice mask slipping just enough to let me glimpse the warm skin behind it.

He kisses me like he means it.

Then a chill breaks the spell.

I have no idea where it comes from. Why goosebumps are spreading on my arms like wildfire. It should be desire, not terror—not *this.*

But when I look up, I realize why.

At the other end of the hallway, a figure is staring. A man dressed in white, fists clenched at his sides like he wants to punch a hole in the nearest wall.

Brad.

"Mia?"

"He saw us," I murmur. "He saw the kiss. He…"

Panic spreads in my heart. The same panic that gripped me whenever a guy friend dared say hi to me, whenever my dad's buddies would hug me, whenever a man on the street would stop me because I dropped something.

"… He saw everything."

37

YULIAN

That fucking mudak.

I couldn't care less that he saw us. I don't give a fuck that he knows I've claimed his ex-girlfriend as more than arm candy, more than just a girl to show off.

But clearly, Mia does.

I grit my teeth. The Baldwin family is the second richest in New York, just a notch under my own empire. They have generational wealth, deals with prominent mobsters, hands in every cookie jar across the tri-state area. They pay off cops, feds, judges—everyone they need to keep raking in billions while keeping their hands clean of mafia activities.

They don't scare me.

Fuck it. Let Baldwin come at me with all he has. I don't give a shit what he does to me—I'll repay it a hundredfold.

But Mia is a different matter.

Mia lives alone in Brownsville. She has a small kid his father must never find, a job where anyone and everyone can come waltzing through the door, a predictable schedule.

And right now, she's scared.

So I gather her up in my arms, leave the investors to Tikhon, and tuck her into the backseat of my car.

"Drive," I tell Maksim.

He doesn't need to ask where we're going. There's only a place Mia would want to be after this ugly mess.

Home.

~

It's a long drive from Manhattan to Brooklyn. Mia spends the first half of it in silence, squinting out the window, as if terrified that Brad's car will appear right behind us. As if he could do anything to us that I couldn't protect her from.

Why should you? that cold voice in me demands. *She's no one to you.*

I clench my fists and don't reply.

Instead, I keep replaying the scene in my head, over and over. Mia's face when he appeared at the end of that hallway was pure dread. It was the way my enemies look at me. The way a prisoner faces their executioner.

Whatever went on between them wasn't just a bad break-up. I'd known that before—it was far too obvious in the way Mia flinched away from him at the wedding.

But seeing it with my own two eyes? Feeling Mia gasp for air, clawing at her own throat, in the grip of the most vicious panic attack I've ever fucking seen?

It makes my blood boil. It makes my gun hand itch. It makes me want to murder that son of a bitch with my own bare hands, feel his body kick uselessly as I squeeze, watch the life fade from his goddamn eyes.

But Mia needed me. And at that moment, she mattered more than payback.

On the Brooklyn Bridge, her voice finally breaks the silence. "I'm sorry," she whispers.

It catches me by surprise. "You're apologizing again."

"Well, I ruined your night again." There's sadness in her words. Regret. "That deserves an apology, doesn't it?"

"No."

She blinks at me, stunned. "What?"

I cup her face. Force her to keep those blue eyes on me—*only* me. "I already told you, *kotyonok.* Either you stop apologizing for things that aren't your fault, or I'll make you."

Her body goes slack in my grip. Pliant, like clay. Right now, I could do anything to her, and she'd let me.

I could push her into the backseat. Could work my hands up and down her body, touch her just the way she likes. Make her gasp, moan, scream my name like it's the only one she's ever known.

But I won't.

Not tonight.

Instead, I pull her forehead close to mine. Touch our heads together like Kira used to do to me, back when we were kids, back when she'd find me crying in a corner of the garden because I saw something I shouldn't.

I was soft back then, too soft for the role the world had carved out for me, but she never held it against me. Never.

I won't hold Mia's softness against her, either.

"Yulian?" she whispers.

"Close your eyes."

She does. Tonight, she won't question anything I ask of her.

"Breathe."

She obeys. I can feel the warm air leave her nose, brushing my lips on the way out.

"You're safe here," I tell her. "As long as you're with me, Brad can't touch you."

"And after?" she asks in a small, quivering voice.

After. Somehow, I'd forgotten there was one. A future where Mia isn't on my arm, in my car, in my bed.

"After," I begin, stroking her cheek in time with her breathing, "you'll be free. You'll decide who touches you."

Every instinct is screaming to claim her, pull her close and never let go, but I can't trust that part of me. It's the part that makes mistakes. The part that fails.

That part of me needs to die.

Once the Maybach rolls to a stop, I walk Mia upstairs. I don't want any surprises. I won't let her out of my sight until I know she's truly safe.

The irony of that stabs me right in the gut. If there's anyone Mia should be afraid of, it's not Brad Baldwin—it's *me*. I'm the one putting her in danger. The one shoving her into the line of fire, one trap after another.

"Mia."

She turns, eyes rimmed with red. "Yes?"

"Our contract—"

"Mommy!"

A little ball of energy careens towards us, straight into Mia's legs. "Hey there, munchkin." Mia smiles, ruffling her son's hair. "Why aren't you in bed yet?"

"I was waiting for you," he says with a pout. "You didn't kiss me goodnight."

Mia's face falls. "Oh my God, you're right. I'm sorry, baby. Work ran so long, I couldn't make it back home."

"You're here now," he points out. Then his eyes, blue like his mother's, zero in on me. "Hi, Yulian."

I blink. "You remember me."

"You're really tall."

"Alright!" Mia blurts out. "How about we let Aunt Kallie get back home and order some pizza?"

"Yay!" Eli squeals. "I want pepperoni! With extra cheese!"

Mia shakes her head, laughing. "Fine, you can have extra cheese. But just for tonight, you hear?"

But he's already turned to me again. "What pizza do you want, Yulian?"

For a second, I'm too stunned to speak. "Pardon?"

"Pizza," he repeats, like he thinks I might not be familiar with the concept. "It's big, round, and it's got slices. But it's not a cake, because it has cheese."

"Honey," Mia blurts, "I'm sure Yulian's too busy to—"

"Sure."

Mia stares at me, eyes wide. I'd stare at me like that, too, because why the hell did I just say that?

But I've said it now. It's out.

And the warm smile spreading on Mia's face is far too beautiful to take it back.

38

YULIAN

There's warmth here.

It's the first thing I notice. Mia's apartment is nothing like what I'm used to. It's small, messy, chaotic like a toy box. And yet, it's warm.

Warmer than I deserve.

"Okay!" Eli chirps. "You sit here, Mommy can sit here, and Garfield—"

"Garfield's already eaten," Mia says. "Kallie told me."

"Oh." Eli pauses for a moment, then promptly puts Garfield back in his designated chair. "Well, he might be thirsty. Here, Yulian, you can sit next to him."

I steal a glance at Mia. She's trying so hard to fight back a smile, it's ridiculous. "I'd be honored," I say.

We order food by phone. I try to wrest back control of this improvised family dinner by suggesting I foot the bill, but

Mia won't have it. "You're our guest," she insists. "At Winters House, we feed our guests."

"Aunt Kallie didn't stay to eat," Eli complains. "She always stays."

"Well," Mia says, ruffling her son's hair as she walks by, "Aunt Kallie heard her friend Maksim was waiting downstairs. She didn't want him to eat alone."

"Too old for her," my ass.

That answer seems to pacify Eli. He goes back to playing with his worn Garfield plushie. Occasionally, his eyes will flit up, studying me. Every time they do, I'm struck by the resemblance. Aside from his hair—too curly, too light, too much like Brad's—he's the spitting image of Mia.

"Are you really not a spy?"

I almost choke on my water.

"Eli!" Mia scolds. "That's rude. We talked about this."

"It's fine," I tell her. Then I turn back to her son. "Wanna know a secret?"

"A secret?"

"I've never even been to Russia."

He gasps. "No way!"

"It's very far." I shrug. "My parents came from there, but I never went."

"They won't take you? Not even for a holiday?"

They can't. Not anymore. "Someday, perhaps, I'll go."

"Can we come?"

This time, it's Mia's turn to choke on her water.

It makes something playful flare inside me. Something that hasn't been stirred in a long time. "Aren't you afraid of the spies?"

"I wanna meet them!"

"Then, yes. If your mom says it's okay."

He turns to Mia with pleading eyes. "Can we, Mommy?! Can we go to Russia to play spies?!"

"Well, you don't have your passport yet. So why don't we put a pin in it until then?"

"Okay," he concedes. "But I really wanna go."

Eli chats my ear off some more, with Mia chiming in every now and then. It strikes me how quickly we've gone from awkward to comfortable. How quickly *I* did.

Growing up, kids were like aliens to me: tiny beings with huge eyes and secret languages I couldn't decipher, let alone speak. The fact that I'd been a kid once too had slipped so far below the surface, I barely remembered how it went.

Now, it's all coming back.

The pizza comes. We sit down to eat. Garfield has a little plate for himself, too, where Eli discreetly pushes his crusts.

Then, from outside the window, light flashes into the room. "Mommy!" Eli jumps down from his chair. "That phorogopher's here again!"

"Photographer," Mia corrects. "And I think that's just the light from a blowtorch, munchkin. You know there's always some road work around here."

At night?

My instincts kick in. I feel that prickling at the back of my neck again.

"I forgot something in the car," I tell them. "I'll be right back."

Mia tries to say something, but I'm already off.

I fly down those stairs. Like a bolt of fucking lightning, I rush down into the street.

And there he is.

No trench coat. No crooked tie. Just a dark pullover and equally dark pants, with a camera slung around his neck, but I know exactly who it is.

Or rather, *what* he is.

"Hey! What the hell, man?!"

Within seconds, I've got him backed against the wall. "I should be the one asking that, *man.*"

"I don't want any trouble."

"You were taking pictures of that family," I snarl. "You just asked for trouble."

Light from a flickering lamppost hits his face. Suddenly, I realize I've seen this guy before. When I was jogging in the neighborhood that day, and then earlier tonight, right outside the StarTech building.

It's the paparazzo. The one Mia pointed out to me.

I should've fucking listened.

"Look," he babbles, covered in sweat, "I'm just doing my job."

"Good," I growl. "I'm just doing mine, too. So I hope there won't be any hard feelings."

Then I punch him in the face.

The guy crumples against the brick wall, but my grip on his collar holds him up. Blood spatters from his nose, hitting my suit jacket. Luckily, I always wear black.

I'd be lying if I said this wasn't the reason why.

"Tell me who sent you," I demand. "Or I'll take your teeth next."

"Shit!" He spits out a glob of blood and staggers to his feet. "Look, I promise I'll quit, alright? But I can't just give out the name of—"

"Yes, you can," I snarl. "And you will."

Then, for good measure, I punch him again.

This time, a tooth goes flying. Never let it be told I don't make good on my promises.

"Fuck!" he hisses. "Fine, fine! It's that guy from the construction company! The one on all the fucking billboards!"

Brad.

I let the poor bastard go. He falls into the heap of trash at our feet, coughing and rolling as he struggles to stand back up.

"You're lucky," I tell him. "I'm in a good mood tonight. So I'll just let you off with a warning." I crouch down, grab his face, and force him to look at me. "Never come back. Not to this place, not to mine, not anywhere within a ten-mile radius of me. If you do, I'll know. And next time, I won't be so nice."

He glares at me. No doubt, he cannot see what I just did to him as mercy.

Good. Ignorance is bliss.

I pocket his camera and stride back towards the apartment, straightening myself up on the way.

When Mia sees me, her eyes go wide with concern. "Everything okay?"

"It is now." She doesn't need to know the details, especially not with Eli within earshot.

Her eyes flit to my knuckles. I've wiped away the blood, but it takes more than that to fool a nurse. "Oh my God. Did you just—?"

"Later," I whisper.

She presses her lips together, but eventually nods. Mia's always been too smart for her own good. No matter how badly I want to keep this from her, it's looking less and less likely. She saw those flashes, saw my bruised knuckles, probably heard that P.I.'s screams. She's probably put two and two together already.

But Eli's here, so she doesn't press.

"Did you get what you forgot?" Eli asks.

I pause. "You know what? I think I forgot again."

He giggles. "You're silly."

"You're the first person to call me that. Though your mom had some choice things to say about me when we met."

Mia shakes her head. There's still worry lines on her face, but they're fading quickly. "Can't imagine why."

"You've got sauce on your shirt," Eli says. "Right there."

I glance down. *Shit.* So it wasn't just my jacket that got sprayed.

Mia goes pale for a second, but I dab at the stain with a wet napkin until it's unrecognizable from actual tomato sauce. "I'm a clumsy eater."

"You should wear a bib," Eli suggests. "Like me."

"Good idea. Next time, I'll borrow one."

That draws a snort out of Mia.

Dinner goes smoothly after that. Eli's a tiny talking machine, always coming up with a topic or a question, all suspiciously related to spies.

To keep him entertained, I tell him about StarTech and the "gadgets" we make. He's excited to learn all he can about it. By the end of the conversation, he extracts a promise from me to show him around the place.

Belatedly, I realize I actually want to.

Don't be an idiot, that cold voice inside me snarls. *You're dangerous to be around. And these two? They're a danger to you. They make you want things. Things you've lost.*

Things you can never have again.

"Sweetie?" Mia calls, perhaps noticing how quiet I've gone. "Why don't you go pick a movie?"

He doesn't make her ask twice.

Once he's out of earshot, she draws closer to me. "Please tell me that's not my ex's blood on your shirt."

"Would it bother you if it was?"

She pauses. "I don't know. Depends on how much, I guess."

"That doesn't sound very Hippocratic of you."

"Technically, I'm not a doctor."

I hand her the camera. "It's not his."

Her eyes go wide as she flips through the pictures. I've already checked them once, so I already know what she's seeing: herself, photographed by the kitchen window. Herself on my arm, at various events, then at work in her faded scrubs.

Eventually, she sighs with relief. "Thank God—there's no Eli."

"He got lucky," I agree. "Couple of inches taller, and that window shot would have caught him."

"There'd be pictures of him at school, right? If Brad knew."

It's not that simple, I should tell her. *This is just one camera. We have no idea what else that P.I. gave him.*

But I don't. I don't want to be the reason the relief on Mia's face morphs into worry again. After that panic attack earlier, I've realized just how thin a thread she's been hanging from all these years.

If Brad wants anything from her, he'll have to go through me.

"Mia."

She turns to me. "Yeah?"

"About our contract—"

"Mommy!" Eli calls. "Can we watch *Skyfall*?"

"For the millionth time? Sure. Let's break all records."

"Yay!"

"Sorry," she smiles apologetically. "You were saying?"

Tell her, the human part of me screams. *Tell her you don't want her to keep working for you. That she doesn't need to. That you'll pay her anyway, give her everything she needs to go far, far away.*

Give her back her freedom.

But I don't.

I *can't.*

I need her.

"Nothing," I say.

"Oh, okay." Her face falls, just a little, but she schools it quickly.

"I'll have my men follow Eli tomorrow," I tell her. "Just to make sure."

"You'd do that?" The gratitude in her eyes is blinding. "Really?"

"Of course. You're my employee."

She rolls her eyes, but fondly. "So you treat all of your employees to private bodyguards?"

"Only the ones who matter."

A shiver runs through her. She's beautiful like this, in the chaos of her home, with gratitude in her eyes and flour at the corners of her mouth. If temptation has a face, it must be Mia's.

"Thank you," she whispers. "For everything you did for me. Today, and every day since we met."

My chest goes dangerously warm. "It's nothing."

"No, it's not nothing." She takes my hands in hers. Her thumb strokes my bruised knuckles, uncaring of the blood that stained them. "It's more than anyone has ever done for me. For us."

It's like the static before a storm. I can feel it in the air between us, that spark of electricity, ready to ignite into something bigger than either of us.

If I let it, it just might consume me.

Mia's eyelashes flutter like butterflies. I lean in, close enough to kiss—

"The movie's starting!"

Eli shouts. The spell breaks. The moment passes. The electricity fades away, just enough to let us compose ourselves again.

Just enough to let me wonder…

What the hell am I doing?

39

MIA

Five minutes into *Skyfall,* Eli conks out.

I had no doubt he would. It's way too late for him to be up, and besides, he's just stuffed himself full of pizza. That's a guaranteed nap formula.

"Sorry," I whisper to Yulian, who just ended up with a lapful of little boy's legs. "I'll move him in a minute."

"No need." He shrugs, careful not to displace Eli from his nest. "He's comfortable. Let him sleep. He'll be cranky if you wake him now."

"Sounds like you're speaking from experience."

"My sister was a terror." A small smile quirks his lip, but it's gone as quickly as it came. "Alina. She always wanted to pick the movie, but never stayed awake long enough to finish it."

The way he says it makes my heart go tight. "I didn't know you had a sister."

"It was a long time ago."

I have no family. That's what he told me back then.

"I'm sorry." It's all I can think to say. Every time the topic of Yulian's family comes up, I feel like a bull in a china shop, all those broken shards cracking loudly under my feet.

"Don't be." Yulian's tone is casual, but I can tell it's just practice. A pain like that never goes away, no matter how long it's been. It's the one thing no nurse or doctor can fix. "And I thought I said I didn't want to hear those words from you anymore."

That drags a smile out of me. "Fine. Then I'll say something else."

"About time."

"Thank you." I squeeze his hand. "For being so patient. For being here, tonight, despite everything else you've got going on."

"It's—"

"Don't say 'nothing,'" I catch him. "That's my rule."

He fixes me with his CEO glare. A soft version of it, anyway. "You've gotten bossier lately."

"Been learning from the best."

"Is that so?"

His rough knuckles shift under my palm, still tender from the fight. There's no blood right now, but I know there was. I know it ended up there for me.

It should make me feel horrible as a nurse, but as a mom, I'm glad whoever threatened my family got his just desserts.

And as a woman…

I won't lie, it's a little hot.

"So, as I was saying," I blurt before I let that train of thought reach Horny Station, "thanks. I really needed this. Though I promise I won't make a habit of it."

His fingers flex. I feel like he wants to say something, but he's keeping himself in check.

I shouldn't get my hopes up, though. Earlier, when he mentioned the contract, my fantasies carried me so far away I had to hitch a cab back to reality. Because the truth is, I thought he wanted to break it. To do away with it all and just—

What? Keep you? The ugly part of me, the one that sounds so much like Brad, sneers. *Right. As if.*

He's right, though. Yulian is basically a Forbes Prince Charming on steroids, with none of the charm and all of the guns.

Whereas me? I'm nobody. I'm poor, broken, used. I've got baggage for two lifetimes.

I've got a son.

And Yulian made it clear he doesn't want that.

It's so easy to forget, though. He's so good with him. With *us.* So patient, kind, and every other good word I never thought I'd use to describe Yulian Lozhkin.

But I can't pretend this is more than it is. We have a contract, and that's not going anywhere. We have sex—amazing, Earth-shattering sex—but that's it.

It doesn't mean we're ever going to be anything else.

I should let it be enough.

"Fire."

It's a whisper, small and weak. My head turns instantly to Eli. "Honey?"

"Fire," he whines again. His eyes are squeezed shut, his tiny body tossing and turning in his sleep. "There's fire everywhere..."

Yulian's immediately on high alert. "What's wrong with him?"

"Nightmares." I don't elaborate any further, waking Eli up instead. "Eli," I call as I gently shake his shoulders. "Baby, wake up. You're dreaming."

His eyes blink open. Instantly, they fill with tears. "Mommy," he sniffles. "I'm sorry. I used the stove, I—"

"Hush," I whisper, gathering him up in my arms. "It's okay. It was just a dream. Mommy's got you now."

It goes on like this for a while: Eli apologizing, me comforting him. It doesn't matter how many times I tell him it's not his fault, that he's got nothing to apologize for. That day is etched in his mind, in fire and smoke and all that came after.

Because of me.

Yulian shifts. I can tell he's uncomfortable, that he has no idea how to handle this. It must be a first for him—not knowing what to do in a crisis.

But I get it. He didn't sign up for this. Nor for any of the mess I've put him through.

"Where's Garfield?" Eli mumbles. "He didn't burn, did he?"

"He's fine," Yulian says. "I'll go get—"

"No!" Quick as lightning, Eli's small hand grabs Yulian's. "Please, don't go."

Yulian stares at Eli's fingers. His tiny knuckles, white with effort. "Okay," he says eventually. "I won't. I'll stay right here."

It takes a few more minutes to calm him down. Even longer to convince him to let Yulian go. I'm mortified, but the motherly side of me can't spare much thought for how awkward Yulian must be feeling.

Right now, all my focus is on my son.

My son, who needs me.

"I'll go put him to sleep," I tell Yulian.

I tuck Eli into bed and push Garfield into his arms. "See?" I force a smile. "Safe and sound."

The truth is, all I want to do right now is cry. I want to curl up and sob, curse myself for being such a horrible mother, for letting my kid put himself in danger like that. For giving him nightmares for the rest of his life.

But Yulian's still here.

So I wipe my eyes, wait for Eli's breathing to even out, and go back into the living room.

I find him in the kitchen.

"I made some warm milk," he says. "To help him sleep."

It's the sweetest thing he could have done. "Thanks," I whisper. "He's down again, but I'll take that."

Yulian offers me the cup. Our fingers brush as I take it. His fire, I've come to learn, is almost as dangerous as his ice.

Even now, when it's warm as a hearth, it's more dangerous than ever to me.

Because all I want is to curl up into that warmth, sob into Yulian's chest, let him hold me. Like he did earlier tonight.

But that's not part of the deal.

I pour honey into the milk. Yulian's eyes go wide when he sees how much.

"What?" I ask.

"Nothing. Just wasn't aware you were courting diabetes."

I roll my eyes. "We all have our vices."

"And yours is milk and honey." His eyebrow rises. "Most people would go for something stronger."

"Cheap wine tastes horrible." I sip my drink, relishing the sugary warmth on my tongue. "So does beer. Too bitter."

"I feel like you're taking the concept of 'sweet tooth' to a whole other level."

"You're not the first," I sigh. "Brad loved to tease me for it."

Realization dawns in Yulian's eyes. "That's why he calls you—"

"'Sweet thing'? Yeah." I grimace. "Can you believe I used to like it? Now, I can't hear it without wanting to throw up."

"That doesn't surprise me." He makes a disgusted face. At least we've got this in common: not being able to fucking stand Bradley Baldwin. "Has he always been that slimy?"

"Oddly, no." My mind goes back to that summer. To the sweet way it started. "He was kind of a dick, but no more than any other Hamptons guy. He still thought himself human, back then."

"When did he stop?"

I grip my cup tighter. "When his father died."

Yulian pauses. Perhaps, for the first time, he's feeling something close to kinship to Brad. This is the one thing *they* have in common—losing someone they shouldn't have lost, too young to know what to do with the void it left behind.

"What happened then?"

"He inherited everything. He wasn't supposed to, you know. His dad believed you had to make your own fortune, even if you were born lucky. Brad was supposed to graduate business school and then support himself. Become an asset to the company, or fund his own. He didn't seem to mind that at the time. Said he'd rather be a capable rich jerk than a useless rich jerk." The memories keep flooding in. "But then his dad died, and overnight, he was worth billions."

"And it went to his head," Yulian fills in.

"Yeah. Guess it did."

We go back to silence for a while. I keep an ear out for Eli's nightmares, but for once, they seem to be leaving him alone.

"You're worried," Yulian guesses, following my gaze.

"Not more than usual." I force a small smile. "It's gotten better lately. He has them less and less. But last year…"

His hand touches my shoulder. Without thinking, I lean into its warmth. "Tell me," he says, but for once, it doesn't sound like an order. "If you want."

And suddenly, I realize I do want to tell him.

"It's not much of a story," I exhale. "Eli was three. I'd just gotten hired at the hospital, with an actual contract and all. Before that, I was pulling triples at several nursing homes, but it was almost all off-the-books. Getting a real job at the hospital—it was like a dream." I take another sip, then sigh. "But I was still on probation. Even a small mistake, and I could have lost it."

Yulian nods. "Go on."

Somehow, his voice grounds me.

"I was at work that night," I say. "I'd gotten a sitter for Eli, of course. It was this seventeen-year-old girl Dorothy, the daughter of a neighbor. She could use a few bucks, and I could use the convenience of ten dollars an hour. She'd watched Eli before. But that night..."

"She bailed," Yulian realizes.

"Yeah. Texted me halfway through my shift, said she had to go pick up a friend, that it was an emergency. It was past midnight—I couldn't possibly find someone else."

"And you couldn't leave."

"They'd have fired me so fast." Tears bubble up at the corners of my eyes, but I wipe them away. "In hindsight, that's what I should've done. It would have been hard on us, but still better than what happened."

"The fire?"

I nod tightly. "I told myself Eli was asleep, that I'd be back before he woke up. He wouldn't even realize I was gone. But then the shift ran long, and by the time I made it home, he'd gotten hungry." I give Yulian a watery smile. "He tried to make himself pancakes."

I can see it in Yulian's eyes—the second the horror dawns. "The stove."

"Eli said a rug had caught on fire. He'd tried to toss it out the window, but then the curtains caught fire, too. He was smart enough to run to Dorothy's place and tell them what happened. The family called 911." I bite my lip. "Dorothy was passed out drunk in her bed. But she was technically a minor, so…"

"So the blame fell on you."

Yulian's hand squeezes my shoulder. Guilt pierces me—for what happened back then, for what's happening now. For leaning on this man who owes me nothing.

"When I came back," I rasp, "I still didn't know any of this. I just saw smoke rising from my window. The fire department was on the scene. I had to be held back by neighbors because I tried to run inside. I thought my kid was still in there, you know?"

There's no use fighting back the tears now. But Yulian simply hands me a tissue, not leaving me for a second.

"Thanks," I whisper. "Anyway, then the police came. And then there was Child Protective Services. It all happened so fast. It's a miracle I didn't lose him—to the fire or to them." I blow into the tissue and crumple it. "Wanna know what the worst part is?"

"Tell me."

"Eli blames himself. Even now, he still does. Every time he wakes up, all he does is apologize to *me.*"

"Sounds like someone I know," Yulian remarks.

It almost makes me laugh. Almost.

"I'd spent years thinking Eli would be better off with me. That I'd be a better parent than Brad. And then, when that happened… It just made me feel so arrogant. Because I knew something like that never would have happened on his watch."

"You don't know that." Now, Yulian's closer than ever. "In all the time I've known you, you've always put your son first. And that man…" His fist clenches at his side. "He hurt you."

I don't deny it. I can't.

By now, Yulian's seen enough to put two and two together.

His thumb strokes my scars. "You shouldn't blame yourself. You protected Eli from a monster."

"But I put him in danger," I whisper.

"Because you're human. Because you tried your best and for one night, it wasn't enough." Somehow, his words feel raw. Personal. Like they're about more than just my story. "But that doesn't mean you get to stop trying."

We're so close now, our lips are touching with every word. I want him to kiss me so bad. Want him to take me to bed and make me forget.

"Go," I beg him instead. "Before we do something we'll both regret."

His hand comes up to my cheek, stroking my face, brushing away the tears. "Like what?"

"Fall," I whisper. "I've fallen once already. I know what it feels like when there's no one there to catch you."

"That's what you think?" he asks. "That I won't catch you?"

"I think," I murmur, stroking his face right back, "that we have a contract."

He pulls away then. Not abruptly—not with anger. Just does what I asked him to do, even if it guts me. Even if it guts us both.

"Okay."

"Thank you," I whisper.

He heads for the door. There, he hesitates.

I wonder if he'll say I'm wrong. If he'll shred that contract to pieces and pull me into his arms. If he'll tell me he wants me, all of me, the baggage and the broken parts, and take me to bed to fix what needs fixing.

Instead, he says, "Goodnight, Mia."

"Goodnight, Yulian."

And then he's gone.

40

YULIAN

Headstones flank me as I walk.

My link with death is usually more subtle than this. I feel it like a knife in the ribs every second of every day, but for others, it's just a chill in the air that surrounds me.

Today, though, I walk with death. Beside it. Among it.

The cemetery is quiet. Unchanged since the last time I was here, a whole trip around the sun ago. There's an unnatural stillness in the air, the leaves, everything that should be moving but isn't.

Here, every living thing is waiting.

"Mama." The word scrapes like sandpaper on my tongue. "Otets." My gaze flicks from one headstone to the other, then drops to the last one. Much lower. Much smaller. "*Sestra.*"

Mother. Father. Sister.

I kneel in the dirt and start cleaning the graves.

Kneeling is such a foreign concept for me. Men like me don't kneel: we break everybody else, knock them down until their only choice is to curse me looking up.

But here—for them—I kneel.

I wet the rag in my hand and touch it to the cold, smooth stone of my mother's grave. Grime sticks to the fabric, a year's worth of it, staining my fingertips the color of gray earth.

"I met someone."

No one else is here, so my words echo. It's the crack of dawn on a Monday and not a soul in sight. Maksim is standing just a little way off, ensuring I won't be disturbed, but he could have saved himself the walk.

"Her name is Mia." I don't know why I'm telling my mother this. Why my first words to her are about the woman I hired to pretend to be my fiancée. "She's a nurse. An insufferable, stubborn nurse with zero bedside manner and the mouth of a sailor. Can't imagine how she even got the job, really."

I trace the letters of my mother's name. *Olga Lozhkin.* The dates of her birth and death, too close together to be fair.

But this world has never been fair. That's the greatest lie of all: *fairness.* Justice. Balance.

If you want balance, you have to even the scales with your own fucking hands.

"I hired her," I confess. "To draw out the ones who did this to you."

I move on to my father's grave. My fingers follow the edges of his name. *Yevgeny Lozhkin.* Every year, they feel smoother.

"I put her in danger." The words claw their way out my throat, leaving blood in their wake. It's all I can taste lately—the blood I've shed. The blood I *will* shed. "Every time I walk with her, speak to her, *look* at her, I'm putting her in danger. Her, and her son."

I'm a liar. That's part of the job description. When you're a *pakhan,* you can't afford to wear your heart on your sleeve.

Hell, you can't afford to have a heart at all.

But this is the only place where I can't bury the truth.

Here, where I buried my family.

"It's what I need to do," I grit. "I have to avenge your deaths. All these years, I've been trying. Now, I'm finally closing in on them—the *mudaki* who did this to you. I can't stop now. I won't."

But what if you did, Yulian?

That last thought comes in Alina's voice. She died too young to know anything else. She never knew her toys were paid for by someone else's blood. She was…

Just like Eli.

I banish the thought as I move over to her grave, the smallest one of the bunch. But no matter how hard I try, Mia's son keeps crashing into my thoughts the way he crashed into her knees when she came home.

Faded memories bubble back to the surface: a marble staircase, a huge hall. The front door opening on my father's shadow, back from yet another trip to Russia.

I'd slam into his legs, too. I'd tell him I missed him, that I wanted to come along next time.

When you're old enough, he'd say.

Then Alina was born. My little sister, tinier than a loaf of bread, with the lungs of a fucking opera singer. She could scream all night long if something bothered her. I watched her grow, saw her turn into a two-legged creature, transform into a bright kid filled with joy.

We'll take you both, my father started promising then. *Once Alina's older.*

But she never got older.

And the sons of bitches who did it are still out there.

I rise from their graves. I place fresh flowers in fresh water, even though it won't last. Even though it's a meaningless gesture that can't even soothe them.

Then I shift to the next grave.

It's right by Alina's, just separated enough to signal that it belongs to another family. The name etched in the stone isn't Lozhkin, but it might as well have been.

Kira Morozova.

This time, I don't kneel. "Hi, Kira."

Hi, Yuli.

I can hear her voice in my head like it hasn't been a day. Her amused lilt, like there was always something funny to find in every conversation. Even when she was sad, or angry, or in one of her gray spells that the weight of her birthright brought about, the ones that made her cold and indifferent to everyone and everything, she never lost her humor.

I take in the details of her grave. It isn't as dirty as my

family's, but the flowers—camellias, her favorite—are far from fresh. They're dried, stiff things on cracking stems.

One touch and they'd crumble into dust.

"I see your sister hasn't been by," I remark, touching my fingers to the thin layer of dust on the headstone. Another sign Nikita hasn't been here in a while. "I'm to blame for that. I lost her."

You lost my sister?

"Yes. But I'll find her."

If Kira was here, she would have raised a skeptical eyebrow. But unlike her voice, Kira's is blurry in my memory. Indistinct. Like I'm gazing at her through water. It should be the clearest of them all, with Nikita being a living reminder by my side, but for some reason, it's not. The only time I can see her again is once a year, when I stare into the eyes of her portrait.

I wonder if this is why Nikita comes by every week.

Because she doesn't want to forget.

Fuck, what wouldn't *I* give to forget?

"There's someone else I might lose." I don't put fresh flowers into her vase. It's not my place to. I was never family to her, not a boyfriend or a fiancé or anything else like that, not that her killers cared enough to ask.

"Someone who's got nothing to do with me." *Like you.*

"Someone who might die for it." *Like you.*

"Someone I don't want to lose." *Like you.*

The *pakhan* in me is silent. Usually, it'd be sneering already, mocking my weakness. Reminding me of what I need to do and why.

But here, in front of the graves of everyone I've lost, even the *pakhan* side of me has no place.

Here, I'm simply human.

"I lied to her." My voice goes hoarse around the lump in my throat. "I let her believe I had nothing to do with that shooting."

The flashbacks from that day overlap with the ones from twenty years ago: the bullets, the roar, the blood. Carbon copies of each other.

"She almost died. I almost turned her son into an orphan. I shouldn't give a shit, but God help me, I do."

You always give a shit. Her tone is light, joking, with a note of truth underneath it. *That's why I had to look out for you. You were way too soft for a Bratva kid.*

That wasn't a bad thing, you know.

I turn deaf to that last part. I don't want to hear all the reasons why being weak is a luxury I can afford. Not when it so clearly isn't.

Not when it cost me what I cared about most in the world.

"Without her, I can't avenge my family." I clench my fists at my sides, bloodthirst mounting with every second. "I can't avenge *you.*"

Would that be so bad? Letting sleeping ghosts lie?

"Yes."

Why?

"Because I can't do that to you."

But you can do that to her?

"I have to." My teeth grit, my knuckles pop. "If I let her go, I'll lose them."

And if you don't, you'll lose her.

"I'll lose her anyway."

Kira's ghost falls silent. If she were truly here, she'd know what to say. She was always wiser than me. If she were here, she would have known what to do. About Nikita, Mia—about everything.

But she's not here.

She isn't the one who survived.

I am.

And I'm going to hunt the motherfuckers who took her life to the ends of the fucking Earth.

No matter what it costs me.

No matter what it costs anyone.

41

MIA

ONE MONTH LATER

"I need a gurney here!"

"BP's 70 and dropping. He's hemorrhaging from—"

"Where's the goddamn cart?!"

I rush to the ambulance doors. The guy strapped to the EMTs' gurney has definitely seen better days.

So has his stomach. Specifically, the giant rebar-shaped hole in it.

"This the hypotensive patient?" I ask.

"Yes, but Dr. Adams said to wait for—"

I ignore the paramedic and push one microgram of epi.

"Nurse Winters!" Dr. Adams comes thundering through the doors in his pristine white coat. My scrubs are soaked in blood from head to toe, but his clothes, like usual, don't have a single goddamn spot on them. "I gave specific instructions for this patient!"

I try to bite back my irritation, but I fail. "If we'd waited, he'd be dead," I hiss through my teeth, making sure the patient doesn't hear me. The last thing we need is to add an anxiety attack on top of hemorrhagic shock.

"He's a patient of *my* OR—"

"Then get him into your OR!" I snap. "Right now would be good, actually!"

Dr. Adams's eyes flick between me, the patient, and the EMTs still applying pressure to the wound. I can tell he wants to argue more, because that telltale popping vein on his temple is promising a scolding for the ages.

But he must realize what everyone else in the room has clocked three minutes ago: this guy cannot afford to wait.

"Get him prepped," he orders his terrified residents with a bossy wave of his gloved hand. "I'll be waiting in OR 2."

Then he stalks off.

The residents glance nervously at each other, unsure of what to do. They're fresh out of med school—probably started today, judging by the lost expression on their faces—but God forbid Adams actually do his job and *teach* them.

I take a deep breath and take charge. "C'mon," I tell them, grabbing the gurney on one side. "Help me roll him inside. I'll show you how to prep him."

I go as quickly as I can, giving instructions to the young team of doctors, letting them handle the minor stuff and showing them everything else, including how to plug a rebar hole with their fingers to staunch the blood flow. It's not the most effective lesson—we're up against a ticking clock, after all—

but by the time we're heading to the OR, they seem to have regained their composure and remembered their training.

"Thanks," one of them—a young woman with glasses—exhales as we roll the gurney through the white hallway. Her white coat reads *Dr. Park.* "Dr. Adams can be a bit..."

"Pain in the ass?" The two guys suppress a snort at my comment. "It's okay," I continue. "I know. Best surgeon out there, though, much as it pains me to admit it. Make sure to learn all you can from him."

"Are you a surgical resident, too?" one of the others—a Dr. Shaan—asks with bright eyes.

"Nope." I grin. "Nurse practitioner."

"OR nurse?" the last young doctor asks, with a thick Scottish accent and hope in his eyes. "We could use you in there. Keep Adams in line and the patient breathing."

"Sorry." I shrug. "The ER owns my soul. But feel free to shout for me if you ever need help with anything. God knows it's hard to find your feet in here."

After I've dropped the surgeon puppies back on Adams's doorstep with the patient, I grab a fresh set of scrubs and head back to the ER.

"Crisis over?" I ask Kallie, noticing much less shouting than before.

"Yeah," she sighs. "At least until the next impalement. Ever feel like we're in 1400s Romania?"

"Maybe that's what the R in ER stands for."

"And the E?"

"The E stands for Enough Chitchat," Gwen's steely voice cuts in, making us jump. "Nurse Kathri, help the patient in Bay D to the Maternity Ward. Nurse Winters, Bay C is all yours."

"Yes, Gwen," we answer in glum unison.

Kallie's patient is already in a wheelchair. She wheels her into the elevator and disappears from Gwen's all-seeing eyes.

"Hello!" I greet brightly, pulling back the curtain on Bay C. "What seems to be the—?"

Problem.

The word gets stuck in my throat. Like a splinter, or a rusty piece of rebar.

Because there's no way, right?

There's no way *he's* here.

"There you are, sweet thing." Brad's smile slices his face in half, sharp as the crescent moon. "I've been waiting forever."

~

It's been a month since that night.

A month since I've hide or hair of Yulian.

A month of my texts getting radio silence or the rare noncommittal answer about how the next event hasn't been fixed yet, how he'll let me know if he needs me again.

And a month since Brad saw us.

He looks perfectly healthy in his crisp, cream-colored suit. After all these years, it's still all he seems to wear: shades of white, blinding enough to mask the darkness lurking beneath.

"Well?" he demands, crossing his legs impatiently. "Aren't you going to examine me?"

Fucking hell. Even his tone is begging to be punched. "I'll go get another nurse."

"No." He grabs my wrist as I turn, keeping me there. "I want *you.*"

It roots me to the spot—his touch, the memory of it. The force of his death grip. Any tighter, and the pressure will turn into pain.

But this time, I don't freeze. This time, an unfamiliar fire keeps my limbs from falling numb. A fire I haven't felt in a long time.

Rage.

I turn back to Brad, eyes blazing. "Leave," I spit. "Or I'll have security throw you out."

"On what grounds?" His sardonic smile hasn't wavered for a second. "You don't have a restraining order. You never asked for one."

Because I thought I was done with you. "That can be fixed."

"After five years?" He laughs. "No, sweetie, it can't. No judge in their right mind would take you seriously."

"Try me."

He leans in, voice low and smug. "I'm a patient," he whispers. "I have every right to be here. So, you can either do your job, or I can report you to your bosses. Bet they'd like an excuse to get rid of you. From what I hear, you're quite a handful."

"I do what needs to be done," I say flatly. "Now, let me go, or I'll scream."

"I'll let you go if you visit me."

"Fuck off, Brad." I wipe the sweat from my brow with my free hand. "This isn't the place for your games!"

"But it's the place that signs your paychecks." His grip tightens just a little. A warning: *Do not test me.* "So do your fucking job, or I'll make sure no hospital in the country will ever hire you again."

Pain sears up my arm, but I bite my lip and bear it. Because it's nothing compared to what I've endured in the past—and to his threat.

Brad isn't the kind of man who bluffs. He's the kind of man who'll scorch the earth just to rob you of the feeling of grass under your feet.

And right now, I can't afford to be burned again.

Because it's not just about me anymore.

"Fine. You first."

Pleased as punch, Brad lets me go. "Excellent. You may begin."

I rub my sore wrist. I can already tell it'll bruise. Add it to the tab, I guess. "You haven't told me what's wrong with you."

As if wanting to mock me, he lifts his own wrist. "This hurts," he says with a fake whimper.

I sigh and pick up a fresh pair of gloves. "Let's see it, then."

"No."

"'No'?"

"No to those." He nods towards the gloves. "I'm… allergic to latex."

My eyebrows high-five the ceiling. "Are you now?"

"It's new."

"It's not in your chart."

"No gloves." This time, his tone is final. "Or else—"

"You'll throw yourself to the floor and scream like a toddler." Angry, I dump the gloves. "Don't worry, I got your memo."

Then I pick up Brad's wrist.

And my hands start shaking.

Stop, I bark inwardly. *Stop that. Don't let him see.*

Don't let him get to you.

But it's useless. The memories are too strong. My body's stuck in fight-or-flight response, waiting for the blow to land. For that hand to escape my hold and just—

"You're looking a little pale," he comments.

"I'm fine." It's a lie. "There's nothing wrong with your wrist."

He hums, considering it. "Then the pain must be coming from somewhere else."

Without warning, he grabs my hand and moves it to his crotch.

I snatch it away. My elbow hits the supply cart, toppling it in the process.

Everyone in the room turns to stare at me.

"Nurse Winters?" Gwen asks, half-glaring from behind a stack of patient charts. "Everything alright?"

"Yes," I lie through gritted teeth. "Sorry. I just—tripped."

"You should pick those up," Brad drawls, eyeing the scattered mess of supplies all over the floor of Bay C. "Unless you want someone else to trip over them."

Hot, burning humiliation courses through me.

Without a choice, I crouch and start picking up everything.

"Not like that," Brad murmurs, a dark, heated edge to his words. *"Kneel."*

My old defense mechanisms try to kick back into gear. *Do as he says. Stay calm, shut up, wait for it to be over.*

It always hurts worse when you fight.

But something's changed. For some reason, those old boundaries that kept me safe back at Montauk are starting to chafe.

Now, my pulse isn't racing out of fear, but out of fury.

I wonder if it's because of Yulian.

When he stopped Brad at the wedding, he wasn't scared. When he faced him again at StarTech, he wasn't scared, either.

So why should I be?

Because you're not as strong. Because you've been hurt before.

Because you're hiding his son.

"No need," I rasp, forcing the words past the lump in my throat. "I'm done."

Brad's dark eyes fix on me. Thoughtful, considering. "You've changed," he observes.

"If you say so."

"I've changed, too."

I bark out a laugh. "Yeah, right."

"Is that so hard to believe?" His fingers catch a stray lock of hair and start to play with it. "That I've become a better person?"

My arms break out in goosebumps. "You just asked me to kneel. That's not 'changed.'"

"That's on you." I try to move away, but he doesn't let go. Instead, he leans in, smelling it. "You know what you do to me." He smirks, leading my gaze between his legs, where I see—

He's hard.

Disgust floods me. I yank my hair away, not caring that it hurts as a few strands stay caught in his grip like wings ripped off a butterfly. "I'm leaving."

"No, you're not."

"Yes, I am."

"Because I'm not *him?*"

He spits out that word like it's venom. Like Yulian's nothing but a parasite, feeding on what's rightfully his.

"No, Brad," I croak. "It's because you're *you.*"

"Liar." He gets up from the stretcher, following me to the front desk. "You're hiding things from me. But I'll find out, sweet thing. I'll find all your dirty little secrets."

That promise turns my veins to ice.

I don't remember what happens next. What I write on his chart, what he says as he leaves. All I know is that, moments later, I'm hunched over in the bathroom, dry heaving into the toilet.

I don't even remember picking up my phone. Dialing the number. Pressing "call."

But I must have. Because, at some point, a voice cuts through the fog.

His voice.

"... Mia?"

42

YULIAN

The kid's footwork is all wrong. Too much weight on his front leg. I see the opening before he even finishes his swing.

I sidestep. He stumbles forward, making himself the perfect target.

It'd be rude not to take him up on the invitation.

With a vicious crunch, my fist finds his gut. Not full strength—I don't want to break him. Just enough to teach him what happens when hard knuckles meet soft insides.

Air rushes out of his lungs in a sharp, panicked wheeze. His eyes go wide, pupils shrinking to pinpricks. He staggers, tries to stay upright, fights the pain and the nausea and the gravity—

And then he folds, dropping to his knees.

I give him a second. Then: "Up."

The recruit looks up, face twisted in humiliation. He knows the others are watching. Knows he just got put down like a fucking amateur. It's the point of these sparring sessions: teaching these wet-behind-the-ear kiddos what it's like to fight against a man. To fight *like* a man.

Shame is a damn good motivator for that.

I hold out a hand. After a moment's hesitation, he takes it, letting me haul him up. "You've got good instincts." I nod at his stance, taking in the distance between his feet, the symmetry with his shoulders. It tells me it's not his first fight.

Not his first loss, though, either.

"Watch your left flank," I order him. "It's wide open."

His eyes flicker with understanding. "Thank you, sir."

Sir. Good boy. He'll make it.

I step back, rolling my shoulders, wiping sweat from my brow. The Goldenrod's ring smells like stale blood and adrenaline. No underground fights yet—it's too early for that—but my recruits are training, running drills. I need them sharp. Ready.

Maksim is leaning against the ropes, arms crossed. "You're going to break them before they even see a real fight."

I grab a towel from the corner and wipe the sweat off my face. "The enemy won't go easy. Neither will I."

"Guns settle most fights these days."

"They do until they don't." I toss the towel aside, grabbing my bottle of water instead. "If they can't handle themselves, they'll die."

Maksim doesn't argue. He knows I'm right. "You're actually a big, hunky care-bear underneath all that muscle, aren't ya?"

"Say that again if you want to be next."

He barks out a laugh. "No, sir. This suit's brand new. Wouldn't want to mess it up before I've had a chance to use it."

"You're using it now."

"For an audience of *men.*" He grimaces, wrinkles his nose at the ripe smell of recruit musk. "Not exactly the target demographic I had in mind when I bought it."

I don't quite roll my eyes, but it's a close thing. "I take it things are going well with Cammie."

"Kallie." He gives a soft, forlorn sigh like a teenager in love. "Or, as her tasteful parents named her, *Kalinda.*"

I shake my head. Maksim's annoying on most days, but when he's got a special lady in his life? Absolutely fucking unbearable. "Thought you said you were too old for her."

"I am."

"Then what's the suit for?"

"Dinner." He shrugs. "Entertainment. Flirting. Smelling that sweet coconut oil scent."

"So you're going to wine and dine her, but not fuck her?"

"You're so uncouth." He checks the wrapping on my hands, makes sure it's still nice and tight. "Ever thought about gargling with soap?"

"You're changing the subject." I stretch my arms, then my torso. My back gives a satisfying *pop.* Nothing clears my head like fighting, even if it's in the junior leagues. "According to you, that's *my* job."

"Which reminds me." Maks's eyes light up. "I haven't seen Mia around lately. Finally came to your senses and tore up that contract?"

"No."

"Then I'd say she's skimming from the register."

My fists clench. I don't appreciate Maksim's tone one fucking bit. "Shut up."

"Hey, just trying to get some clarity here." He cranes his neck and searches my gaze. "Is she fired? Is she not? Is she the fake next Mrs. Lozhkin or the real one?"

I tune out Maks's questions. He doesn't call the shots—*I* do.

But his words stick in my brain nonetheless.

Mia. For a month, I've been ghosting her. Cold. Clinical. Careless.

Except I'm anything but.

Because Mia Winters has crawled deeper than my skin. She's in my head, in my brain. In that ugly crevice at the center of my chest I'd long thought empty.

She's everywhere.

And yet, she's not here.

For good fucking reason.

That night at her apartment, and then that day at the cemetery—they've left me with nothing but questions. Haunting, relentless questions, ones I cannot answer without raising many more.

What is Mia to me? What am I going to do about my plan?

Am I going to avenge my family, or am I going to protect hers?

Am I going to lose her to a bullet or to the truth?

"Boss," a recruit calls from the benches. "Your phone."

"Ignore it," I bark. Another fresh face is already stepping into the ring, ready to let me vent my frustration on his lousy footwork.

But Maksim clears his throat. "Yul? I think you're gonna wanna take this."

There's an edge to his tone that I don't like. Knowing. Urgent.

Irritated, I grab the phone.

And then I see who it is.

A bad feeling creeps up my spine. Horrible, sinking.

Without wasting one more second, I answer. "Mia?"

A gasping breath comes from the other end of the line. A ragged, sharp intake of air. Like she's fucking drowning.

Dread fills me. "Tell me what's wrong."

I hate the way my voice strains at the end. Less anger, more fear. An emotion I can't afford.

"Mia. Answer me."

Finally, a whisper. "He was here," she croaks. "At the hospital."

It's all I need to hear.

My vision swims with red. My fists clench so hard I could snap my own bones. My pulse thunders, fury mounting hot and bright, the kind that won't be satisfied with a measly pound of flesh.

Bradley Baldwin is a fucking dead man.

"Stay where you are," I bark.

Maksim flanks me as I jump down from the ring. "I take it I'm bringing the car around?"

I don't answer. He doesn't need me to.

My thoughts are a mangled mess. Nothing like the cold lucidity of the *pakhan* I should be. I told myself I didn't care about this woman, that I could use her as a human shield and feel nothing. That I could dangle her in front of my enemies and not give a shit if they managed to sink their teeth into her.

All lies.

Mia's in danger, my instincts are screaming, raw, animal. *She's hurt. She's scared.*

She needs me.

Before my heartbeat evens, I'm out the fucking door.

43

YULIAN

Kallie meets me in front of the ER doors. “She’s in there,” she says, nodding towards the ladies’ changing room.

Smart girl. I can see why Maksim likes her. She must have guessed I’d start barking orders the second I came through those doors, demanding to be taken to Mia. It wouldn’t have been pretty.

However, those thoughts end up buried deep under the urgency that moves me.

Nothing else matters. Nothing but Mia.

I find her huddled with a blanket around her shoulders and a young man handing her tea. He takes one look at me, wolf-whistles, and says to Mia, “Girl, you weren’t kidding. I’d grate all sorts of dairy products on that washboard.”

She chokes on her tea. “Thanks, Reese,” she coughs, half sincere, half *I’m going to murder you later for that. It will not be quick. It will not be painless.* “You should go. I don’t want to get you into trouble with Gwen, and—”

"And I'm one wheel too many," he finishes for her. "Got it, babycakes. But if I see you back out there wearing purple again, I swear to God, I'll file a sexual harassment complaint against you and get you sent home the hard way."

Far from feeling threatened, Mia squeezes his hand. "Thank you," she whispers, this time genuine. "Seriously."

"Treat her well, Mr. Hunk," he tells me as he passes by, making an *I see you* gesture. "If you don't, I'll know."

Then we're alone.

Mia's blue eyes peer up at me. They're rimmed with red, puffy from crying. She takes in my sweaty appearance, the gym clothes and ruffled hair, and guilt immediately blooms on her face.

"I'm sorry," she says. "I shouldn't have called you, you were busy, I—"

"You did exactly as you were supposed to do."

I kneel next to her. It's a new thing, even for me, with all I've seen and done. A *pakhan* doesn't kneel—ever. It's too close to a show of weakness. Submission. Everything I am not.

But today, for Mia, I do.

She won't look at me now. Her fingers tighten around the cup, shoulders curling inward like she wants to disappear into the blanket wrapped around her.

I fucking hate it.

"Mia."

She still won't meet my gaze. Her eyes fall to her wrist, and I follow them reflexively.

A sharp exhale escapes me. "He hurt you."

"It's nothing—"

"It's not fucking nothing." I reach for her hand, take it in mine, turn it over to examine the purpling bruise around her wrist. Her pulse is erratic under my thumb, rabbit-quick. Like she's preparing to bolt any second now. Her old defense mechanism, roaring back to life. "He hurt you."

Her breath shudders. "It's not that bad. He just—"

"Don't lie." My voice drops, steel beneath it. "Do not fucking lie to me, Mia Winters. I know you. I can tell when you're feeding me bullshit."

I can tell when you're too scared to speak.

Her eyes snap to mine. Heat floods her cheeks. "It wasn't— He didn't *touch* me, Yulian. Not in the way you think. He was just here to scare me." Her throat works, gaze wandering nervously around the room. "I swear, nothing happened."

But he wanted it to.

I can see it in her face. In the way her body trembles, the way her breath hitches.

Fury coils in my chest. Hot, bright, seething fury.

If Brad was here now, every doctor in the hospital combined wouldn't be able to save him.

I shift closer, until there's barely a breath between us. "I should have killed him at StarTech," I growl. "I shouldn't have let him walk out of there. Not on his own two legs."

She swallows hard. "You can't fix everything by killing."

"You'd be surprised."

Her lips part, but she doesn't argue. Instead, she drops her gaze to the floor again. "He threatened him," she confesses, her voice a whisper. "He threatened Eli."

My blood goes cold. "He knows?"

"I don't think so. Not yet. But he said…" Her hands start shaking around her paper cup. "He said he'll find out about my secrets. All of them." Panic fills her voice. Her breaths grow short again, quick, too quick. "I have to take him away, Yulian. I can't stay here with this threat hanging over our heads. I have to run, I have to—"

"You have to calm down." Once again, I touch my forehead to hers. Like I did back in the car, a whole month ago.

That night, I was the one who ran. *Me.* The fearsome *pakhan,* the shadow king of New York, the untouchable CEO, sent running by a wisp of a woman in a crumbling Brownsville apartment. By the words she whispered to me in the dark.

"Go. Before we do something we'll both regret."

"Like what?"

"Fall."

How fucking cowardly.

"Breathe," I command, tone steady. My hand finds the back of her head, holds her gently through it. "In, hold, out."

With a breathless nod, Mia obeys. Always obeys, no matter what I ask her. No matter how bright the fire in her burns, that riotous part of her soul that never wants to yield.

I thought I'd tamed her, in that room at the Goldenrod, but I didn't have a clue, did I?

Mia Winters doesn't break.

Not for anyone.

Not even for me.

And that's what scares me most of all. That I might not want her broken. That I might want her whole, exactly as she is, fierce and indomitable and the worst pain in the ass I've ever fucking met.

That I might want her at all. Not just to use, but to *keep.*

To have and to hold.

"Thank you," she whispers, steadier now. Her perfume lingers around her, violets and candy and something else I can't place. Something uniquely hers. "I'm okay now."

"Good."

I don't want to part from her. To let go of her scent, her warmth.

But if I don't, I'll never be able to do it again.

I push to my feet, take the tea from her hands and set it aside. Then I hold my hand out. "Come."

She hesitates. "Where?"

"Away."

"With…" She hesitates. "With you?"

"Yes. For the weekend." She needs a place you can recharge, clear her head without that *mudak* looming over her. Otherwise, she actually might run.

And I'll never see her again.

That thought shouldn't bother me. It shouldn't cause me more than a passing annoyance, for losing money and losing an asset. For the hassle of having to replace her.

Instead, it fucking guts me.

Mia's brows knit. Disappointment flits on her face, but it's gone as quickly as it came. "Yulian, I can't."

"Yes, you can. You're free for the next two days."

She blinks at me. "You know my schedule?"

"I make it my business to know things."

Something warm spreads across her face. Soft, rosy—*alive.* "I… I really can't," she whispers again, with a twinge of regret. "I can't just leave Eli on his own. Especially not now."

"I'm not asking you to."

Her eyes widen. "You—you want me to bring him?"

"I do."

You're crazy. The rational part of me is banging its head against the wall. Drop everything and leave? My Bratva, my duties, my company? Just to spend one weekend with Mia?

No—*with Mia* and *her son?*

If Maksim were here, he'd call me insane. Remind me of my plans, my goals. Tell me I can't have it both ways, that I have to *choose.*

But I don't have to choose quite yet.

She's watching me now. Trying to gauge if I'm regretting my words, if I ever truly meant them. After a month of radio silence, she's got every right to doubt me.

"Yulian—"

"Pack a bag," I cut her off. "We're leaving tonight."

She stares at me, and I see the conflict war in her gaze. The need to be strong, to be independent. To care for her job and her kid more than her selfish desires.

To *refuse* me.

But she's exhausted. And scared. And deep down, she knows I won't take no for an answer.

So, after a long moment, she nods. "Okay."

"Okay."

Only then can I finally let out the breath I didn't know I was holding.

44

MIA

The whole ride, I rack my brain for a way to turn down Yulian's offer.

It's too much. I don't deserve it—and he certainly doesn't have the responsibility to fix my messes.

He's my employer. My side-boss. He's…

Kind. He's being kind to you, dummy.

The engine purrs under me. I sink into the warm leather seats, Yulian's touch still buzzing under my skin. He's in the driver's seat now, having sent Maksim off to hold down the fort for him—whether the company fort or the shadow fort, I'm not certain. Some things are better off staying mysteries.

Except the mystery of why Yulian's doing this.

It can't be to sleep with me. One, because he's already slept with me plenty; two, because by now, he's probably aware he doesn't need to wine and dine me to sleep with me at all; three, because you can't really get frisky with a kid on the road. Hyperactive four-year-olds with a habit of crawling into bed with Mommy don't exactly qualify as aphrodisiacs.

Which leaves me with only one possible explanation.

He cares.

I shake my head. I'm not ready to accept that. Because, if I let myself be lulled by this, I'll fall into something much worse than a false sense of security.

I'll *fall,* period.

And I can't have that. Not with Mr. Hot-and-Cold here, not with anyone.

Because Brad will find out.

And when he does, it won't just be me who pays the price.

The car slows to a stop. Upper East Side greenery greets me wherever I look, reminding myself of how different two worlds can be.

Mine and Yulian's, for instance. They should never have touched, but here we are, a fluke of fate that's unlikely to repeat itself. Unlikely to last.

But he came for you.

Yes. He did.

And I have no idea what that means.

"Mommy!"

I'm startled out of my thoughts by a small, happy voice. The only voice in the world that can make all my burdens melt away.

"Hey, munchkin." I smile, getting out of Yulian's car and walking up to Eli at the school gate, where a teacher stands off to the side, supervising the pick-up.

Eli's eyes widen at the sight of the Maybach. "Is that *ours?*"

It drags a laugh out of me. "Nope. Bit too big for our parking space."

"You should listen to your mom," a deep voice rumbles from the driver's seat. "She knows all about tow trucks."

"Yulian! You're here!" He doesn't quite crash into Yulian's knees, but it's a close thing. "Are we getting pizza again?"

"If you want," Yulian says. He has this way of speaking to Eli, like he's a slightly tinier adult, that Eli seems to absolutely adore. No baby speak, no cooing, no beating around the bush. It warms my heart to see it—how unexpectedly good Yulian can be with kids. With *my* kid. "But first, how'd you like to go on a mission?"

Eli's face lights up. His mouth falls open into the biggest grin I've ever seen, gap-toothed and filled with joy.

Happy.

And I realize I could never let anything get in the way of that.

Not even the doubts gnawing at my heart.

"Mommy! Can we bring Garfield, too?"

We've been packing for five minutes, and already, Eli's suitcase is filled with more toys than essentials.

"You can pick *one* plushie," I tell him. "We're going away for the weekend, not the rest of our lives."

Though it'd probably be the smarter thing to do.

Eli's face falls. "Just one?"

"I think we can make that three," Yulian chimes in from the doorway. "We'll be flying on my jet. No need to pack small. That is, if your mom's okay with it."

"Please?" Eli puts on his best puppy eyes.

I roll mine and give a resigned smile. "Fine. But only because Yulian's got his personal sky cab. Soon as we're back to flying coach, Garfield guards the door here."

"Thanks, Mommy!"

He didn't listen to a word I said after "fine," but the happiness in his voice still fills my heart to the brim.

"Thank Yulian," I say. "He's the one who invited us."

"Thanks, Yulian!"

As Eli goes back to the hard task of picking three toys for the road instead of three hundred, I slump against the doorway and exhale. Finally, the day's exhaustion has caught up with me. If walls were pillows, I'd be snoring already.

"Last chance to back out," I whisper. "Once he's picked his travel buddies, he'll be unstoppable."

"I'm a man of my word," Yulian drawls back. "And you look like you could use a getaway." His hand touches my cheek, resting just below my eye. "When's the last time you had a full night's rest?"

I try to ignore the way my heart quickens. The way heat blooms in the wake of Yulian's touch, lighting me up from the inside.

"I don't know," I answer honestly.

Ever since what happened the night of the StarTech investor gala—with Brad, with Eli, with Yulian—thoughts have been crowding my mind like moths dancing around a bonfire, refusing to step back from the flame. Whenever I try to close my eyes, it's never darkness that greets me on the other side. Just smoke from a window, cigarettes sizzling on flesh, and that almost-kiss in the kitchen. The kiss that could've changed everything.

The kiss I didn't let happen.

"You can catch some rest on the jet," Yulian murmurs. "I'll make sure Maksim flies it in circles for a while before landing."

"And doom the environment in the process?" I tease.

"I'll buy some carbon offset to atone for our emissions sins." His voice drops low, his face draws closer. Not quite enough to kiss, but enough to let me yearn for it. For everything this could be. "I assume that was the last of your excuses?"

"You're right," I whisper. My gaze keeps flitting from his ash gray eyes to his flame-licked lips. Summer's heat has long faded, and yet, I've never felt more like bursting into flames. "Joke's on me."

Eli's in his room. We're alone in the hallway. We could close the distance right now, steal this moment, make it ours.

We almost do.

And then the doorbell rings.

"*Blyat*," Yulian curses under his breath, right against my parted lips. "Must be Maksim."

"I'll get it." I make my escape like a thief: head low, feet light, heart pounding in my ears. What the hell is wrong with me? Have I learned nothing from last time I woke up in Yulian's bed? That I let him squeeze my heart until there was nothing left?

Have I learned nothing from my ex?

He's different. You know he is. It's that tiny voice at the back of my mind, the one I've tried so hard to suppress. My constant companion in all these sleepless nights. *He's far from perfect, but he cares about you. He cares about Eli.*

He wants you to be happy.

Soothed, I throw the door open. "I hope you've got snacks for the road, because—"

But it's not Maks.

"Ms. Winters," the frosty, nasal voice of Howard Lee greets me. "May we come in?"

45

YULIAN

The guy at the door looks like someone jammed a stick up his ass and then left it there, indefinitely, to fester.

He sounds like it, too. His words may be polite on the surface, but his tone isn't. Snotty, holier-than-thou, an idealist who thinks he's never made a mistake in his life and, therefore, believes people who do are inferior.

He isn't talking to Mia—he's talking *at* Mia. *Down* at her, specifically.

Next to him, an older woman with thick glasses and a cane smiles up at me.

I don't smile back.

"Right! Introductions," Mia interjects quickly, sliding between me and the rat-faced prick at the door.

Smart. She must have caught my death glare and decided she didn't have enough medical supplies in her home to reattach a head to a body, nor enough bleach to hide the fact.

"These are Mr. Lee and Mrs. Deloera," she explains. "Eli's caseworkers."

"Charmed."

I don't offer my hand to shake. The smiling old lady seems to know better than to expect it, but Rat Face turns up his nose. "And this would be…?" he demands.

"Him? Well, he's, err—"

I reach for my business card, but Mia stops me, white in the face.

"Boris!" she blurts. "He's, um, Boris."

Lee eyes me with impatience. "Boris what?"

"Uhh—" she falters. "J-Johnson."

What the hell?

She squeezes my hand, a silent plea to play along. I decide she must have a good reason to conceal my identity from her caseworkers.

Although, I won't lie: She could have done a less shit job of it.

Predictably, Lee's eyebrows scrape the ceiling. "This is *Boris Johnson?*"

"Well, obviously, not *the* Boris Johnson," Mia laughs awkwardly. Her palm has started to sweat. "Just, you know… *A* Boris Johnson."

Lee's gaze fixes on me, filled with suspicion to the brim. For once, I can't fucking blame him. "I see."

"I don't believe you were due for a visit," I say, swiftly changing the subject. "Not until the end of the month."

Mia's eyes widen, just a fraction. If she's shocked that I memorized her CPS appointments on top of her work schedule, she clearly has no idea what I'm capable of. When someone's mine, they are *mine.*

"I, um… yes," Mia stammers. "Guess this must be a drive-by." She's trying to make a joke, but only Mrs. Deloera offers a polite chuckle.

"I'd like to see the child now," Lee cuts in, practically sniffing the air.

Jesus Christ. I've never seen a more punchable face in my life, and I've been in a room with Bradley Baldwin.

My fist clenches at my side, but Mia's hand quickly skims over my knuckles. A silent *"please, don't make this worse."*

Reluctantly, I let out a breath and unclench. If there's one thing I've learned in my years as a Bratva *pakhan,* it's to recognize when I'm stepping into somebody else's fight. It's one of the rules of our creed: never rob a brother of their battles.

And Mia might not be a brother, but here, on her personal battlefield, she's as much a soldier as any of my men.

Lee's foot starts tapping the floor. "Now would be good," he presses. "If you don't mind."

"Not at all." Mia's smile is tight, twitchy. Her *you're lucky I swore an oath* smile, with a side of wistful thoughts about morgue drawers in need of a new occupant.

She leads the two caseworkers into Eli's room. "Eli! You've got visitors."

The boy's head pops up from a pile of clothes and plushies. "But we're gonna be late," he protests.

"Late for what?" Lee prods. His eyes dart immediately from the clothes to the open suitcase on the floor. "Going somewhere?"

Mia's face pales. "Not rea—"

"We're going on a mission!" Eli squeals. "To be spies!"

Lee's brow knits. "And where, exactly, will this mission be taking place?"

"Russia!"

His gaze zeroes in on me. "Is that so?"

"Of course not," Mia laughs awkwardly. "That would be—"

"None of your business," I cut in. Letting Mia fight her own battles and letting her take psychic damage from this *mudak*'s attitude are two very different things. She's had two panic attacks in front of me—I won't let this become the third. "Would it, *Mr. Lee?*"

His jaw flexes. "Actually, it is, Mr. Johnson. It just so happens that Eli Winters is in our custody as well as Ms. Winters's. And if you're taking him to Russia—"

"Montana," I correct.

"Montana?"

"I own a cabin there."

Technically, it's a ten-thousand square foot chalet made of cedar and oak, at the center of a thousand acres of woods, with a private landing site and hunting grounds.

But as far as Mr. Lee is concerned, "cabin" works just as well.

"Ms. Winters and her son will be back here by Sunday. He will not miss school."

"That's good to know," Lee says with a touch of sarcasm, "but I'm afraid it doesn't matter. Montana isn't in the state of New York."

"I wasn't aware we were debating middle-school geography."

"We're not. But unfortunately, Ms. Winters's probation is very clear on the relevance of *middle-school geography* to her case." He whips out a file from his suitcase and hands it to me. "Page 4, paragraph C: *The Respondent Mother shall not remove the subject child from the State of New York without prior written authorization from the Department of Child Protective Services and the express permission of the Family Court.*"

Next to me, Mia's face drains of all color.

"I'm assuming from Ms. Winters's face that she was not yet aware you were taking her there," Lee says with a pointed look at Mia. "Am I correct, Ms. Winters?"

"Yes," she says right away. "We hadn't, um—discussed it. Yet."

"Good." He checks a box on his clipboard. "Because, if you had, I would have had to report you."

"I'm sure Mia just forgot," Mrs. Deloera chimes in. "Right, dear?"

She gives the quickest nod in history.

"Then that's settled." The older woman waves at Eli, then at the rest of us. "Have a wonderful weekend within state lines! I'm sure you'll find another exciting place to visit."

"Ms. Winters," Lee says by way of goodbye. "Mr. Johnson."

Then they're both gone.

As soon as the door clicks shut, Mia leans against it. "*Blyat*.*"*

I frown. "Did you just swear in Russian?"

"Took a page from your book," she exhales. "Turns out, it's useful when you're around kids."

"Mommy?" Eli comes trudging over, his eyes lucid. "Does this mean we can't go to Russia? Or Montana?"

"That's right, honey." She crouches, gathering him up in her arms. "I'm so sorry. We'll go another time, okay?"

"It's because of Mr. Lee," he spits. "I *hate* him!"

"He's just doing his job. He wants you to be safe, okay? That's why he's so strict all the time."

"But I'm safe with you," he argues. "I'm safe with Yulian."

"Then we'll just have to prove that, won't we?" She kisses the top of his head. It's such an affectionate gesture, so uniquely *them,* I feel the urge to look away. Tear my gaze off this family that doesn't belong to me. "And how do we do that?"

"By being good," he recites.

"That's right. By being good." She presses one more kiss to his brow, then smiles. "Now, why don't you go pick tonight's dinner? You can have whatever you want."

"Even ice cream?"

"Even ice cream."

He doesn't look happy, but at least he's pacified. He trudges to the takeout menu drawer. He can't read yet, but he must know what the logos stand for, because he starts sorting the leaflets into "yes/maybe/no" piles.

Regret grips my chest. I'm not used to it at all, let alone in situations like these. Low stakes, where no one's bleeding out on a dirty warehouse floor, or under a white-clothed table.

I'm not used to apologizing, either.

"I talked too much. I shouldn't have."

"You couldn't have known." Mia finds my clenched fists and rubs them, softly smoothing over the tension. One by one, she unfurls the fingers of my right hand until she can intertwine them with hers. "Thank you, though. For offering this. I'm sorry we couldn't make it happen."

Next time. It's on my tongue, but it's also a lie. Because I have no idea if there will be one. If Mia will ever be by my side again.

What kind of piece of shit would do that to her? Put her in danger all over again, just because he's scared to let go?

You, the ugly voice inside me sneers. *You would.*

Not anymore.

"We should talk," I tell her, steeling myself. "About your contract."

Mia blinks up at me. There's hope in her eyes, a spark that dances around the blue like a firefly lost at sea. "What, um… what about it?"

Do it. Break her heart.

Break her, and then save her.

"Mommy! Can Yulian stay for dinner?"

Eli's voice shatters the moment. He trots to me, two takeout menus in hand, like he can't quite decide.

"I..." I swallow around the lump in my throat. "I have to get to work."

"Oh." His face falls, eyes downcast. "Can we come, then? And eat later?"

"Eli," Mia starts, "Yulian's very busy. He can't just—"

"Alright."

Her eyes bulge. "What?"

All my life, I've fought against weakness. Before I was *pakhan,* and then after, building a fortress around me every day. One that couldn't be pierced by bullets, or knives, or cracked by the same feelings that almost broke me once.

Grief.

Loss.

Love.

Tonight, I lose that battle.

Willingly.

"I've got to check on Tikhon. Make sure he hasn't blown up the lab." I crouch low, as close as I can to Eli's height. "Would you like to see how spy tech is made?"

His eyes brighten on the spot. Blue pools of light, just like his mother's. "Really?!"

"If your mother says it's okay."

We both turn to her. "Can we, Mommy?" Eli pleads.

Guilt has never gripped me tighter. I was supposed to protect them. To end the contract. It would crush their hearts, but in doing so, it would save their lives.

But I'm not ready to let go yet.

One more night.

Just one more night, and I'll do it.

One more night with the family I'll never have.

Mia's face melts into a smile. Soft, warm, like milk and honey. "Okay," she whispers.

One more night, and then it's over.

46

MIA

The second we step into StarTech's R&D floor, Eli tugs himself free from my hand and hurtles towards the glass cases. "This is *sooo* cool!"

I have to agree. This place is, in fact, pretty damn cool. Like waking up in the year 3000. A whole floor tiled in seamless black, with overhead lights shining down in cold, classy hues on the prototypes on display. Every glass case contains a different gadget, all sleek and high-tech.

Predictably, Eli starts zapping from one glass case to the other. "Slow down, honey!" I caution, but to no avail.

"It's okay," Yulian promises. "We take extreme precautions to make sure safety measures are always in place. No one can get hurt in here."

"But won't he bother the engineers?"

"They're on the upper floor." He nods towards the sleek gray ceiling. "Key readers in front of every lab door. He couldn't stumble in if he tried."

The weight on my chest immediately lifts. "Thanks," I exhale. "Seriously, I don't know how I'm ever going to repay you. First for the trip, and then this."

"The trip tanked because of me." He shrugs. "This was the least I could do."

I don't know if I'll ever get used to this—Yulian's softer side. The warmth he radiates, like the sun itself, reserved for the few privileged ones he lets close enough to feel it.

We should talk. About your contract.

I shouldn't let myself hope. I know better than that. But the way he said those words, the intensity of his gaze as he spoke them—I can't get them out of my mind. What if…?

What if he doesn't want to keep this up anymore? The farce, the charade?

What if he wants something real?

"Hey there!" Tikhon's voice crashes into my thoughts. "Nice seeing you back here, Mia! Wanted to check on the PulseCheckr?"

"The, um, what?"

"Your idea!" His eyes light up. "I've been tinkering with a prototype; you should see it! Such a beauty. Smaller than a fingernail."

"Oh," I blink, trying to process the mile-a-minute speed of Tikhon's speech. Warmth spreads in my stomach at the idea of having been useful—to him, to the company, to *Yulian.* "That's amazing. I'm glad I could—"

"So far, ingestion hasn't proved to be a problem," he

continues, completely unaware I've spoken at all, "except for Dave. But you know Dave, always choking on his food—"

"Tikhon," Yulian cuts in impatiently. "Not now."

"Yessir! Sorry, sir!"

"And stop poisoning your coworkers. You're one HR complaint away from me having to transfer you to Siberia."

That seems to actually terrify him. "Not Siberia! They're still looking for me there!"

"Then I guess you'll have to leave the break room fridge alone."

His shoulders slump. "I should've taken the job with Neura. *They'd* have let me put chips wherever I liked."

"Go on, then." Yulian says it with the confidence of someone who knows it's never gonna happen. "See what they offer."

"No way. Last time, the HR gal threw up when she saw my BGC. Besides, they wanted me to work for *six* figures. What am I gonna do, starve?"

"Then go dig up whatever you stuffed in Dave's pierogi." Tikhon starts to trudge away, but Yulian puts a hand on his shoulder, spinning him back where he was. "But first, you're going to give someone a tour."

Then he points to Eli, whose face is currently plastered against a glass pane.

"Oh!" Tikhon beams. "What have we here? A young fan, perhaps?"

Eli unsticks himself from the case. "Hi," he mumbles shyly, half-hiding behind me.

"Eli," Yulian says, "this is Tikhon, my chief engineer. He's the one who makes all the spy gadgets."

"Spy—?" A glare from Yulian shuts Tikhon right up. "O-of course! The *spy* gadgets!"

Eli's face instantly brightens. "Really?!"

"Really." Tikhon crouches down, quick to play along. "Wanna see more of them?"

"Can I, Mommy?!"

"Knock yourself out," I grin. "But behave, you hear me? Don't give Tikhon any trouble, or I'll know."

"With the Mommy-Sense?"

"Precisely."

He scurries off excitedly with Tikhon, who also looks like he's having the time of his life. Where else is he going to find someone who'll actually *listen* for five minutes in a row?

Knowing Eli, he'll "ooh" and "aah" in all the right places, too. If anyone can match Tikhon's crazy about nanotech, that's the kid I've raised on pizza and James Bond.

"'Mommy-Sense'?" Yulian asks as soon as they're gone.

"It tingles when he's naughty."

He shakes his head, but I catch the hint of a smile there. Dimples don't lie.

Yulian catches me staring. His smirk turns wolfish, hungry and knowing.

"So," I say, eager to redirect this buzz in the air literally anywhere else, "is tech all you do here?"

"That's a bold question to ask."

He draws closer. His cologne fills my lungs, making it really hard to steer my thoughts away from where they're headed. Every time that scent hits my nostrils, the memories come flooding back, reminding me of how *close* I've been to the source of it.

His skin, his body.

No clothes in between.

Get it together, Mia. You can't jump him in a room full of nanotech. That's got to be a health code violation.

"Well, you're not any other CEO," I say, staring with interest at the black-tiled floor. "I'm guessing there's a rotating bookcase somewhere that leads to the bowels of the Earth?"

"Where I keep my torture dungeons?" That dimple deepens, amusement lighting up every corner of his face. It's so subtle, most would miss it. But then again, "most" haven't been on this man's arm for enough dates to make it feel so damn *real*. "Flay my enemies alive for their secrets?"

"Something like that."

He seems to consider something. Pauses just long enough to make me wonder if I've overstepped.

Then, as if winning a mental argument with himself, he gives a single nod and beckons me to follow.

We walk up to the far edge of the room. The glass cases with the prototypes grow bigger here, turning into floor-to-ceiling tubes.

"Maybe I was wrong about the dungeons," I quip, more to

calm down my nerves than anything else. "Maybe you've got a secret lab."

"Sounds interesting. What would I make there?"

"Beats me." I shrug. "Replicants. Androids. Pokémon."

With a final curve of his lips, he pushes on a tile.

And the wall. Freaking. *Moves.*

I catch my jaw before it can shatter on the floor. My eyeballs, too, lest they roll under the conveyor belts.

Because there's conveyor belts *everywhere* in here.

The low whirring of printing presses catches my attention. "I assume you're not making Peppa Pig stickers here?"

"I'm sure that could be arranged." He puts a hand on my shoulder, steering me in the right direction. "Look closer."

I lean over the railing and squint. From this high up, it's hard to see the details, but at the same time, you just can't miss it. Can't mistake what they're printing for anything else.

"Money," I whisper.

"Bingo." His palm moves to my back, rubbing circles into it. Soothing, maybe, or keeping me from bolting out the door with all his secrets. "Want a private tour?"

I shouldn't. This is why spousal privilege was made, and guess what? Fake fiancées don't have it. I should squeeze my eyes shut, plead the Fifth, clutch the concept of plausible deniability with both hands.

Instead, I freaking *nod.*

What the hell is wrong with me?

I don't get to explore that thought further, though. Soon, Yulian is guiding me down a steel staircase, each of my steps echoing like a gunshot. My pulse keeps thundering in my throat, louder with every heartbeat.

Am I afraid? Excited? A kinky mix of both I should probably bring up with a therapist?

I have no idea. All I know is that *this*—whatever it is—is Yulian, too.

And I want to know every part of him.

We get down to the conveyor belts. My eyes bulge when I realize just how many currencies are being slapped on what has got to be the most expensive stationery paper in existence: euros, pounds, francs, yen. Freaking *rubles,* too.

"No dollars?"

"I don't shit where I eat."

"Smart." I shrug. "OSHA-compliant, too."

He gives me a disbelieving laugh. "I'm showing you my secret dungeon. The least you could do is act cowed."

"Oh, I'm cowed, believe me," I reply, with a tone that isn't cowed at all. "Full cow. One-hundred percent premium beef."

"A nurse *and* a comedian. Talk about a triple threat."

"What's the third?"

Suddenly, Yulian's palm crawls down to my ass. He squeezes. "Right here," he drawls.

I bite my lip bloody not to moan. The way those hands are kneading me—*God,* where's a bed when you need one? Or even a flat, non-moving surface without stacks of illegally forged foreign banknotes on it?

I'm about to settle for the floor when I realize we aren't alone. *"Dobryy vecher, pakhan."*

Yulian answers with a nod. Not for the first time, I wonder if it's not too late to download Duolingo.

A few more men greet us as we pass, but not as many as I'd expected in a place this big.

Yulian seems to read my mind. "We're striving for full automation. Fewer accidents that way."

"Are we talking smudged edges or limbs crushed under the presses?"

"Both."

The way he says it makes a chill run down my spine. So business-like. So… cold.

And yet, at the same time, I realize that can't be all there is. Because who would care enough about maimed Bratva grunts to actually tweak things to prevent it? Why invest in state-of-the-art machinery like this instead of cutting corners unless you actually gave a shit?

Unless you actually *cared?*

"Is this why you're running StarTech?" It's a hunch, a wild guess, nothing more. "Because you're concerned with… safety?"

He doesn't meet my gaze. "Every Bratva needs a good cover."

"Not this good. Not with a CEO dropping by every day to check on his prototypes."

"If the CEO isn't involved with his company, the company won't stay profitable for long."

"Would it matter?" I point with my thumb towards the piles of fake money. "It's not like you need it to be."

His throat works. I can tell I've hit the nail on the head, but also that he wishes I hadn't. That whatever secret I've stumbled upon isn't one he intended to share. Not tonight. Perhaps not ever.

Eventually, he exhales. "You're a nosy little thing, you know that?"

"Got it on a bumper sticker."

"Of course you do." His lip twitches, but only for a moment. "I lost people."

It's just three words, but they hit like bullets. "Soldiers?"

He shakes his head. "No. That comes with the territory. The ones I've lost—they shouldn't have been targeted to begin with. At least two of them were completely innocent. And those who weren't..." a sharp intake of breath. "They still shouldn't have been killed that night."

Finally, realization dawns upon me. I've held the hands of too many people in waiting rooms not to recognize the sadness in Yulian's eyes.

"Your family," I whisper.

He doesn't deny it. "They were after me. Instead, they got them. My parents, my sister." His fist clenches and unclenches, as if trying to squeeze out the emotions like bad blood from a wound.

For a man like Yulian Lozhkin, there is no worse infection than a beating heart.

"My best friend, too. Kira. She had nothing to do with our family, but she took a bullet for me anyway."

"Why?"

"They thought she was going to be my fiancée." A cold, bitter laugh. "They didn't know the first thing about her. We were like siblings. And she never would have let herself be tied down by marriage. Not to me, not to anyone."

He thinks it's his fault. He thinks he's why they died.

A lump settles in my throat, but I force myself to swallow it. This isn't my pain. This isn't my guilt. No matter how familiar it feels, how white-hot and burning, it's nothing compared to what I've gone through. I only *thought* I'd lost my child—but to actually lose him? To lose the only family I've got left, and feel like I was responsible?

I'd never feel at peace again. Not as long as I was alive.

"I'm sorry." It's the only thing I can think to say. The only thing worth saying in the face of all this pain. I knew Yulian had no family—I had no idea he'd lost them so violently. "You shouldn't have had to go through that. It was unfair."

"Life's unfair."

"It didn't have to be. Not for you."

Hesitantly, I touch my hand to his shoulder. I'm prepared to feel him flinch away, shrug me off like an insect, crush me for even daring.

But he doesn't.

"I couldn't catch their killers then," he growls instead, filling the well of his pain with something easier, something manageable: anger. "But fuck if I'll ever let that happen again."

"That's what StarTech is about," I whisper. "Making people safe."

"No one should ever be unsafe in their own homes," he snarls. "At the office. At school. War should stick to war zones. Casualties shouldn't be random. That's why we have soldiers."

I get the feeling he isn't talking about the U.S. Army. That his wars have always taken place on much different battlefields, away from the sunlight and the surface.

That's where he wants to keep them—in *his* world.

Away from *ours.*

Away from mine.

"It's a noble thing to do."

"It's not. It's the least I could do."

"But you're doing it." I give his shoulder another soft squeeze. "That's more than most in your position have tried."

"How would you know?"

"I work at the ER. I've lost more patients to guns than cancer." I give a watery smile. "So, if someone's trying to fix that? I don't care who they are. I don't care what they've done. They're doing it. That's what matters."

Yulian's gaze flickers from me to the floor. I've never seen him so evasive—so obviously uncomfortable.

"What happened with Kira..." he starts, throat working around words that won't come. "I cannot guarantee it won't happen again."

I wonder if this is why Yulian doesn't have a girlfriend. A real one, without contracts and timestamps. If losing Kira scarred him so badly he's afraid to ever try.

"It was a long time ago," I try to reason with him.

"It's who I am," he counters. "I'm a powerful man, a dangerous man. As long as I'm *pakhan,* I'll have enemies."

"I've been your fake girlfriend for a couple of months now." I slide my palm down his arm, tug on his hand. Coax his gaze back on me instead of the cold tiled floor. "I'm still here. Nothing's happened to me."

"That's not—"

"Here." Slowly, I move his hand to the center of my chest. Slightly off to the left—right over my heart. "See? Still beating."

He swallows. His jaw flexes, but it doesn't look like anger, for once. It looks like conflict.

It looks like—

"Mommy!"

From above, Eli waves down at us. Tikhon's there, holding on to his hand, preventing him from trying to run off somewhere he shouldn't.

"Sorry about the interruption!" he laughs. "This little scientist was wondering about pizza. And ice cream?"

The spell breaks. Yulian's hand slips quickly from my grasp, his composure returning like a veil of ice.

"Yes," he says. "I believe that's what was promised."

"Lucky you," Tikhon sighs wistfully. "I wish I had pizza and ice cream in my contract."

I shake my head, but can't help smiling.

As we make our way back up, I press myself close to Yulian. "Thank you," I whisper. "For telling me."

"I hadn't meant to." His eyes are still wandering away from mine. "I was supposed to tell you about the company."

"You have. You've told me more than you think."

"Have I now?"

Yes. You've told me you want to make the world a better place. That you don't want the darkness of the underworld to spill into the surface. That you'll do everything you can to prevent it.

You told me you care.

Before I can answer, we get ambushed by a tiny ball of excitement. "Tikhon says I can work here when I grow up! I can be his append—appro—"

"Apprentice?" I laugh. "That sounds wonderful. But you have to work hard, okay? Do all your homework once school starts."

"I will!"

We bid goodbye to Tikhon. "Thanks for doing this," I tell him. "It means the world."

"Are you kidding? I loved having a little intern around. Best brainstorming companion I've had since Pyotr took his sabbatical."

We each take one of Eli's hands and walk out of StarTech. Yulian suggests he treat us to the snazziest pizza in town.

Yulian. A brutal, hardened *pakhan* with no morals. That's who I thought he was at first.

Now, I realize I couldn't have been further off from the truth.

Because he's also the man who saved me. The man who protected me from a rain of bullets, who shielded me with his body and dragged me to safety when he barely knew me. The man who stepped between me and Brad twice. The man who dropped everything to care for me and my kid when I needed it.

The man I love.

47

YULIAN

I take them to my favorite restaurant.

It's a pizza place in the heart of Manhattan: white tablecloth, wine glasses, complimentary champagne. Not exactly hole-in-the-wall goodness.

Nor is it suited for a child.

But Eli is so busy staring at everything with wide eyes that he ends up behaving impeccably. He leaves most of his pizza uneaten because "the sauce is not right," but practically inhales the crusts.

"You should take it as a compliment," Mia laughs as we're taking a walk around the block, Eli snoozing on her hip. "He *never* eats the crusts."

She's beautiful. She always is. But tonight, there's something about her I just can't place. Something that makes her face shine brighter, her eyes light up like stars.

Soon, she won't be looking at me like that anymore.

By the time we're back at her place, Eli is still sound asleep. I start to ask, "Do you need—"

Help carrying him upstairs? The words stick in my throat halfway out. I've got no right to ask that. Not when I've been placing his mother in unspeakable danger.

"—anything else?" I finish instead.

"Like the moon?" Her laugh echoes in the darkness of Brownsville night. A sound so pure has no place there, in the depths of everything dirty and discarded, but it rings out all the same. "Nah, thanks. I'm fine here, down on boring ol' Earth."

"Too bad. Had my spaceship parked down the road."

"Parked or double-parked?"

"If I didn't know better, I'd say that sounds like you're threatening me with a tow truck. Again."

We're close enough to kiss. I can tell she wants to. One sign from me, one look, and her eyes will fall shut, lashes fluttering like blue-winged butterflies.

I draw back. "I should get going. Business to be finished."

"Yeah," she says, quickly bouncing back from the moment. "Me, too. Got an early shift tomorrow."

"I know."

Her eyes narrow, but her lips curve playfully. "Are you stalking me, Mr. Lozhkin?"

Yes. All the time. Even when I'm elsewhere. Even when I shouldn't be thinking about you at all.

"If I was, you'd never know."

"Guess I'll have to catch you in the act, then."

It's a promise. Soft, dark, alluring.

I don't let myself be tempted.

"Goodnight, Mia."

"Goodnight, Yulian."

Then she's gone.

Afterwards, I drive for hours. Just on and on, drawing circles around New York, burning gas like it's free.

By the time I make it back to the office, Maks is waiting for me. "Back so soon from your trip?"

"Couldn't go. CPS showed up and vetoed it." I shrug off my jacket and hang it. "But you already knew that. Otherwise, you wouldn't be here."

"Eh. Little bird might've told me."

"Little bird by the name of Kalinda?"

"What can I say? Girls text each other. Like, all the time."

I circle my desk. Maksim stands, makes room for me at my seat, and I squint at him. "Did you call them? CPS?"

"Me?" He barks out a laugh. "Fuck's sake, no. Though it might've been smart."

"It would have kept me here," I say suspiciously. "I know how you feel about Mia."

"Okay, one: I'm no rat. Would I take candy from a baby? Yes. Would I tell their mom if they took candy from me? No way in hell."

"Hm." I'm not the trusting type, but it fits. "And second?"

"Second: I don't feel any particular way about Mia. I feel about the way *you* feel about Mia."

"If you're trying to give me a headache, you're succeeding."

"Did you even need me for that?" He peers at me. "From where I'm standing, it looks like you're doing fine yourself. Unless those narrowed eyes are a sign of sudden onset astigmatism."

"Maybe I'm suspicious."

"You always are. But you rarely let it show."

Game, set, match. As always, Maks knows me way better than I wish he did. That's on me for letting him, but then again, only one person was there when my family was turned into Swiss cheese in front of my eyes.

Maksim Goncharov—my late father's freshest recruit.

Everybody else ran, but he didn't. He got me out of there. Even as I was screaming and kicking, clawing at the carpet to stay with the bodies of everyone I'd ever loved, he got me out of there.

He hasn't let go since.

It's the only reason I don't punish him for his insolence. The only reason I let him get away with commenting on my relationship with Mia.

Deep down, I know Maksim is the only person who will never lead me astray.

Of course, there was Nikita. But Nikita is lost in the wind, and her scent isn't exactly blowing this way.

"You can rest easy," I sigh, slumping into my chair. Maks is right—there's a killer migraine right behind my temples that's torturing me worse than my enemies ever could. "I'm done. I'm ending the contract first thing tomorrow. We'll find someone else to play bait."

"You can't."

My head snaps up. "Excuse me?"

"Before you bite my head off, look." Without the slightest hint of a smile, Maksim slides a file my way. His tone is dead serious, which tells me this must be, too. "While following Nikita's trail, I stumbled upon something. I was going to call you once you landed, but this is better, actually. I never thought I'd say it, but thank God for cops."

In the dim light of my office, I have to squint to see what he's talking about. The page he's showing me is filled with numbers. Dates, figures, timestamps.

"Tell me what I'm looking at."

"Our enemies are moving." He points at a few key rows. "I'm afraid we must've spooked them. Warehouses emptying out, street corners freeing up all of a sudden, warlords looking for new weapon suppliers." When he speaks next, he stares me dead in the eyes. "They're leaving, Yulian. They're packing up shop, retreating overseas."

Maksim's words freeze my blood. "You can't know that."

"With people like these, you can't know anything. But what else could it be?"

Anything. Literally anything else. But no matter how badly I wish it, I know he's right. Fuck me, I *know.*

"How long until they're gone?"

"Two weeks, maybe three."

Shit. Shit, shit, shit. Fury fills my thoughts, swirling with a panic I haven't known for a long while. Cold, all-encompassing, gutting.

I'm going to lose them.

I'm never going to find Nikita.

I'm never going to avenge my family.

"*BLYAT'!*" I slam my palms on the desk, sending papers flying. "How did we not notice sooner?!"

"Because they're damn good at what they do," Maksim replies, unfazed by my outburst. "So if you want to get them, Yulian, you're going to have to lay a damn good trap. With damn good bait."

I know what this means. Deep in my gut, I've always known. I've tried to run from this, rewrite the story, reshape reality to suit whatever I wanted to believe. That I could save her *and* get my revenge.

But that would have been fair.

And the world has rarely been fair to me.

Maksim draws closer. "You have to choose, Yulian." For once, his voice is quiet. Pained. "Either you end the contract, or you end Prizrak. There is no more time."

Choose. Between Mia and my family. Her safety, or my revenge.

It's an impossible choice. It's absurd. It's cruel.

But it's the hand I've been dealt.

It was never going to end any other way.

48

MIA

After that Friday night with Yulian, the weekend flies by. When I get home from my early shift the next day, I spend the rest of my free time curled up on the couch with my kid, watching cartoons and guzzling popcorn, with the occasional trip to the park to pet other people's dogs and play hopscotch with the potholes.

It's the most relaxed I've felt in ages. It's *fun.* It's...

Missing something.

No, not "something."

Someone.

I try to brush the thought away. Ever since Friday night, Yulian hasn't been in touch. I've texted once to thank him again for everything, but he hasn't replied. Not to that, not to the daily selfies, nothing.

He's probably just busy. And maybe, just maybe, he's feeling raw about what he shared.

Yulian doesn't strike me as the type to ever have a heart-to-heart, least of all in a money-printing basement, under the whir of machinery, with the woman he hired to play girlfriend.

But is that still all I am to him?

I shake my head, force myself to think about literally anything else. What's brewing between me and Yulian could be a love story or a recipe for disaster. Either way, I can't afford to let it distract me.

Because today, I'm going back to work.

As I walk through the ER doors, my heart starts pounding against my ribcage. I keep stealing glances towards Bay C, half-expecting the curtain to move and reveal that razor-sharp smirk, those dark eyes filled with cruelty.

"Nurse Winters?"

Gwen's voice snaps me out of my thoughts. "Y-yes?"

She pauses in front of me, arms crossed, considering. There's a trace of impatience on her brow, but also concern. It dawns on me she might have called my name more than once before I finally heard her.

Shit. Great first day back, Florence Nightingale.

After what feels like interminable silence, Gwen sighs, "You're wanted upstairs."

"Upstairs?"

"Seventh floor."

I blink. "The *admin* floor?"

"Unless they've been wheeled into the basement overnight, then yes. The admin floor."

I'm used to Gwen being snappy and sarcastic, but today, something feels off with her. Like she isn't just being mad at the world at large, but at something very specific.

On the off-chance that it's me, I give the quickest nod in history and hurtle towards the elevator. I don't even get changed first. Just bolt for the closing doors and squeeze in.

The seventh floor. Come to think of it, I haven't been back there since my contract was made permanent. It's where the hospital's bureaucrats reside, scalpels traded for ballpoint pens and red tape.

Which means this can't be good.

Calm down, Mia. Maybe there was a typo in your last patient's chart.

Maybe they're finally giving you that raise you asked for last year.

Or maybe they're firing your ass.

Before my anxiety can win the Olympic gold for jumping to the worst possible conclusion in the shortest amount of time, I slam the brakes on my thoughts.

Then, when the elevator goes *ping* at my floor, I fling myself out of there.

And collide with a horribly familiar white suit.

The scent hits me first. Expensive, artificial, sanitized, like the chemicals used at the morgue to mask the smell of death.

Then his laugh.

Grating. Mocking. *Close.*

He catches my forearms, "helps" me back upright. Only I can feel the way his hands linger, snakelike, feeling the soft skin of my inner arm before slinking away like silk.

"Speak of the devil," he croons.

That's my line, asshole.

"Brad." I step back, my teeth gritted so tight I might need a trip to Orthodontics. "Fancy seeing you here. Again."

"Excuse me." An older man with gray hair and a pair of half-moon glasses steps between us. "Please refrain from addressing my client directly."

"'Refrain from'—?" I balk. "Smithers, you *know* me."

"I have no such recollection." The man adjusts his glasses and fixes me with a cold, impassive stare. "Now, if you'd please step back, Ms. Winters."

Swallowing my frustration, I do as he asks. One, because I don't actually mind being *further* away from Brad.

And two, because I know exactly who this man is: Theodore Smithers, the Baldwin family's infamous shark lawyer.

Which begs the question of what the fuck he's doing here.

A bureaucrat in a brown suit clears his throat. Someone who works for the hospital, though I don't recognize him. "Seems like we're all here," he says. "If you'd kindly follow me, gentlemen, Nurse Winters."

"Wait," I say. "What's going—?"

Then I see him

Dr. Adams.

If the Chief of Surgery is here, it means this is bad. Like, earth-shatteringly bad. He loathes his bureaucratic duties like no one else. Doesn't move from his OR unless the MRI machine is on fire or the hospital's about to get sued into the ground.

And since I can't smell barbecue...

I'm fucked, aren't I?

"Gentlemen. Thank you for coming." He shakes both their hands. "Nurse Winters," he adds, sans handshake and with the sourest tone I've ever heard.

Fuck. Fuckity-fuck-fuck, with a side of duck with an F. I have no idea whether my contract of employment includes an exclusivity clause, but clearly, it must, right? Because there can only be one reason we're all here.

Brad found out about my *other* contract.

The one with Yulian.

And he's here to rat me out to whoever will listen.

We're made to sit on a C-shaped leather couch bigger than my whole living room. It goes around a glass coffee table. No coffee is provided, but then again, why would it? I'm about to face my doom. Meet my maker, at least career-wise.

God, I'll never work in this city again, will I?

I brace myself for the inevitable. Consider begging, too.

"As you all know, there was an unfortunate incident last week which we're all here to resolve. Mr. Smithers, the floor is yours."

An unfortunate incident? For a second, I allow hope to bloom in my chest. Hope that, in some counterintuitive way, this whole circus is actually for my benefit.

Because what other incident could have happened last week, if not Brad trying to send me fishing for his trouser trout?

"Thank you, Dr. Adams." Smithers fixes his papers on the coffee table before rising. "Last week, Ms. Winters provided my client with ineffective care. As a result, he's suffered."

I blink. Resist the urge to stick my fingers into my ears and dig for wax, because clearly, I can't have heard right. "What?"

"Please, do not interrupt." He flicks his beady gaze to me, then goes back to his papers. "At the hour of 2:13 P.M., Mr. Baldwin came into the ER of this hospital with acute pain in his left arm. It was aching, swollen. There, Ms. Winters examined him—if it can even be called that. She sent him home with a prescription for, I quote, 'a cold shower.'"

"Hey!" I snap. "He was perfectly healthy. Only *one* part of him was aching and swollen, and it wasn't his damn—"

"Ms. Winters, if you can't keep silent during these proceedings, we will be forced to put this in the hands of a judge."

"For a sore wrist?!"

"Quiet down, Winters!" Adams barks at me. "You'll have your turn to respond."

I bite my lip and reluctantly obey.

"Very well." Smithers clears his throat. All the while, Brad sits cross-legged, perfectly silent and triumphant, happy to let others do his dirty work for him. "As I was saying, my client was not provided effective care. Later in the night, his chest pains grew worse—"

"He never mentioned any chest pains," I cut in, but they ignore me.

"He then drove himself to Manhattan General, where he was promptly put under observation," Smithers drones on. "An EKG revealed he was in the early stages of a heart attack."

My face drains. *"Heart attack?"*

"Here." Smithers provides both Adams and me with a copy of the EKG. "As you can see, he should have gotten immediate care. Luckily, the staff at Manhattan General took him seriously before the damage done by Nurse Winters here could become... irreparable."

My hands are shaking as I hold up the EKG. Guilt swallows me whole. Arm pain—that's textbook early heart attack. There are clear signs here, signs I shouldn't have missed, signs that—

Wait. Did he say his *left* arm?

"When you came here," I say to Brad, "you said it was your right arm that hurt. Specifically, your wrist. Didn't you?"

Brad opens his mouth, but Smithers cuts him off. "Don't answer that."

"Why not?" I retort. "He's the patient. He should remember what brought him into the ER. Better than that, it will be in our records."

Brad's eyes widen in realization. "It's possible I misspoke at the triage desk," he says briskly. "But when I saw Nurse Winters, I am certain I informed her of exactly where the pain was."

No shit. You forced me to cop a feel, too.

"There's a smudge on this EKG," I point out. "Right here, next to the patient name. And this data isn't consistent with a man of your age and—"

"Ms. Winters," Smithers growls, "if you insist on denying your mistake, we'll have no choice but to take this to court."

"I'm certain Nurse Winters knows better than to cost this hospital a lawsuit with its newest, biggest donor," Adams hisses, his tone like ice. "Especially when she's already facing a month's suspension without pay."

"What?" I say. "You can't suspend me. I didn't do anything wrong. I need this job, I—"

"I don't care," Adams snarls. "You made this mess. A month off will teach you respect. Now, Mr. Smithers, is there anything else we can do to ease your client's recovery?"

"There is." He fixes me with a condescending gaze. "In his infinite generosity, my client is prepared to overlook the incident."

"Great," I rasp. "Then we're done here. If you'll excuse me—"

"*Provided,*" he interrupts, "that Ms. Winters apologizes."

I'm seething. Burning with rage like never before. "No," I spit.

"Excuse me?"

"I said no." I stand up and get in Smithers's face. "He comes here with fake analyses, trumped-up charges, and then expects *me* to apologize?" I point at Brad, still sitting leisurely on the couch, like a king on his freaking throne. "Like hell I will."

"Nurse Winters." Dr. Adams stands up too, his voice like ice. "Do it."

"No."

"Apologize now," he growls. "Or I won't stop at a suspension."

Betrayal burns behind my eyes. I knew Adams hated me, but to this point?

It's not that, the rational part of me says. *Brad's a donor now. Adams isn't going to piss on the hand that feeds him.*

If I refuse now, I can kiss my job goodbye. I can kiss my *life* goodbye.

And I won't let Brad take that from me again.

I swallow the lump in my throat. Then, staring Brad right in the face, I grit out, "I'm sorry."

"Didn't sound like you meant that, *Nurse Winters.*"

"I. Am. Sorry." I spit each word like venom. "Are we done now?"

"I believe so." Dr. Adams shakes their hands again. "Gentlemen. My assistant will show you out."

"See you soon, sweet thing," Brad drawls on his way out.

I clench my fists. Humiliation is burning in my veins. I'm this close to crying, but I won't let the tears fall.

I won't let him see me break.

49

YULIAN

Cards slap down in quiet rhythm. A flick, a breath, the shuffle of chips.

"More vodka," Rurik snaps at a tux-wearing waiter.

Same old Rurik. Utterly unsuited to this game as he is to everything else that requires more than thirty seconds of deliberation.

Russian poker isn't about luck—it's a test of patience. Reading your opponents before they get a read on you.

I needed a distraction, though this wasn't my first choice. If it were up to me, I'd be shooting targets in the woods tonight. *Moving* targets, ideally. Spies we caught, enemies we saved for later like canned beans in a doomsday bunker.

But it's been too long since I've kept tabs on my *vory*. Leave this bunch alone too long, and they'll start plotting your demise. Fucking sharks, but that's exactly why I have them.

The Goldenrod's private lounge is thick with smoke and vodka. It's overbearing, but it helps.

Anything to chase her scent away.

Kazimir lounges back, a smug grin plastered on his face. He tosses a queen of hearts over a half-built straight. A bluff. As always.

Slavik leans forward, fingers steepled, eyes hawkish. He plays a slow, deliberate game, folding a full house just to bait Rurik into false confidence.

The Volkov twins sit across from me. Zhenya pushes her luck with a bold raise on three of a kind, her poker face perfectly unfazed.

"Damn, Sis. You got me." Anton flashes his cards before folding with a wink.

Rurik knocks back his third shot of *horilka* and sneers. He tosses a messy pile of chips forward with a jack-high hand.

Maksim grins like a madman, a Cuban cigar hanging from his teeth. He's playing recklessly, but then again, when isn't he?

"Nice hand," he whistles at Rurik. "Not as nice as this one, though." He tosses two queens on the table.

I tap my knuckles against the felt. "I raise."

"Our *pakhan* plays a dangerous game," Kazimir teases. "Someone bolstering your courage, boss? Perhaps your girl?"

The mention of Mia is enough to make my knuckles go white. *Fucking Kazimir.* Never knows when to shut his vodka hole.

"Shut up and play," I growl.

"She's not his," Rurik grumbles. The ice in my voice seems to have gone way over his head. "Not yet."

"You're so old-fashioned," Anton sighs. "He will marry her. It's only a matter of time. And when he does, it will be good."

"Will it?" Rurik grumbles. "If you say so."

"Of course it will," Slavik bristles. "A married *pakhan* sends a message. It tells our allies we're strong, stable. Most of all, it tells our enemies."

"You bunch sure love to talk." Maksim barks a laugh. "I thought we were here to play, not gossip like bridesmaids."

"How about you put your money where your big mouth is?" Rurik snaps.

"Sure." Maksim pushes all his chips in the center. "How's this? All in."

Whistles slice the air. Slavik and Rurik follow suit, too competitive to let someone else steal the spotlight. Kazimir, too, because he's an agent of chaos and thrives on it.

Anton folds. Zhenya keeps her cards close, lost in thought, and doesn't say anything.

"Something on your mind, *sestra*?" Anton asks.

"Maybe she misses the gossip," Kazimir says. "Maybe she actually wanted to play bridesmaid."

Zhenya shoots him a glare that says *I'll turn you into a bridesmaid if you don't shut the fuck up.* But then her face turns thoughtful again.

"The wedding will be good for us," she says.

"Forgive me if I don't take your word for it," Rurik snarks.

"Then don't. Take history's. Empires strengthen with bonds," she observes, as if reading off a goddamn textbook. "And heirs."

That word lands heavy.

"That's a bit premature," Anton laughs awkwardly, aware of how dark my glare has turned. "But sure, I suppose that'll come, too."

"Of course it will," Slavik grumbles. "That's the whole point."

I don't respond. But inside, something twists horribly. Rage, loss. Guilt.

Mia.

I'm playing a game with her, too. With her goddamn life. She deserves better than that.

In another life, perhaps, I could have given her more. I could have leaned in on Friday night, stolen that kiss off her lips, walked her upstairs. Let her put the kid to bed before taking her to bed, no tucking in involved.

I could have stayed the night. Woken up to the scent of half-burnt pancakes in the morning. To a *family*.

I could have given her everything.

But I had a family once already. It was taken from me, ripped from this world in the cruelest way.

And I won't rest until the *mudaki* who did it are six feet underground.

Can you really do it? It's the cold, dark voice inside me, questioning my every move. *Can you really stomp on your feelings for her, when you don't even know what they are?*

Can you stop caring about Mia Winters?

I have no fucking clue.

I tell myself I'll protect her when the time comes. That I've saved her once. That I can do it again.

It's the only thing that keeps me sane.

"C'mon, people," Maks yawns. "Less chattering, more playing. I'm dying of old age here."

"Before Rurik and Slavik?" Kazimir grins. "That's a feat."

"Laugh all you want," Slavik sighs. "But if I died tomorrow, I'd die without regrets. I've built my legacy."

"As have I." Rurik puts down his cards, still covered. "Now, our *pakhan* will." He squeezes out a raucous laugh. "Let's just hope the girl isn't taken off the board before she's done her duty."

The room stills. Silence falls like a guillotine.

My chair scrapes back with a scream. I rise, slow and deliberate, every muscle tight with rage.

"Say that again," I order.

Rurik scoffs and doubles down. "It's not like it's a secret. You're still in the crosshairs of your old man's murderers. They won't let you sire an heir without taking a shot at your lady. In fact, they've already tried." He downs the rest of his vodka. "It's not a question of 'if,' but 'when.'"

"Careful, brother."

"I'm just telling it like it is. Sure, she's a spitfire and all, but even she won't survive a bullet to the skull." A cold, piercing laugh echoes in the room. "The least she can do is shit out a son before—*blargh*!"

The punch leaves my body before I'm even aware of my arm moving.

The table jolts, cards fluttering to the floor. Rurik's body hits the ground with a dull thud.

"No one touches her." My voice cuts through the smoke. "As long as I draw breath, no one will so much as *look* at her wrong. If you imply otherwise again, Rurik, I'll take that breath from you myself."

His face drains of color. He sees it now—that I'm not bluffing. Beneath the title of *pakhan* is still the man who carved his empire out of the blood and bones of his dead family.

Even Kazimir stops smiling.

I look around the table. "Any other thoughts?"

No one speaks.

No one dares.

I nod once, then turn to Maksim. "We're done here."

He moves without a word, falling in beside me as I stride out of the lounge. On the table, where I sat moments before, my cards rest uncovered.

Ace of spades, ace of hearts.

I don't stop to collect the pot, though. I just force my feet to move before my itching hand can reach for my gun and leave me one *vor* short.

The door swings shut behind us, silence falling in our wake.

"Was that wise?" Maks asks once we're out of earshot, on our way back to the car. "Making an enemy of your oldest *vor*?"

"He's the one who made an enemy of me."

"No. He was crass and rude, but he wasn't lying." Maksim steps between me and the car door. "I'm serious, man. You've made your decision. Either change your mind, or learn to live with it."

I don't answer him.

I can't.

Because I know, as I fold into the Maybach and slam the door hard enough to crack it, that he's fucking right.

50

MIA

I bite back tears the whole rest of my shift.

Despite my suspension, I knew I couldn't just leave Gwen to scramble for a last-minute replacement. That's what Adams never thinks about: that we are actually *needed* here. Might as well be the tagline for nurses everywhere.

First in line for the grunt work. Dead last for credit.

I've never cared about any of that—just seeing patients get better has always been enough for me.

But it makes rage coil tight in my gut that he thinks we're *this* disposable. That he can just put my head on the chopping block and the ER won't suffer for it.

By the time I've hung up my scrubs, I've turned my rage into purpose.

One month, unpaid. Before Yulian's advance, it would have been unthinkable. I would have had to take out another loan just to survive, and what bank in its right mind would have given it to me?

But now, I can breathe a little easier. Sure, the anxiety of five years of food insecurity won't disappear overnight, but at least I know I'll survive. That *Eli* will survive. My boy will lack for nothing.

In the car, my hands tremble around my phone. I've wanted to text him all day, but haven't had a single break.

Now, I'm hesitating.

What's he gonna think? Worry crowds my mind, mixing with the anxiety I was already nursing. I don't want to be the girl who only texts or calls when she's in trouble. I've never needed a knight in shining armor to bail me out of my messes before.

But with Yulian…

With Yulian, it's different. It isn't about need—I *want* to call him. To share how my day went, the good parts and the shitty parts. Tell him he can stop sending Tamara over and invite *him* over instead.

He hasn't replied to any of your texts. That simple truth burns on my fingertips. *What does that tell you? That he's been busy, or that he doesn't want to get involved with you?*

I have no clue what it tells me. Just that this is how Yulian has always been with me: warm one second, cold the next.

Does it drive me crazy? *Yes.* Capital Y, cherry on top.

But he was always there when I needed him. I can't just forget that.

Finally, my fingers start typing. I channel all my courage into that simple gesture, try to find the words to start—

"Drive."

—and then feel a blade against my throat.

51

MIA

My first thought is, *Fuck.*

My second thought is actually also *Fuck.*

But my third is, *Shit. That's a surgical blade.*

My breaths turn shallow. It's only thanks to years of ER work that I manage to fight down the panic. One wrong move, and I'm as good as dead.

Slowly, I turn my gaze up to the rearview mirror. I can't see the full face of my attacker clearly from here, only the half that's not hidden by the headrest of my seat.

"Who are you?"

My attacker doesn't answer. "I said drive."

It's a woman. That surprises me more than the fact I'm being attacked. After all, would I really put it past Brad to corner me in my car with a sharp object and force me to bend to his will?

But this isn't Brad. And he must have really fucked me up, because just knowing that brings me a short burst of relief.

Then I remember the blade against my throat.

"Okay," I whisper. "You don't have to hurt me. I'll take you wherever you need to go."

Something flickers in her eyes. There's a haziness there, like she's struggling to stay awake. Her hand isn't the steadiest I've ever seen, either, which worries me more than anything else.

She's sick, I realize. *Drugged. An addict, maybe.*

But then why isn't she asking for money?

I turn my key into the ignition. Rhonda the Honda splutters to life, making the blade wobble dangerously in the air, far too close for comfort to my jugular.

"My wallet's in my purse," I tell her. "You can take it."

"I don't need your wallet." Her ferocity feels more like that of a cornered prey than a predator's. It strikes me as odd, but I can't afford to think too long. "I just need you to drive."

"Okay. Where to?"

"Anywhere."

Odd answer. Very, very odd answer.

"Alright," I whisper, trying to keep my voice calm. "I'll drive. Just put the blade away."

"N-no," she coughs. "You'll—you'll take me to the cops."

"I'm a nurse." I force a small smile. "I wouldn't harm you. Can't, really. Swore an oath and everything."

"Oaths can be broken."

"No offense, but so can my jugular. And New York traffic isn't exactly smooth sailing." I pull out of the parking lot as carefully as I can. "Way too many potholes here."

"Just... dri..."

Her head sways in the rearview mirror. Her arm wanders away from my body, but not intentionally.

She's about to pass out.

I see my chance. Before she can recover, I jab two fingers into the soft spot under her elbow. The blade clatters under the passenger seat, stuck between the car floor and the mat.

I'm expecting retribution, but the woman doesn't attack me.

Instead, she slumps all the way to the right.

I hit the brakes in the middle of the parking lot. Cars are honking madly around me, but right now, I don't care.

Hesitantly, I reach for her wrist. She doesn't stir when I touch her. She's built strong, but her skin is sallow, not as tense and elastic as it should be, like she lost a bunch of weight all at once. The clothes she's wearing don't fit her. An oversized t-shirt, a large leather jacket, both sweaty and stained.

When I take her pulse, it's as weak as they come.

I should get her to the hospital, I realize. *I should get her help.*

But when I grip the door handle, my hand stills.

She said "no cops." That's not a phrase you'll hear unless a patient's in trouble with the law, on the run, or has good reason not to trust a uniform. Getting her into the ER would mean questions. Risks. Possible identification.

And I can't do that to her.

Of course you can, my rational mind snaps. *She held a blade against your throat!*

But I don't listen. Instead, I turn the key into the ignition again, pull out of the jammed parking lot, and head for the Brooklyn Bridge.

Rain starts pouring halfway through, full sheets clashing into the windshield like lashes.

I don't stop driving until I've reached my destination.

I ring the doorbell. I wait in the pouring rain, my attacker's arm draped around my shoulders, her unconscious body lilting to the side, head bowed lifelessly forward.

Then he opens.

Dark hair. Unkempt scruff. A pair of eyes as gray as snowy skies. "Mia?"

"I need your help," I rasp.

He doesn't ask. Doesn't protest.

Just moves to the side and lets me in.

Once the door clicks shut behind us, I let Yulian guide me towards one of his guest bedrooms. His shining Manhattan penthouse turns into a swamp with all the water and mud I'm tracking in, but he doesn't say a word about it. When the pristine white sheets of his guest bed go damp with the rainwater clinging to my new patient's body, he sucks in a sharp breath, and I feel a stab of guilt.

There you go again, taking advantage of his kindness. Bringing your messes to his doorstep—literally.

"I'm sorry about this," I say. "I promise I'll clean up, but I'm going to need a few supplies first. This woman isn't well, and I need to—"

"Why do you have her?"

"What do you mean?"

"Mia." Yulian's gaze is cold, hard steel. "Just answer me."

I blink, confused. "She… she attacked me in my car. She had a blade. She wanted me to drive."

Yulian's eyes sweep over me as I speak, concern taking over his features. "Did she—?"

"I'm fine," I say quickly. "She didn't touch me. But who is she, Yulian? Do you… do you *know* her?"

His jaw flexes. His fists clench and unclench at his sides, betraying his nerves.

"Yes," he rumbles. "That woman is Nikita Morozova. A lieutenant of my Bratva… and the soldier who's been missing since July."

Say what now?

52

YULIAN

Nikita.

Three months we've been looking for her.

Three.

Fucking.

Months.

And now, here she is, soaking my hardwood floors.

Not that I could give less of a shit about that. What's ridiculous is that a whole army of my men couldn't track her down, but somehow, *Mia* did.

Mia, who knew nothing about her.

Mia, whom I'd sworn I wouldn't see again unless it was part of the plan.

Mia, who's now working tirelessly to save her.

She has no idea who Nikita is, aside from the fact that she apparently held her at knifepoint and tried to carjack her.

How Mia is even still alive after that, I have no clue. Nikita is a trained killer.

Granted, she's not the type to cut up nurses in parking lots, but I doubt Mia could have overpowered her even without lethal intent on her part.

The fact that she apparently did?

It means Nikita's on death's doorstep.

At least, that's the assumption I'm working on as I watch Mia dart around my cabinets, gathering up battlefield supplies to treat her. It must be far from what she's accustomed to: dry beds, clean tools, a full pharmacy waiting on her. But she doesn't utter a single word of complaint.

"Mia."

She doesn't answer me, still rummaging for God-knows-what in place she won't find it.

"Mia," I repeat, harder.

"What?" She doesn't quite snap, but the urgency in her tone is clear. She needs to take care of her patient. Here, she is on *her* battlefield, fighting a war I know nothing about: the war against death. She has no bandwidth for distractions.

Good thing that I'm not planning to be one.

"Tell me what you need."

Her eyes light up at the realization of what I'm offering. "A bedside monitor," she answers quickly. "A pulse oximeter will do in the meantime. You probably have one already."

"What else?"

"IV bags," she says. "A pole, too, ideally. We need to give her fluids, nutrients, and intravenous acetaminophen for her fever."

"Nutrients?"

"She's severely malnourished." Mia holds up her arm, showing me the skin hanging from her upper forearm.

That's all I need to hear.

I call Maksim and order the supplies. He doesn't question me, nor the urgency of my command.

"Twenty minutes," I tell Mia. "Is that good? Will she hang on for twenty minutes?"

"Yes," she exhales. "She's not in immediate danger."

"Good." I turn back to Maks on the phone. "You've got your twenty minutes. No delays."

As we wait for him, Mia busies herself taking care of Nikita. She towels off her short black hair, borrows one of my sets of pajamas, and changes her into it.

It's odd, seeing my worlds collide like this. Seeing Mia taking care of one of my soldiers.

"Is there anywhere else we can put her?" she asks at one point. "Somewhere dry?"

"You can use my bedroom."

She blushes, but doesn't argue. We carry Nikita on my bed, much larger and more comfortable than the one she'd been shivering in.

Fury crowds my mind. Concern, too. I'm itching to *do*

something, find the people responsible for this and make them pay. There are too many mysteries surrounding this.

I've never been good at sitting still, letting others do the work. If I'm not dirtying my hands, I'm not doing it right.

But tonight, I force myself to stand back and watch. Watch Mia's hands expertly move over Nikita's body, feeling her vitals, countering the fever with a damp cloth and ibuprofen. She's working in battlefield conditions here, but she's still—

Incredible. She's fucking incredible.

Maks arrives with five minutes to spare. He's carrying the monitor on his shoulder, a machine that's clearly been recently unhooked from somewhere, but I know better than to ask questions.

"Geez," he huffs. "If I'd known she was in your bed all along, boss, I would've cut down on the overtime."

"Shut up and bring that," I order, not in the mood for games. "Help Mia with anything she needs. As long as we're in this room, *she's* your boss. Got that?"

"See what I've got to put up with?" His tone is light, but there's a gravity to his expression as he finally sees Nikita's ashen face that echoes mine. "*Blyat'.* Someone sure did a number on her."

"They're dead," I growl. "Soon as I fucking find them, they're—"

"Can you please hold off on your mafia talk until I'm out of the room?" Mia interrupts. "Here. Help me sit her up."

She works several IVs into Nikita's arms with speed and precision, then hangs the bags. When the monitor's finally plugged in, I watch her exhale with relief.

"Vitals are rising," she murmurs. "She's still weak, but she'll pull through."

I let out a breath I hadn't known I'd been holding. By my side, Maksim does the same.

"Notify the others," I tell him. "And search the hospital's parking lot. I'll handle things here."

"Sure." He throws one last glance at Nikita. "When she wakes up, tell her I said hi. And that I called dibs on gutting the sons of bitches who did this to her."

"You'll have to fight her for the privilege," I mutter. "And me."

"Guys?" Mia pleads. "Seriously, plausible deniability? Ever heard of that?"

I wave Maksim out and sit down next to Mia. "So, she's fine now?"

"I wouldn't go that far, but at least she's not burning up anymore." I watch her bite her lower lip, worry all over her face, her gaze wandering over Nikita's shivering frame. "What was her physical shape before this?"

"Not that skinny," I tell her. "She's been fit forever."

"She'll need help walking at first," Mia says, hands deftly moving from Nikita's biceps to her calves, assessing the damage. "There's still something, but chances are, she's eaten away at it. There are all textbook signs of starvation and immobility. We see this in coma patients, but—"

"Coma patients?"

"Not exclusively," she amends. "But yes. Patients who spend a lot of time bedridden, being fed through an IV. Look." She shows me the inside of Nikita's left arm. "See the holes? Either she's been using like crazy—"

"She would never do drugs," I say. "Not Nikita."

"—or she's been kept somewhere for weeks."

Kept. The thought fills me with rage. I take a deep breath to dominate myself, fists clenched into the sheets.

It doesn't take long for Mia to notice. Her brow creases, pain and guilt waging a war in her eyes.

"Yulian... Are you and Nikita...?"

It takes me a few heartbeats to realize what she's really asking. In the end, her cheeks give it away, flushing hot pink with embarrassment and a touch of anger.

I fight down a smile. "Is that jealousy I hear, *Nurse Winters?*"

She tears her gaze away, chin held up with pride. "I'm not—"

"Because," I cut her off, cupping that prideful face and turning it back towards mine, "I wouldn't mind it if you were. It's a good look on you."

More color rushes to her face at my words. She looks so delicious like this—positively edible. "Don't play games with me," she rasps. "Not about this."

I don't tell her that I want to play all sorts of games with her. That, right now, Nikita's unconscious body in my bed is the only thing keeping me from pushing her down and showing her exactly how little reason she has to be jealous.

"You tell me," I croon into her ear. Faint notes of her perfume hang in the air, sweet as cotton candy. It drives me fucking crazy. "Am I toying with you right now?"

She's breathless. Red. "Sure feels like it sometimes," she whispers, but her heart's not in it. She isn't doing a thing to resist me, not even as I dive into her neck and fill my lungs with the sweetness of her scent.

Blyat'. I was supposed to cut off all contact with her. To stop seeing her, stop thinking about her, stop wanting her perfect fucking body under mine.

I've never turned to drugs in my life, but I imagine this is what it must feel like: to be hopelessly in the clutches of something else, something you can't live without. Something that consumes you.

I angle her head towards mine, fit my mouth over those perfect lips—

—and my fucking phone rings.

"Is that...?" Mia gasps, breaking away from me.

I roll my eyes and pick up. "Talk, Maks."

"Nikita's trail is nonexistent," he says without any preambles. "Someone beat us to it."

Fucking hell. Just what we needed. Our enemies are shipping off to greener pastures, and somehow, they're still quicker and more efficient than us.

"Look harder," I bark. "Or else I'll kick you all to the streets and hire a bunch of nurses to replace you."

Far from cowering at my threats, Maksim laughs. "Heard that, boys? Grease your elbows. It's gonna be an all-nighter."

"Keep me posted."

"Aye aye, Captain."

By the time I shove my phone back in my pocket, Mia has scooted a little further down the bed. Embarrassment still colors her face.

I find myself grateful for the distance. It gives me time to get my bearings, get my riotous body back under control.

"I should go," Mia says, rising all of a sudden. "I'm already late as it is, and Eli—"

"He needs you."

I stand up with her, show her to the door. Even as every instinct is screaming at me to keep her here. *With me.*

I could send for Eli. I could make up a room for each of them. I could build us a house, bigger and better and safer than any fortress. I could—

But you can't. Not in this life.

Right. I've already made my choice. No point putting it off. Better to rip off the Band-Aid here and now.

Mia's blue eyes find mine. She looks uncertain. Like she's tiptoeing on the edge of a cliff. "So, you'll be okay on your own? Both of you?"

"Yes."

"I can stay if you—"

"There's no need." *This is it,* I tell myself. My chance to cut her loose. "Mia, our contract—"

"I was suspended," she says out all of a sudden. "From the hospital."

I blink. "Suspended?"

"Brad's little plan," she says. "He fed the admin some lies about what happened when he came in. He's a big donor, so..."

Rage fills my veins. "He came to hurt you again."

I'll kill him. I'll fucking kill him for real.

Suddenly, I don't care about my revenge anymore—all I want is a different pound of flesh.

Mia seems to read it on my face. "He couldn't," she whispers, putting her arm on mine. "Not this time. Because I had you."

It's a knife right between the ribs. "Mia..."

"Our contract, I mean." She's stumbling on every word, as nervous as I've ever seen her. Like she can feel me stepping back, but has no intention of letting me. Every time I try to push her away, she only pulls harder. Without an agenda, without hidden motives. "Your advance—it saved my life. Literally. So... thank you."

Tell her, my conscience screams at me. *Tell her the truth. All of it.*

But the words don't come.

"You were saying...?" Mia asks. "About the contract?"

"Right." I swallow the lump of cement in my throat. "I'll need you for an event. Tomorrow. I realize it's short notice."

"Not gonna be a problem," she grins. "Lucky for you, my schedule's wide open. Text me the details."

"I will."

"Thanks."

She hovers at the door for a moment, undecided. Then, as if gathering up all her courage, she stands on her tiptoes.

It's the shortest kiss of my life. The lightest, gentlest kiss.

It hurts like a thousand cuts.

"Goodnight, Yulian."

"… Goodnight, Mia."

Then she's gone.

The second she disappears behind my front door, I stride back to my bedroom, stopping only to pick up a bottle of ice water from the fridge.

Then I dump the contents on Nikita's face.

"FUCK!" She jolts upright, gasping for breath. "What the—?! Oh. It's just you."

Not many people on this Earth would react like that upon seeing me. For most criminals in this city, I'm the Grim Reaper incarnate.

But Nikita's different. Nikita knows what binds us. She knows it's sacred.

She also knows how to tell my moods. And right now, even through the haze of her situation, she can tell I'm in my darkest one yet.

"Start talking," I snarl. "Now."

53

YULIAN

As a *pakhan,* I'm used to giving orders. More than anything, I'm used to them being executed swiftly and flawlessly. Without questions—without hesitation.

That all goes to shit when Nikita's involved.

"I want a milkshake," she yawns, still fighting the anesthetic in her system. "With whipped cream. Then I'll talk."

I could fight her on this. Pull rank, remind her who's in charge. Or better yet, I could simply *make her* talk. She's too weak to fight back, let alone win.

Soft, the beast in me mocks as I turn on the blender. *You've gone too fucking soft, Yulian.*

Maybe so. But I've sworn an oath. On Kira's grave, the day of her funeral.

That I'd always look out for her little sister.

She drags herself to the kitchen counter, IV in tow. I don't try to help her walk, and she doesn't ask. Wounded or not, Nikita's still one of my top lieutenants. A soldier.

Her pride needs healing, too.

"Ew!" She pulls a face at her first sip. "Is there protein powder in this?"

"According to your nurse, you've been eating your muscles."

"My nurse?" Her brow knits, then realization dawns on her face. "Oh! The one with the shitty car and balls of steel."

"Her name's Mia. She's the one who brought you to me."

"Seriously?" She takes another, careful sip. Her lips are all cracked with dehydration. She almost chokes a couple of times, struggling to swallow. "Wow. Did I just happen to carjack the nurse you're fucking, or did you develop a scrubs kink while I was gone?"

"If you're going to choke on that, at least say something useful."

"Hey, I'm on the mend. You should indulge me with sweets and gossip. How else am I supposed to get better?"

"I've indulged you plenty." I fix her with a hard look. "Now, talk."

She rolls her eyes, but obliges. "Fine. What do you want to know?"

"Everything."

"Figures." She stretches in her chair, careful not to displace the IV in her arm. "It's gonna be tough. My memory's still hazy."

"Try."

"Gee, thanks. That's helpful."

"Start with the Ws. You know how it goes."

Back when we were kids, our parents preferred belt and cane over shrinks. Mine never went that far, but the Morozov patriarch wasn't very tolerant. As such, Nikita's frequent lapse in memory and focus were written off as laziness, lack of intelligence, and occasionally disrespect.

She didn't get an ADHD diagnosis until she was well within her twenties.

Nikita purses her cracked lips. "Right. Okay, well, I've got no proof about who took me."

"But you have a guess."

"Same guess you must have." Her voice hardens on those words. It tells me we're on the same page about this.

Only one common enemy turns her tone to ice like that.

Prizrak.

That's the "who."

"One W down," I tell her solemnly. "Four more to go."

"I remember *where* I was taken," she says, deep in thought. "I was following a lead. I'd been getting reports of homeless people disappearing without a trace, all in a single area."

"Brownsville," I fill in.

"Yeah," she frowns. "How'd you know?"

"GPS in your phone."

She doesn't seem particularly surprised or even offended. "Oh, cool. I forgot you installed that."

Nikita is infamous for her ability to get lost in a glass of water. Once, she went hiking and dropped off the grid for a whole weekend because she couldn't find her way back to the path.

It was a beginners' trail.

"Anyway," she says, "I went to check out this construction site. Seemed like a promising place to start."

"You shouldn't have gone alone," I growl. "You know how we operate. Our rules exist for a reason."

"It was just a teeny-tiny building!"

"It was a Prizrak *nest.* If you'd told someone, we could have made real progress. Instead, they made you disappear." I clench my fist on the counter. "I don't have to explain to you what I thought happened, do I?"

She considers me, her green gaze fixed on me like water. Calm, unfazed. "I knew you'd never stop looking."

Damn right I didn't. And yet, in the end, I wasn't the one who found her.

It was Mia.

"I made a promise to your sister," I tell Nikita, eager to steer my thoughts away from Mia. "I wasn't going to let some *mudak* put you in the ground next to her."

"I love you, too, Yuli."

I hold up a hand. "Don't."

"Sorry for triggering your feelings allergy." She doesn't sound sorry at all. "As for our Ws..."

"Go on." I'm eager to get to the end of this conversation, find out where to strike. If we hurry up, we can still find traces. Traces we can follow.

But Nikita dashes all my hopes with a single sentence. "I have no idea where I was kept. And before you start barking with your alpha voice, I was drugged out of my mind."

I ignore her provocation and clench my teeth. "I find that hard to believe, considering you escaped."

"I got lucky," she shrugs. "Someone must have fucked up my dose. I woke up, freed myself, hobbled away with the first weapon I could find. I was too high to get a car in motion, so I waited in the backseat. The rest, as they say, is history."

Fuck. "You're telling me we don't even have a trail."

"Sorry to disappoint. Next time I have to run for my life, I'll make sure to bring breadcrumbs."

"I don't think you understand the reality of the situation," I snarl. "Our enemies are packing up, Nika. They're shipping themselves overseas. If we don't catch them now—"

"Overseas?" Her face goes pensive. "So that wasn't a dream, then."

The hell...? "Explain yourself," I demand.

"While I was under, I heard voices. Just now and then, between doses." She purses her lips, eyes narrowed, trying to grasp a memory just out of reach. "They were talking about leaving. Said they had one last job to finish, and then they'd be gone."

One last job.

My blood freezes. It can't be anything else.

All these years, they've kept close tabs on me. I couldn't figure out why they hadn't struck yet, but now, it all makes sense—they were preparing their escape hatch.

And if it's ready, so are they.

Conflict grips my stomach, twisting hard. Every drop of guilt I've been suppressing rises, a torrent of acid burning up my throat.

Suddenly, my phone buzzes with a text. I check it distractedly, not even looking who it's from.

And then I see it.

A selfie—from Mia.

She's grinning, carefree and light despite the hellish day she just had. Her hair is still damp from the shower. I can almost smell her shampoo through the screen, creamy and sweet.

In her arms, Eli is giving the camera a gap-toothed grin, his Garfield plushie held tight in his arms.

Looking forward to tomorrow!

P.S.—Your biggest fan says hi.

Time slips through my fingers. I have no idea how long I spend staring at the screen, lost in the image of Mia and her son.

Smiling.

Happy.

Safe.

"I need to make a phone call."

Nikita doesn't say anything. She knows better than to get in the way when I'm like this. Dark, rumbling thunderclouds are gathering above my head, a storm in the making.

I walk out into the balcony and dial Maks's number.

"Calling again so soon?" Maksim laughs on the other end of the line. "If I didn't know better, I'd say you were growing soft on me, boss."

"Shut up," I say. "I need you to put guards around Mia's building. Better yet, make it the whole fucking block."

He curses under his breath in Russian. "We're in the endgame, then?"

"The end of the endgame."

"Then you'd better hurry. Move up our schedule, set a date with Mia for an engagement party or—"

"No."

Maks falls silent for a moment. "'No'?"

If what Nikita said is true, then I can no longer take the risk of involving Mia. Things have officially become too dangerous—too unpredictable.

I thought I could stomach putting her on the line. Told myself I'd be able to protect her again. But if things are at this stage, then...

This time, Prizrak won't miss.

And I can't do it. I can't sacrifice her on the altar of my revenge. I can't let her son grow up an orphan.

I can't let him turn into *me.*

"I'm letting Mia go." The words claw my throat to ribbons on the way out. "Tomorrow night."

For a long while, my second-in-command doesn't speak. He doesn't need to. I can hear his disappointment through the line.

So be it. I'd rather be weak than a coward. I won't spend one more second hiding behind a single mother's skirts to draw my enemies to me.

Revenge be damned.

Eventually, Maksim finds his voice again. "That's your choice, then?"

"That's my choice."

More silence. "Very well." He clears his throat. "I'll arrange the perimeter."

Then he hangs up.

I walk back inside and toss Nikita a spare burner phone. "Stay inside," I warn. "If anything happens, call me."

"You're going out?"

I can't stay one more second cooped up like this. If I do, I risk shattering every piece of furniture in my penthouse. I need to clear my head—to *hit* something. Someone. Anything.

Anything to keep my mind off what I'm about to do.

Because, tomorrow, I will lose Mia Winters forever.

54

MIA

Yulian doesn't say a word the whole way to Manhattan.

It's unnerving. More than that, it *hurts.* I have no idea what I've done to piss him off, but here we are, stuck in the same cold silence.

Maybe it's not about you, says the voice at the back of my mind, not without a touch of mockery. *Maybe it's about Nikita.*

Right. Nikita. She was the one Yulian was supposed to take to Brad's wedding last summer. Now that she's back…

Does he even need you anymore?

I tell myself it's not true. That my mind is just being mean to me. After all, didn't Yulian say so himself? Last night, in his bedroom, his face inches away from mine?

You tell me. Am I toying with you right now?

The truth is, I've got no fucking clue.

I told him things I'd never told anyone. Opened my heart to him like I hadn't in forever. More than that, he's opened up to me, too. He's laid his bloody history at my feet and trusted I wouldn't trample it, that I wouldn't turn his vulnerability into a weapon.

It was huge.

It *mattered.*

I've dreamed of his lips more times than I can count. And I could see it in his eyes, last night, that he was dreaming of mine.

But what if none of that is enough anymore?

I hate this burning pit of jealousy. I've never been this person, this needy, insecure girl. But I'm quickly discovering how good Yulian is at pulling out sides of me I hadn't been aware of.

"How..." I swallow around a dry throat. "How is Nikita?"

It feels hypocritical to ask, after the direction my thoughts just took. But Nikita was my patient, however briefly. Part of me can't help worrying about her. I may have been suspended from the hospital, but some habits are hard to break.

No matter what, I'm still a nurse. A caregiver at heart.

Yulian's gaze flicks to mine. The gray of his irises is flat, unreadable, a steely mirror to mine. It betrays nothing. "She's fine."

"That's a pretty curt diagnosis." I try to laugh, but it comes out brittle. "Gonna need a little more to work on, Dr. Lozhkin."

His lips quirk imperceptibly. That precious dimple of his makes a late appearance, filling my chest with unexpected hope. "You drive a hard bargain, Nurse Winters."

"What can I say? I'm the bane of every hospital."

"Then it's a good thing we're not in one."

His body leans into mine reflexively as he speaks. I lose myself to the warmth radiating through his suit, the husky notes of his voice rumbling through me. His cologne, always so present everywhere he goes.

"She woke up," he says. "Demanded a milkshake. Took my blender hostage."

Relief seeps through me. The way it was looking last night, I kept fearing the worst. Couldn't sleep a wink all night, caught between worry for my patient and other, less noble types of thoughts.

"Good. That means she's recovering well. It wasn't a given she'd still be able to swallow on her own."

"Clearly, you've never tried getting between Nikita and her midnight snacks."

"You're making it sound like *I'd* become the snack if I did."

"Yes." He turns to me, heat burning through his gaze. "Which would be a problem. I'm not in the habit of sharing my food."

His rough tone turns my legs to jelly. "Are you calling me a snack, Mr. Lozhkin?"

For a second, hunger flashes in his eyes. That gray curtain melts into a haze—a brand of desire I'm only too familiar with.

He's gonna kiss me, isn't he?

But then, at the last second, something else takes over his face.

It's like watching a gust of wind snuff out a candle. His jaw flexes, his dimple disappears, and the heat in his gaze dims to a forgotten ember.

With perfect timing, the car rolls to a stop. "We're going to be late," Yulian says, fixing his cufflinks. "Let's—"

"Did I do something?"

He turns to me. For a moment, surprise flickers on his impassive mask of steel. "Do something?"

"To upset you." I swallow around the lump in my throat. "You keep doing this—this *thing* where we're fine, we're talking, we're joking around, and then suddenly…" The nerves are eating me alive as I speak, tearing chunks off my thoughts, but I force myself to put them into words nonetheless. "Suddenly, we're not."

There—another flash of *something.*

"You've done nothing wrong, Mia."

"Then what's going on?" My tone turns pleading. I've never been good at turning myself into a salt statue, not like Yulian is. "Is it about Niki—?"

All of a sudden, Yulian's hand cups my face. He tilts it up, forcing me to look into his eyes—to bare myself to him.

I have no idea what he sees there. But whatever it is, it softens the ice in his features.

"This charity gala is very important," he says. "To the company, and to me."

"To you?"

"Mm." His touch is scalding, sending sparks of heat between my legs with every stroke of his fingertips on my chin. "Tonight will determine a great deal of things. It may very well lead to... changes."

"Changes," I echo.

"Yes." There's a wistful note in his voice, one I can't quite place. "For better or worse."

My heart is pounding now. If he doesn't kiss me within the next five seconds, it might actually explode. Which wouldn't be very good for his Maybach's sleek leather interiors, now, would it?

So really, he should just get on with it.

I close my eyes. My lashes flutter, my fingers dig into the leather of the backseat. I can feel the *thump-thump-thump* in my chest growing louder, deafening—

HOOONK!

—and then it nearly *does* explode.

"Get a move on, lovebirds!" Maksim hollers from the driver's seat. "Or else all the food will be gone."

I can't think of anything I want less than food right now. My stomach's so full of knots, I could sail right out to sea.

Predictably, Yulian pulls away. I mourn him immediately—his warmth, his touch.

"Let's go."

He gets out of the car, then holds out his hand for me to take. Like he's asking me to dance.

And, like all the times before, I take it.

55

MIA

Fifteen minutes into the event, I lose sight of Yulian.

It's not my fault. Or, well—it's not *completely* my fault. It's just that there are so many donors, all elbowing each other for a word with the head honcho, and at one point, his suit melts into the sea of white shirts and black ties.

Seeing as StarTech's rooftop is practically a small European village, finding my way back to him soon proves to be more than my Louboutins can handle.

But there's another reason I don't mingle again. Another reason I keep myself on the edge of it all, elbows against the railing, eyes vigilant, scanning every face I see.

Because I'm afraid the next will be Brad's.

It isn't unthinkable. He's already snuck in once. He could do it again.

"Fancy a tart?"

I nearly jump. I'm so nervous, I didn't even notice anyone approach. "What?"

"Tarts." The woman who just spoke holds up a perfect circle of puff pastry with a fat, round shrimp curled in its center. "I'm kind of off solids for now. Doctor's orders, apparently."

Finally, the dots connect.

Green almond eyes. Porcelain skin. Black hair cropped into a short, homemade pixie cut, something that looks like the lovechild of kitchen scissors and a stolen electric razor, but somehow still manages to give off a stylish vibe.

And a black dress that's practically hanging off her too-thin figure.

"Relax, *malyshka*." Nikita winks. "I left my knives at coat check."

"That's… good?"

"I'd hope so. Unless they're serving steak, in which case, it might prove to be a colossal lapse in judgment." She waves the pastry in my face again. "Anyway, tart?"

I want to say no, but that's when my stomach decides to chip in with a growl.

Nikita looks encouraged. "It's got a cute little shrimp in it," she says, like she's trying to convince a little kid to eat her veggies. "C'mon. Take it off my hands. You don't want me to break my liquid diet and choke, do you?"

It's a pretty persuasive argument.

I take the pastry. It's savory, with a crunchy and airy texture that you really can't get out of store-bought dough. Not for the first time, I realize how filthy rich Yulian is. This single appetizer is probably worth more than a full day's pay at the hospital, isn't it?

Not that I'm gonna go back there any time soon.

"Good, right?" Nikita sighs wistfully. "I used to crash these charity things all the time. The open bar is to *die* for." She shoots a mournful glance at the waiters carrying trays of delicacies all over the rooftop. "Too bad I missed your presentation dinner. I heard the chef went all out."

It strikes me as odd, how easygoing she's being. Last night, she was practically feral. Dosed to hell and back, unable to stand, to focus her gaze beyond the knife in her hands. She's wearing makeup today, but I can still see the faint shadow of the dark circles under her eyes. God only knows what she went through to earn those.

"Are you sure you're up for this?" I ask, suddenly filled with concern. "Being here? Walking around?"

"Yeah, so long as I sit down every now and then." She gives a careless shrug, like her brush with death is not that big a deal. "Yuli threatened me with crutches, but I told him where I'd shove 'em if he bought a pair."

Yuli. Such a familiar form of address. It fills my heart with ache all at once, dull and throbbing like a bad tooth.

Only, I'm not quite certain I'll be able to rip this one out.

"Not a fan of walking aids?"

"Only when they come in hospital gray." She makes a gagging motion. "One word: *barf.*"

Somehow, I'm not surprised. Her outfit may be a little ill-fitting, but it's curated down to the last detail: black dress, black boots, black studs. A black belt cinched tight around her waist, looking to disguise how loosely her dress hangs. Not a drop of color breaks the pattern.

My gaze wanders to her arms. Black tattoos snake up from her wrists to her shoulders. They're different from the ones on Yulian's chest, but they carry the same aura, the same weight of meaning and purpose.

And danger, too.

She was born into his world, I realize. *She was born to be Bratva.*

But I was not.

Suddenly, I can't keep it inside anymore. I *have* to know. No more of Yulian's half-answers—no more guesswork.

"Look," I start. "I know it's none of my business, but—"

"Love the start of that question," she says. Somehow, she doesn't sound like she's mocking me. "Go on."

Her eyes fix on me with a bright, amused sort of curiosity. I swallow around a dry mouth and force myself to ask the question that's been on my mind ever since last night.

"Are you Yulian's girlfriend?"

It comes out all at once—*AreyouYuliansgirlfriend?*—which isn't very dignified. Part of me wants to dig through all fifty floors of the StarTech skyscraper just to find a hole to crawl into.

I can feel Nikita's eyes on me, burning holes in my face with her dumbfounded staring. I'm on the verge of blurting out an excuse and running back into the fold, Brad danger be damned.

But then…

Is she laughing?

Nikita doubles over. I can hear her wheeze, struggling to catch her breath, holding on for dear life to the railing.

"*Fuck* no." She pulls herself together and lifts her face again, wiping tears from the corners of her eyes. "Not in a thousand years. That'd be a fucking nightmare."

"I… Oh."

"No offense."

"None taken." Then I realize why she's said that. "I mean, not that I'd have any reason to be— It's just, we're not—"

"Relax." Nikita waves off my ramblings. "He told me what the deal is with you two."

"He did?"

"Well, no. Maks told me. He's way more talkative than our mutual BFF."

I can't fight the smile off my face. I tell myself it's because hearing Yulian being called anyone's BFF is too ridiculous to ignore, but it's only half the truth.

The relief is much stronger than anything else.

I let out a breath I didn't know I'd been holding. Mentally, I cross Nikita off the list of reasons for Yulian's weird behavior lately. It doesn't leave me with much, but if nothing else, it leaves me with hope.

I turn back to her, much more at ease now. "Sounds like you're all caught up."

"That I am." She steals two glasses of champagne and hands one to me. "So, wanna get out of here?"

I blink. "Like, ditch the party?"

"Oh, believe me, this isn't the party. This is a corporate sausage fest. The *real* party's downstairs."

"Downstairs?"

"You'll see. It's where Yulian hides all his actual friends."

"I—" My gaze darts to the crowd, to where Yulian is. But the sea of suits remains unchanging. And the cold dread of running into Brad without him by my side—

It makes Nikita's offer incredibly inviting.

Besides, I want to know more about Yulian. What kind of company he keeps when he isn't wearing his CEO mask. What his friends are like.

"C'mon." Nikita hooks her arm through mine. "Gotta pay you back for last night somehow, don't I? Consider this my rescue mission to you."

And, well. *That'd* be rude to refuse.

So I let Nikita drag me through the crowd, push me into the elevator, and push the button to the basement floor.

56

YULIAN

I catch sight of Mia just before the elevator doors close.

What the hell is she doing?

"Maks." My second is at my side in an instant. "I just saw Mia leaving."

"That's odd." He touches his chin with faux pensiveness. "Could it have anything to do with you ditching her all night?"

"I didn't *ditch* her," I snap. "I kept getting dragged away. Why the fuck did we even invite this many people?"

"For their money," Maksim supplies unhelpfully. "You know, like we do every year?"

I grind my teeth into dust. Without a word, I start swimming through this sea of faces and suits, every single one vying for my attention.

I should have kept better tabs on Mia—I know that. With all

that's at stake, I should have kept her glued to my fucking side.

And yet…

You couldn't look her in the eye, could you? That cold, merciless voice laughs in my ears. *You couldn't bring yourself to. It hurt to have her close, didn't it?*

Knowing it'll be the last night you ever get to?

I shake my head and rush to the elevator. "I have to find her."

"Relax, man. She's with Nikita. She's perfectly—"

"Safe?" I snap. "Tell me, Maks, how long has Nikita been missing for?"

He frowns. "What's that got to do with it?"

"I'll tell you how long: *Three. Fucking. Months.* You don't think that's long enough to be concerned?"

The second he understands, his expression sobers. "You think she's been reprogrammed?"

"Can't fucking rule it out, can I?" I mash the buttons, impatience coursing through my veins hand in hand with rage. "*Blyat'.* Too slow."

"Calm down," Maksim sighs. "You're not wrong, but you've got no reason to think that. No proof. When I talked to her, she seemed fine."

"They always seem fine."

"By your logic, *I* could be an enemy plant, too." He covers the buttons with his palm, preventing me from crushing them with my urgency. "There's no reason to panic."

"I'm not panicking."

"Could've fooled me."

"Maks, I swear to God, if you don't shut up right this second—"

"What?" He gets between me and the buttons. "You'll find every excuse under the sun to bury the truth?"

"What *truth?*"

"That you love her."

It's like getting sucker punched. All the air goes out of me, leaving only anger in its wake. "You have no idea what you're talking about."

"Don't I?" He crosses his arms. "You gave up your best shot at revenge for her. You chose her over twenty years of single-minded obsession. And now, you're afraid it's not going to matter."

"I'm not fucking—"

"Yes, you are!" Maksim raises his voice to match mine. "Goddammit, brother. You know it as well as I do: You've painted too big a target on her back. It's too late to pull the plug now. That's why you're scared out of your wits, seeing enemies in every shadow. Even your best friend's."

It hits too close for comfort.

Too close to the truth I've been burying deep inside my conscience, where I can no longer feel it clawing at me.

"Shut up," I snarl.

"You love her," he repeats, undeterred. "And you didn't realize soon enough. And now you're trying to undo it all, but you *can't,* Yulian! You—"

I grab Maksim by the lapels of his jacket and slam him against the elevator wall. The powder keg of my fury is this close to exploding, and he keeps dangling the match close enough for sparks.

"I said," I growl into his tattooed face, "shut the fuck up, or I'll make you."

"Fine." He spits that word like it's an insult. "Just don't come crying to me when you've got two more graves to clean."

I hit him before I can stop to think why I shouldn't.

Blood spatters on my shirt. Maks clenches his teeth, but doesn't cry out—he's made of stronger stuff than that.

I let him go and slump against the opposite wall, panting hard.

He's right.

It's all I can think of. I thought I'd made a choice last night, but the truth is, I didn't. I didn't even make a choice when Maks came to me in my office a week ago, telling me about our enemies' movements.

There was only one choice to be made, and I made it the second I let Mia climb into a car with me, the night of Brad's wedding.

Put a target on her back, or spare her.

"Fuck." I drag my hands over my face. "FUCK!"

Maksim spits a bloody glob on the elevator floor and cleans his face with his sleeve. There are no tooth fragments, nothing broken.

"Yeah," he echoes. "'Fuck' is right."

"You should have stopped me earlier."

"Earlier, you didn't give a shit about her." He mirrors my posture on his side of the elevator. "Now, you've grown a rather inconvenient heart."

"You're one to talk."

"That's fair." He lets out a sigh, bone-deep and tired. For once, he actually looks his age. "But I never had any illusions, Yulian. I know where I stand with Kalinda. She's young, pure, untouched by this world. What we have won't last 'til dawn."

"But you're still buzzing around her like a goddamn fly to honey."

"And when the time comes, I'll stop doing that. I'll let her go." He takes one step towards me. When I don't glare at him, his hand touches my shoulder. "Sometimes, the best thing we can do for the people we love is to let them go."

"So what exactly are you suggesting?"

"Ship her overseas." His tone is dark, serious. "Put her and Eli on a plane. Give them fake names, new lives, and burn their addresses afterwards. Never go near them again. Only then can you truly keep them safe."

Maksim's words are a butcher's knife. It guts me to listen, to hear the reason behind them—but he's fucking right. I've got no other choice.

I have to let them go.

The elevator doors slide open on the basement floor.

"Good luck," Maksim tells me. "And don't punch anyone else. They're not all as tough as me."

I stride into the basement.

Suddenly, I hear a scream.

Her scream.

I dash through like a madman. What if I'm already too late? What if Mia's—

"Fuck, Missy!" A bald man with head tattoos whistles. "You sure know how to hold your liquor."

Laughing.

She's laughing.

I take in the sight before me. The basement floor is where I host Bratva gatherings—away from the limelight and the cameras. Whenever there's a party elsewhere, my people make sure there's one here, too.

It's a stupid little thing, but this way, no one feels left out. Too many *pakhani* have been cut down by their own men after playing too hard at being CEO and forgetting to be leaders.

That won't be me.

"Bartender!" Nikita calls, perched on a stool next to Mia. "Another round!"

The stupidity of my earlier suspicions hits me all at once. I hate Maksim's habit of butting in, but I hate it even more when he's right. Nikita's weakened right now, but she's far from broken.

I should know that better than anyone.

I move my gaze back to Mia. She's radiant like this: a shot glass in her hand and laughter on her lips. She's joking with my men like she was born into a Bratva bar, not even flinching when they slam their palms on the counter or break out in vulgar choruses.

There's even a little brawl going on off to the side, but Mia looks unfazed, only keeping an eye out for injuries.

"Keep still," she orders once the losing party trudges back to the bar, dabbing at his broken nose with a cloth thick with alcohol. "Otherwise, it'll sting worse."

She's beautiful.

She's perfect.

She's…

The woman I love.

It hits me all at once, like a goddamn freight truck.

I love her.

I fucking *love* her.

And I cannot let her go.

"Yulian!" She waves at me when she sees me, eyes bright with delight. "You're here!" She jumps down from the stool and runs to meet me. "I'm sorry, I didn't mean to leave. It's just, Nikita said this is where your friends hung out, so I thought—"

"Marry me."

She blinks once, twice. "What?"

Maksim was wrong. Shipping Mia overseas is one choice, but it's not the only one. There's another way to save her—one that doesn't involve fake IDs and burned addresses and me never seeing her again.

It's almost stupidly simple. All this time, we've been playing the part of future husband and wife.

But when it comes down to it, isn't that an option, too?

If Mia becomes my *pakhansha,* she will have the full force of my Bratva to protect her. She will live under my roof, have 24/7 security, with private bodyguards for her and Eli.

She will be safe.

She will be mine.

That's not a reason to marry someone, the voice at the back of my mind mocks. *It's possession. It's just one more contract.*

Maybe so.

But I'm willing to sign it in blood.

"Marry me," I repeat to her stunned face. I have no idea what else to say to her—to convince her to give me the *yes* that will save her life. Right now, I'd say anything. "Be my wife. For real."

It's the only way I can keep her alive. The only way I can keep her *here.*

"Yul—"

"I love you."

The only way I don't lose her.

57

MIA

My head is spinning. My pulse is racing. I can feel the *thump-thump-thump* in my chest like a drum, loud, deafening.

And his words, ringing in my ears over and over again.

Marry me.

Be my wife.

I love you.

Yulian looks breathless. Like he's been running down all those flights of stairs instead of riding in his cushy elevator. He's ruffled, tie askew, hair a mess, but his eyes...

His eyes have never burned brighter.

"This is the part where you say yes," he rumbles, his husky voice vibrating through me.

"Why?"

"Because if you don't, that means you're going to say no." His fists clench at his sides, not out of violence but something else, something softer. *Hope.* "And I really don't want to hear that word coming from your lips right now."

"That's not— I mean, *why?*" I take a trembling step towards him. "Why would you…?"

Why would you propose to me? Why would you ask me to be your wife—your real *wife—when I've got nothing to offer you? No money, no power, no advantage?*

Why would you want me, when nobody else ever has?

I have no idea how to even begin to say all of that. To cut this tangle of emotions out of my heart and pick out the threads, one by one, until they make sense.

But Yulian doesn't wait for me to do it.

He takes a step towards me. His face is burning with a kind of urgency I've never seen on him before—never since the night of Brad's botched wedding, when he was fighting to save both our lives.

Does this feel equally important to him? A matter of life and death?

"Because you've made a mess of me," he answers.

"Wait, what?"

"You heard me," he almost snarls. "You've fucked me up, Mia Winters."

"Now I'm confused. Is this a proposal or are we fighti—?"

"I used to think I didn't have a heart anymore," he interrupts. "That it died that night, bleeding on that floor, the same way my family did. Cold, full of holes. Unfixable." His gray gaze fixes on mine, burning like the ash of a fireplace. "Then you came along, with your disrespect and your attitude and your fucking tow truck—"

"I said I was sorry for that!"

"—and I could *feel* it. I could feel it beating again." He takes my hand and places it over his chest. The strong *ta-thump, ta-thump* of his heart echoes through me. "I've been killing myself trying to find a way to keep you without hurting you. A way to save you from this life—*my* life. And from my choices, too."

"Your choi—?"

"I'm Bratva," he cuts me off. "It will always be dangerous to be with me. Always, Mia."

A small, watery smile twists my lips. "Haven't I already signed up for that?"

"You have no idea what you signed up for." His voice nearly cracks on those words. "But if you'll let me, I'll use the rest of my life to protect you from it. And from Brad. And from anything else in this world that so much as dares to fucking touch you."

I'm so anxious I could burst. A small, cautious flame of happiness is starting to kindle at the center of my chest, and suddenly I'm terrified.

Because when's the last time I've had that?

When's the last time I've had *hope?*

"Today, someone told me that the best thing you can do for the people you love is to let them go." He squeezes my hand tighter, his anxiety almost matching mine. "But I don't want to let you go. Not for a goddamn second."

I can't remember the last time he spoke for so long. I'm afraid to break the spell—afraid I'll say the wrong thing, that I'll ruin it. Like I've ruined everything else in my life.

"Yulian..."

I want to say *yes* so bad. I've never wanted anything more.

But then, reality comes crashing down on me. "I have a son," I rasp. "I can't put that on you. I can't ask you to be Eli's father."

"You won't have to."

"What are you saying?"

"I'm saying you're my family—*both* of you." He cups my face with his free hand. "You're the family I never thought I'd find again. And I don't want to lose you."

Something keeps needling at me about the way he's talking. Like we're one step away from being whisked into nothingness, Eli and I. Like he's speaking out of fear.

But then I remember his family. What happened to them, and how. The horrors he's had to live with all his life.

Is it really such a wonder that this is how a man like Yulian loves? Strongly, fiercely, afraid to ever lose you?

Just like that, I stop hesitating.

Just like that, I know exactly what I want.

And for the first time in my life, I reach out and just take it.

"Say it again," I whisper. "What you said before."

"Marry me."

"The other thing."

Realization dawns in his eyes. "I love you."

"Again."

"I love you."

"*Again*."

His dimple flashes. "I fucking love you, Mia Winters."

"Fuck." I can't take it anymore—it's too much. Too many feelings bottled up inside me, begging for release. "Then show me."

He doesn't make me say it twice.

We crash into the elevator like teenagers, groping and kissing all the way up. It's like breathing again after drowning—each kiss brings me back to life, lighting wildfires under my skin.

"*Blyat*," he curses between kisses. "You still haven't given me an answer."

"You still haven't shown me you mean it."

His eyes go dark and hooded. "Oh, I will."

Suddenly, the floor disappears from under my feet. Yulian's palms dig into my thighs, hoisting me up against the elevator wall, and then he's on me again, kissing me like his life depends on it.

Like mine might, too.

His lips slide down my neck, teeth scraping against my pulse. I gasp for breath, clawing at his shoulders, his hair, his everything.

I'm distantly aware of my nails digging crescents into his

scalp, but Yulian doesn't seem put off by it. If anything, his kisses only grow wilder.

"Fucking hell, *kotyonok.*"

He starts sucking bruises into my neck, biting into the curve of it. I can't see straight—I can't *think.* Heat is pooling low between my legs, robbing me of all reason.

"Please," I gasp. "Touch me."

He doesn't. Not with his hands, at least. "Patience, kitten." He rolls his hips against mine, so slow I could miss it if I wasn't this keyed up. But I am, and the feeling of his clothed cock rubbing against me drives me fucking wild.

"Patience," my ass.

When the doors slide open, we don't even look where we're going—he just carries me out of here and into his penthouse.

It takes us a couple of moments longer to realize it's *not* his penthouse.

"*Blyat'*," Yulian curses, glaring at the desk and bookshelves. "Wrong floor."

I glance around. There doesn't seem to be anyone else, the whole floor made up like a large, empty study. "Where are we?"

"My office."

He starts heading back for the elevator, but I stop him. "No," I whisper, tugging at the lapels of his jacket impatiently. "I need you now."

A wicked glint appears in his eye. "What happened to patience?"

"It died. Funeral's tomorrow." I grab his face with both hands. "Now, fuck me."

His gaze goes dark, liquid. "Have it your way."

Then he throws me on the desk.

Okay, maybe "throw" isn't the right word. It doesn't hurt—his hand is at the back of my head, and the fall isn't too steep—but *fuck* if it doesn't feel like he just grabbed me by the hair and dragged me into a cave to have his way with me.

In other words: *Hot. As. Fuck.*

I stare up at him, my skirts bunched up at my waist, my breasts half-spilling from the plunging cleavage of this dress. Yulian, on the other hand, is still impeccably dressed.

Somehow, that offends me personally. "Take off your clothes."

"You don't give the orders here, kitten." He gathers my wrists in one hand and pins them above my head. "That's not the way this works."

His free hand slides down my body, stopping to tease one stiff nipple through the fabric. The sensation is electric, and I let out a little cry, arching into his palm.

I can practically feel him smirking down at me. He pinches the nipple through the fabric of my dress, twisting until a sharp, delicious pain shoots down to my clit.

Fuck. I want him now. No—I need *him.*

My legs part wider, begging for his touch, but he doesn't give it. Not yet.

Instead, he keeps playing with my breasts, his deft fingers

making quick work of my dress. He pushes down a shoulder strap, then the other.

Just like that, cold air hits my naked nipples.

He stares down at my bare breasts, his eyes burning with want. With *need.*

He wants me. He wants me as badly as I want him.

Not just today—forever.

He bends his head to my chest, licking and sucking until I'm writhing on the desk beneath him. Until I'm going insane with pleasure. My wrists are still caught in his grip, and fuck if it's not the hottest thing I've ever done. I can feel the wetness building between my legs, feel my inner muscles clenching on nothing.

If he doesn't fuck me within the next five minutes, I might actually die.

Eventually, he releases me.

But not to take off his clothes.

I don't even manage to exhale with relief before I feel his mouth on me. His wicked tongue, lashing through the drenched folds of my pussy. I can feel his teeth, his tongue, his lips—*everywhere.*

Every inch of skin he touches burns like fire, like lightning.

He lifts my legs onto his shoulders, pressing even closer. The new angle gives him better access, and he uses it, fucking me with his tongue.

I dig my nails into his hair and try desperately not to come.

But it's useless. With Yulian, it always is. It isn't long before I'm shaking on the desk, trembling with the force of an orgasm I'm still trying to stave off.

"Yul—!"

"Come for me, kitten." He doesn't stop, not for one goddamn second. "Come, or I won't fuck you next."

It's a threat I can't ignore.

When his mouth sinks into me again, I'm lost.

I come—*hard.*

"Good girl."

The praise washes over me like touch. I tug his head down to mine and kiss him hard. I can taste myself on his lips, on his tongue. I can smell my scent on his beard.

"Asshole," I gasp afterwards.

His hands slide around to cup my ass. "Is that a request?"

The thought of prying that particular door open sends a thrill of excitement down my spine. "Maybe someday," I concede, trying not to sound too eager.

But my words only darken his gaze further. "Is that an answer, then?"

I fix him with a liquid stare. "Not yet."

He understands what I want immediately. Like always. Like our bodies have learned to speak with each other of their own accord.

When he finally goes to unbutton his pants, I push myself up to a sitting position and reach for him. Then I rub his cock through his pants.

He bites his lip, letting out a harsh, heavy exhale. "*Blyat*."

I smirk.

And keep rubbing.

"Mia." It's the first time he's called me by my name since we've started fucking on his desk, and it's a warning. One I fully intend to ignore.

"Yes?"

"Behave."

"Make me."

He lets out a growl, grabbing my face and pulling me in for a deep, dirty kiss. "You asked for this."

He pulls me off the desk and spins me around, bending me over it. The polished wood is cold under my breasts, the air hot and sticky against my bare back.

He presses himself up behind me, grinding his erection against the curve of my ass. His mouth finds my ear, his breath hot and damp against the shell. "Are you ready for me, *kotyonok*?"

I arch into him, reaching back to grab his hair. "Always."

"Always," he repeats. There's an emotion in his voice I can't quite identify.

He pushes the tip of his cock against my slit, rubbing it through the folds. My wetness coats the head, easing his passage, and the thick length of his cock begins to fill me up.

I gasp at the sensation. *Fuck.* The stretch is almost unbearable.

And I fucking love it. The impossible girth, the pressure—all of it.

He slides out slowly, then thrusts in again, deeper this time.

I'm already close. My legs are trembling, my hands grasping for purchase on the desk. Yulian's hand is firm on the back of my neck, pinning me in place, while the other is reaching around between my body and the desk, seeking my clit.

It's too much. It's not enough.

"Yulian," I whine, too far gone for dignity. "I wanna see you."

"Only if you have an answer for me."

"Yes."

Within seconds, he's flipped me onto my back. His gaze is burning as he slides back into me with a single thrust.

"'Yes' what?" he demands.

"You—*ah!*—you know what."

"Say it." He starts fucking me in earnest, hard and fast. "Say you'll be my wife."

"Ahh—"

"Say you'll marry me."

"I—*I*…!"

"Say you'll be mine."

And it's too much.

"Yes," I moan. "Yes, I'll marry you, I'll be your wife, I'll—*ahh*—!"

He thrusts into me again, the tip of his cock brushing up against that spot that makes my vision white out. Over and over, he hits it, driving me closer and closer to the edge.

"Say it again."

"Yes."

"Again."

"Yes!" I scream. "I'll be yours!"

He traps my mouth into a violent, filthy kiss. I can feel my orgasm tightening in my core, can feel his cock slamming into me, filling me with his release. *Claiming* me.

"Mine," he snarls.

"Yours," I breathe. "Only yours."

'Til death do us part.

58

YULIAN

I should feel like the happiest man in the world.

I'm in my jacuzzi with Mia, under the stars, on the balcony of my penthouse. I can hear the noises from the rooftop party, but no one can see us here.

"Should we be going back?" she asks, nestled into my arms. "To the party?"

"No."

She lets out a little laugh at my tone. "Can't say I've ever met anyone who wants to work less than you."

"Only when you're around."

"That might prove difficult, considering the terms of our contract."

Right.

That.

"You shouldn't worry about that anymore," I rasp, guilt catching in my throat. "I'll liquidate you first thing in the morning. You won't have to—"

"No," she says, touching my arm. "No more money."

I frown. "You've earned it."

"And now, I'm telling you I don't want it." She forces confidence into her voice. "I think this hasn't been about work in a long time," she says, gesturing between us. "Don't you?"

"You still—"

"I don't want to cheapen it," she whispers. "What we have. To me, it's worth more than any number."

Her blue eyes gaze back into mine, trembling and uncertain. Like she's scared that I'm going to change my mind, pull back on my promise, even now.

Like Brad did.

Fury coils in my gut, but I force myself to push past it. Right now, it isn't my fury Mia needs.

"We can table this discussion for another time," I tell her. "For now…" I reach for the tray behind me and pick up a chocolate-covered strawberry. "Open wide."

She blushes at my choice of words, but obeys. I push the fruit into her waiting mouth. My cock twitches with interest at the sight, despite all the work I've put it through tonight.

But I'm no longer surprised. When it comes to Mia, I'm insatiable.

And I should be happy.

She said yes. She's marrying me. She's *mine.*

But all I can feel is guilt. Because I know, if she ever found out the real reason I proposed to her tonight, she'd never forgive me for it.

Nor what I've done.

Used her. Lied to her. Put her in danger.

Marrying her feels like the least I can do.

And fuck me, I *do* love her. Enough to forsake all my plans, all my bloodlust. So why can't that be enough?

Why can't I just be *happy*?

Because you know this is wrong, that cold voice at the back of my mind whispers. *You're still lying to her. You're still putting her at risk.*

You're just dressing her in white for it.

I want to call it a liar, but I can't. Even now, Mia is still in unspeakable danger. She's still the lamb I paraded around for the slaughter.

And because of that, I need to make her my wife as soon as possible.

Mia closes her lips around the strawberry. I feel her tongue lapping at my fingertips, just enough to tease.

She has no idea what kind of monster she's about to marry. What kind of beast is feeding her treats while tightening the noose around her neck.

"When did you get these?" Her hands start tracing the tattoos on my arms. Jagged lines, soft lines—her fingers don't discriminate, following each with reverence.

"Eighteen," I answer, covering her hand with mine. "My swearing-in ceremony."

"Sounds important."

"It is."

"What's it like? A swearing-in ceremony?"

"You'll see one eventually."

"As your *pakhansha?*"

Yes. And my prisoner.

"You've learned that word very quickly."

"I'm a quick study." She grins big. "Wanted to go into foreign languages when I was a kid. Then…" She takes a long, deep breath. "Dad got sick one day. It was all very out of the blue. I was fourteen."

"Sick?"

"He collapsed," she explains. "While we were down at the beach. Everyone was saying it was just the heat, to put him in the shade and give him some water, but I knew that wasn't it. In my gut, I just knew."

"You called 911?"

"You bet I did." She slumps against my chest. "Dad was furious. Said we were making a scene in front of the neighbors, running up a bill for nothing. Mom and Ginny backed me up, though. We stuffed him in the back of that ambulance and followed by car."

"Ginny?"

"My sister." Her tone turns wistful. "I haven't seen her in five years. None of them, really."

Realization dawns. "Because of Brad."

She gives me a weak smile. "Couldn't let his goons put a tail on me back to New York, could I? Especially not with…"

A kid in tow with curly blond hair and the perfect age to be his.

"You won't have to worry about that anymore," I growl. "Brad isn't stupid enough to fuck with a *pakhan*'s wife. He knows what I am. What I can do to him."

"I don't know," she sighs. "He's been pretty bold regardless."

"He thought I wouldn't care." I tip up her chin, hooking her gaze. "After the wedding, he'll know I do. And once I adopt Eli, he won't have a say in your life anymore. Either of your lives."

Mia's eyes widen. "*Adopt*?!"

"Of course." The picture she sent me last night pops up in my head. I remember Eli's face, all gap-toothed and joyful, his tiny hands clutching the Garfield plushie. "That is, unless—"

"I want it," she says. "I—*yes.* I mean, I'll have to talk to him—about the wedding and all this—but I don't think he'll have a problem with it." Her expression turns anxious. "God, I hope he doesn't have a problem with it. His therapist said I shouldn't make sudden changes to his life. What if—?"

"We'll figure it out," I reassure her. "We can break it to him gently later. He doesn't have to be involved from the get-go, if you think it won't be good for him."

I don't tell her we don't need to get married right away. Because, as a matter of fact, we do.

Mia purses her lips, deep in thought. "I don't want to lie to him," she whispers. "But I don't want to lose this, either." She squeezes my hand tightly.

I return the gesture and kiss the top of her head. "You won't."

"I'll talk to him tomorrow," she says. "I promise."

I nod. "Want me to be there?"

"Maybe not right away." She gives me an apologetic smile. "Better let Mommy handle this one."

"Keep saying it like that, and you're not getting out of this tub."

She laughs. "God, you have such a dirty mind."

"Are you saying you don't like it?"

"Not at all," she croons, rolling over in the water to face me. "Just wonder what it's gonna mean for our wedding night."

I hook my palms behind her thighs and pull her on top of me. "I can show you right now, if you'd like."

Her eyes go dark. "You'll be the death of me, Mr. Lozhkin."

Not if I can help it.

"That'll teach you to tow the wrong car."

"You are never going to let it go, are you?"

"No." I wrap my arms around her waist. She's so close now—closer than I deserve. "You never finished your story."

"Huh?"

"About your dad."

"Oh, right." She straightens up. "Turns out, it was a heart

attack. Caught it early enough, though. He had a stent put in, some bed rest, an outrageous medical bill—but lived."

"And that's why you decided to become a nurse instead of a linguist."

"Doctor," she corrects. "I wanted to become a doctor. But then..."

"Brad."

"Yeah." She shrugs. "Turns out, lots of stuff in my life can be summarized by those three words. *'But then, Brad.'*"

"We'll deliver your family's invites personally, if you like," I murmur. "I'd love to meet them."

Her smile turns sad. "I would have loved to meet your family, too."

My chest clenches. "I know. They'd have loved you."

"Yeah?"

"Yeah. Alina especially. She used to play nurse with her dolls all the time."

"Really?"

"Really. Had me patch up half a dozen teddy bears."

Mia cups my face. "I love you, too, you know."

"Because of my sister's teddy bears?"

"No," she laughs. "Because of *you.* I hadn't said it back yet."

She rolls her hips once, twice. Soon, we're kissing again, out of breath and out of our minds. Soon, I'm sliding into her again.

"Three days from now," I murmur as I fuck up into her, "there's a swearing-in ceremony. New recruits. I want you to be there. To announce our engagement."

She moans, head thrown back, hanging on for dear life. "Isn't that—soon? I mean—*mhh*—!"

"I don't want to wait," I whisper. "Not one second longer than I have to. All you have to do is say yes."

She's riding me now, chasing the high of her pleasure. "Yes," she gasps. "Yes, yes, *yes*—"

Three days from now, it'll be out in the world. We'll have a date, a place, a claim staked for all of New York to see.

After that, Mia will be safe.

And mine.

59

MIA

"… and then Ally said she wants to play basketball, too!"

I half-listen to Eli's school tales, my mind elsewhere. The ice cream cone in my hand is melting, strawberry stickiness sliding down between my fingers. Somehow, I completely forgot I was holding it.

Strawberry. Memories flash before my eyes: chocolate-covered strawberries and promises under the stars. Everything a girl could ever wish for.

But can I truly have it?

"Mommy?"

Eli's voice snaps me out of my reverie. "Yes, munchkin?"

"You're not listening," he says, arms crossed over the picnic bench. "You're ADHDing again."

"I'm not sure that's a real word."

"Marcus uses it."

"Oh, well, if *Marcus* uses it…"

"Mommy!" Eli half-giggles, half-pouts. "Stop teasing!"

"No can do." I grin. "You're just that teasable."

Then I activate the Tickle Monster.

"Mommy!" Eli squeals as I reach over the table to tickle him between neck and shoulder. "Stop! Your ice cream!"

"My ice cream will feed the grass. Then the grass will turn pink, and they'll make more ice cream with it. It's the circle of life."

"That's not how ice cream *works*!"

"No?" I let my cone fall and tickle him with both my strawberry-stained hands. "Maybe *I* should go back to school, then."

We keep horsing around like that for a few more seconds. By the time the Tickle Monster has reached full power, Eli is rolling on the grass, squealing and kicking like a piglet. "I yield! I yield!"

"Wise choice." I wipe my hands on my jeans and join my kid on the grass. "So? What have we learned today?"

"You can't beat the Tickle Monster."

"That's right. It's unbeatable."

We stay like that for a moment, gazing up at the sky. It's so sunny today, it doesn't feel like Halloween is just around the corner at all. Instead, it feels like an echo of summer.

Last summer. The summer that changed everything.

"Mommy?"

"Huh?"

"You're thinking again."

"Oh, no. Is that bad?"

"Yes." Eli pouts. "Because it means you're worried."

Guilt needles at me. Is it that obvious? Have I been worrying my kid all along, even while trying to hide the truth?

Silly girl. You can't lie to him, remember?

Right. We made a pact.

And our pact means more to me than anything else.

"You're right." I take a big breath and sit up on the grass. This park is usually full on Sunday mornings, but we got here bright and early, so it's just us and a few frisbee-chasing labradors. "Mommy's had something on her mind lately."

"Is it bad?"

"No," I answer quickly. "No, baby, it's not. Actually, it might be very good for us."

Eli sits up next to me. He's frowning, his little face all the cuter for it. "Then why are you worried?"

"Because…" I sigh. "It's a big change. For both of us. And I want to make sure you're okay with it before—"

"Are you getting married?"

I choke on air. "What?" I ask, a little too shrilly to be convincing. "What gave you that idea?"

"It's Yulian, isn't it?"

Dammit. "You kinda stole my thunder there, buddy."

"What thunder?"

"Nevermind." I look him in the eye. "You're not wrong. Yulian… he did ask me to marry him."

"Did you say yes?"

"Not yet."

Okay, that's not the full truth. I *did* say yes—over and over and over again—but somehow, it doesn't feel kid-appropriate to mention that.

Besides, there's only one "yes" that matters.

My son's.

Eli's brow knits. "Why not?"

"Because I wanted to talk to you first."

"Why?"

"Because it's a big decision. And not just for me." I ruffle his hair, wondering how in the world did I get so lucky. To have a kid like Eli. He's everything bright and kind in the world, and he shows me that every day. "So, if you don't want me to do it…"

"Will we go live with him?"

"Yes. At some point. But we don't have to rush it—not until you're ready."

He gives a thoughtful little nod. "I think he's got a bigger house than us."

"I think so, too."

"I'm okay with a bigger house."

"But are you okay with Yulian being there?" I search his eyes, making sure he understands what he's saying. What *I'm* saying. "Every day? Having breakfast with us, dinner with us, driving you to school? Coming with us to the park on weekends or needing us to be there for his work events?"

"Work events?"

"It's like picture day, but much more boring."

He purses his lips. "Can I skip picture day?"

"You can skip whatever you want, buddy. That's why we're talking right now." My heart clenches as I prepare to say what comes next. "And if you want to skip all of it… if you want things to stay as they are—"

"Do you love him?"

It's not the answer I was expecting. "I…"

"It's a simple question, Mommy. Yes or no."

"Hey! Watch the attitude." But even as I say that, I can't help laughing. And I can't help realizing that, no matter how long or hard I think about it, there's only ever been one answer. "Yes, munchkin. I love him."

"That's gross."

"Right? So gross. Mega-ultra-yuck."

"Yeah." He makes a face. "But you should get married."

"Are you sure?" I whisper. "You can say no, you know. I won't be mad. This is your life, too."

Eli's gaze drops to the grass, tormenting a few stalks between his fingers. Like I do with my sleeves whenever I'm nervous. "You're not happy, Mommy."

"What? Of course I—"

"No, you're not. All you do is work and take care of me." His little fists clench in the grass, ripping out the stalks. Suddenly, he looks close to tears. "You have to see Mr. Lee because of me and work late because of me and put up with Vanessa—"

"Tamara."

"Whatever. I hate her."

His words break my heart. His *face* breaks my heart—into a thousand tiny little pieces. He's red, teary, and so nervous he could burst.

I shouldn't have asked. I shouldn't have put this on him.

"Baby—"

"But when Yulian's there, you're happy." He looks at me again. "You get all pretty and go out and have fun, and then you take me for fancy pizza and ice cream. And in the morning, you sing while you're making pancakes."

Tears start welling at the bottom of my eyes, too. All this time, I've been trying to protect him from the harshness of our lives. To keep it hidden as long as I could.

But I never fooled him, did I?

And maybe—just maybe—I was never the one protecting him.

He was the one protecting *me*.

"I don't want you to leave Yulian because of me," he sniffles. "I like him. You like him. Why didn't you say yes already?"

A watery laugh bursts out of me. "I told you, I wanted to talk to you first!"

"And now, you have!" He crosses his arms, all angry-looking and reproachful. Like he's the parent, scolding an unruly child. "So what the heck are you waiting for?!"

I gather him into my arms. He doesn't resist, letting me hug him tight and stroke his head as he breathes harshly, working hard to school his feelings.

"You shouldn't say that word," I whisper.

"Waiting?"

"Heck."

"Oh." He blinks. "Marcus says it, though."

I don't tease him this time. I just hold him close to my heart, thanking the stars for sending him to me.

My son.

My treasure.

"Okay." I press a kiss to his head. "I'll marry him. But don't think for one second I'm doing it because I'm not happy being your mom." I squeeze him a little tighter. "It's the best heckin' job in the whole world."

He doesn't say anything for a while. Then, with the smallest voice I've ever heard: "... Will he be my dad?"

Guilt mixes with hope in my chest. "He'd like to. But only if you're okay with it."

"I'm okay with it."

"You're sure?"

"Mhmm." He burrows further into my embrace. "I'd like to have a dad, I think. I've never had one before."

Don't cry, Mia. You've only just stopped.

Seriously, enough with the waterworks already!

But I can't help it. This time, I'm crying mixed tears—happy because of my son, sad for all the pain I've put him through. For that one horrible lie hanging over our heads.

Your dad died.

"I'm sorry, baby," I rasp. "I'm so, so sorry."

"For what?"

"For never giving you a dad."

"It's not your fault." Eli's head peeks up. "You're giving me one now."

That drags another laugh out of me. How do kids do it? Always see the bright side, no matter what?

"Yeah," I whisper. "Yeah, I am."

And just like that, my choice is made.

I'll marry Yulian. I'll be his bride. I'll be his wife.

And together, we'll be the family we never had.

60

MIA

"Kallie! Have you seen my earrings?!"

"Yeah!" Kallie calls back from the bathroom. "They're on your ears!"

"Oh." I touch my lobes and find the cut edge of a diamond. "Right."

"Mommy!" Eli shouts from the living room. "You're gonna be late and then Yulian will change his mind and we won't go live in a big house anymore!"

"Don't you love it when your kids are supportive?" Kallie snorts.

"I suspect that's his way of showing support," I laugh. "Besides, he's been incredibly cool about all this. He's earned the right to be sassy."

"I have to say, I didn't think the wedding bells were gonna come *this* early." Kallie steps out of the bathroom in a gorgeous burgundy sari and silver hoop earrings. "Thought there'd be, like, flowers first. Or chocolates."

"What can I say? We're a modern couple."

"I'm lowkey jealous," she sighs. "At least your guy's decisive. Mine hasn't so much as kissed me yet."

"Seriously?" I fix her neckline in passing. The scent of coconut oil fills my nostrils, sweet and comfortingly familiar. "I didn't peg Maksim for a 'wait until marriage' kind of dude."

"The word 'marriage' would probably give him a heart attack." She grabs her brushes and sits me down on the bed, picking out a sleek gold eyeshadow to match my jewelry. "I have no idea what goes on in that guy's mind. One second, it's like he can't get enough of me, and the next—"

"He turns into a cold, unfeeling asshole?"

"Worse. He *panics.*" She shakes her head, her long black braid whipping side to side with the motion.

"Maybe he's got a complex." I close my eyes and let Kallie work her magic. "You *are* twenty years his junior."

"What can I say? I like my men how I like my beer."

I frown. "German?"

"Bitter." One final flick of her brush, and she's all done. "Girl, you're ready to *eat.*"

"I'm not sure there's gonna be food."

"Regardless." She makes a *chef's kiss* motion. "Mwah. Perfection. You're going to slay harder than any mafioso tonight."

"Did someone say slay?" Reese walks into the bedroom. His jaw drops. "O-M-G. Now, *that's* a five-course serve."

"You guys need to stop watching *Drag Race* without me. I swear, by next week, I'm not gonna be able to catch a single word you're saying."

"By next week, you'll be wearing a diamond ring and picking out bridal boutiques. If there was ever a time to binge *Drag Race*, it's now."

"Good point."

I walk up to the mirror. The dress Yulian sent me for tonight is royal blue, with high-heeled sandals to match. Somehow, it feels fitting. After all, tonight isn't just a Bratva swearing-in ceremony—it's the night I'm announced as future *pakhansha.* As Yulian's queen.

My stomach knots. I haven't thought too deeply about that—what it means, what it makes me. There's already so much to figure out with Eli, I'm not sure I have the bandwidth for Bratva-related craziness.

But I mean, surely I won't be asked to shoot someone? Surely *Yulian* isn't going around doing much of that, either?

He prints money. That's what he does. I've seen it with my own two eyes. If that's the extent of his "crimes," then…

Then we'll be okay.

"Thanks for doing this before your shift," I tell Reese. "Yulian was going to send Tamara right away, but…"

"Eli hates her." He shrugs. "Don't worry. I'll stay with the little munchkin until midnight, like a good fairy godmother. This way, when Tamara comes, he won't have to deal with her."

"He's been so understanding with all of this, I feel bad ignoring his wishes," I sigh. "After tonight, I'll have to talk to

Yulian about interviewing replacements. I never liked Tamara much either, but it's not like she does anything *wrong.* I can't put my finger on it."

"Kids are sensitive," Reese says. "Maybe he's picking up on evil witch energy."

"Or evil b—"

"Language, Kal."

She pouts, but doesn't look like she regrets what she was going to say. In these past few weeks, Tamara's been popping by every time I have a shift, regardless of whether I need her or not. I assumed it was Yulian's way of making up for his silence and let it happen—after all, I could use the help.

But now that Eli's made his mind known, I can't just ignore it. Whether he's just being difficult or Tamara actually makes him uncomfortable, he deserves to be heard.

Just like he heard me.

I do feel a little bad for Tamara, though. If anything, the apartment has never been shinier.

The doorbell rings. I hurry over, tripping on a stray toy car on the way, and throw open the door.

And my breath catches.

Oh. My. God.

Sleek black tux that looks tailored to every inch of his body. A crisp white shirt, so fine and tight you can see the ripple of muscle underneath. Perfectly shined shoes, like any good CEO worth his salt.

And a face worth a billion bucks.

His expression is wicked. Like, seriously wicked. He's got eyes like cinders and a smirk like the wolf that ate Grandma, but somehow, I doubt he's here to prey on old ladies tonight.

My eyes travel over his stubble, still as *GQ*-worthy as the day we met. I want to touch it so bad, feel its graze on my fingertips and remember what it felt like in other places. I can smell his aftershave, faint notes of musk and pine over the amber and cedarwood of his cologne.

It's unfair for a guy to look this good. Illegal, even.

Maybe that's his *actual* crime—hotness in the third degree.

Oh, and Maksim's here, too.

"Gentlemen," I say, trying to sound suave and failing.

"Ladies," Yulian echoes in plural, but his eyes don't so much as look for Kallie.

For all his playboy reputation, I've never seen him look at another woman once. It used to feel odd, but in light of his recent declaration… Well, it makes all the sense in the world.

He frowns when he glances down. "Why is there a toy car skewered on your heel?"

"Towing," I say. "It's a hard job, day and night."

"Hm." He steps into the apartment, followed by Maksim. That cheeky dimple is back on his face, just in time to make fun of me. "I suppose someone's gotta do it."

He takes my hand, helps me out of Eli's death trap on wheels. My heart somersault when his face comes close to mine.

Get a grip, Mia. You're going to marry this guy. Keep your cool, goddammit.

"Thanks."

"Anytime."

"I hear congratulations are in order." Maksim winks. "Didn't think I was gonna live to see the day."

"You're forty-five," Yulian deadpans.

"Means nothing in our line of work."

"That's incredibly reassuring," I mumble.

"Oh, don't be nervous." He pats me on the shoulder. "You're in great hands. If anyone's good at dodging bullets—"

"Who's good at dodging bullets?"

Maksim's words die in his throat.

In the bedroom doorway, Kallie stands in all her glory, her burgundy sari wrapped around her curves like a hug. Her long braid rests on her shoulder, shiny and sleek with coconut oil, and her hoop earrings catch the light in an almost playful way, matching her coy smile. Her makeup is, of course, flawless.

Maks swallows. I've seen him flirt with my best friend left and right, but tonight, it's like he's forgotten how that song goes. His mouth is hanging slightly open, none of the earlier sass coming out of it.

He catches himself quickly, though. "Kalinda," he greets, once again the epitome of long-dead chivalry. He picks up her hand and kisses it, careful not to break the henna lines on her knuckles. "You look as radiant as the sunset over Mumbai."

"Flatterer," Kallie smirks, hand outstretched for her kiss like the Viscountess Bridgerton.

I can practically smell the nerves on Maksim. One exchange of glances with Yulian tells me he can, too. He probably knows a lot more about his mixed feelings towards Kallie than he lets on.

I'll have to pry into that later.

"Yulian!" Eli's voice crashes into the hallway, soon followed by the little man himself. "You're dressed like James Bond!"

I hide a laugh behind the back of my hand while Yulian fixes his bow tie, feigning ignorance. "I am?"

"Yes, you are!"

"Well, that's good then," he says, crouching to Eli's height, "because I've got a gadget for you."

He gasps. "A secret spy gadget?!"

"See for yourself." Like a seasoned magician, Yulian produces a small box from his jacket pocket. "C'mon. Open it."

Eyes wide with delight, Eli obeys. He fumbles with the box until he's got out the contents, then lifts up a tiny, kid-sized smartwatch.

"A laser watch?!" he squeals.

"One of a kind." He secures it around Eli's wrist, then taps a button to the side. "Try pointing it at the wall."

Eli does.

A tiny red dot appears on the peeling wallpaper. His jaw falls. "It's real!"

"Very real." Yulian steals a wink my way. "Can't cut through steel yet, but once you're older, I'll upgrade it for you if you like."

For a moment, Eli doesn't say anything. Then, suddenly, he does something he's only ever done with me.

He throws himself into Yulian's arms.

"Thanks, Yulian! I love it!"

Yulian seems taken aback. But after a heartbeat, his arms wrap around Eli's frame, hand resting gently on the top of his head. "Anytime, buddy."

My heart double-clutches in my chest. I find myself blinking back tears to avoid ruining Kallie's makeup. But the emotion in me is rising fast, a whirlwind of guilt and gratitude all at once.

He's so good with him. He'll be so good for *him.*

For us.

"Okay!" I say, forcing cheer back into my voice. "We've gotta go now, munchkin. Be good for Uncle Reese, alright?"

"Yes, Mommy." He hugs my knees. "Have fun. Don't be late."

"Since when did you become the parent here?" I joke, ruffling his hair.

"Uncle Reese says Yulian's car will turn into a pumpkin at midnight. I don't want to wait 'til Halloween to see you again."

"He said that, huh?" I shoot Reese a faux-mad look across the kitchen doorway.

"Hey, I saw it on TV," Reese justifies. "It must be true."

I squeeze Yulian's hand. "Ready?"

He squeezes back. "Ready."

"Treat her well, Mafia Daddy!" Reese calls from the kitchen. "Otherwise, I'll know!"

Eli frowns. "What's a 'Mafia Daddy'?"

"Nothing you should worry about," I answer quickly. "Or repeat. Like, ever."

"Oh. Okay." He shrugs. "Bye, Mommy! Bye, Aunt Kallie! Bye, Yulian!"

"What about me?" Maksim says, feigning hurt.

"Bye, Mad Maks!"

"That's more like it."

It feels surreal. Like a dream wrapped in silk and hope. It's more than I ever thought I'd get—all of this, here, right now.

"Thank you," I whisper to Yulian on the way to the car.

"What for?"

"Everything."

And then we head off.

61

YULIAN

The Goldenrod's gardens aren't in bloom right now, but they might as well be.

Because Mia makes everything around her look alive.

She steps out into the grounds with wide eyes, her royal blue dress puffing as she twirls. "This is…"

Beautiful. Not the gardens, not the decorations—*her.* She's everything I've ever wanted and didn't know I needed.

And tonight, she might die.

I took every precaution. Picked a terrain I was comfortable with, one I know like the back of my hand. My men have secured this place a thousand times before. Tonight, I've tasked the best soldier I know with their leadership, the quickest draw and smartest head.

"How's Nikita doing?" I whisper to Maksim as we let the girls overtake us.

"She's practically performed a colonoscopy on this place. Every exit is as secure as Fort Knox."

"Fort Knox was broken into."

"Yeah, by her. And they still haven't got a clue."

I shake my head and check my phone. No messages from her. Her GPS is green and bright on the map, along with everybody else's, a sea of dots guarding us from the inside and out. We've never had security this strong in the history of the Lozhkin Bratva.

Which is exactly what makes me so fucking nervous.

"Relax," Maksim murmurs. "You'll give yourself away like this."

I hate that he's right.

Slowly, I exhale and force myself to regain control. The worst thing I can do right now is bleed my anxiety onto Mia. If she catches my worry—if she demands an explanation—then I'm fucked.

She won't be satisfied with half-answers. She'll demand the truth.

And I can never give her that.

"Yulian!" Mia calls. "Come take a look at this!"

I stride into the garden. My men are already buzzing around, excited about the ceremony, but they all give Mia and Kallie a respectful berth.

Predictably, Nikita is nowhere to be seen.

"Look!" Mia grins, pointing excitedly at a tree branch. "I've never seen a fruit like this before. What do you think it is?"

I pick the round, brownish fruit from the branch. "Foxish pear," I answer. "It's not native to here. The Goldenrod prides itself on its orchard of ancient fruit."

"That sounds like such a rich people thing to do."

"It is." My lips curve without my permission. I've never met someone as painfully honest as Mia—not as long as I've lived. "Want a bite?"

"Wait, it's *edible?*"

"It's fruit. It's not there to be looked at."

Then I push the pear towards her lips.

She hesitates for a moment, but then opens her mouth. I watch her with rapt eyes as she bites into the pulp, her face going from uncertain to delighted. Her throat bobs as she swallows.

"It's sweet," she whispers, licking the juice off her lips.

If it weren't for the crowd, I would have pushed her up against the tree trunk and started fucking her already. Everything she does, even something as innocent as eating fruit, has the power to draw out the worst, most primal instincts in me.

I'm not sure I dislike it.

She finishes off the pear in a couple of bites. "What do I do with this?" She dangles the core. "Do I just—toss it?"

"Yes," I tell her. "But first..."

I pull her to me and kiss her. The sweet taste of the pear lingers on her lips, but it's her own I'm after. Her unique, addictive taste.

Soon, whistles and whoops rise around us. I distinctly recognize Kazimir's voice starting the *"Kiss! Kiss! Kiss!"* chant.

"Hate to interrupt, lovebirds." Maksim clears his throat. "But it's time. Should we kick off the ceremony?"

I don't want to part from her, but I can't stay glued to Mia all night, no matter how badly I wish I could. The sooner we get this over with, the better.

"Let's."

"Good luck," Mia whispers against my lips. "I'm really curious to see what this infamous swearing-in ceremony is about."

"The good part's after that," I rumble. "When I tell the world."

We've decided to get married a week from now, in a small private ceremony. We'll have a big wedding afterwards, but getting the bureaucracy out of the way will allow me to start the adoption process immediately. This way, when we celebrate publicly, Eli will already be under my protection, and Brad won't be able to do shit.

And a week from now, Mia will be untouchable.

What makes you so confident? the cold voice inside me sneers. *You've been avoiding marriage exactly because of the target it'd paint on your wife's back. Now, you're marrying Mia to protect her. Isn't that ridiculous?*

"Things are different now," I mutter under my breath. Before, I didn't know my enemies were leaving. I thought they'd always be sticking around, in the shadows, waiting for me to find happiness again before snatching it right out from under me.

Now, it's only a matter of time before I'm free of them.

And until I am, I'm not letting Mia out of my sight.

"Recruits!" I call from the stage.

Six men walk up to me, standing at attention, their nerves palpable. A couple of them are older, but most are barely out of boyhood—caught in this life by the harshness of the world. My Bratva will give them a place to sleep, food to eat, strength to protect what they love.

Most of all, it will give them purpose.

I beckon the first one from the left. He walks up to me on unsteady legs and kneels at my feet.

"Do you swear your loyalty to the Lozhkin Bratva?" I demand.

"Yes."

"Do you swear your loyalty to your comrades?"

"Yes."

"Do you swear your loyalty to me?"

"Yes, *moy pakhan!*"

I make a mental note to change up the oath. After tonight, these men will no longer be swearing themselves to me alone. Mia will be their *pakhansha*—they must vow to obey her as much as me.

I get out my pocket knife, hold it under the flame, and make a small cut on the tip of my left thumb. Then I push it onto my ring on the opposite hand, where the Lozhkin sigil gleams.

I press the sigil to the recruit's forehead. "I accept you as my brother in arms," I recite.

"Spasibo, pakhan."

"Vstavat'."

He obeys my command and rises.

Recruit after recruit kneels before me. I search Mia's gaze in the crowd to see her reaction. This isn't a particularly violent ceremony, but it's still intrinsically Bratva. Will she approve? Or will she be disgusted by the man she's about to marry?

But when I meet her blue eyes at the front of the crowd, it's not disgust I see.

She's smiling. No, not just that—she's *beaming.*

With pride. For me.

I know, at that moment, I will never love anyone as much as her.

The last recruit receives his mark. As he blends back into the rest of my men, who welcome him with claps on the shoulders and open arms, I straighten myself on the stage.

Then I gesture for Mia to join me.

She hesitates, but takes my outstretched hand after a heartbeat. "Am I getting marked, too?" she jokes.

"Not unless you want to."

"I mean, it feels a little unsanitary, but—"

I silence her with a kiss.

That's it. That's our announcement.

When she parts from me, breathless and surprised, I address the crowd. "You have all heard of my engagement," I say. "But you've all thought it was business. That it was the CEO of

StarTech Industries who was getting married." I take Mia's hand in mine. "Tonight, I'm here to tell you that's not the case."

She draws herself up towards me. I haven't told her to do it, but she knows. She understands how important it is to project strength.

"Next week, you'll have a new *pakhansha,*" I rumble. "Mia Winters. My fiancée—and soon to be my wife."

Then I take out the ring.

It's not the most romantic proposal in the universe. It's a rite—a tradition.

But Mia still looks like the happiest woman in the world.

She drinks in the sight of the ring in my hand. A flawless, round-cut diamond, easily five carats, sits on a platinum band lined with smaller stones.

My mother's ring. The only thing they could salvage from her.

Mia offers her hand, eyes wide and shiny with tears. Her smile is watery, wobbly, but certain. It makes that old muscle in my chest flare back to life, start pumping blood again, after twenty years of dormancy.

I slide the ring onto her finger.

And then it's done. We're engaged. Officially.

Just in time for the gunshots to ring out.

62

YULIAN

There's no time to think. No time to do anything but act.

So I act.

My hands are around Mia before the second gunshot. I drag her behind the stage and cover her body with mine, drawing my gun as I hold her close.

"Stay down," I snarl.

"What's happening?" Mia's voice is laced with panic. "Yulian, talk to me."

But I can't. Whatever words are in my heart, they don't make it past my lips. They just pound on the walls of my skull.

It's happening again.

I did this.

I put her in danger.

"Nikita!" I bark into my phone. Security tonight was

supposed to be perfect—whatever's going on out there, heads will roll for this. "Nikita, answer me."

But there's no answer.

Only silence.

Mia buries her head into my neck, a flimsy protection against the hail of gunfire. I can feel her shaking, terrified, even worse than on the night of Brad's wedding.

Back then, she had no time to process what was even going on.

Now, she knows perfectly well what this is.

The past overlaps with the present. That hot, blazing guilt I cradled in my chest twenty years ago comes back as roaring fire, ready to burn me alive. I remember my parents' bodies, my sister's bloodstained dress, and *Kira*—

"Oh my God," Mia gasps suddenly. "Kallie's out there. I have to get to her! I have to—"

"No!" I roar. "You will not move from here."

She stares at me with wide, teary eyes. Like I've betrayed her. "She is my friend."

"She's not you."

Mia's gaze hardens. She struggles against my grip, her eyes darting between me and the crowd. There are bodies on the ground—I recognize one of the recruits from earlier, the blood mark on his forehead as bright as day. The *pakhan* in me aches for my soldiers, my brothers, but the man—

The man only needs Mia to be safe.

It's precisely the kind of conflict I could never afford. The one I've been running from my whole life—the day I'd be asked to *choose*.

Duty or love. Love or duty.

What a cruel trap to get caught in.

Mia starts pounding my chest with her free hand. "Let me *go!*"

I strengthen my grip. "You're not going anywhere."

"That's not for you to decide!"

"YOU'RE MY WIFE!"

Mia flinches at my shout, then steels herself. "I'm not your wife yet," she whispers.

Then she slaps me.

It's a cold, hard strike across my cheek. It couldn't hurt if she tried. I'm trained for pain—it's my oldest companion.

And yet, at that moment, something else fills me.

Shame.

I let go. I don't mean to, but I do.

"Mia—"

Then I hear it.

Her scream.

Mia's face falls. Her eyes fill with cold, naked horror as she watches her best friend fall to the ground.

And then she starts running.

In the rain of bullets. With no protection, no vest, no weapon.

Straight towards her friend.

My heart stops. Time slows to a crawl. I can see every moment amplified, every bead of sweat frozen as if caught in amber.

Then I see the bullet pierce Mia's arm.

She staggers. Blood spurts from the wound, bright and red and terrifying.

My veins fill with ice.

This is it, I think. *This is how I lose her.*

And then, *No fucking way.*

I follow the trajectory of the bullet. It's instinct more than anything else, a split-second decision.

Then I fire into the trees.

The noise stops. Something falls from a branch—a man. Dressed in camouflage, disguised, perfectly blended with his surroundings.

Dead.

The rain of bullets ends, as abruptly as a summer storm. Mia stumbles forward, clutching her left shoulder, but doesn't stop moving. Instead, she starts crawling on the grass, dragging herself towards her friend.

"Kallie!" She's panting hard, her free hand darting towards Kallie's wrist, searching for a pulse. "Can you hear me? Stay with me, Kal. Please."

Blood is oozing from her side, dark in the moonlight. Her sari is torn at the height of her stomach—a round, perfect hole quickly covered by Mia's hand.

Next to them, Maksim is on his knees. I've seen a lot of expressions on his face over the years—joy, anger, mockery.

But I've never seen him look so empty.

Slowly, I drag myself over to them. Force my feet to move, even when they feel like twin blocks of cement. Even with the memories weighing me down every single step.

This is your fault, the voices of my dead family hiss in my ears like vengeful spirits. *You did this. You killed her friend.*

Like they killed yours.

I don't realize I've spoken until Mia says, "What?"

"It's my fault."

There's a phone in her bloodstained hand. *She must've called 911.* I have no memory of her picking it up, or taking off her coat to press against Kallie's wound. No memory of Maksim clutching Kallie's hand and whispering sweet nothings in her ear.

All I can think of is the blood still gushing from Mia's shoulder.

"You're hurt," I rasp.

"It's nothing."

"It's not nothing."

"Kallie takes precedence," she snaps.

"Let me look at it."

"Later."

"No. You need—"

"I don't care what I need!" she cries out.

"I do," I croak. "I—"

She ignores me, applying more pressure on Kallie's wound instead. Her phone drops to the grass as she uses her other hand to slap lightly at her friend's cheeks. "Stay awake, Kal. I need you to stay with me now. Don't fall asleep."

"Listen to her, love," Maksim murmurs. "It's too soon to leave the party. They haven't even brought out the cake."

Kallie's eyes are glazed over, her lips pale. She's shivering from head to toe, gurgling out words that aren't words, her pupils wide and unfocused.

"I did this," I whisper, barely realizing it. "I should've taken more precautions. I shouldn't have taken you here. After Brad's wedding, I knew this might happen, and I still—"

Mia's head snaps towards me. "What did you just say?"

Shit.

Clarity returns to me. "Mia—"

"You *knew?*" Disbelief flashes across her face, then realization. "Brad's wedding," she whispers. "That was you?"

I've felt the world crumble around me once. I had no idea it could happen a second time. That it could feel like this.

Like I still had something left to lose.

"Let me explain—"

"You—" I can see her mind working, connecting dots I've prayed she never would. "Your enemies. The ones who killed your family. You never told me what happened to them."

"Mia, please."

"They're still around, aren't they?" Her eyes go wide with horror. "They're trying to finish what they started. And this whole time—" Her voice catches, every piece finally falling together in her head. "Were you *using* me?"

I keep silent.

"Say I'm wrong," Mia begs. "Say it's a lie. Say you didn't know."

I don't say a word.

"Oh my God." She covers her mouth, tears gathering in her eyes. "I was bait. For your enemies—for your revenge."

"It wasn't supposed to go like this."

"But it's true, isn't it?!" she cries out. "That's why you put me under contract, why you had me go out with you—"

"Mia—"

"—why you wanted the whole world to think I was your girlfriend, why you asked me to *marry* you—"

"That's not true," I snarl. "I asked you to keep you safe. It was the only way I could think of to protect you. To have you and Eli live with me."

It's the wrong thing to say.

Mia falls silent. There's heartbreak in her eyes, and it kills me to look at it. To face the consequences of everything I've done.

"You said you loved me," she accuses.

"I—"

"You didn't mean it." Her free hand curls on her thigh, nails digging deep. "You just wanted to clean your conscience. All that talk about adopting my son—that was just to get me to say yes, wasn't it?"

"That's not—"

"He thought you were gonna be his father. That we were going to be *family.*"

"We can still be that." I've never begged in my life, but right now, it fucking feels like it. "We can still—"

"You used him!" she seethes. "You used *me.* Just like Brad did."

I reach out to her—

And she flinches away from me.

"Don't touch me," she hisses. "Don't you dare fucking touch me again."

"Mia, I—"

"Here." She slips the engagement ring off her finger and hurls it on the ground. "Keep it. And keep your money, too. I'm done."

The sirens become deafening. Within seconds, paramedics are rushing through the garden, hauling Kallie onto a stretcher.

Mia says something to them. Moments later, she's climbing into the back of the ambulance and pulling Maksim along with her.

"Mia, stop," I growl. "We're not done talking."

"Yes, we are."

"I—"

"Goodbye, Yulian."

Then the doors slam shut.

63

MIA

Kallie stays in surgery for two hours.

It's not long by any standard. I've once seen a surgery run fourteen hours straight. No breaks, no pauses.

But those two hours feel like infinity to me.

I spend them in the waiting room with Maksim. He's still shaken up, speechless, eyes fixed on nothing. Taking care of him is the only thing that keeps me sane.

Because, if I'm not doing that, then I have to think.

And I really don't want to be thinking right now.

Yulian. The shooting. The confession.

The lies.

Lies, lies, lies—all of them lies.

Finally, at two minutes to midnight, the doors open back up.

I spring to my feet. "How is she?"

Of all people, it's Dr. Adams who is on call tonight. I never imagined our first interaction after my suspension would be like this. That I'd be begging him for anything.

But for Kallie, I'd beg the devil himself.

He walks up to me. He's still wearing his surgical mask, making his expression even more unreadable than usual. When he puts a hand on my shoulder, I nearly burst out crying.

But then he rips off his mask—and *smiles.* "The surgery went well. She's okay."

Tears fill my eyes. "She—she'll be fine?"

"Good as new. Soon as the anesthetic wears off, you can go see her."

"Thank you." More words I never thought I'd say. "I—*Thank you,* Dr. Adams. I know we haven't seen eye to eye lately, but—"

"Don't mention it," he says. "This is medicine. We will always agree on medicine." Then, with one last squeeze of my shoulder, he heads off.

Maksim appears at my side. "Did I hear right?" he rasps. "She pulled through?"

"Damn right she did." I quickly wipe my eyes. "Kallie's a fighter. It takes more than one bullet to take her out."

But it almost did.

I ignore that thought. Right now, I don't want to process what could have been.

I just want to see my friend.

A coworker smuggles me into her room. Under the circumstances, it would be a "family only" situation, but Kallie has none. All she has is me.

And now, Maksim.

He sits on her left. I take the chair to her right. Kallie is deathly still in her bed, an oxygen mask secured to her face, IVs everywhere. I'm used to seeing people like this, but never her. In my mind, Kalinda Kathri is invincible.

"I thought I'd lost her." It's my thoughts, but not my voice. Instead, it's Maksim's. "I never even kissed her."

"Yeah. She was pretty pissed off about that." I force a small smile. "So make it up to her."

"If it's the last thing I do, I will."

"Good. That's what I wanna hear."

Maksim's gaze fixes on me. "I don't suppose you want to talk about what happened with Yulian?"

The wound in my heart rips open again. "As a matter of fact, I don't."

"He didn't mean it, you know. What he said at the end."

"Maks, I really—"

"He loves you." His tone is firm, certain. The most certain I've heard him all night. "He's been wrestling with demons all his life. Dark things straight from the pit of hell, stuff that most people can't even imagine. When he met you, he had no idea how to handle it."

"He made me bait," I whisper bitterly. "That's how he handled it."

"And he's regretted it ever since."

"He still did it, though."

"Yes," he murmurs. "He isn't that good at handling regret, either. Last time he felt it, there was nothing to be done about it."

Uncertainty mixes with the pain in my heart. It makes the fortress of my anger waver, if only just a little.

"Did you know?" I ask with little emotion. "About his plan?"

"I suggested it."

I fist my dress. *Of course he was in on it. They were all in on it.*

Only I was stupid enough to believe it.

I try to turn my anger at Maksim, but it fizzles out like an old lightbulb. "Don't tell Kallie," I warn him. "She'll never forgive you."

Maksim's smile turns sad. "If tonight's taught me anything, it's that secrets don't lead to good places."

"So you'll tell her?"

"All of it. As soon as she's well enough."

I shake my head with fondness. Leave it to Maksim to redefine the standards for Bratva boyfriends. "It's your funeral."

"Who's dead?"

We both turn towards the third voice in the room.

"You're awake," I whisper.

Kallie gives me a shit-eating grin and lifts her oxygen mask.

"Ding-dong, this witch hasn't kicked it yet. So stop planning my funeral."

"We wouldn't dream of it," Maksim says, hoarse. "You'd have opinions about everything."

"Damn right. I want elephants."

"Is this the drugs talking?"

"Nope." I smile through the tears. "That's all her."

"Wanted them since I was four. The elephants, not the drugs. Those didn't come up until my Sweet Sixteen wish list." She tries to sit up and winces. "Ouch. So, what's the damage?"

I update Kallie as best I can. Letting the nurse in me take over is the only thing keeping me from bursting into tears again. I don't mention Yulian, nor our final argument.

If she notices the lack of a ring on my finger, she doesn't say anything.

"So *Adams* was inside me? Damn. I'll never live that down."

"You took a bullet to the spleen," I murmur. "He had to remove it. I'm sorry."

"Spleen? Pfft." She waves me off. "Nothing I can't live without."

"You'll have a scar."

"Cool. I'll get a tattoo around it."

"You're impossible, you know that?"

"I do." Her smile turns soft. She squeezes my hand once. "Learned it all from you."

I stick around a little more, until Kallie's eyes grow droopy. "I'll stay with you tonight," I promise.

"No way in hell," she says. "You've got a kid at home."

"Tamara can handle it."

"Okay, let me rephrase that: You've got a *bed* at home. Go use it. Sleep. Hug that hunk of yours for warmth if you have to."

I don't let my smile waver. She doesn't need to deal with any more of my messes tonight—she's already taken plenty of damage from them.

"Alright," I whisper. "I'll keep in touch with Maksim."

"Don't answer her texts until the sun's back up," Kallie instructs him. "I mean it. If you do, I'll eat your phone."

"That'd be one surgery too many, Kal."

"Try me."

I roll my eyes. "Fine. You win. I'll see you both in the morning."

After bidding goodnight to both, I head back out into the parking lot. I spend five whole minutes looking for my Honda before remembering I didn't drive here. That I didn't take my car at all tonight.

Because Yulian came to pick me up.

I banish that thought and hail down a cab.

The whole ride home, all I can think about is Eli. I've never missed him so much. I want to hug him so bad. Bury my head in his perfect curls, smell his shampoo-and-Cheez-It-dust cologne.

The thought of having to tell him about Yulian is enough to break my heart all over again.

I climb the stairs two by two. It's well past the time Reese should have headed off. He's the one person I want to talk to right now. With Kallie out of commission, he's the last emotional support human I've got left.

Tomorrow, I tell myself. *We'll talk tomorrow.*

Except that, when I open the door, he's still there.

On the floor.

Bleeding.

"Oh my God." I rush to him, tossing my bag on the ground. "Reese, talk to me. Are you okay? What happened?!"

His face is swollen, his nose bent at an awkward angle. One eye is puffy and bruised, and his teeth are stained red.

Fear grips my heart. For a moment, I'm terrified this will be Kallie all over again. That he's too hurt, that it's too late.

But then Reese's good eye cracks open. "Mia…?"

Relief rushes through me. "I'm here," I whisper.

Abruptly, Reese sits up. "Eli," he stammers. "Where—where's Eli?"

My breathing stops. "What?"

"Tamara," he says. "She—she wasn't who we thought she was. She grabbed him. I tried to stop her, I—"

The fear in my heart grows into dread. "What did she do, Reese? Where's my son?"

"She took him," he murmurs. "She must've."

I spring to my feet and rush to Eli's bedroom. "Eli?!" I call, desperate. "Eli, are you—?"

But he's not there.

The bed is empty. The room is empty. I trip on his Garfield plushie on the way back to the living room, abandoned on the cold hard floor. The sight makes my heart sink faster.

I search the rest of the apartment, but he's nowhere.

Panic grips me. My breaths start coming in short, my vision tunneling.

He's gone.

He's gone, gone, GONE—

"Mia."

Reese's voice snaps me out of it. "What?"

"Look at this."

He's dragged himself to the counter. His leg is a little wobbly, but aside from that, it looks like his face took the brunt of the injuries. A bad beating—nothing more.

Relief bursts in my heart, but it's a short reprieve.

He holds something out to me. A piece of paper—a note. The handwriting is girly, curated. Perfect the way Tamara always seemed. But the words…

The words, I recognize.

And they're not Tamara's at all.

Did you really thing you could hide him from me forever, sweet thing?

Come to our love nest, or you'll never see him again.

The world spins.

He's got him. He's got my son.

He found him because of me.

"It's him, isn't it?" Reese hisses through gritted teeth. "She was working for him. For Brad."

Brad.

Fury rises within me. Bright, burning, fire and brimstone and the goddamn meteor that killed the dinosaurs.

I hand Reese a bag of frozen peas and pick up my bag. "Wait," he says. "We need to call the police. We—"

"They won't help. Not with this."

"Then we call Yulian!"

"He's not who we thought he was, either."

"Then—" Reese stammers, eyes wide. "Where are you going?"

"To get back my son."

64

YULIAN

The scotch glass hits the counter hard.

The bartender doesn't need any more encouragement than that to bring the bottle again. His eyes are scurrying away from mine as he pours, terrified. If I'd been any other client, he would've cut me off already.

But I'm not any other client. I'm the deadliest son of a bitch in New York. A piece of shit with too many zeroes in his bank account and too many guns shoved through his belt.

I'm a monster.

And tonight, Mia saw it, too.

"You used me."

"Don't you dare touch me again."

"Goodbye, Yulian."

The liquor burns down my throat, chasing away the pain. Trying to, at least. But pain is a stubborn bitch.

“Have you tried gasoline yet?” a female voice chimes in. “I hear it tastes just as bad.”

“Go away, Nikita.”

“I’ve been away for three months.” She shrugs, slides into the empty stool next to me at the counter. “I’m not staying gone longer than that.”

Her sass hits all the wrong notes. “Then where the fuck were you tonight?” I snarl. “You were supposed to stand guard. This happened on *your* watch. I swear, if we didn’t have the history we do—”

“I know,” she overrides. “I’m sorry.”

I couldn’t miss the guilt in her voice if I tried. It makes me feel like shit. “‘Sorry’ won’t cut it, Nika.” I grimace. “You didn’t get the color of the napkins wrong; you left a hole in our defenses. Someone took a bullet. *Mia* almost—”

“I know!” There’s a desperate, pleading edge to her tone. “I’m really fucking sorry, Yuli. I don’t know what else to say.”

“You could start with an explanation.”

She takes a brittle exhale, then gestures to the bartender for a drink. When it comes, she downs it in one go. “I passed out. During my rounds.”

“Bullshit.”

“Is it?” She lifts up her sleeve, showing me the constellation of needle marks in her arm, the bruises still bright purple. “I’ve been fed through a tube for three months, Yulian. I haven’t been walking, standing, or even being awake for more than five minutes at a time. Tonight, I could barely sit down.”

"You said you could handle it."

"I did. And that was my mistake." She passes a hand through her hair. There's white in it now, sprinkled into the black like midnight snow. "Look, I'm not here to make excuses. I fucked up. That's on me. My whole team is dead—that's on me, too."

Dead. That's news to me. Though, to be fair, I didn't exactly stick around for damage control. "How?"

"Single bullet to the head. We were surrounded before we even took up our posts."

"How's that fucking possible?" I growl. "We checked the perimeter. We re-checked a dozen times. We—"

"There were holes in the ground," she whispers. "They'd buried themselves, Yulian. With tiny tubes to breathe, hidden in the foliage. They were everywhere."

The image sends a cold chill down my spine. *Buried.* I try to picture it: an army of corpses, rising from the earth, turning my worst nightmares into reality. And Nikita, in the middle of it all, reliving it all over again.

Suddenly, my anger at her fizzles out. I promised Kira I'd take care of her sister, that I'd keep her away from the monsters that took her. Instead, I shoved her right into their gaping maws.

"How many?" I ask, exhausted.

"Seven."

"*Blyat'.*"

"Yeah. *Blyat'* is right." She finishes her second drink and pushes away her glass. "I woke up because of the screams. I'd passed out in the brush—that's probably the only reason they didn't get me, too. When I tried reaching out, there was only static on the line."

Jammed comms. "And then?"

"Then I crept through the orchard and took them out one by one."

Despite the disaster that was tonight, I can't help the spark of pride that flickers through me. "I got the one in the trees."

"You got his shoulder. I blew his brains out when he fell."

"Good job."

"Not good enough." Her nails dig into her palms, short and bitten. "That girl got hit. Mia's friend."

The mere mention of Mia is enough to rip my wound open all over again. "And Maksim's girl," I whisper, trying to focus on literally anything else. Anything that isn't *her.*

"Damn."

"Yeah. Damn."

"I saw the ambulance. How's she doing?"

"I don't know."

"You didn't ask?"

"His phone's off."

"And Mia's?"

Cracks snake up the glass in my grip. "She's no longer our concern."

"What does that even mean?"

"It means she's done with this." I grind my teeth and set my jaw. "With me."

"I don't believe that."

Without a word, I fish out the engagement ring and set it down on the counter.

Nikita's eyes widen at the sight. "Fuck. Seriously?"

I don't bother answering.

Instead, I turn towards my phone, left unlocked next to me on the bank's app, ***$900,000*** blinking at me from the screen.

It's not an oversight. It's stalling.

Once I pay her, it's all over.

She said she didn't want it. *Keep your money*—those were her words. Right as she was slipping her engagement ring off, she spit those words to me.

Suspended. Jobless. Cashless. And still, she turned down a million dollars.

That's how much she fucking hates me.

It's not right to keep the money. I won't do it. She can give it all to charity if she chooses; I don't care. But she needs to get it.

She needs to get something for all I put her through.

Idiot, the cold voice inside me growls. *Do you really think it's money she wants? That a wire transfer will fix what you broke?*

After all this, do you really still think Mia Winters is for sale?

No. She isn't.

But she's a mom. Before anything else, she's always been that. A mother to her son. To Eli.

And Eli needs that money.

She'll take it. I know it in my gut. After the storm has passed in her heart, she'll take it and move far away from here. She'll take her son, her life, and disappear under a new name again.

And I'll never be able to reach her.

It's why my fingers are still hovering over the screen, unwilling to press down. The second I do, it's goodbye.

And I'm not ready to say goodbye.

"Look." Nikita's voice snaps me out of it, but not all the way. "She's angry. You lied to her, and her friend got shot. She needs time to process. That's all this is, Yulian."

"You weren't there."

"No, but I was in her car. I was in your bed, under her care, and then I was in the StarTech basement doing shots with her. I was there when you proposed—shit job, by the way, but at least it was original—"

"If there's a point, get to it."

"Sure." She turns to face me. "She loves you, you big idiot. She had stars in her eyes when you asked her to marry you. It was the worst proposal on earth, and still, she said yes. Do you have any idea how many women would've done that?"

"Pretty much every socialite looking to marry into wealth and power."

"No. Those would have demanded a diamond and candlelight. And you would have given it to them, because you wouldn't have cared if they lived or died. But with Mia, you did."

"I put her in danger."

"You were trying to save her."

"From myself!" I snarl, palms slamming on the counter. "I was trying to save her from *me,* goddammit—where the fuck's the love in that?!"

"Everywhere." Nikita does something bold then, something risky at best and suicidal at worst: she takes my glass away and grabs my hand. "So don't let it go to waste, brother. Don't let these *mudaki* take yet another family from us."

Us.

Not "you"—*us.*

In the short time she's been around, Mia has already become family to everyone who matters most to me.

And she's become family to me.

Don't let these mudaki *take yet another family from us.*

My parents, my sister—they're all beyond reach. Kira, too, alive only in memory and in the flowers Nikita brings her every week.

But Mia is here. She's *alive.* She isn't a memory yet.

And I'll be fucked if I let her become one.

"I have to go."

Nikita grins. "Go get her, you big idiot."

"Call me that again, and I'll have you thrown into a dungeon."

"Attaboy."

I pour my last drink into a plant, grab my coat, and head out into the night.

The whole way to Mia's apartment, my pulse is thrumming. I'm more lucid than I've been in ages. *Awake.* I have no idea how I'll get her to forgive me. But fuck me, I'll try. I'll try as many times as it takes. Until she's either on a plane or in my arms.

Because I can't imagine a life without Mia in it.

I take the stairs of her shitty apartment building three by three. I'm out of breath when I get to her floor, the alcohol and exhaustion weighing me down, but I still push open the door.

Wait. *Push* open the door?

Why isn't it locked?

"You."

I almost draw my gun, but then I recognize the voice. *Reese.*

"Where's Mia?"

He strides towards me, fists balled up with rage. He isn't imposing by any means, but the black eye is new. "Why don't you ask Sitter Ratched, you dickhead?"

"Sitter what?"

"Tamara. That psycho you sent to watch her son."

Dread sinks into my gut. "I never sent anyone."

"Bullshit," Reese growls. "That night, when Mia stayed over at that rich boys' club with you, you sent—"

"No one," I cut in. "I thought Kallie was staying over. Mia didn't ask for a sitter, so I didn't send one."

"But..." Reese's eyes widen. His fists uncurl. "But Mia said it was in the contract. She said—"

"If she'd asked, I would have done it. But she never did, Reese."

"Because she thought you'd already sent someone!"

Impatience mixes with terror in my veins. I scan the room. Everything looks haphazard in a panicked sort of way, like there's been a search and seizure. It's unlike the warm chaos of Mia's home—unlike anything I've ever seen before.

Then, on the floor, I spot it.

Eli's Garfield plushie.

I pick it up without thinking. It's cold, I realize. It must have been on that floor for hours.

Eli never would have left it like that. Not if he had any choice. In fact, he wouldn't have left it at all.

My fingers dig into the fabric. "Reese, I need you to answer me now. What happened here?"

And finally, he tells me. About the woman named Tamara, Eli's kidnapping, the note on Mia's counter.

When he's finished, my knuckles are marble white.

Brad.

I should have killed that *mudak* when I had the chance. I never, ever should have let him walk out of StarTech, or even his own wedding. That stunt at the hospital—it should have cost him both his legs.

Instead, for Mia's sake, I let it go unpunished.

A mistake I won't repeat.

"Where did she go, Reese?"

"She didn't say. Just that she was going to get Eli back."

She's going to him. To bargain—to plead.

Fear grips me as hard as fury.

"Wait!" Reese calls after me as I turn to leave. "Where are you going?"

"To get my family back."

65

MIA

I park Rhonda the Honda into the snazzy driveway of the Baldwin family's Hamptons villa.

It's not where Brad lives now. According to every Forbes article I've read, the young heir to the Baldwin construction empire favors his Manhattan penthouse, right in the heart of Soho. Closer to business *and* pleasure—that's how he answered in that interview.

But I know he's not waiting for me there. Because I've never been in it.

Come to our love nest. Those were the instructions. That can only mean one place.

As I walk up to the gate, I can hear the crashing waves around me. It's been ages since I could. It gives me strength—the roll of the tide, the scent of the sea—for what I'm about to do.

Face my past.

"Let me in, you sack of shit."

The buzzer goes off. The iron gate slides open, like many times before, its metallic noise digging up memories. My heart starts hammering in response, remembering how unsafe this place was for us, how hard we've worked to put it behind us.

But I won't run anymore.

Not if my son needs me.

I walk into the garden. It's a bare, aseptic thing, curated by some landscaper who probably got to fund their retirement with it. The Baldwin family never spared expenses. Brad used to make fun of them for it—millions of dollars burned in vanity projects to look good in the eyes of their Hamptons's neighbours. He used to be *different*.

Now, he's worse than they ever were.

I get to the door. I lift my hand, gathering courage through long, steady breaths. *In, hold, out.* I can practically hear Yulian's voice chanting those words, low and gravelly, the scrape of nails and the warmth of touch.

I chase the memory away and knock.

"It's open."

Of course. Why bother getting up?

When I close my fingers around the handle, I hesitate. Every instinct is screaming, *Don't go in.* The scars on my forearm are tingling. Even if I've shut off my mind, my body remembers.

But I'm not the girl I was. There's nothing he can do to me today that will hurt as much as it did then.

Because now, I know who he is.

I twist the handle.

I open the door.

And there he is.

Blond curls. Dark eyes, darker than sin. He's lounging in an armchair by a crackling fireplace, a drink in hand, clad in a perfectly pressed white suit. The flames lick at the shadows, painting him red in the low light. Like the devil himself waiting to strike a bargain.

"You're late," he says.

I roll my eyes. "My friend got shot."

"Really? The brown one?"

"Her name's Kallie, asshole."

"Right. Candy. Hope it was quick." He waves his hand and forgets her. "Sit."

"I think I'll stand."

"Don't make me mad now, sweet thing."

"I have a name, Bradley." I cross my arms and stand my ground. "You might want to learn to use it."

"Right." He rises, whiskey swirling in his glass. There's no ice —it must have melted while he waited. There's a lot of things you can accuse Brad of, but lacking a flair for the dramatic ain't one of them. "More than one, now."

"Mia's just fine."

"See, I don't think it is, Euphie."

That nickname shoots through me like ice. I clench my fists, steel myself. *Don't let him rattle you.*

"I want to see my son."

"Your son?" He laughs, grating and unpleasant. "Don't you mean *our* son?"

"He isn't—"

"Don't lie to me." His tone drops low, dangerous. I can see his fingers grip the glass tight, angry veins bulging on the back of his hand. "I had a paternity test done. He's mine."

Cold dread grips me. This is it—the nightmare I've been desperately trying to avoid.

He knows. Beyond a doubt, he knows.

Calm trades places with panic in my heart. "You had no right—!"

"I had every right!" he snarls. "He's my blood, Euphemia. He's *mine.*"

"He's not yours," I growl. "He's his own person. He's—"

"He's my heir. He belongs to me, Mia." An icy, sickening smirk spreads across his face. "And now, so do you."

I take long, steadying breaths. I can't let him get the better of me like this—not now. Not when Eli's life is on the line.

"Show him to me, or I'll call the police."

"Sure." He smiles at my words, amused. No doubt, he's had every Hamptons cop in his pocket since the day he became the new head of the family. "Right this way."

He puts down his drink and struts off, further into the house. For a split second, I hesitate and glance back to the front door.

Get out. Get help. Don't do what he wants.

But the thought of leaving my son is more than I can bear.

I follow Brad into the hallway. I remember the ins and outs of this place like it was yesterday—sneaking in at night, sneaking out in the morning. A Montauk girl playing hooky with the local playboy billionaire.

He always talked of changing up the decor in the house once he took over. Warming it up a little, making it more personal.

And yet, everything is the same as it was back then: white, rich, impersonal.

So is the room he shows me.

There's a glass wall separating it from the hallway. A studio, hurriedly converted into a guest room, a single bed shoved in between a bookshelf and a desk.

And in that bed—

"Eli!"

I press myself up against the glass. My hands are shaking, my own eyes staring back at me, wide with horror.

He's sleeping. In that empty bed, without a single plushie, not a splash of color anywhere. It's not a room fit for a child. For Eli, who loves mess and chaos and star stickers on the ceiling.

"Nice digs, hm?" Brad says, standing closer than I'd like. "Definitely an upgrade from that shit hole you call an apartment."

"He doesn't have a nightlight." That, more than anything, puts me on high alert. "He always sleeps with a nightlight."

"Ah, yes. He did say that."

"Then why's it so goddamn dark in there?"

"He's almost five. He's got to grow up at some point."

I stare at his frame, motionless under the covers. "You gave him something," I realize. "You—you *drugged* him."

Brad clicks his tongue in distaste. "'Drugged' is such an ugly word. I just tweaked his milk to help him get over that whole nightlight business. Couple of drops of Valium, three at most."

"He needs an ambulance if you gave him any more than that." Cold sweat breaks at my back. "Let me in. I need to check his pulse."

"He's fine." Brad's tone is annoyed now, bordering on pissed. "For fuck's sake, give me some credit. I'm his *father*. I—"

"You haven't been his father a single day of his life."

"And whose fault is that?" he snaps.

"Yours!" I'm yelling now, but I don't care. If Eli wakes up, even better—I can get him out quicker if he's walking. "You forfeited any right to him. Or do you not remember what you did when you found out I was pregnant?"

He averts his gaze. "Let's not dredge up the past."

"No, actually, let's."

"Mia—"

"You kicked me in the stomach." The memories come flooding back as if it was yesterday. "You threw me to the ground, stomped on me, yelled that you'd never stand for—"

"That's enough."

"—a bastard child with a whore for a mother. You called me a gold-digger, said he wasn't yours, and that if he was, I'd better get rid of it or you'd kill m—"

"ENOUGH!"

His fist connects with the glass wall. Spider cracks spread from the point of impact, ugly and jagged like the line of his snarl. He's red-faced, panting, eyes bulging, hands twitching like he wants to—

I step back. One step, just in time to avoid his other hand swiping for me.

"Don't touch me," I croak. "Don't you fucking dare, Bradley Baldwin. Not unless you want your son to see exactly what kind of monster you are."

His eyes clear at those words. With difficulty, he puts his right hand back down, unclenches his left fist on the glass. "I'm not that man anymore, Mia."

"Could've fooled me."

"Always so high and mighty," he huffs. "You want to know what Eli thinks of you? He thinks you're a fucking liar."

"Whatever you told him—"

"I told him the truth. Nothing else."

His gaze flicks to the sleeping figure on the bed, too drugged to be disturbed by our argument. My heart clenches for him —my son, my world, unable to even hear me. No doubt, this was exactly what Brad wanted.

"The truth is complicated," I rasp.

"Actually, he didn't find it so hard to understand." His sneer is back now, as cold and sharp as the edge of a blade. "You lied to him. You told him I was dead. Apparently, that was a big blow for the little guy. He kept going on about a promise —that you'd never lie to him, or something."

Guilt pierces me. "It was the only lie."

"It was enough." He's smirking now, victorious. "He doesn't want to see you anymore. He hates you, Mia. You betrayed him. How can he ever trust you again?"

I want to call Brad a liar.

But I know, in my heart, he's not lying about this.

Eli's pure. He's too honest for his own good, and very strict about it. I've been dreading the day we'd have to talk about this—how he'd react, if he'd ever forgive me. I wanted to wait until he was old enough. Until he could understand.

But now, that choice has been taken from me.

"Face it," he says. "You've lost him. He doesn't want you anymore, and I'm sure as fuck not going to give him back."

Those words light a fire under me. "Yulian will never let that happen," I say. "He's far more powerful than you, and he cares about us. He—"

"'*Cares*'?" Brad barks out a laugh. "Oh, please. Don't tell me you haven't figured it out yet."

"Figured out what?"

"That he's been working for me, too. Isn't that right, Tammy?"

Suddenly, a figure slips out from the shadows. Blond, slender, pretty. Smiling like she's sipping cocktails at a pool party, dressed in nothing but an oversized men's shirt I immediately recognize as Brad's.

Tamara.

I've never wanted to punch someone in the face so bad.

"Tell her," Brad urges, grinning. "Tell her how Yulian hired you. Tell her what instructions he gave you."

"I was supposed to earn your trust." Her delicate Russian accent rolls off her tongue like sugar. "Keep the boy close, wait for the right time. Then I'd take him back to his father, and he could keep you instead."

"You're lying," I grit. "Yulian would never—"

"He wanted bait and a squeeze," Brad cuts in. "He never signed up for a kid in the mix. He'd fuck you until you got sniped, maybe get a legitimate heir out of you, but that's it. In exchange, he'd get an exclusive contract with Baldwin Construction."

"I don't believe you."

"No?" He opens his arms wide. "Then how do you explain all the coincidences? He took you to *my* wedding. I popped up at *his* investors' meeting—how could I have done that unless he'd invited me?"

"But you fought. You—"

"The fights were staged," he explains, a bored note to his tone, like he's fed up that I don't get it yet. "He needed to gain your trust for this to work. Seriously, you never suspected? God, you're even dumber than I remembered."

I want to spit in his face. Want to call him a liar again, louder.

But then I remember Yulian's behavior. His hot-and-cold flashes that never seemed to make sense, his initial discomfort towards Eli. The coincidences Brad just talked about, a little too convenient to make sense.

And then his words tonight.

"I guess you never learned your lesson."

I don't want to believe it. I *refuse.*

But what if it's true?

Tamara—Yulian hired her. He sent her to me. If she was a spy, he'd never miss it.

Which can only mean…

He used me. Not just for his revenge—for everything.

Bitterness pools in my stomach. I have no idea what to believe. All I want right now is for Yulian to come bursting through that door, explain himself to me, tell me he loves me. That he'll make it all okay.

But he's not here. And if Brad's right, he's not coming at all.

So I need to fix this on my own.

"Send her away," I murmur, gesturing to Tamara. "Then we can talk."

"Fine. You, back to the bedroom."

"With pleasure," Tamara winks, hips swaying as she retreats behind closed doors.

Finally, we're alone again.

"It's game over, Mia." Brad steps towards me, close, looming. I can smell alcohol on his breath, and I hate it. Hate the memories it drags back up for me. "I can take you for everything you have now. I can sue you for damages, petition the court for Eli's custody, report you to the State Board for unethical conduct. You'll lose your job, your license, your parental rights. You'll be penniless and alone, just like you deserve."

Brad's words sink into me like claws. They're not idle threats—they're a preview. I can see that future unfolding plain as day: Adams giving me the pink slip, my landlord evicting me, CPS declaring me an unfit mother. I could never work again as a nurse in the State of New York. I could never see my son without supervision, without Brad's approval.

And yet, at the same time, I'd never leave the city. Because leaving would mean losing my son for good. I'd be homeless, reduced to begging on the streets, surfing between Kallie and Reese's couches on the coldest nights of the year.

Until they got sick of me, too.

And then I'd really have no one.

"Please," I find myself whispering. "Please, Brad, don't do this."

He cups my chin. I want to jerk away so badly, but I force myself to keep still. Because right now, he has all the power, and I've got nothing.

Just like back then.

"There's another way, you know." He drops in close, his whiskey breath acrid on my nostrils. "A way for you to earn Eli's forgiveness. A way to keep him."

Hope sparks in my chest. "What's that?"

"Come back to me." He drags his thumb across my bottom lip. "Let us be the family we were always supposed to be. I never liked Yulian's part of the plan—fucking you until you died. It was a bit much, even for me."

"You shouldn't have agreed to it, then."

"I did what I had to do. But now, I don't have to play nice with him anymore." He lowers his lips to mine, speaking right against them. It makes my stomach roil. "You deserve better than a lie, Mia. We all do." He glances towards Eli as he says this. "Don't you agree?"

My heart is hammering now. A drum of war. "And how am I supposed to believe you've changed?"

"You give me a chance to prove it." He starts playing with my hair, like he used to do back then. It gives me the chills, but I let him. I've got no other choice. "I didn't hit you tonight, did I? Even if you made me angry."

"What do you want, a fucking medal?"

"I want you to trust me." He takes my hand, squeezes it just on the wrong side of too hard. "I want us to be whole. You, me, Eli—our family. Let me mend what you broke."

I've never wanted to run so bad. Every instinct is screaming at me that I can't trust this man—this monster pretending to be a father to my child.

"Don't look so afraid," he tuts. "I won't touch you until you're ready. Consent is all the rage these days, didn't you hear?"

"No offense, Brad, but that sounds like the bare minimum."

"God, you're never happy, are you?" He rolls his eyes, steps back from me. "Maybe this will motivate you."

Then he pulls out a gun.

My blood freezes. "Brad, put that down."

But he doesn't aim it at me. Instead, he presses it on the glass, right at the heart of the spider cracks he made. Right towards…

Eli.

"Let's see if this works better," he says with an eerie sort of calm. "Either you do as I say, or I'll shoot the little bastard in the head. How's that for a deal?"

"Don't you call him that," I snarl. "Don't you *ever* call him that."

He taps the gun to the glass. The spider cracks grow wider. "Tick-tock, Euphemia. What will it be?"

I've never felt so outraged in my life. Never been so fucking furious. But all of that pales in comparison to the terror of seeing my son—my world—being held at gunpoint in his bed.

"Three," Brad counts down.

I rack my brain for a choice—*any* choice.

"Two."

Trust Brad. Trust Yulian. Are those really my only options?

"One."

I open my mouth to speak…

66

YULIAN

It takes me all night to search Baldwin's properties across the city.

He's got his name on deeds everywhere—company buildings, construction sites, condos. My men are too busy handling the aftermath of the shooting to do the legwork, with Nikita filling in for me, juggling the *vory* and organizing funerals. And Maksim is with Kallie at the hospital, so there's no question of dragging him in.

Tonight, for the first time since I became *pakhan,* I'm on my own.

I kick down every door with the Baldwin name on it. I keep my gun drawn, my fury fresh, and don't forget for a single second what I came to do.

Get my family back.

I was an idiot. I ruined the only good thing I had. But fuck me, if it takes me the rest of my life, I'll earn Mia's forgiveness. I'll put a ring on her finger again—for real this time. I'll adopt Eli, give him everything he needs, treat him as my own. *Love* him as my own.

And love Mia, too, the way she deserves to be loved.

It's nearly dawn when I get to the last property on the list—a vacation house in the Hamptons.

This time, I don't kick down the door. I don't need to. There's nowhere else he could be, and I don't want to frighten Eli uselessly.

His Garfield plushie is on my backseat, waiting to be reunited with its owner.

I swear on all that is fucking holy in my life that I'll get it back to him.

"Open up, Baldwin," I snarl, banging on the hardwood with my fist. "Or else I will."

Seconds tick by. I grip my gun with both hands, forcing them to steady. All night, behind the wheel, all I could think about was Brad's sick smile, his hands on my woman. I could read it in his eyes every time we met—what he wanted to do to her.

What if I'm already too late?

That thought is too much to bear. I take a step back from the door, ready to kick it down with all my strength—

"Hi."

—and it opens.

Only, it's not Baldwin on the other side.

"Mia."

My stomach drops at the sight of her. She's wearing a white pianoforte dress, fastened tight at her throat. It's not one of mine. It's not one of hers, either.

Her eyes meet mine. Blue, rimmed with red—she's been crying. No, she's been holding back. Her tears are still there if you know where to look, trapped behind long lashes and recently refreshed makeup to hide the bags under her eyes and any bruises Brad might have gifted her.

The mere thought is enough to send my blood pumping, seeking blood in return.

Fuck me, she looks like a doll. A cold, lifeless doll, perfect in its emptiness.

When she returns my stare, there's nothing there. "Yulian."

I used to love the way she said my name. It sounded so much gentler on her tongue.

Now, it sounds like nothing.

"What did he do to you?" My fury mounts, the dread in my gut burned to ashes by the sheer need to make someone *pay*. "Where the fuck is that *mudak*?"

"Brad is sleeping." It's a lie. Mia's never been good at lying. Even their whole charade only worked because she cared. Because, deep down, she hadn't needed to fake the love at all. "He had a big day."

"Kidnapping children from their beds? Yeah, I bet it's busy fucking work."

I stride past her and into the house. Whatever's up with Mia, there isn't a doubt in my mind that Brad is behind it.

She's scared—I can tell. I've learned what fear looks like on Mia's face. Burned it into my fucking retinas.

Whatever he did to her, it's nothing compared to what I'll do to him.

"Yulian, stop." She cuts me off in the hallway. "I'm serious. You can't be here."

"Where's Eli?"

"Sleeping," she says. "Like we all should be."

I push past her again. There's something she doesn't want me to see over there—something she's desperately trying to keep hidden. "He's in that room, isn't he?"

"*Who,* Yulian?"

"Eli."

I spy a glass wall behind the corner. Transparent—perfect for prisoners.

But before I can turn it, Mia's hand closes around mine.

The contact is electric. It forces me to look back, chase it to the source, turn my back to the mysterious glass room. "Please, Yulian," she whispers. "Just… stop."

"I'm afraid you'll have to be more specific than that."

"Pretending that you care." She draws herself up, shoulders tight, expression unreadable. "I know everything."

"Know—?"

"About your plans."

Of course you do. I told you about them. Bared my fucking heart to you—every cut, every scar.

I clench my fists. Now isn't the time to demand forgiveness. Not yet, not in the enemy's lair. "We can talk about that later. Now, we need to get you to safety."

"There's nothing left to talk about."

"Whatever Brad told you, Mia—"

"I'm back with him."

It takes eternity for those words to sink in. "Excuse me?"

"I'm back with Brad," she repeats, voice cracking around every vowel. "For good this time."

My first instinct is *never* to laugh. I rarely use those muscles at all. But tonight, I have to fight the urge to curl my lips and lift my eyebrows to the ceiling.

Because there's no way that's true, is there?

But Mia's face is dead serious. "We're going to be a family, Yulian. Like it was always supposed to be."

"Bullshit."

"I don't care what you believe. It's my choice."

"At the cost of repeating myself: *Bull. Shit.*"

Her lips press into a tight line. "Eli is Brad's son. He deserves to have a father."

"A father who beats his mother to a pulp?" My knuckles pop. "A father who'll turn on him the second he screws up?"

"That's none of your concern."

"Like hell it isn't," I snarl. "I care about Eli. I—"

"He was never yours, Yulian." Mia's hand clenches mine. "Just like I wasn't."

It cuts deeper than I thought it would. Loss. Heartbreak. I think back to that little boy in his room, glow-in-the-dark stars on his ceiling and that battered Garfield plushie held tight in his arms.

When exactly did I start thinking of Eli as mine, too?

And why does it hurt so fucking badly to let go?

"You're lying." I tip her chin up. It's a bad idea to turn my back to an empty hallway, where the enemy could be lying in wait, but right now, I don't give a shit. All I care about is searching for the truth in the sky blue of Mia's eyes. "You've been mine since the day I met you."

She swallows. I can feel her throat work against the back of my hand. "It's over, Yulian," she rasps. "It was never real. It couldn't be."

"I'll decide what was real."

"Yul—"

"I'm getting Eli," I say. "Then you're going to get in my car, and we're going to talk at your apartment. You're free to do whatever you want after that."

Mia's eyes widen with terror as I start turning back to the glass room. I follow the scared flick of her gaze, take a step towards the shadows—

"I'm pregnant."

And I stop.

Time stills. My breath, too, just below the sternum.

I turn back to Mia. "What?"

"I'm pregnant," she blurts. "With Brad's child."

For a second, the world spins. "That's a lie."

"It's not. I can prove it."

"If Brad did anything to you, it would have been tonight." *And if that's the case, he'll wish he was dead.* "That's not long enough to get pregnant."

"We've been meeting in secret," she rasps in a dead, flat monotone. "Behind your back."

"Have you now?" An angry vein starts pulsing at my temple. Of all the lies tonight, this one is the laziest, most disgusting one I've had to hear. "Tell me, when would that have happened? Where? I've had a camera at your door, a guard downstairs—"

"The hospital." Her hand has gone white around mine. "There's an old supply closet no one uses."

"You're lying."

"It's on the second floor, right next to—"

"You're fucking *lying*!" I tear my hand from hers. "That didn't happen. I would have known, I—"

"You were distracted." Her voice cracks, eyes brimming with tears. "You were desperately trying not to think about me. You had your job, your Bratva—"

"You wouldn't have done that to me." Jealousy like I've never felt before grips my chest, its burning claws sinking deeper than I knew they could go. "You wouldn't have done that to yourself."

"But I did," she croaks. Her face looks so guilty—so filled with shame. "I'm sorry, Yulian. We were both lying to each other."

My certainty starts to waver. The image of Mia in my heart —strong, kind, loyal—abruptly finds itself at war with this other Mia: a weaker, selfish, treacherous version of herself, dressed in white like Brad's little toy.

And suddenly, I can't tell which one's real.

"It's over," she repeats. "I want you to leave now."

"You don't mean that."

"I do."

"You don't mean a word you just said."

"Guess that makes two of us, then." Her features turn hard. "Because you didn't mean a word you said to me, either."

"Like hell I didn't," I snarl. "You're my *family.* You and Eli, you're—"

"Your family's dead!" she bursts. "They're dead, Yulian. Dead and buried because of your failure. And we are *not* yours."

It's the last straw.

All this time, I've been killing myself not to love her. To forget the girl in the parking lot, the spitfire nurse who stood up to me when no one else would.

But if this is what she thinks of me…

Then perhaps she's right.

We really have been lying to each other all along.

"He won't change, you know." I grind out those words like grit from a wound. "He'll never change. Not for you, not for him. People don't change, Mia."

"I know." Her gaze turns to steel on me. "I've finally learned my lesson. Looks like I've got you to thank for that."

I don't stay a second longer after that.

I push past her. She doesn't stop me.

I throw open the door. She doesn't stop me.

I drive off. She doesn't stop me.

The Garfield plushie rolls down under the front seat. Cold, battered, abandoned.

Lesson fucking learned.

67

MIA

"I'm getting Eli." Yulian sounds mad, mad, mad, angrier than I've ever heard him. "Then you're going to get in my car, and we're going to talk at your apartment. You're free to do whatever you want after that."

He turns. No, no, no—don't turn. Don't go into that room.

My eyes flick, terrified, past the glass and the shadows. I can see him in the dark, because I know where Brad is: by the bed, in a crouch, right next to Eli.

And he's pointing a gun at his head.

Make him go away. *That's what he ordered me. Brad knew Yulian would be mad tonight; knew he wouldn't stand a chance in a race to the quickest draw.* Make him leave, or I blow your boy's brains out.

But Yulian is almost there now. He's about to see.

Brad glares at me from the dark, half his face illuminated by a single ray of moonlight. I can feel his cold gaze on me, can feel the pressure of the trigger next to Eli's head like it's my own.

I have to save him.

"I'm pregnant."

Yulian turns back to me. "What?"

My lie burns on my tongue. It's the only thing I could think to say. The only way I could stop him.

"I'm pregnant," I repeat. "With Brad's child."

"That's a lie."

"It's not. I can prove it."

I can't, actually. But I have Reese and access to the maternity ward —stealing ultrasound pictures won't be too hard. He'll do it for me. He's my friend.

He'll do whatever I ask to save Eli.

Yulian would, too. *It's a sinking thought, one I can't let myself trust. Because what if Brad's words are true?*

What if it was really all a lie?

Why would Brad be hiding from his business partner? *My brain keeps nagging, throwing proof in my face that he was lying, too. But I can't risk it. Yulian is mercurial, possessive—the kind of man who's prone to changing his mind on a whim.*

If that's what Brad is afraid of, he's right to be.

So I sell the lie. I tell Yulian every ugly thing he needs to hear to believe me—to want *to believe me.*

"We've been meeting in secret."

"Your family's dead."

"We are not yours."

That's what finally breaks him. Yulian, the Ice King—fucked over by the only vulnerability he ever dared to share.

And then he leaves.

I want to go after him, but I don't.

I want to run, but my feet stay rooted to the spot.

Because, one room over, Eli's still got a gun to his head.

"Good job," Brad whispers, now close to me again. The tip of his gun slides across my cheek, trailing along my tears, and it feels good *to have it there. Because at least that means it's not on Eli. "Always knew you could do it, sweet thing."*

I want to throw up, but I resist.

Brad opens his mouth. I can feel his lips on my neck, then his teeth. Only, they're not human teeth—they're monstrous.

He unhinges his jaw.

He swallows me down.

And I scream, scream, scream into the void inside him as he devours me, scream because I know what's next, and with the last of my breath, I beg him...

Please, don't take my son, too.

68

MIA

I spring up in a cold sweat on the bed.

The dream sways before my eyes. My hands are white-knuckled, gripping the covers so tight it's painful. My heart is hammering in my chest, hard enough to burst through, hard enough to *hurt.*

Please, don't take my son, too.

I force myself to take steadying breaths. *In, hold, out,* like he taught me.

Even after a whole month, I'm still hearing Yulian's voice whenever I need it.

Slowly, my vision clears.

I'm not in my bed. Haven't been for a few weeks now. My fingers curl into an impersonal set of sheets—another one of Brad's guest rooms. White, bare, cold.

Matches how I feel.

"Calm down," I whisper to myself. "Eli's safe. As long as you play your part, he's safe."

Though I wonder how much longer I can keep this up.

I kick off the comforter and step into the ensuite bathroom. It's still dark out, but lately, I've been preferring it, getting up earlier than the rest of the house. The maids, the cook—they're all noise.

At least, before dawn, it's just me.

I step under the shower spray and wince at the scalding temperature. But soon, I grow used to it, just like every other uncomfortable thing in this house.

Brad's house—the Hamptons mansion he swore I'd never step foot in, gold-digging whore that I was.

Oh, how the tide changes.

Outside the window, the ocean rocks. It's the only thing that keeps me sane, sometimes: the song of the ocean. A last scrap of home to keep close to my heart, reminding me who I used to be.

Who I can *still* be, if I play my cards right.

I throw open my wardrobe. There's nothing but white in it—white dresses, white jackets, white underwear. I pick out a white cashmere turtleneck dress and slip it on, then pad into the kitchen.

"Good morning," Rosie greets. She's one of the maids. Young and pretty, and as polite as they come.

"Good morning." I smile back. It's a little forced, but I won't be rude to anyone who doesn't deserve it. It's not Rosie's fault I'm in this mess, after all.

Louis, the French cook, isn't here yet. Usually, breakfast would fall under his purview, but Brad decided to spice things up since I moved in.

You're going to be my wife, he declared. *Wives make breakfast for their husbands.*

If it wasn't for Eli, I'd have smashed a frying pan into his face on day one.

Eli. This is all for him. I have to remind myself of that fact every day, all day long, like a mantra in my head. Otherwise, I'll never keep my sanity.

It's good, in a way, that I'm the one making breakfast. The first few days, Eli wouldn't eat a single thing that came out of Louis's kitchen. I tried explaining it to the chef and Brad that he's particular about textures, that his foods need to be separated so the flavors won't mix, but he wouldn't listen.

You're spoiling him. Look, he's turned into a mumbling idiot because of you.

I grip my pan tighter. One day, I'll make him eat those words with a side of maple syrup.

But not today.

I start with the pancakes. They're delicate work—getting them just the way Eli *and* Brad like them. Eli loves a little burning on the edges, but Brad won't eat anything that's not basically raw. For him, his food must be as white as his clothes.

I make Brad's batch first, then Eli's.

"Hmm. What's that smell?"

It's Brad, coming up behind me. His arms try to wrap around my middle, but I slip away, busying myself with the food as an excuse.

"Pancakes," I answer, trying to sound light and happy, the way he wants me to be.

He isn't fooled. "Fuck, you're such a cold fish. You should be more grateful—I let you keep your own room to give you time. But now, I'm wondering if I shouldn't be taking that privilege away."

Shit.

"I'm sorry," I whisper, forcing myself to peck him on the cheek. Just once. Just to sell it. "But I'd just bother you if we shared. You wouldn't want me to wake you up at the crack of dawn, would you?"

He tries to twist his head to capture my lips, but I'm already gone. Sleep, I've learned, still makes Brad as sluggish as it used to.

"Damn right," he exhales. "I'm not like you. I need my sleep to function at work."

Right. Busy job you've got there, sitting at your desk looking important all day.

I bite my tongue and force another smile. "Speaking of work—"

"Don't even try it," he interrupts, stealing a pancake off Eli's plate and pulling a face because, *surprise,* it's not to his taste. "We've already gone over this. Being a mom is a full-time job. You'll be handing in your resignation tomorrow, once your suspension's over. God, you suck at cooking, don't you?"

Think. Quick, think.

"I have some PTO left over," I say. "Be a shame to waste it. Maybe I could take it and then resign?"

He fixes me with a thoughtful stare, as if gauging whether I'm trying to fuck him over. Which I very much am.

"Sure. It'd be dumb not to. Looks like it's not all cobwebs and makeup in that pretty little head, huh?" he says at last.

"Morning."

We both turn towards the voice in the doorway. "Morning, *what?*" Brad asks with a saw-toothed grin.

Eli cringes. "Morning… Dad."

Brad nods in approval. "Better. How's that new pillow working out, sport?"

"It's too soft," Eli mumbles. "My neck's all stiff."

Brad's smile tightens. "It's a thousand dollar pillow. Get fucking used to it, Jesus."

Eli's brow knits. I can tell he wants to argue, which is not a good idea right now. Brad's never more volatile than when he's had a drink or when he's just woken up. "But—"

"No 'buts,' munchkin," I chime in. "Now c'mon, time for breakfast."

Eli doesn't reply to me. He barely even looks at me. Just climbs into the designer stool that's clearly too tall for him and starts pushing food around on his plate, lips sealed like the tomb.

My heart cracks, but I don't let it show.

Eli. My son, my world. The first few days we were here, he'd gone completely non-verbal. Brad blamed it on me, of course.

Look what you did to him. He's gone stupid because you're such a shitty mom.

He was about to strike me, that night, when Eli spoke again.

"Dad. ... Please, don't hurt her."

Five words. Just five, but Brad lit up like a Christmas tree.

Because, for the first time, his son had called him "Dad."

He has no idea how bad that is—that he's not throwing himself into his arms, yelling 'Daddy' at the top of his lungs, filling his ears with chatter. Only I see how withdrawn he's become, how wan, how blue.

His dad is unpredictable. His mom is a liar. His house is unfamiliar, filled with strange smells and fabrics he's never felt before. His Garfield plushie isn't here—we have no idea where it ended up, after that night at the apartment.

Maybe that's a good thing, though. Brad never would have let him keep it. He would have bought him a new one and tossed it in the trash. Eli would have cried. Brad would have lost his temper.

It's a good thing Garfield left.

If only we'd been half as smart.

"You're not eating."

I startle back to the present. "I'm not hungry," I tell Brad.

He considers my words for a second, sipping his morning coffee. "Good. You should watch your weight. Your body's not what it used to be."

Oh, you mean after I had a fucking kid?

I grind my teeth into dust. *Keep quiet. Don't engage.* But it still makes me furious to hear him speak like this in Eli's presence. All the effort I put into raising my boy away from such nonsense, teaching him to be respectful of women, of everybody—all of it is going up into smoke.

But it's just temporary. There'll be time to fix it.

Once we're out of here, I'll fix everything.

If that ever happens.

"Okay!" I force another smile and clear away the plates. "Time for school, munchkin."

"I still don't get why you insist on sending him to that nonsense school," Brad grumbles as soon as Eli's out of earshot. "I could have him enrolled into Riverdale with a snap of my fingers."

"Well, he's already made friends there," I say, trying to dance around the heart of the subject: that Eli's got special needs and Brad needs to get that into his thick fucking head. "And the year's paid out."

"Hmph. Well, we'll have to reevaluate next year."

We won't be here that long, sucker.

"Sure. We can do that."

He gives a pleased hum. "See? Housewife life's agreeing with you. Leave all the big decisions to me, sweet thing. No need to worry your pretty little head with the hard stuff."

"Of course. Whatever you say."

He doesn't like that answer. I can tell he knows I'm not being genuine—that I'm just playing the game. But pride is pride, and Brad's never been the type to question when things are going his way.

If he can have his cake and eat it too, he'll never look closely enough to see if there's rat poison in the batter.

After a few minutes of forks scraping plates and me idly imagining Brad's face going gray as he choked to death on his undercooked pancakes, he clears his throat and stands.

"C'mon, bud. The driver's waiting," Brad says.

Driver. Eli's eyes dim at that word, like they always do.

I decide to risk it. "Why don't you take him today? Just to see the place."

Brad fixes me with a stare that says, *Are you stupid?* "I've got work. I don't have time for that bullshit."

Which Eli immediately translates into his head into, *I don't have time for you.*

Fucking hell. He wanted his son so badly, and now, he can't even be bothered to drive him to school?

I open my mouth to argue, but Eli cuts me off. "It's fine, Dad. Let's just go."

"See?" Brad ogles me. "He gets it. Why can't you?"

Deep breaths, Mia.

You can't whack your child's father in front of him, Mia.

Think of the therapy bills, Mia.

I smooth the creases out of my face. "Bye, munchkin," I whisper sweetly. "Have a wonderful day at school."

I try to kiss him on the head, but he ducks away.

My heart cracks just a little bit more.

I wait for the car to leave the driveway. Wait for the engine's rumble to fade into traffic.

Then I dart to Brad's computer.

"Okay," I breathe, sticking in my trusty thumb drive. "Time to get to work."

Brad isn't stupid. He takes his laptop with him every day. His home computer is linked to his cloud, but it's password-protected.

What he doesn't know is that I still remember it.

Perhaps not that smart, then.

This is what I do every day: log in, look for dirt, save every file I can. There are five terabytes of data on here—only so much I can go through in a single day. But I still do it.

Because this is how we get out.

Dirt. That's what I need. Information, shady deals, sensitive data I can trade for my freedom. Baldwin Construction's activities have never been completely above-board, not even when Brad's dad was in charge.

If I look hard enough, I'll find what I need.

Then I'll take my son far away from here, and we'll be a family again.

Family. That word stirs uncomfortable memories inside me. Memories of him.

Yulian.

For four weeks, I've been searching for proof of Brad's claims that they were in on it together. So far, I haven't managed to find anything.

But that doesn't mean I can trust him. He still lied to me, after all. And I'm sure as fuck not going to trust Brad.

Which leaves only one person left to trust.

Myself.

My stomach churns. It's been doing that a lot lately. I put my hand over it, try to calm down the wave of nausea.

That night, I didn't tell Yulian the truth, either.

"I'm pregnant. With Brad's child."

It was supposed to be a lie. An eye for an eye, just to get him to leave.

Turns out, I was only lying about half of it. Two pink lines on a plastic stick confirmed it last week.

Only, this time, the baby isn't Brad's.

It's Yulian's.

TO BE CONTINUED

WICKED PROPOSAL is Book 1 of the Lozhkin Bratva duet. Yulian and Mia's story continues in Book 2, WICKED REFUSAL.

ALSO BY NICOLE FOX

Akopov Bratva

Filthy Promises

Filthy Lies

Ozerov Bratva

10 Days to Ruin

10 Days to Surrender

Litvinov Bratva

Inked Adonis

Inked Athena

Groza Bratva

Cashmere Cruelty

Cashmere Ruin

Kuznetsov Bratva

Emerald Malice

Emerald Vices

Novikov Bratva

Ivory Ashes

Ivory Oath

Egorov Bratva

Tangled Innocence

Tangled Decadence

Zakrevsky Bratva

Requiem of Sin

Sonata of Lies

Rhapsody of Pain

Bugrov Bratva

Midnight Purgatory

Midnight Sanctuary

Oryolov Bratva

Cruel Paradise

Cruel Promise

Pushkin Bratva

Cognac Villain

Cognac Vixen

Viktorov Bratva

Whiskey Poison

Whiskey Pain

Orlov Bratva

Champagne Venom

Champagne Wrath

Uvarov Bratva

Sapphire Scars

Sapphire Tears

Vlasov Bratva

Arrogant Monster

Arrogant Mistake

Zhukova Bratva

Tarnished Tyrant

Tarnished Queen

Stepanov Bratva

Satin Sinner

Satin Princess

Makarova Bratva

Shattered Altar

Shattered Cradle

Solovev Bratva

Ravaged Crown

Ravaged Throne

Vorobev Bratva

Velvet Devil

Velvet Angel

Romanoff Bratva

Immaculate Deception

Immaculate Corruption

Kovalyov Bratva

Gilded Cage

Gilded Tears

Jaded Soul

Jaded Devil

Ripped Veil

Ripped Lace

Mazzeo Mafia Duet

Liar's Lullaby (Book 1)

Sinner's Lullaby (Book 2)

Bratva Crime Syndicate

**Can be read in any order!*

Lies He Told Me

Scars He Gave Me

Sins He Taught Me

Belluci Mafia Trilogy

Corrupted Angel (Book 1)

Corrupted Queen (Book 2)

Corrupted Empire (Book 3)

De Maggio Mafia Duet

Devil in a Suit (Book 1)

Devil at the Altar (Book 2)

Kornilov Bratva Duet

Married to the Don (Book 1)

Til Death Do Us Part (Book 2)

Heirs to the Bratva Empire

**Can be read in any order!*

Kostya

Maksim

Andrei

Princes of Ravenlake Academy (Bully Romance)

**Can be read as standalones!*

Cruel Prep

Cruel Academy

Cruel Elite

Tsezar Bratva

Nightfall (Book 1)

Daybreak (Book 2)

Russian Crime Brotherhood

**Can be read in any order!*

Owned by the Mob Boss

Unprotected with the Mob Boss

Knocked Up by the Mob Boss

Sold to the Mob Boss

Stolen by the Mob Boss

Trapped with the Mob Boss

Volkov Bratva

Broken Vows (Book 1)

Broken Hope (Book 2)

Broken Sins *(standalone)*

Other Standalones

Vin: A Mafia Romance

Box Sets

Bratva Mob Bosses (Russian Crime Brotherhood Books 1-6)

Tsezar Bratva (Tsezar Bratva Duet Books 1-2)

Heirs to the Bratva Empire

The Mafia Dons Collection

The Don's Corruption

MAILING LIST

Sign up to my mailing list!
New subscribers receive a FREE steamy bad boy romance novel.

Click the link below to join.
https://sendfox.com/nicolefox

Printed in Poland
by Amazon Fulfillment
Poland Sp. z o.o., Wrocław

53716301R00304